IN
DARKNESS,
LOOK
FOR
STARS

BOOKS BY CLARA BENSON

ANGELA MARCHMONT MYSTERIES
The Murder at Sissingham Hall
The Mystery at Underwood House
The Treasure at Poldarrow Point
The Riddle at Gipsy's Mile
The Incident at Fives Castle
The Imbroglio at the Villa Pozzi
The Problem at Two Tithes
The Trouble at Wakeley Court
The Scandal at 23 Mount Street
The Shadow at Greystone Chase

ANGELA MARCHMONT SHORT STORIES
Angela's Christmas Adventure
The Man on the Train
A Question of Hats

FREDDY PILKINGTON-SOAMES ADVENTURES
A Case of Blackmail in Belgravia
A Case of Murder in Mayfair
A Case of Conspiracy in Clerkenwell
A Case of Duplicity in Dorset
A Case of Suicide in St. James's

OTHER
The Lucases of Lucas Lodge

IN DARKNESS, LOOK FOR STARS

CLARA BENSON

Bookouture

Published by Bookouture in 2020

An imprint of Storyfire Ltd.
Carmelite House
50 Victoria Embankment
London EC4Y 0DZ

www.bookouture.com

ISBN: 978-1-83888-200-6
eBook ISBN: 978-1-83888-199-3

To my parents, Tony and Hazel.

PROLOGUE

Somewhere near Le Bourget, September 1941

His right leg was bleeding, and a feeling of warm stickiness in his hair suggested his head was too. Flight Lieutenant Alec McLeod didn't stop to ponder the question – there was no time for first aid, as he had come down in the middle of a wheat field that was exposed on all sides. Anyone might be watching from the road that ran alongside it, or the farm buildings to the north, or the little cluster of cottages to the east. It was just after five o'clock, but already the hazy dawn light made him uncomfortably visible to anyone who might be passing, so it was vital to move. McLeod struggled to his feet and tested his weight. There was a nasty burn and a gash on his right shin, and his lower trouser leg was torn to shreds, but no bones were broken, thank God. Ignoring the blood that had now begun to trickle down his neck, he set about gathering up his parachute. That done, he glanced about. He needed to find cover, and quickly. The nearest shelter was a little patch of woodland two hundred yards away, and he headed towards it. If he was lucky enough not to have been seen, he could rest there for a few minutes and examine his injuries.

Once in the shelter of the trees he sat on the low-hanging branch of a large oak and took stock. He felt the back of his head gingerly. The blood was still running, but he was almost sure it was nothing more than a superficial wound. The gash on his leg was another matter, as it was unpleasantly deep. McLeod dug in his knapsack, brought out a roll of gauze bandage from his supplies, and bound himself up as best he could, cutting away the shredded fabric of his uniform with his pen-knife. He was longing for a cigarette, but the smell of smoke would give him away. Instead he ate a couple of squares of regulation-issue chocolate as he considered his next move.

The Germans would come searching soon. When he'd bailed out of the Spitfire and left it to its fate he'd waited as long as possible to open his parachute, mindful of visibility. Fortunately there was some cloud cover, but it was touch and go, and he couldn't have been more than five hundred feet from the ground when he'd finally pulled the ripcord. But they'd soon figure out where he must be. He had a map, and he was fairly sure he could pinpoint his current location reasonably accurately, but he was a little woozy and his faculties weren't working as efficiently as usual. It must have been the bump on the head. The question was whether it was safe to stay in the wood until nightfall, or whether, despite his RAF uniform and his bloodied appearance, he'd be better off trying to get away as quickly as possible.

He stared at the map for some minutes and tried to think clearly, aware that whatever decision he made could be the difference between escape and months in a prisoner of war camp. But before he could come to a conclusion there was a crack behind him, like a twig snapping, and he realised it was too late. He started to his feet and whipped round, ready for fight or flight. How had they found him so quickly? But it was not the Germans at all; it was a girl. She was small – not more than five foot two – with clear brown eyes that darted warily left and right. She was wearing an old pair of overalls and battered wellington boots, and had a brightly patterned scarf tied around her dark curls. She wore no lipstick and there was a streak of something that looked like oil on her face. She couldn't have been much more than about twenty. She held up her hand to indicate silence as she tipped her head to one side, listening. Then she relaxed slightly and smiled.

'*Bonjour*,' said McLeod, feeling self-conscious. His French was a little rusty, and he hadn't had much cause to use it in the field until now.

'I saw you come down. We'd better get you out of here,' she said. Her English was perfect, cut-glass, without a trace of a French accent.

'You're English?' he asked in surprise.

'My mother is. I suppose you'd call me half-and-half. Where's your plane?'

He shrugged. 'In pieces in a field somewhere, I hope. Rather that than sticking out of the side of a block of flats.'

Her lips twisted. 'Rather,' she agreed. 'No bombs, I take it? There were no raids here last night as far as I know.'

'No, I'm reconnaissance.'

'Section C? I met one of your chaps a few months ago. Can't remember his name. Ingram, or Ingleby or something.'

'Ingram.'

'Did he make it back in the end?'

'No,' said McLeod grimly. 'He got picked up and sent to Düsseldorf. He tried to escape and was shot for his pains.'

'Oh.' There was a touch of sadness tinged with resignation in her voice. 'What a pity. I rather liked him. Well, if you don't want the same to happen to you we'll have to move quickly. You haven't picked the best place to come down, but we'll do what we can. I know someone close by. We'll go by road. There are bushes you can hide in if we see anybody. Can you walk?'

'Yes.'

'What about your head? No dizziness or anything?'

'It's nothing serious. Heads always bleed.'

'Hmm,' she said, giving him a sharp look. 'We'll see. Now, let's go. There aren't many people out at this hour, except farmers, and they'll look the other way.'

She turned, and he followed her to the edge of the wood, where she had left her bicycle leaning against a tree. There was a basket on the front, covered with a blue and white checked oilcloth that had a cigarette burn on it.

'What are you doing out at this time, by the way?' he asked.

'Best not ask,' she said with a short laugh. 'It was your good luck, though. I'm not strictly supposed to be here, but the Germans usually let me pass. Comes of having friends in high places, you see.'

'Oh?' he said curiously.

'My father was a very well-known musician. He died a few months ago but Maman makes damned sure nobody will ever forget him.' There was a harsh note to her voice as she said it. 'Still, I oughtn't to complain. Before this mess all began I used to go to any lengths to avoid the association, but now it comes in rather useful, and I blurt out my name to every German I meet. Now, you stay to the hedge side and I'll wheel the bike, and if anybody comes, dive into the undergrowth. And for God's sake try not to pass out before we get there!'

He didn't know how she'd spotted it, but she was right that he was starting to feel unwell. Perhaps the bang on the head had been harder than he thought. But it was no time for a concussion, so he took a deep breath and set off after her as she pushed the bicycle down a scrubby incline towards the road.

She stopped and peeped out through a gap in the hedgerow. 'Nothing. Let's go. It's only a few hundred yards.'

They walked along the road, trying to hurry without seeming to do so, but luck was with them and they met nobody. At length they came to the cluster of cottages he had seen from the field.

'It's that one on the end,' she said. 'He's a grumpy old so-and-so, but I can usually talk her round. Now, pretend there's nothing doing.'

It was easier said than done, given the state of him, but they strolled casually past the little group of houses. A dog behind a fence barked at them, and McLeod jumped.

'*Tais-toi!*' said the girl, in seeming unconcern. The dog ignored her, the barking becoming more frantic until they had passed. 'Here we are.'

They were now outside a tumbledown house with peeling green shutters and crumbling plaster. The front garden was an unkempt and overgrown vegetable patch.

'It kept getting requisitioned, so they stopped bothering,' said the girl, by way of explanation. 'Here, anyway. If they grow anything they do it elsewhere, out of sight.'

She parked the bike at the side of the house then came back and rapped sharply on the front door, which was the same faded dark green as the shutters. After a minute it was opened just a crack, and McLeod glimpsed the suspicious face of an old woman through the gap.

'Open up, Suzette,' said the girl in French. 'It's Maggie. I've brought you a present.'

The door opened further, and McLeod saw the woman in her entirety. Despite the early hour she was fully dressed. Her hair was grey and her face was worn and tired, but her bright blue eyes missed nothing. She gave a bark of laughter when she saw McLeod, then stepped back and opened the door to let them both into her little kitchen.

'Oh, so this is what you call a present. We can't eat him, can we?'

'No, but you can look after him for a day or two, until we can get him out. It won't be long, I promise you.'

'That's what you always say,' said Suzette. 'But what about the man last December? Almost a month we had him, and he ate so much! These British men are always hungry.'

'Now, you know you liked him,' said Maggie. 'You told me so yourself. And he was awfully grateful.'

'Gratitude's all very well, but you can't make an omelette out of it,' grumbled the old woman. Then she smiled. 'Come here and give me a kiss, child, and think yourself lucky I forgive you for only coming to see us when you want something.'

'I promise next time I won't bring anyone except myself. Where's Pierre?'

'Out,' said Suzette, casting a wary glance at McLeod, who judged she didn't want to speak in front of him. She started as she noticed for the first time the blood which was still trickling down his neck onto his collar. 'Oh, but he's bleeding!'

'*Ce n'est rien*,' said McLeod, although he wasn't sure whether she was worried about him or merely concerned for her linoleum.

'You do look peaky,' Maggie said to him in English. 'I'll bet it's concussion. You ought to lie down.'

He was about to reply when the kitchen door opened and in came a large, morose-looking elderly man, who smelt suspiciously of horse manure. He took one glance at Maggie and her companion and cleared his throat as if to spit, although without completing the action.

'What are you doing here?' he asked. 'You know we told you not to bring any more. So this is why the Germans are out this morning, eh? Well, you can go away. We don't want any trouble.'

'They're coming now?' said Suzette in dismay.

'Out on the road.' He cocked his head in that direction. 'Four of them. They'll be knocking on the doors soon.'

'We'll have to hide you,' said Maggie to McLeod.

'*Non*—' began Pierre, but Suzette stopped him.

'Of course,' she said. 'He can hide in the coal cellar.' Pierre raised his voice to protest, but she talked over him firmly. 'Don't worry, we won't say a word. Did anybody see you coming here?'

'I don't think so,' replied Maggie. 'Not on the road, at any rate. Someone might have seen us from one of the windows along the row.'

'Well, if they did, they'd better not say anything or I'll give them what for,' said Suzette fiercely. It sounded comical, coming from such a frail-looking old woman, but there was no time to laugh, because she was already shoving McLeod through the house, towards a side door. At the side of the cottage was a coal bunker with a wooden hatch and rusting hinges.

'We don't have much coal any more, so there'll be plenty of room for you,' she said. 'Now, in you get, and for God's sake keep quiet!'

The coal cellar was deeper than it looked from the outside. McLeod stepped in and eased himself down a flight of steep steps. He had just enough time to see that it was almost empty of coal when Suzette banged the hatch down, shutting out all the daylight except for a tiny, crescent-shaped sliver where the wood had warped. He listened, but heard nothing. He closed his eyes. Sparks and stars and kaleidoscopic patterns floated before him. Opening his eyes did nothing to dispel them. He forced himself to take deep breaths, then rummaged in his knapsack and finished the chocolate. It tasted like sawdust in his mouth, and at that moment he wanted nothing more than to go to bed and sleep for a month.

He waited. After a while he heard voices outside the bunker and strained to distinguish them. They were not ones he recognised; two men, he thought. Germans. Then he heard Maggie. They were speaking French.

'There's nobody here, as you can see,' she was saying. 'Why would he come this way? If he has any sense he'll have hopped on the first passing farm truck and headed south. That's what I'd do.'

'Never mind what you would do,' said a bored-sounding male voice. 'What about this coal cellar?'

There was the crunch of footsteps, and something blocked out the sliver of daylight. McLeod held his breath and pressed himself against the back wall of his refuge as the hatch creaked and rose a little way. Then there was a crash of metal. It sounded like a bicycle falling over.

'I'm sorry,' said Maggie hastily. 'It was an accident.'

The hatch dropped and the cellar went dark again, leaving only the comforting crescent of daylight.

'What is that you just picked up?' demanded the first German, no longer sounding uninterested. 'Show me. Tobacco? Where did you get so much? What else is in the basket?'

'Nothing much,' replied Maggie.

There was a pause. McLeod imagined the two Germans pulling off the checked oilcloth and peering inside.

'These jars of jam and honey are only available in German shops. And this coffee. Did you steal it?'

'No. It was all mine, from before the war. I brought it to give to Pierre and Suzette.'

'Well you have no right to it,' said the first German. 'This belongs to the Reich. Show me your papers. And you two also.'

'They're in the house,' came Pierre's voice.

'I'll get them,' said Suzette.

'Go with her, Bauer, and check that she's not hiding him in there. Now, *mademoiselle*. Marguerite Brouillard. Is this you? I know the name.'

'I expect you do. It ought to be familiar enough. You've probably heard of my father.'

'Ah!' There was a moment's silence, as though he were looking her up and down. 'Very well, Mademoiselle Brouillard of the famous father, what are you doing out of Paris?'

'These people worked for my family before the war. I came to give them the things in the basket. I have permission to travel this far.'

'So I see, but this is a very strange time of day to do it. You must have left home before the end of the curfew.'

'No, it doesn't take long to get here by bike – less than an hour. And I have to go to work later. This was the only time I could come.'

'Well, it seems you have wasted your journey. We will take these things, and you had better watch out. If we find out you were lying about where you got them, then... you understand?'

'Perfectly, sir.'

The soldier gave a snuff of approval. McLeod heard the voices of Suzette and Pierre a little distance away. Then there was silence. He waited for what seemed like an hour, before footsteps approached and the hatch was lifted.

'They've gone,' said Maggie.

She held out a hand to help him up the steps, and he was glad of it because his legs were starting to feel like rubber. They went back into the kitchen and found Pierre and Suzette sitting at a rickety wooden table that had a folded magazine shoved under one leg. There was a certain tension in the atmosphere, and McLeod guessed they had been discussing him.

'We can't keep him,' said Pierre stubbornly.

'It's just for a day or two,' replied Maggie. 'Look at him, he's had a nasty whack on the head and his leg is in shreds. He needs bed rest. You can keep him in the attic for a little while, surely? We'll get him out of here as soon as we can, but he's in no fit state to travel at the moment.'

They all stared at him, Maggie dispassionately, the other two nervously. McLeod opened his mouth to tell them there was no need for them to put themselves out – he was quite all right and perfectly capable of looking after himself – but even that slight movement brought on a wave of nausea, so he said nothing.

'You'd better sit down,' said Maggie, and that was the last he remembered before he blacked out.

*

He woke to find himself lying on a narrow iron bed in a dim attic. Maggie was standing across the room, peering out through a dirty window. He watched her for a few minutes, and heard her give a sigh. She turned around.

'You're awake, then,' she said, and her voice was brisk enough. 'You gave us a fright just there.'

'How did you get me up the stairs?' he asked.

'Pierre slung you over his shoulder, I'm afraid. I'm sorry we couldn't manage a stretcher, but the stairs are narrow and he's as strong as an ox so we had to make do with what we had. No, don't try and get up. There's no need, and it won't do you any good.'

'I thought they wanted me to leave.'

'Oh, take no notice of Pierre. He's hungry and grumpy but as loyal as they come. And Suzette, too.'

'I'll pay them.'

'What use is money to them? There's nothing to spend it on. I'll get them some extra food, and they'll be perfectly happy, you'll see.'

'But where will you get it?'

'From my own rations, probably. And I know people.'

'I'm sorry you had to sacrifice the jam and the tobacco.'

'Don't worry. I always carry something of the sort. It's a kind of decoy. They see the goodies in the basket and I clutch my hair and pretend I'm terrified about the cigarettes and it distracts them from searching me. Food isn't all I carry, you see.' She grinned conspiratorially at him.

'I see,' he said. 'I won't ask any questions.'

'That's probably wisest.'

'Thanks, anyway.'

'Don't thank me now – we're not out of the woods yet. You ought to be safe enough here until you've recovered, and then we'll see about getting you out. I don't know which routes they're operating lately. I doubt we can get you to Brittany – they're more likely to send you south to Marseille, then back via North Africa, or perhaps across into Spain. Stay here and do as Suzette tells you. She'll probably try and mother you. She lost her own son on the Somme, you see, and for all her talk she really wants to help. She and Pierre will give you your instructions when you're better. It'll probably involve shivering by the side of the road at three in the morning, and two days of sitting crammed in the back of a truck under a tarpaulin, but I'm sure you've survived worse.'

His eyes were already growing heavy again. 'Marguerite Brouillard,' he murmured drowsily.

'Oh, you overheard them, did you? Yes, but everybody calls me Maggie.'

'Maggie. And you're half-English.'

'I spent a lot of my childhood in Hertfordshire. Went to school there. But Paris is my home now.'

'You're a loyal Frenchwoman.'

'Perhaps. Although sometimes I wonder whether it's worth it – all this fighting, and lying, and sneaking around, I mean. Sometimes I wonder whether it mightn't be easier just to do as they say. It doesn't look as though we've any chance of winning.'

'Don't talk like that,' he said. 'You mustn't give up. It will all be worth it – you'll see.'

'I wish I could be as certain as you are.'

He felt himself starting to drift off. 'Shall I see you again before I go?' he asked.

'Probably not. It's safer that way.'

'Then thank you and goodbye. Perhaps I'll come and look you up after this is all over.'

'I'll look forward to it,' she said, and with that he fell asleep.

*

It was well after six now, and Maggie ought to have been on her way back to the city, but the British airman had held her up. She'd be late for school but she couldn't go back without carrying out her errand, so they'd just have to start lessons without her. She said goodbye to Pierre and Suzette, but instead of fetching her bike and heading back the way she'd come, she followed the path down the lane a short way and then turned right down an overgrown footpath which led to some farm buildings. One of them was a hay barn, open on one side. Inside at one end was a ladder which led to a hayloft. Maggie went across to it and glanced about.

'Emil!' she hissed. 'It's me.'

There was a scuffling sound from above, and a shadow passed across the hatch in the ceiling. Then a man's face looked down at her.

'About time,' he grumbled. 'Where have you been? I'm dying for a smoke.'

'Well, I've bad news for you,' she said, climbing the ladder. 'The Germans got all my tobacco.'

'What?'

She stepped out into the hayloft, and Emil threw himself back onto the straw mattress that had been laid down for him in one corner.

'I told you it was better to put you here rather than at Suzette's,' said Maggie. 'I found an airman on the way and the Germans came looking for him. If you'd been there they'd have caught you.'

'Did they catch him?'

'No.'

'Well, then.'

'All right, but if they'd got *him* they'd have sent him to a PoW camp. If they catch *you* they'll send you to Drancy with all the other Jews – that's if they don't shoot you on sight. Better here where it's safer.'

'Colder and more uncomfortable, you mean. Have you heard any news of Filip?'

'I'm afraid not. Nobody's talking, and it's difficult to find out what's happening. But I'll let you know as soon as I hear anything.' She went over and sat down on the mattress next to him.

'I'm bored,' he said. 'I'm sick of kicking my heels here. I want to get out and do something useful.'

'And so you shall. Here.' She felt inside her overalls and brought out a screw of paper with some tobacco in it. 'I kept some back, just in case.'

'You're wonderful.' He made to grab the little package but she held it away from him.

'Before you set fire to the barn we need to talk about where you're going to go next.'

'I'm staying in Paris.'

'Oh, no you're not. It's far too dangerous, and I'm sure they're keeping an eye on Club Madagascar. You want to keep doing useful work, don't you?'

'I can see by your face that you've had one of your ideas,' he said, taking the tobacco. 'Come on, then, out with it.'

'What about going to Nice?'

'Nice?'

'My sister is there. You remember I told you? She won the Prix de Rome for music, and she's studying at some fabulous villa or other. There are no Germans there, but lots and lots of Jewish refugees who need help getting out of France. You know all the unofficial channels, and the loopholes, and which visas to get, and whatnot. You could help so many people.'

'But my home is in Paris.'

'I'm sure that's what all those people in Drancy thought, too,' she said practically. 'And now look at them – stuck in a concrete prison camp, and probably about to be deported.'

He looked at her.

'So you want me to go to this sister of yours?'

'Yes. I've written her a letter to take with you. Once we've got you smuggled across the demarcation line, go and find her and say I sent you.'

'Is she safe?'

'Well, she won't inform on you, if that's what you mean. She's not a Resistant, but she's not a collaborator either. To be honest, she's in her own little world most of the time, and sometimes I think she hardly even knows there's a war on. But she'll give you a place to stay. She's shy, though, and isn't used to men, so make sure you don't frighten her.'

'She sounds delightful.'

'Don't be unkind. She's my sister and I adore her. Now, here's the letter.'

He took it and glanced at it, tucking it in his inside pocket.

'You've got it all organised, haven't you?'

'I hope so.'

He pulled her down on top of him on the mattress. 'You'll make some man a wonderful wife one day.'

'Well, I should *hope* that man will be you,' she said, laughing.

He kissed her, and she returned the kiss fiercely, tangling her fingers in his hair. After a minute he rolled her over onto her back and started to undo the straps of her overalls.

'Emil!' she said, half-laughing, half-exasperated. 'Not now. Not here. We should wait.'

'If you ask me, we should get our fun while we can,' he replied, but she slapped him away and sat up.

'There'll be plenty of time for all that. Go to Nice. Cécilia will look after you and send you back safe and sound once the war's over.'

'Are you sure of that?'

'Of course I am,' said Maggie. 'She's my sister. I'd trust her with my life.'

Chapter One

It was a world of fog. A counterpane of silver-grey gauze had descended upon the landscape, wrapping itself around the trees, the road signs, the fences, the telephone boxes. It enveloped houses and cars in its caress, sinking like a dying breath onto the road ahead. Nothing could withstand its gentle advance – not even the low autumn sun, which struggled to penetrate the grey, making only an occasional pale appearance through the dense swirls.

Harriet put down her suitcase to adjust her gloves, which were second-hand and pinched at the wrists. She had come all the way from the station on foot, and her arms were aching. Not that her luggage was so very heavy, but it was quite enough to make the two-mile walk less pleasant than it ought to have been. And the weather didn't help; droplets of water attached themselves clammily to her coat and hat, settling delicately on the curls she had tried her best with that morning. She thought of her destination. It was not far, and there would be a fire, or perhaps even central heating if the place had been modernised. The woman at the agency had spoken enthusiastically if vaguely of Chaffingham. A gorgeous old house, she'd said: big, but not so big as to be unaffordable or unmanageable. And the people were nice enough. Mrs Brouillard (she had pronounced it Broolard) was a bit formal, perhaps, but very polite and well-mannered.

'French?' asked Harriet, glancing at the paper she had been handed, and noting the spelling of the name.

'I don't think so. She sounded English on the telephone. Her husband was, though. He was a well-known musician, she said, although I've never heard of him.'

'Jean-Jacques Brouillard?'

'That might have been the name. They were living in France but came over after the war. You don't mind the stiff type, do you? She probably just wants softening up a bit.'

'I'm sure I can manage her,' replied Harriet. She was trying to sound calm and uninterested, as if she had a whole selection of jobs to choose from and didn't desperately need this one.

'Well, we'll see,' said the woman, giving Harriet an assessing stare. 'They've been through a few secretaries lately, and to be perfectly honest I wouldn't have put you forward given your recent performances, but they want someone who speaks French and German, and we don't have anyone else at present. But do try and make an effort this time, won't you? We've no use for someone who can't cope, and if you keep on proving unsatisfactory I'm afraid we won't be able to keep you on our books.'

'I can cope. I'm sorry about the other jobs, but…' There was no use in explaining. Harriet wasn't the only person with problems, after all. 'I promise I won't let you down,' she finished. She was sitting up straight, trying to put on the face of the old, competent Harriet she'd once been.

'You'd better not,' said the woman, and so it was agreed.

It didn't take Harriet long to make arrangements – it wasn't as though she was leaving much behind, after all. Her landlady had been only too glad to see the back of her after one too many late rent payments, and there was nobody to say goodbye to, except her fellow lodgers, most of whom were transients like her: fleeting acquaintances to exchange meaningless pleasantries with over breakfast, who would leave for parts unknown after a month or two. She was lucky to have got this position, she knew; they hadn't been exactly unkind at the agency but they weren't in the business of curing broken hearts, and if she couldn't do the work then they had no use for her. She'd try harder this time.

She picked up her suitcase and pressed on. According to the directions she'd been given it was only another quarter of a mile or so, but the fog made the walk more of a struggle. At last she saw something that looked like a stone pillar looming out of the dimness in front of her which, as she approached, proved to be a pair of gate-posts. A worn stone plaque on the nearest one bore the words 'Chaffingham House'. Harriet turned in and set off up the drive. It was rough and unpaved – more of a muddy track than anything – but after a short distance the going became smoother and the road split off into a path that curved round through a thick clump of trees and eventually emerged at the front of the house. Harriet was too anxious to get out of the cold and damp to look at it closely, but she had the general impression of weathered grey stone, sharply gabled roofs and tall chimneys. The doorstep was uneven and dipped in the middle, worn away from hundreds of years of visitors, but the front door was modern and solid enough, with an electric bell, which was at length answered by an elderly woman wearing a black dress and grey apron. She peered at Harriet for several moments even after she had announced her name, then suddenly stepped back to allow her into a dark entrance hall.

'One moment, I announce you,' she said, and hurried off.

From her accent she sounded French. Harriet looked around for a seat, but on second thoughts decided to remain standing. The house was silent except for the ticking of a grandfather clock, sonorous and echoing in the emptiness, and Harriet surveyed the hall in which she stood. The walls were half-panelled in dark wood, while above the panelling the paint might once have been white or cream, but seemed to have yellowed with age. The floor was tiled in black and white squares as far as the green-carpeted staircase, which led up from the centre of the hall and split into two directions on a landing at the top. It was too dark to see where it went from there. On one wall was a chimney breast and a stone fireplace, above which hung two crossed swords. Below that was a certificate in a frame.

Harriet stepped forward to look at it more closely, then stopped as she heard something. It was the sound of a piano playing from the depths of the house. The music was like nothing she had ever heard before: as it began it was soft and melancholy, mournful yet soothingly melodic and calming. Gradually, though, the mood changed to become something altogether different – Harriet could only have described it as though the music had melted and sagged to one side. The melody was the same underneath, but now it was joined by something not atonal, exactly, but which jarred, as minor and major chords came together in a sound that was more eerie than anything else, almost like a cry of pain.

'Miss Conway,' said a voice behind her. Harriet started violently and turned as the music cut off abruptly. Before her was a very straight, very slim woman of fifty-five or so, dressed in a dark turquoise dress in the style of a few years ago, cut in a fabric that spoke of expense. At one time Harriet might have looked at it with envy and regretted her own shabby outfit, but she was beyond such things now. Nobody ever looked admiringly at her these days, and nor did she want them to.

'Mrs Brouillard?' she replied, pronouncing it carefully. The other woman gave a quick inflection of the eyebrows that might have indicated approval.

'The agency said you spoke French. That's what they said about the last girl too, but it seems they had overstated her ability. I hope we shall have more success this time.'

This last sentence was in French. Harriet replied fluently and Mrs Brouillard's brow cleared further.

'Very well, that will do for the present. Let us go into the sitting room where it is more comfortable. You look rather damp. Have you walked here? I should have thought a taxi would have been more sensible.'

Her manner was distant, careless. Harriet knew the type. Mrs Brouillard would not understand the idea of sacrificing luxuries for want of money.

'I preferred to walk,' Harriet said.

'The active sort, are you? Then you will find it pleasant around here. The countryside is said to be very attractive. I don't care for such things myself.'

Although perfectly correct, her English was a little stilted, perhaps the result of having lived so many years in France. As she spoke she looked Harriet up and down openly. There was no malice in it; rather, it was the action of one assessing a new acquisition for its suitability. What the result of her examination was Harriet couldn't tell, but Mrs Brouillard turned abruptly and led her along a short passage to a door which opened into a small sitting room.

'I prefer this room to the drawing room,' she said as they entered. 'It used to be a study but I took it over myself when we came here, since the view is much pleasanter. Sit.'

Mrs Brouillard took a comfortable easy chair and waited. Harriet sensed this was a test, and paused before choosing a seat herself. The logical choice was a thinly upholstered seat opposite Mrs Brouillard's chair which was far too low and would put her at a distinct height disadvantage. The other chairs were mostly plush, soft and brocaded, for guests rather than secretaries. In the far corner of the room was a chair of just the right height, comfort and appropriateness. Harriet fetched it, set it down a respectful distance from her new employer, and sat down. Mrs Brouillard didn't smile exactly, but the corners of her mouth relaxed, and Harriet judged she had passed the test. The room was not as warm as she would have liked, but it was better than being outside, and she took the opportunity to glance around while Mrs Brouillard looked down at the references Harriet had handed her. They must have brought the furniture over from France, because there was a curved opulence to it that was decidedly un-English, with a preponderance of white and gilding. It was far more suited to a Parisian apartment than to this old, traditional country house in the Hertfordshire countryside.

'What have you been told about us?' asked Mrs Brouillard, looking up from the references. 'Do you know who we are?'

'I know a bit about you,' said Harriet. 'Your husband was famous, of course. I saw him in London shortly before the war.'

'Oh, you did, did you? You must have been quite a child then.'

'Not exactly. It was my eighteenth birthday. My mother took me. She was very fond of music.'

The eyebrows lifted.

'Eighteen? Pardon me, but you don't look much more than that now.'

'I'm nearly twenty-nine,' said Harriet in answer to the not-quite-spoken question.

Again came the assessing look, but the older woman made no reply.

'My husband's death was unfortunate,' Mrs Brouillard said. 'He made an enormous contribution to the world of music – it's not an exaggeration to say that he was one of the most important composers and conductors of his time. It is a great pity that he is not here to see his children follow in his footsteps. Or, rather, his *child*.'

Harriet waited. Mrs Brouillard went on.

'I don't suppose you have heard of my daughter, Cécilia Brouillard. She had only just begun to make a name for herself when the war intervened.'

'I think I have heard of her. She is a violinist, I believe?'

'She *was* a violinist,' Mrs Brouillard corrected her. 'And a composer, too. She was one of the first women to win the Prix de Rome scholarship, but she has retired from the profession. My eldest son, Marcus, who was a talented cellist, chose to enlist and was killed in the Battle of France.'

'I'm sorry,' said Harriet dutifully. Mrs Brouillard waved it away.

'Such things are part and parcel of life. I dare say you have had your own personal tragedies. Don't take that as an invitation to cry on my shoulder, by the way, Miss Conway. I must warn you now that I have no interest in mothering my employees.'

'That suits me,' replied Harriet. 'That's not why I'm here.'

'Good. At any rate, now that the rest of the family have proved something of a disappointment in carrying on the Brouillard name, we are left with only Sébastien. I believe he has just as much talent as the other two – perhaps more – but he is delicate and requires careful handling. Since we left Paris his musical education has been somewhat piecemeal, but he is in the hands of the best tutors I could find, in Cambridge and London, and I hope he will very soon be in a position to enter the professional world.'

'How old is he?' asked Harriet.

'He turned nineteen in August.'

Nineteen seemed a perfectly suitable age to be earning a living. Harriet wondered what they were waiting for, but didn't ask.

'Is he a pianist? I heard someone playing the piano when I arrived.'

'He is not here today,' said Mrs Brouillard. 'I expect that was Rex you heard practising.'

'Who is Rex?'

'My grandson. Cécilia's son. He is seven and unfortunately not very promising musically.'

Mrs Brouillard seemed to judge people solely by their musical ability. Harriet hadn't been told that there were young children in the house, and she wasn't especially pleased at the idea. She'd come to Chaffingham to act as secretary to Mrs Brouillard, but she knew how these things went – had experienced it too often in the past: before she knew it her duties would be extended to include acting as unpaid nursemaid to a spoilt child. She felt a pang of disappointment, but beggars couldn't be choosers, and she couldn't afford to lose this position.

She wanted to ask more about Rex and his care. Where was his father, for example? But Mrs Brouillard, although perfectly polite, had a reserve about her that discouraged questions. The older woman seemed to think Rex had been dealt with, and began to enumerate the duties that Harriet would be required to carry out as her secretary.

Harriet listened, and studied her employer as she did so. Rose Brouillard was a handsome woman still, although she couldn't be called beautiful in the classical sense, since her profile was a little too patrician for that. She had large, grey eyes under heavy eyelids, and her chestnut hair had few traces of grey. She wore it swept back from her face, which accentuated her fine bone structure and perfectly smooth brow. When she smiled, which was not often, the effect was quite dazzling. She had been much younger than her husband, Jean-Jacques Brouillard, who had famously died of a heart attack on stage at the Salle Pleyel concert hall in the early days of the Occupation, when he was already well into his seventies. Mrs Brouillard had lived through difficult times – as had everybody – but her face bore few traces of it, for it was almost unlined, and were it not for the severity and imperiousness of her demeanour she might have passed for a much younger woman.

Mrs Brouillard finished talking about the job, which sounded straightforward enough, and went on to question Harriet closely about her experience.

'I see you didn't stay long in your last three positions, although they speak reasonably highly of you at the agency.'

She looked up questioningly. Harriet thanked her stars that she'd been so good at her job once; that fact had given her a certain amount of credit with the agency, although it was swiftly running out.

'We didn't suit each other,' she said, and it was true enough.

Mrs Brouillard didn't press for details, but seemed more interested in making absolutely sure that Harriet's French was as good as the agency had promised, which came as something of a relief; Harriet didn't want to have to explain that she'd spent the last year and a half in pieces, and was only now beginning to glue herself together again. She didn't know quite what to make of Rose Brouillard, but the woman was polite, if a little chilly – which she'd been warned about anyway. If this was as bad as she got, then Harriet thought the two of them would get on very well together. Mrs Brouillard was obviously thinking the same.

'Well, you seem to have your wits about you,' she said at last, once she had finished questioning Harriet. 'We'll see how it goes. I expect a week or two will be enough to tell whether we shall be able to work together. The last two girls were worse than useless, especially when it came to speaking French, as I mentioned. Where did you learn it, by the way?'

'My father was a professor of languages,' replied Harriet. 'He made us speak French in the house. He said being bilingual was good for the brain.'

'He was right. Is he still alive? What about your mother?'

'They're dead,' said Harriet shortly.

'Ah, that is your particular personal tragedy, I see.' Mrs Brouillard looked at her more closely.

One of them, Harriet wanted to say.

Her new employer rose and rang a bell. 'Estelle will show you your room. I'll give you today to settle in, but from tomorrow I shall expect you to be ready to work first thing. You'll dine with the family at seven. Sébastien isn't here today but he is meant to return tomorrow. I don't suppose you've met many geniuses in your life, Miss Conway?'

'No,' replied Harriet, surprised.

'They are not like you and I. You will find Sébastien rather highly strung, especially when he's preparing for an audition or a performance, but don't take it personally if he's a little difficult to live with. There is a price to be paid for talent such as his, and Sébastien has suffered for his music.'

Her face lit up as she spoke, her eyes shining with repressed excitement, and Harriet was almost shocked at the change in her employer, at the joy she evidently took from her youngest son. She suddenly felt awkward, as though she had just witnessed something intensely private. Then the elderly Frenchwoman entered, and Mrs Brouillard's face returned to its habitual unemotional expression.

'Show Miss Conway to her room,' she ordered in French. 'And turn on the heating. I expect she'd like to warm up and change before she meets the family.'

'*Oui, madame,*' said Estelle.

She led Harriet out into the hall. As they ascended the stairs the grandfather clock chimed four suddenly, making Harriet jump. The chimes were still echoing when the eerie music started again, the sound of the piano floating through from some unseen part of the house as though played by an invisible hand.

Chapter Two

Harriet's bedroom was not one of the best ones, that was obvious, but it was very pleasant, situated at the end of a corridor on the first floor. It was smallish and narrow, with a brown patterned carpet that was a little worn but not unduly so, and walls painted in a pale pink. A copy of Constable's *The Hay Wain* hung on one wall, while a reproduction of one of Degas's ballerina paintings was on another. The single bed was covered in a bedspread of soft, pea-green candlewick, and next to that was a bedside table with one drawer. The bathroom was just across the corridor. The water was heated daily, Estelle had informed her, so she might have a bath as often as she chose. It was all so much more comfortable than the boarding house, and Harriet was determined not to mess things up this time.

She sat on the bed to test it, then unpacked her few things and placed them in the wardrobe and the drawers, which smelt faintly of dried lavender. When she had finished she stood looking out of the window for some time. The light was sinking with the afternoon, but the fog had lifted slightly, and in the twilight she could see that they had put her in a room overlooking a clump of fruit trees that was too small to be called an orchard. The leaves were falling, but a few apples lay on the grass underneath the trees – brown and rotting now, half-eaten by wasps and other creatures. To the right she could see a terrace which looked like a more recent addition to the house, although it was in a state of disrepair, with moss growing up through the stones and patches of lichen on the balustraded wall. Beyond that stretched a long lawn, but it was too misty to see all the way to the end of it. As far as she could tell, the house was divided into two wings – a main one, in which the sitting room she had just been in and most of the bedrooms were situated, and a smaller one, which branched off the main entrance hall. Harriet liked what she'd seen of the house so far, and was pleased with her accommodation, which was positively luxurious by comparison with that in some of her previous positions. Her room was warm, thanks to a small gas heater, and not stuck out of the way. Some employers considered secretaries as not much better than servants, but Mrs Brouillard had mentioned dining with the family, which was an encouraging sign.

Harriet glanced in a mirror that stood on the chest of drawers. She was looking a little dishevelled from her journey; the damp had made her fair hair look darker than normal, and her curls had gone limp. After attending to her hair and reapplying her lipstick, she left the room, intending to explore the house. Outside in the corridor everything was quiet. Harriet listened, but whoever had been playing the piano seemed to have stopped for now. If it was the seven-year-old Rex, then Mrs Brouillard had done him a disservice in saying that he had no musical ability, since the music Harriet had heard, although eerie and disturbing, had been played by an obvious expert.

She descended the stairs and entered the dim hall, looking about her. The framed certificate she had seen before caught her eye again, and she moved over to it.

'*Ordre National de la Légion d'Honneur*,' she read. The certificate was filled out in a grand, swirling hand, with the name Jean-Jacques Brouillard, who had been awarded the distinction of Chevalier of the Legion of Honour by the French government in 1928 for his great contribution to music. Harriet now noticed something she had missed before: on the wall to the left of the certificate hung a painting in oils. She moved to look at it more closely. It was a portrait of a man and, to judge from his clothes, it had been painted in the early years of the century. The man himself looked to be in his forties, perhaps, for his forehead was somewhat lined, and the grooves between his nose and the corners of his mouth were deeply scored. His hair was still dark, however, with no sign of grey, and long for the time, almost touching his collar. It was clear that no attempt had been made to flatter the subject, but even so it was evident that the man was, or had been, quite an exceptional person.

He was gazing straight out of the canvas at Harriet, an uncompromising stare that seemed to challenge any and all comers. His mouth was set in a firm line, with not a sign of a smile. As though he disdained the need to sit down he was shown standing by a chair, upon which was laid a musical score and a violin. If Harriet had had any doubt that this was a portrait of Jean-Jacques Brouillard, his name was etched on a plaque at the bottom of the frame, together with the year '1907'. This was how the famous French conductor had looked more than forty years ago.

Harriet remembered seeing him towards the end of his life, grey-haired but still full of passion and vigour as he conducted the London Philharmonic Orchestra in Berlioz's *Symphonie Fantastique*. Age had not shrunk him or diminished him in any way, and the newspapers had written of it as one of his finest performances. They'd walked the mile home afterwards, Harriet and her mother talking non-stop about the concert all the way. That had been a good night, and it was just a pity her father hadn't been able to make it because he was tied up with some important meeting or other at the university. Mrs Conway would have been thrilled to know about Harriet's job with the Brouillards, and Harriet would have loved to telephone her and tell her. But she was dead now, and there was nobody else who would be interested. Jim hadn't cared about classical music, and he certainly would never have heard of the Brouillards. But that was part of the reason she'd fallen in love with him – after a childhood spent among academics, his uncomplicated personality and lack of intellectual pretence had been like a breath of fresh air wafting through the stale, dusty scent of ancient books. He'd swept her off her feet quite unexpectedly one day, and that had been it: her introduction to a life that promised adventure and excitement, but which had ended with one ten-second nosedive that had wrenched her heart out and torn the ground from under her.

Harriet grimaced. She wasn't supposed to be thinking about all that. Jim and her parents were dead, and she'd accepted that and was trying to be happy in her new life. She had a new job that promised well, with an interesting family.

'Are you Grand-mère's new secretary?' came a voice behind her. She turned and saw a small boy hovering uncertainly at the bottom of the stairs, one hand on the banister, a foot poised ready to step onto the hall floor. He was pale, with large eyes and a pointed chin. His dark brown, almost black hair was cut very short, and his brow was drawn together in an expression of worry.

'I'm Harriet Conway. I've come to work for Mrs Brouillard. You must be Rex.'

'That's right.' He came towards her and held out his hand in an oddly formal gesture. She shook it gravely. 'I'm very pleased to meet you, Miss Conway.'

'I heard you practising the piano earlier when I arrived,' said Harriet. 'At least, I think it was you.'

He shook his head.

'I haven't done my practice for today yet. But please don't tell Grand-mère, or she'll be cross. She likes me to do an hour first thing, but I didn't, because—'

He stopped and looked confused.

'Don't worry, I won't say a thing,' she replied. 'Don't you go to school?'

'Not now. I did, but I was unhappy so Grand-mère said I could come home as long as I promised not to be any trouble.'

'Who teaches you your lessons?'

'A tutor comes sometimes, but not this week, of course. It's half-term, you see,' he explained.

'Is it? I hadn't realised. I suppose it is. But if you don't go to school then who do you play with?'

'Nobody,' he said. 'There was a boy who was my friend at school, but he moved to Aberdeen. That's in Scotland.'

'Yes, it is. But aren't you lonely stuck here by yourself?'

'A little, sometimes. But I'm not really by myself. There's Grand-mère, and Sébastien, and Estelle, and there's Maurice and John at the farm. They let me tag along sometimes. Maurice let me drive the tractor once. And there's Maman, too, but I'm not supposed to disturb her.'

The French words sounded odd coming from a boy with such an English accent, but he said them quite unselfconsciously.

'Why aren't you supposed to disturb her?' asked Harriet curiously.

'Because she's not well, and Grand-mère said she's not to be bothered with me.'

'Is she sick? I didn't know.'

'Not sick, but she had an accident years ago, when we lived in France, so we have to make *a-llow-ances* for her.' He said the word carefully, as though to make sure he was pronouncing it right. 'I was quite a baby, so I don't remember it.'

'Do you remember anything of France?'

'Not much. We came here when I was very little, after the Germans left Paris. Sébastien thinks we should have stayed. He preferred France, he says.'

'Sébastien is your uncle, I think?'

'Yes. He's quite young for an uncle – more like a cousin, really.' His face clouded for a second. 'I don't like him much, but he's not here all the time, so it doesn't matter.'

'You don't like him? Why not?'

'Oh – because he doesn't play with me,' said Rex evasively. 'Anyway, I'm glad you've come.' The grandfather clock just then struck five and he froze. 'I'd better go and practise before Grand-mère finds out I haven't done it,' he said. 'You can come and watch if you like.'

There was an appeal in his eyes that Harriet was at a loss to understand. She didn't particularly want to listen to a child practising his scales, but she agreed and followed him into the large drawing room. Here a fire had been laid but not lit; Harriet supposed the family only sat in this room after dinner, since it was too grand to be used in the normal way. It was at least thirty feet square and was furnished ostentatiously, with an eye to effect rather than comfort. Again, there was that suggestion that the furnishings had been shipped from abroad, since they didn't quite seem to fit with their surroundings. In the far corner stood a magnificent grand piano. Rex went across to it, sat down, and began shuffling exercise books.

'You practise on this, do you?' asked Harriet in surprise.

'Yes,' replied Rex. 'Grand-mère can't hear me from the music room and she likes to be sure I'm doing it properly, so I play on this one. It belonged to Grand-père. He composed music on it. Have you heard of him? He was very famous.'

'Yes, I have. I saw him once, before you were born. I don't suppose you remember him either?'

'No. I don't know whether I'd have been afraid of him.'

'He does look a bit cross in that portrait of him, I suppose,' said Harriet.

Rex gave a sudden movement of his shoulders, like a wince.

'Yes. I don't like it much. It looks as though he's watching me. I always hurry past it and don't look at it, especially when my practice hasn't gone well.'

He began playing arpeggios with great concentration. Harriet watched for a moment or two, then began to wander round the room. The heels of her shoes clicked on the dark walnut parquet, and she glanced down in concern that she might be damaging an expensive floor. But she immediately saw that there was no need to worry. It was already dented and chipped, bearing the wear of many years. In fact, the more closely she looked at everything, the clearer it became that much of the Brouillards' appearance of affluence was something of a façade. The opulent cream and yellow silk curtains which hung at the windows smelt of dust, and showed unmistakable signs of moth damage. A polished, inlaid table which stood at the side of the room turned out to have a badly scraped surface. A lamp had been placed carefully so as to hide much of the mischief, but it was still visible. An elegant silver tea set stood on a dresser at the side of the room. It, at least, was obviously polished frequently, but the milk jug and the teapot itself were both dented in several places, and the tray on which the set stood was not solid silver, and the plating had worn off around the edges. Harriet remembered the cracked stones of the terrace and the thin carpet in her room. Rose Brouillard did her best to keep up appearances, but it was evident that the family's circumstances were not what they had been. It was hardly to be wondered at; so many people had lost everything during the war, and France could hardly have been an easy place to live while the Germans were there. The Brouillards were only lucky they had come through it as well as they did. One son had been killed fighting, and Jean-Jacques Brouillard himself, the source of the family's wealth, was dead too, but Mrs Brouillard still had much to be thankful for.

Rex had stopped practising arpeggios and was now doing complicated finger exercises very slowly. One in particular seemed to be giving him trouble, and after the fifth or sixth attempt he stopped in frustration and gave a sigh.

'I have told you time and time again that you will never succeed if you give up at the first sign of difficulty,' came Rose Brouillard's sharp voice from the doorway. Rex gave a gasp of surprise.

'I was only stopping for a rest, Grand-mère,' he said hastily. 'I've got a cut on my finger, and it hurts a bit.'

'What do you mean, you have a cut on your finger?' said Mrs Brouillard, coming fully into the room. She had not seen Harriet, who had been examining some old photographs on a desk in one corner of the room. 'Have you been playing with the pen-knife again?'

'No,' said Rex.

'Then how did you do it?'

'I— I don't know.'

She advanced towards him slowly and stopped, standing over him where he was sitting at the piano, which was so enormous it almost hid him entirely. Harriet glanced at Rex and was astonished at his reaction to his grandmother, as he quailed before her in seeming terror. Mrs Brouillard's eyes were narrowed and Harriet might almost have described her expression as one of menace.

'Show me your hand,' said Mrs Brouillard quite deliberately.

Rex put his hands behind his back and cast his eyes in desperation at Harriet.

'All right, it was the pen-knife. I'm sorry, Grand-mère, I know I promised to be careful with it, but I was trying to carve a piece of wood and the knife slipped. It's not very bad. It'll be better by tomorrow, I promise.'

Rose Brouillard made a sudden movement, as though about to strike him. Rex flinched, just as Harriet stepped forward hurriedly and said, 'I think it was my fault.'

Mrs Brouillard whirled round and saw Harriet for the first time. Her hand fell to her side.

'It wasn't his finger giving him trouble,' Harriet went on. 'He managed the arpeggios quite easily. But I'm afraid I distracted him by asking him questions when he was trying to do the last exercise. I'm sorry, Rex, it was awfully inconsiderate of me. I'll leave you alone in future, but I couldn't resist the sound of this magnificent piano. It's quite beautiful. I understand it was your husband's?'

She was talking to Mrs Brouillard now. Her employer paused for a second, and her eyelids lowered.

'Yes, it was. It is all we have left of him.' She turned back to Rex, and there was no sign of the anger Harriet had seen in her. 'You are supposed to be careful with your hands. They are a musician's most important possession. If you damage your hands then you have nothing. Now, you had better go and fetch the pen-knife and give it to me, since you are obviously not to be trusted with it.'

Rex looked as though he would have liked to protest, but thought better of it.

'Yes, Grand-mère,' he said meekly. He got down from the piano and went out.

'I should advise you not to disturb Rex while he is practising in future,' said Mrs Brouillard to Harriet, without looking at her. 'He is inclined to be lazy and will seize upon any excuse to avoid his exercises.'

'Perhaps he doesn't like playing the piano,' suggested Harriet.

'No child *likes* playing the piano, Miss Conway. It is not a question of liking it, but of doing what must be done. If Rex is to have any future in music, then he must do better. If indulged, he will waste far too much of his time in useless pursuits. I do not intend to indulge him.'

Poor Rex, thought Harriet, his future already decided for him at the age of seven. Rex himself returned just then and handed over the offending pen-knife to his grandmother. Harriet noticed he kept his left hand carefully out of sight.

'Very well,' said Mrs Brouillard. 'You may go and play, but you must do an extra half-hour tomorrow to make up for what you have missed today.'

'Yes, Grand-mère,' replied Rex gratefully, and ran off.

'Perhaps you would like to look around the grounds, Miss Conway,' said Mrs Brouillard. 'There are some very fine views of the house from the west side, by the bridge over the stream. Or perhaps you would like to read quietly in your room until dinner-time. If you have no books of your own then you may have the free run of the library. Many of the books are in French, but there are a few modern novels in English if you prefer to read in your own language.'

Harriet had the feeling she was being subtly reprimanded. She didn't want to go out in the damp and cold again, but she'd had an early start, so the thought of spending an hour or so resting quietly in her room was appealing. She would get a book, she said. The tightness at the corners of Mrs Brouillard's mouth relaxed a little.

'The library is just across the hall. There is no need to dress for dinner if you don't wish it, but I advise you to change into something a little smarter if you have it. If you haven't, there are several reasonably priced clothes shops in Royston, which you may like to visit the next time you go. We don't take the car out very often, since we save most of the petrol coupons for Sébastien, who needs them to get to London and Cambridge.'

'I see,' said Harriet. She was curious to meet this Sébastien – and the mysterious Cécilia, too. But there was no chance of exploring the house at the moment since her employer was clearly expecting her to go up to her room. She went into the library, directed towards some books Mrs Brouillard thought she might like. Harriet didn't particularly feel like reading, but she picked a title at random, came out of the library and went up the stairs. As she reached the first landing she turned involuntarily and saw her employer watching her intently. Harriet gave her an uncertain smile, which Mrs Brouillard did not return. Continuing on her way until she arrived at her room, Harriet didn't enter immediately, however, because her eye had been caught by a sudden movement, a brightening of the light in the dark corridor. She turned and saw Rex standing just inside a room, peeping out.

'Is this your bedroom?' she asked.

He nodded, opened the door wide and stepped back to show her. Harriet looked inside. It was about the same size as her own, and almost as sparsely furnished. Some shelves on one wall held Rex's few toys: a few tin cars and a plane, a battered-looking wooden yo-yo, a chemistry set, a pack of cards, some books. On one of the shelves was a small black instrument case.

'What's in there?'

'A clarinet. Grand-mère wants me to play it, but I can't blow it very well yet. I don't have enough puff.'

'No, I expect your lungs aren't quite developed enough yet.' She went across to the window. Rex's room gave out directly onto the back garden, although it was getting much too dark to see. She drew the thin curtains closed, then was struck by a thought.

'Show me your finger,' she said.

He hesitated, then held out his left hand. She looked closely. Rex's index and middle fingers were swollen and crusted with blood. He must have been bitten by something, because it was plainly not a cut.

'That pen-knife of yours must have a rather odd-shaped blade,' she said. 'You'd better go and get it clean and wrap it in a bandage, or it'll go septic.'

'It's not that bad. It hardly hurts at all.' He was flushed, seeming almost proud of the injury.

'Still, you'd better put some iodine on it, too. Do you have any?' He shook his head. 'I've got some I can give you. Now, quick, off to the bathroom with you!'

Rex ran off to wash his hand, and Harriet went back to her room to dig out her iodine and look for a bandage.

'There,' she said, once she'd finished dressing it. 'Does that feel better?'

'Yes, thank you.'

She glanced at him.

'Do you think it's a good idea to be keeping secrets from your grandmother?'

He went pink again.

'I'm not keeping secrets – I mean, not really. Only Grand-mère is *so* strict, I don't think she'd like it.'

'Like what?'

There was an air of excitement about him, and he seemed to be deliberating about whether to tell her, but just at that moment Mrs Brouillard's voice called him, and all at once he shrank back into himself.

'It's Grand-mère,' he said. 'I must go.'

He ran out before Harriet could say a word.

Chapter Three

It was not quite light when Harriet woke the next morning, but the darkness was a thin grey, and she could see the outline of the curtains where the daylight was seeping in. The rain was pattering heavily against the window, and the fog had mostly lifted. At last she could see to the bottom of the garden, which ended in a wooded area. A path led from a side gate down to the trees, just where they widened into a clearing. Under the canopy of branches was a little wooden bridge over a stream. On a bright day it would be pleasant to look at, but today it spoke of mud and damp and chill. Even the yellow and orange of the autumnal vegetation failed to cheer the prospect, and merely gave the place a jaundiced look.

Harriet went to the bathroom to wash, then returned to dress. She opened the cupboard and gazed at her few frocks in dissatisfaction. They'd ended clothes rationing a few months ago, but she hadn't had the money to do anything about her meagre wardrobe. She remembered Mrs Brouillard's turquoise dress from the day before, and the deep red silk she had been wearing at dinner last evening. Harriet had had to make do with her one good frock, a calf-length button-down affair in dark blue print fabric, with a white collar. It was hardly evening-dress material, but it was smart and business-like, as befitted a dependent secretary. She had hoped to pass muster, but had seen from Mrs Brouillard's expression as soon as she entered the dining room that her appearance was a disappointment. Her employer said nothing, but the all-observing eyes swept over Harriet then glanced away. Harriet was too experienced to be easily disconcerted, but on seeing Mrs Brouillard's reaction she was prepared to admit that perhaps it was time to invest in some new clothes if she wanted to obtain the approval of her new employer. Perhaps she could buy something cheaply in Royston.

There had been only the three of them at the table: Mrs Brouillard, Rex and Harriet. Harriet wondered where Cécilia was, but didn't like to ask. Rex sat meekly and toyed with his food. Harriet had bandaged his fingers for him, and every so often he glanced at his grandmother in trepidation in case she renewed the subject of his carelessness, but it seemed Mrs Brouillard considered the matter dealt with. She made icily polite conversation with Harriet throughout the meal, then afterwards rose and asked Harriet to join her in the sitting room, where she announced she was accustomed to listen to the BBC after dinner. Rex, meanwhile, had been sent off to bed. Harriet sat and paid dutiful attention to the classical music issuing from the wireless. It was heavy-going, and inevitably made her think of the days when her parents had still been alive. Once the war started they'd abandoned the earnest broadcasts of the Third Programme and the Home Service, and had switched over to the Forces Programme, which provided light relief in those dark, early days of the fighting. Harriet couldn't imagine Rose Brouillard ever listening to anything that made her laugh. At ten o'clock, Harriet had discovered she was tired and decided to turn in. As she left the room, she glanced back and saw Mrs Brouillard sitting erect in her chair, watching her with narrowed eyes. The older woman nodded a goodnight, then turned to pick up a book from a table next to her, and Harriet knew she had been duly dismissed.

Today, when she went downstairs at a quarter to eight, she found Mrs Brouillard already in the dining room, sipping coffee.

'I expected you earlier, Miss Conway,' she said. 'There is a lot to do today, and the sooner we start, the better.'

Harriet apologised, and Mrs Brouillard nodded briskly.

'Yes, never mind. I suppose you'd like something to eat. I can't bear breakfast myself, but I shan't insist on starving you if you're one of these girls who likes her food. The bread here is dreadful, but Estelle will make you some toast if you like, and there might even be an egg. We can get hold of some extra ones sometimes from the farm across the way. They're short of butter, though, so you'll have to make do with margarine. Do you prefer coffee or tea? We've stuck with the French customs and have coffee, but you may have tea if you prefer.'

'A slice of toast and some coffee will do nicely, thank you,' said Harriet.

'Sébastien will be home later, and you shall meet him, but this morning I shall show you your duties. They told me at the agency you are very experienced, so I expect you to learn quickly. I don't want to have to spend all my time holding your hand – I had quite enough of that with the last one.'

The shrill ring of a telephone sounded just then from outside in the hall. Harriet glanced at Mrs Brouillard and went to answer it.

'It's Mr George from the BBC,' she said when she returned. 'He wants to know whether you've spoken to the French lawyers yet about the rights for the third and fourth *pièces symphoniques*.'

'Tell him I spoke to them yesterday about it, and I shall call him back when I've had a few days to consider the matter. No – I've changed my mind. Let me speak to him. I'll take the call in the office.'

Mrs Brouillard rose and went out unhurriedly. Harriet saw her disappear through a door at the end of a corridor, waited a second then went to hang up the extension in the hall. As she picked up the receiver, she heard Mrs Brouillard's voice, sounding strange and tinny at the other end of the line.

'Angus.'

'Rose,' came another voice, a deep one this time. 'Don't tell me Radio Luxembourg is digging its heels in again.'

Mrs Brouillard laughed. It was an unexpected sound from such a severe woman. Harriet put down the telephone and returned to the dining room to find that Estelle had delivered two slices of toast and refilled the coffee-pot. Harriet nibbled at the toast, which was limp and flavourless, and sat lost in her own thoughts until Mrs Brouillard returned.

'Terribly tiresome, the BBC,' she said. 'But one must court them at all costs.' She didn't seem inclined to elaborate just then, so after a few moments Harriet asked:

'Where is Rex this morning?'

'Practising, I hope.'

'He doesn't go to school, he told me. What does he do when he's not studying?'

Mrs Brouillard made an impatient noise.

'Whatever small boys usually do, I expect. Gets up to mischief.'

'Doesn't he have any friends nearby?'

'Not as far as I'm aware. Musicians are not like ordinary people,' she went on, seeing Harriet's look of surprise. 'They have little time for play. One must make sacrifices for this life.'

But he's not a musician yet, Harriet wanted to say.

'Have you finished your breakfast? Then I shall show you what there is to be done this morning. I am expecting an important telephone call later, which requires some diplomacy, but I shan't expect you to cope with that sort of thing on your first day. However, there are many letters to be dealt with.'

Harriet saw that she was not to be allowed to linger over her morning coffee. She left it half-finished, then followed her employer along the corridor and into a small office which looked out onto the front drive. The room was furnished with a desk, a chair, and three or four filing cabinets. On one wall was a calendar, while on the window-sill stood a vase of dried flowers which had seen better days. A typewriter and a telephone were on the desk, as well as numerous sheaves of letters and bills, which were piled up at random wherever they would fit. Harriet wrinkled her nose at the sight.

'As you can see, the last girl lacked any sort of discipline,' said Mrs Brouillard. 'I don't know how she managed to get anything done at all.'

'How long did she stay?'

'Ten days. That was quite enough, I assure you. Now, here is today's post. Open it and stamp it with the date. Anything marked private don't touch it, but keep it for me.'

Harriet looked at the top of the pile.

'This letter is addressed to your daughter,' she said.

Mrs Brouillard took it and glanced at it.

'From the Conservatoire de Paris – that's Cécilia's old music school. You may open these ones, but anything else you must leave for her to deal with. Not that she will,' she added almost to herself, and left the room.

Harriet wondered what she meant, but thought she had better make a start on the post. The letter to Cécilia was an official invitation to some function or other in Paris. Harriet stamped it as instructed, then proceeded to work methodically through the rest, sorting it into piles as best she could given her unfamiliarity with her employer's business. She had soon finished, and cast about for something else to do. When Mrs Brouillard returned she found that Harriet had already begun to organise and tidy the contents of the desk.

'I've filed the bills that were marked paid,' said Harriet, indicating the row of filing cabinets. 'I assume these ones haven't been done yet. The rest of the letters I've put into piles according to urgency. I think this one needs to be dealt with today, as the event is on Friday. Are you going? Should you like me to inform them?'

'Oh, that's of no importance,' said Mrs Brouillard, glancing at the letter in Harriet's hand. 'But you might as well telephone them and give them my excuses. Say I'm otherwise engaged – whatever you like.'

Mrs Brouillard's affairs were soon restored to some semblance of order, and Harriet was already thinking of improvements to the filing system, when her employer said approvingly:

'You seem to have a head on your shoulders. What did you do in the war?'

'I spent most of it at the War Office, translating intercepted messages and telegrams,' replied Harriet.

'I see,' said Rose Brouillard, with a sharp look, but made no comment. 'Very well, you may return to these papers later. Now come, and I'll show you one of your other duties.'

She led the way out of the room and turned left and through a door. Now they were entering the smaller wing of the house which Harriet had seen from her bedroom window. The white-painted corridor walls, fluorescent ceiling lights and echoing wooden floors reminded Harriet strongly of a school or other public institution. Only the smell of boiled cabbage was lacking. Mrs Brouillard led her past a set of solid wooden double doors and up a flight of stairs to a long landing. The first floor was much more in the style of the rest of the house – dim, with worn, old-fashioned carpeting and a slight smell of dust. Mrs Brouillard opened a door.

'This is our history,' she said proudly.

They were in a long attic room which must have stretched the entire length of the upper floor of this wing. Three dormer windows let in the daylight, but the other three straight walls were built up with shelves containing hundreds, perhaps thousands, of leather-bound files. A table with a single wooden seat stood in the centre of the room. On it were one or two pairs of scissors, some pens and a pot of glue, while around it were piles upon piles of newspapers, heaped, sliding, toppling to the floor. Half the floor of the room must have been covered in them. Harriet blinked.

'Whenever you are not busy with other things, I should like you to come up here,' said Mrs Brouillard. 'As you can see, the work has not been completed and I should like it done.'

'What is it?' Harriet picked up the nearest newspaper. *Pariser Zeitung*, she read. The date of the newspaper was 22nd November, 1942, nearly seven years earlier.

'You read German too, you said?' asked Mrs Brouillard.

'Yes.'

'That is excellent. You see, during the war it was difficult to find anyone to help us keep up the work. The Germans came and most people had other things on their minds. I did the best I could, but I have a touch of arthritis in my hands and scissors are a trial to me, so I didn't get very far. However, I kept all the papers and made sure they were sent over when we came to England.'

Harriet glanced at the folders on the shelves. 'You keep scrap-books, do you?'

'I should prefer to call them record-books,' replied Mrs Brouillard. 'But yes, if you like, we keep scrap-books. It is of the utmost importance that no information about the family is lost. Jean-Jacques Brouillard may be dead and gone, but I have taken it upon myself to ensure that he will not be forgotten.'

'Then these folders are all cuttings about your husband?'

Mrs Brouillard went across to one of the shelves, selected a folder with deliberation and handed it to Harriet, who opened it.

'Oh!' she exclaimed. 'These are reports of his—'

'Of his death, yes.' Mrs Brouillard was watching to see her reaction. Harriet turned the stiff leaves one by one, seeing page after page of articles, obituaries and commentaries, all relating to Jean-Jacques Brouillard. 'Since you were familiar with my husband's work I expect you read about it at the time. He collapsed on stage while conducting a performance of Beethoven's Fifth, and died shortly afterwards. I used to attend all his concerts, but that night I was not well, and so I missed it. They told me about it afterwards.

They wanted to spare me the details but I insisted. One should never shirk the truth, however unpleasant.'

She took the volume from Harriet and replaced it. 'The cuttings are not all about my husband. Some of them are about Cécilia and Marcus too, although not nearly so many, since neither of them achieved anything lasting to speak about.'

There was a bitterness to this last remark which surprised Harriet.

'Don't you play?' she couldn't help asking.

Mrs Brouillard's mouth tightened.

'I played the violin as a young girl, and I was thought to have talent. I studied as hard as I could, but my parents were not keen on the idea of my pursuing music as a career, and eventually I gave it up. Not all of us are cut out for glory, Miss Conway. Mere talent is not enough. There must be something else – a divine spark, let us call it, for want of a better phrase, and that was lacking in me. I never understood this so well as I did when I met Jean-Jacques. He taught me, and encouraged me, and, I believe, spurred me on to greater heights than I could ever have achieved alone. But next to him I quickly saw I was nothing, and so I gave up my own ambitions and laid them at his feet.'

'What a pity for you,' said Harriet.

'On the contrary, I did it willingly. There is no sense in continuing with self-delusion once the reality has become clear. It would have been a stupid waste of time, and my efforts were much better directed towards helping my husband attain the greatness he deserved.'

Her face was flushed with pleasure. This was the most animation Harriet had seen in her in their short acquaintance, and she felt she was beginning to get some insight into her employer's unusual attitude towards her family. The colour faded from Mrs Brouillard's cheeks, and she resumed her usual serious expression. She gestured at the newspapers piled around the room.

'These are all the newspapers that could be had in Paris during the war – or at least, all the most important ones. As you may imagine, to be an Englishwoman in Paris during the war was not the easiest life, and I was forced to tread very carefully.'

'Why didn't you leave?' asked Harriet. 'You might have come to England.'

'There was nothing for us here,' said Mrs Brouillard, as though it were obvious. 'Had we left France we would have had to sacrifice everything we had worked so hard for. Now, I don't expect you to finish the job at once – and I certainly don't want you spending time on it when there are other things to be done – but whenever you have a spare half-hour or so, I should like you to come up here. A little bit every day and the job will soon be done.'

'Shall I do some now?'

'Why not?' Mrs Brouillard set about showing her exactly how it was to be done. 'Now, I shall leave you to it. I have an appointment this morning and must go out. I should be back just after lunch. Don't wait for me. Estelle will make you a round of sandwiches.'

She left Harriet alone in the long attic room, looking around her and blowing out her cheeks at the size of the task. But that would not get the job done, so she sat down and set to it. She picked up a copy of *Gringoire* from the spring of 1941 and began flicking through the pages. It didn't take long to find what she was looking for. There, in the section dedicated to the Arts, was an article about the posthumous performance by the Paris-Montparnasse Symphony Orchestra of Jean-Jacques Brouillard's final work, Symphony no. 12 'Les Orchidées', which he had completed only a few weeks before he died earlier that year. The piece had been conducted by Lucien Robiquet, who had taken over the role after the sacking of Brouillard's close colleague, the conductor Fernand Quinault, in a purge of Jews from public life.

In the opinion of the newspaper critic, although Brouillard's piece was daring in its modernity and something of a departure from his usual style, this merely demonstrated the composer's immense talent, and was bound to become a classic among audi-

ences and connoisseurs alike. Sonderführer Heinrich Schuster of
the German propaganda office had praised it, and was quoted as
saying that it was only a pity that Brouillard had died when the
degenerate music of the Jews was still too much in the ascendant
in the popular mind, throwing into the shade music composed by
the real geniuses of the time. The Führer himself was an admirer
of Brouillard, however, so it was not to be supposed that his legacy
would ever be permitted to die out.

Harriet read the article, shaking her head. How odd it was
to read old news. Was it really only a few years ago that people
had believed Jews were such a threat to society that they had to
be removed from their jobs? *Les Orchidées* had of course become
world-famous since the end of the war. It had been adopted as one
of the themes of French independence and liberty, and become
almost as recognisable as the 'Marseillaise', the French national
anthem, for a while. And yet the piece had been approved by the
Germans on its first performance in 1941. Presumably the people
of France had found it within themselves to overlook that fact
in the euphoric period that followed the liberation – or perhaps
they had just forgotten it, as it seemed strange to think that they
would have been so enthusiastic about any composer so beloved
of the enemy.

But if she was ever going to get through the pile of papers
there wasn't time to read every article. She quickly fell into a
rhythm, selecting, flicking, cutting, pasting, moving to the next.
She worked for an hour, then stopped for a rest. She was stiff
from sitting, so she stood up and went to the door to look out.
The place was silent. Harriet took a turn or two up and down the
corridor, and was about to return to her work when the sound
of the piano started up again, drifting up from the floor below.
It was the same tune she had heard the day before, but whereas
yesterday it had become increasingly discordant and uneven as it
went on, today it maintained its equilibrium, a soft, melancholy

sound, not unpleasant to the ears. The melody continued and as Harriet listened she thought that whoever was playing must be in a calmer, more reflective mood today. She followed the sound down the stairs to the lower, brightly lit corridor. The music was coming from behind the double doors they had passed earlier. Harriet listened for a moment, then pushed open the right-hand door.

The room behind it was dim, almost dark, as the floor-to-ceiling windows that ran the whole length of the far wall were shielded by heavy curtains. Here and there they had been carelessly drawn, allowing a few inches of light to seep in. The room was laid out as a large sitting room, but in a much more modern style than the main part of the house, although it had the same parquet flooring. There was a matching sofa and armchair in rich ochre, the same shade as the curtains, while against the wall, where a fireplace ought to have been, stood a square ash dresser with spindly legs. Along another wall was a range of bookshelves a good ten feet wide, stacked from top to bottom with books, periodicals and piles of papers. On the top shelf was a guitar in a battered case. But the main thing that caught Harriet's attention was the baby grand piano that stood in the corner by the window, and from which the music was coming. The lid was open, so she couldn't see who was playing it; nor had the musician heard or seen her come in, it seemed, as the music continued uninterrupted in that reflective vein.

'Hallo?' ventured Harriet. The music stopped, and she approached the piano, eager to see this mysterious musician. At the instrument was a young woman of perhaps Harriet's age, who to Harriet's mind was quite extraordinary-looking for no reason she could quite put her finger on. She was thin, almost gaunt, with hollow cheeks, a heart-shaped face and a narrow chin that made her already large, hazel eyes, fringed with long, delicate lashes, look enormous. Her dark hair had one or two streaks of silver, and she wore it cropped short to the sides of her head, revealing delicate ears and a long neck. She was too thin to be a beauty, but there was something strikingly ethereal about her that made her impossible to forget. Her mouth turned naturally down at the corners, and she didn't smile when she caught sight of Harriet. She made no move to get up but merely regarded Harriet with mild interest.

Harriet held out a hand. 'I'm Harriet Conway. I've come to work for Mrs Brouillard. You must be Cécilia Brouillard.'

The young woman neither confirmed nor denied it, but glanced at Harriet's hand and took it limply for the merest second.

'Where is Maman?' she asked, turning back to the piano and starting to play again.

Harriet observed the long, thin musician's fingers, and the delicate wrists that wore no jewellery, not even a watch.

'She said she had an appointment. She'll be back after lunch.'

Cécilia Brouillard did not reply. She seemed to have lost interest in her mother's whereabouts already, and was concentrating on the music, into which that discordant note had once more begun to introduce itself.

'I heard you playing the same thing yesterday, I think,' said Harriet. 'I like it. Who wrote it?'

'Nobody wrote it. It wrote itself.'

Harriet didn't know how to reply to that, but Cécilia seemed to have no idea that she had said anything in the slightest bit odd. Her hands continued to move over the keys, first quietly, then building to a crescendo. Halfway through a sequence she broke off so suddenly that Harriet jumped.

'Enough,' she said, and pushed herself back from the piano. Harriet expected her to stand up, but instead with a sudden shock she saw that the other woman was sitting not on a piano stool but in a wheelchair. Cécilia grasped the large back wheels and turned it away from the instrument, then wheeled herself with apparent ease across the room to an electric bell on the wall, which she pressed. Nothing happened, so she pressed it again.

'She's gone out again,' she muttered in French to herself, then, in English, 'You, miss, I forget your name.'

'Harriet Conway.'

'Miss Conway. Would you be so good as to help me? My nurse has disappeared. I want to sit on the sofa.'

'Of course.'

'I can't stand very well but if you would just hold out your arm so I can pull myself up…'

Two bony hands clamped around Harriet's right forearm, and she put her own left hand against Cécilia's right arm to steady her as she pulled herself to her feet. She seemed to weigh nothing. She stood for a moment, then reached for the arm of the sofa and lowered herself down with Harriet's help.

'If you would just give me that rug,' she said. Harriet arranged the blanket around her knees and ensured she was comfortable.

'Do you want me to send Rex to you?'

'Rex?' said Cécilia blankly, then seemed to recall who he was. 'No thank you, I am tired now. I'd like to read. Can you get me a book from the shelf?'

'Which one?'

'I don't care, any book.'

'A novel, you mean?'

'As you choose,' she said with a shrug.

Harriet was nonplussed. She had no idea of Cécilia Brouillard's taste in literature, so she selected a book at random and handed it to her. Cécilia glanced at it and threw it onto the sofa next to her.

'Thank you, I will read it later.'

Just then a door Harriet had not spotted earlier opened and a middle-aged woman in a nurse's uniform came in. She threw Harriet a sour look, and said in French:

'You wanted me, *madame*?'

'Not now. You are too late as usual. Miss Connor has helped me.'

'Conway,' said Harriet, but they were not listening. The nurse broke into a torrent of speech, of which the gist seemed to be that Miss Brouillard ought not to be accepting help from someone who was not trained and could not be trusted to lift her without injuring her further.

'She didn't lift me,' said Cécilia. 'I lifted myself. And if you are going to ignore the bell every time I ring, then I must make my own arrangements. Now, go away before I get tired of your face and give you notice. And next time answer the bell when I ring it, not when it's convenient for you.'

The nurse opened her mouth to argue, but Cécilia quelled her with a glance. It was the most animation Harriet had seen in her so far. The nurse left the room, muttering, and Cécilia sagged against the cushions of the sofa, her energy seemingly spent.

'Why don't you get rid of her if she's so inefficient?' said Harriet.

Cécilia waved a hand in resignation.

'She's not the laziest nurse I've had by a long way.' Then, as was her way, she lost interest in the subject. 'I'm tired,' she said again. 'You may leave me now.'

'Shall I speak to Estelle about lunch for you?'

'I usually have it here. Léonie brings it to me.'

She picked up the book and opened it, indicating the conversation was at an end. Recognising that she had been dismissed, Harriet left the room. Rex had said his mother had had an accident, but Harriet hadn't expected this. What on earth could have happened to put such a young woman in a wheelchair?

Chapter Four

The sound of minor scales, played heavily, was emanating from the drawing room when Harriet emerged into the hall from the convalescent wing, as she had begun to call it in her head. Rex must be practising.

'Hallo, Miss Conway,' he said cheerfully when she entered the drawing room. 'I've just finished. Is it too early for lunch, do you suppose? I'm ravenous!'

He was in luck, as just then Estelle came in to announce that there was a plate of sandwiches for anyone who cared to eat them. They went into the dining room and found she had also managed to procure a large pork pie, although she was most mysterious when questioned on the subject of its provenance, tapping her nose and leaving the room.

'Grand-mère thinks Estelle has a gentleman friend at the farm,' said Rex conversationally as they ate. 'Sometimes she gets things.'

Now that his grandmother was out of the house he seemed cheerful, much more like a normal little boy.

'That's good luck for us,' said Harriet, cutting large slices for them both.

The pie was delicious, the pastry light and tasting almost buttery, the meat moist and flavourful, and they enjoyed it in silence for some minutes. Then Harriet asked:

'What really happened to your hand, Rex?'

He went pink, then glanced at the door. He seemed to be trying to suppress a laugh. 'You won't tell?'

'On my honour.'

'Well—' he began, but got no further.

'Hallo, hallo, who's this?' came a male voice from the doorway. Harriet, who was facing the window, turned round and blinked. There stood perhaps the most beautiful young man she had ever seen. He was tall and long-limbed, and he leaned gracefully against the dining room door frame as though he had been sculpted in that position. His hair was an unusual shade of dark red that reminded Harriet of the terracotta-roofed houses she had seen in pictures of Florence, and he wore it slightly long so it flopped over his forehead. But where most red-haired people had pale skin, his held a delicate tan that set off the amber colour of his eyes. His bone structure was that of his mother and sister, and his mouth turned down at the corners in the same way as Cécilia's, but where sickness had made her pale and thin, he was bursting with vitality – a young man in the physical prime of his life. He was wearing a crumpled tweed suit and no tie, but it seemed a studied rather than a genuine carelessness, as though he knew perfectly well that no deficiency of dress could spoil his radiant good looks.

He was regarding Harriet with interest, and as she gazed at him his mouth widened into a smile. She had known his teeth would be good.

'Well, hallo,' said this young god easily. 'Are you the new girl?'

'Harriet Conway,' replied Harriet, standing up and offering him her hand.

'Welcome to our little hovel, Miss Conway. It's not much, I know, but you'll have to take it for what it is.'

He held her hand a little too long, and eyed her up and down quite openly as he spoke. His mouth curled up again and his eyes narrowed, as though he were enjoying a private joke.

'You must be Sébastien,' she said, after a moment's hesitation as to whether she ought to call him Mr Brouillard. He was nineteen, she remembered; practically a child, so too young for formality – and besides, there was a knowing, amused look about him that suggested he might become overfamiliar if given an opportunity.

'*Oui, enchanté*,' he said with a mocking bow, then looked across at Rex. 'What were you saying just then? It sounded as though you were about to tell our new guest one of your delicious little secrets. I'd keep an eye on him if I were you, Miss Conway. He's a furtive little devil, forever skulking in corners and hiding things from people.'

The wide smile didn't falter as he said it. It might have been intended as friendly teasing, but Rex didn't take it that way. He flushed and looked sullen, but said nothing. Shortly afterwards he excused himself from the table, and disappeared without looking at his uncle.

'Little beast,' remarked Sébastien to no one in particular. 'I say, is that a pork pie? What did Estelle have to sell to get it? Herself, perchance?'

He laughed unpleasantly, then cast Harriet a glance from under his lashes and threw himself down opposite her at the table. He helped himself to a large slice of the pie, before looking about him. 'What? No tomatoes today? Not even an egg?'

'It seems not,' said Harriet. She had finished her own lunch, so she rose.

'You're not leaving already, are you? Have I said something to offend?'

'Not at all,' she replied pleasantly. 'But I have work to do.'

'Ah, yes. You don't want to get a reputation for slacking. The last one was quite useless. Nice-looking little piece, though. I'd have had a crack at her if I'd thought she'd be willing. But she was the sort to keep her legs firmly crossed at all times. What, you're still going? Aren't you going to stay and keep me company?'

'I have lots to do. Shall I ask Estelle to make you some more sandwiches?'

He waved his hand in a negative, quite unabashed, and she went out. She suspected he had been trying to provoke her with his remarks, but was wise enough not to rise to his bait.

She spent another half-hour or so in the archive, then heard the sound of a car approaching. A glance out of the window showed it was Rose Brouillard, returning from wherever it was she'd been. Harriet supposed she would be wanted now, so went downstairs. Her employer and Sébastien were in the small sitting room.

'I take it you've met,' said Mrs Brouillard, as Harriet entered, then, without waiting for an answer, continued her conversation with Sébastien. 'What did Professor Jarman say about the Amati? Does he think Mrs Dexter will sell it?'

'I forgot to ask,' replied Sébastien carelessly.

'But you were supposed to get him to help us. Adele Dexter has no earthly use for a violin now her husband is dead, but she's as stubborn as a mule and won't listen to reason. The only person who could possibly persuade her to sell it to us is Jarman, but if you don't remind him constantly he'll never get around to speaking to her about it, and it will go to auction and we'll never be able to afford it.'

Her tone was sharp, and Sébastien seemed to squirm under it.

'Oh, well,' he said sullenly. 'I suppose I'll speak to him about it next week.'

'It might be too late by then.'

'Well, there's nothing I can do now, is there?'

He was flushed, and Harriet was secretly amused to note his resemblance to Rex just then. At that moment he was a small boy being told off by his mother.

'Just make sure you don't forget next time,' said Mrs Brouillard. 'By the way, I spoke to the people at King's College this morning, and they're keen for you to do the concert. You'll be playing the second movement of *Les Orchidées*.'

Sébastien's expression changed from sulky to aghast.

'What? I can't do that. You know I can't. I thought they wanted me to do the Prokofiev. I can play that with one hand tied behind my back.'

'Nobody wants to hear the son of Jean-Jacques Brouillard play Prokofiev,' replied Mrs Brouillard impatiently, 'and it's about time you got over this mental block you have about your father's music.'

'But—'

'Enough! Miss Conway, I have some letters to dictate to you,' said Mrs Brouillard. 'Let us go into the office.'

She got up and left the room. Harriet followed, and as she did so glanced back and saw Sébastien rubbing his chin, a dismayed look on his face.

*

The rest of the afternoon was taken up with letters and telephone calls. After that, Harriet was free to go. She went up to her room and read for a while, then decided she had better show her face downstairs rather than shutting herself away out of sight. After all, she was supposed to be staying there as part of the family, in a manner of speaking, although what kind of family they were she couldn't tell yet. They were unlike any people she had met before, with their broken glory and their inner despair and their determination to pretend things were normal despite all appearances to the contrary. Rose Brouillard in particular seemed to be clinging to a past that could never be regained. Her daughter and her grandson had clearly disappointed her, and she had been forced to invest all her hopes in her youngest son. Would Sébastien restore the Brouillard fortunes and bring back something of former days?

She was interrupted in her thoughts by Sébastien himself, who was just emerging from the other wing of the house when she came downstairs.

'Come and talk to me while I practise,' he said. 'This place is dreary enough and I like to have someone there when I'm playing.

Maman does nothing but criticise, and I want someone to listen and admire. As you heard, I have a concert coming up.' He rolled his eyes at her humorously. 'You can pretend to be my audience.'

His manner was pleasant and friendly, without any of the insinuation it had held earlier. Harriet followed him into the music room, which she had not seen until now. It overlooked the garden, and through the window she could see Rex throwing sticks at a tree, trying to bring down a stray chestnut.

'What a lot of pianos you have in this house,' she remarked, looking at the upright one in the corner. 'I've counted three so far. Are there any more?'

'Probably a couple,' he said. 'As you've no doubt guessed, we Brouillards were never allowed to get out of our music lessons as children.'

'I suppose it must be difficult to follow in the footsteps of such a man as your father.'

'You might say that.' He took out a bow from a violin case and tightened it, then applied some rosin. 'Still, I have to try.' He picked up the violin and held it clamped under his chin, bow still in his right hand, as he tuned the instrument with his left. He drew the bow experimentally across the strings, made another slight adjustment, then played a chord with a sudden sweeping movement. 'That'll do. Do you play the piano at all?'

'Not well enough to accompany you,' she said in slight alarm, and he laughed.

'No matter.' He went across to a gramophone in a wooden cabinet. Under the machine itself were stacked some records. He selected one, put it on the turntable and dropped the needle somewhere in the middle.

'Do you recognise it?' he asked as the sound of music drifted out into the room.

'*Les Orchidées*, second movement,' said Harriet. 'The adagio.'

'Well done. You'll be a favourite with my mother in no time. It was the last piece my father wrote before he died, and it made him something of a legend. Now, here's the solo. Listen.'

He began to play along with the record, his brow wrinkling with concentration. Harriet listened. This was not the rousing third movement which had become inextricably associated with the days of the liberation, but was a less familiar part; a haunting, melancholy tune that spoke of suffering and longing for a brighter future. Sébastien closed his eyes as he played, wholly absorbed in his task, oblivious to everything around him. Harriet watched his long fingers move over the strings with ease, then looked at his face, which wore an almost blissful expression. He might have been lying in a soft feather bed, drifting off to sleep, such was his air of contentment. Then the tempo changed and he missed his cue, tried to pick it up too late and played a series of wrong notes. His eyes snapped open.

'Ah, damn it!' he said, suddenly furious. 'I fluffed it.'

He knocked the needle off the record with a bad-tempered swipe. There was a screech and the music stopped. Sébastien threw down the violin and bow with a clatter, strode up to Harriet and thrust his face into hers. She flinched.

'That was *your* fault!' he hissed. 'You distracted me. How can I be expected to concentrate when you're fidgeting with your earrings like that?'

For a second Harriet was quite taken aback, and was almost shocked into stuttering an apology. Then she caught hold of herself. She had not come to Chaffingham to indulge the moods of a temperamental young man.

'I beg your pardon,' she replied, with crisp coldness. 'You invited me to come and listen. I was listening. If you can't cope with an audience of one, I don't see how you expect to cope with an audience of hundreds, all sniffing and coughing and tapping their feet. You won't be allowed to throw a tantrum like that at King's College, you know. At least, not more than once.'

For a second she was just like the old Harriet, and she felt a pang of surprise, followed by triumph, then fear that she might have gone too far. After all, she'd only just arrived, and offending her employer's son was perhaps not the best way to ingratiate herself. He stared at her for a long moment, then to her astonishment burst out laughing and threw himself into a chair.

'Brava!' he exclaimed. 'Round one to you. You're right, of course. I'm sorry. It's just I've been on edge lately, and it's only too easy to take one's temper out on the staff. The other ones would have run off crying, but you're obviously made of sterner stuff. You will forgive me, won't you? Call me a spoilt child if you like.'

'Yes, you are,' said Harriet severely. 'I'll forgive you this time but don't try it again.'

'I'll be good, I promise.' He regarded his violin and sighed.

'It doesn't matter, does it?' she asked. 'You've time to perfect it.'

'But that's just it – I've been trying to perfect it for nearly two years now, and I still haven't got it. You wouldn't think it to look at it, but that's the most complicated passage, and I fluff it at least one time out of three. And this is my father's most famous work. How does it look if I can't even get that right?' He regarded her with wry humour. 'It's a good job Maman's not here. Then you'd see her raging at me and you'd think it served me right. She can't bear the thought of my father's legacy not surviving for a thousand years, you see.'

'She was very fond of him, I think.'

'Oh, she was devoted to him, and ridiculously loyal. Too loyal to mention the fact that when he died he left us in an awful hole. It seems musical geniuses aren't much good at keeping hold of their money, and he used to splash it about as though it were water. He ought to have let Maman manage his affairs, but he was the sort who preferred his women decorative rather than functional, so he showered her with jewels and furs and nobody had the slightest idea that he couldn't afford it. Luckily, once he was gone, Maman had the brains and the sense to make the most of what he *had* left – which was his music and not much else – and keep us afloat by the skin of our teeth. She was much younger than he, you know. He had an inconvenient first wife, but she was mad, or old, or both, and Maman was young and beautiful, so it's no wonder he threw the first one aside for her when she came along.' He was sly now, looking at her to see her reaction. 'They caused quite the scandal at the time. Marcus was born four months after the wedding, although I don't suppose she's realised I've worked it out. At any rate, she has no right to judge Cécilia.'

'Judge her? Why should she judge her?'

'Why, for the little beast, of course. You don't suppose he's legitimate, do you? Why do you think his surname is Brouillard?'

'Is his surname Brouillard? I didn't know.'

'Not that he deserves it, but better that than his filthy father's, I suppose.'

His face was twisted in disgust. Harriet would have liked to ask who Rex's father was, but thought it better not to pry. It was obviously a sore point and she didn't want to provoke him again. Sébastien was feeling in his pockets.

'Cigarette? Oh, do,' he said as she shook her head. 'Don't be prim or I won't believe you've forgiven me.'

She took one, and they smoked in silence for a few moments. He stared out of the window. Rex was nowhere to be seen.

'Ghastly place, this,' said Sébastien at last.

'Then why do you stay? Where should you prefer to live?'

'Why, Paris, of course. But Maman keeps us in exile and won't take us back.'

'You might go yourself.'

'Oh, I couldn't do that. She'd never allow it.'

'But you're old enough, surely. She couldn't stop you. Couldn't you find a job in an orchestra? I understand you're a great talent.'

'So I am,' he replied, quite unselfconsciously. 'But you don't know my mother. She'll find a way to stop me if she doesn't want me to go.'

'But—'

'Never mind,' he said petulantly. 'Don't let's talk about it any more. You've made me think of things I didn't want to think about.'

Chapter Five

Cécilia joined them for dinner that evening. Harriet wondered if she had been browbeaten into it by Rose, because she gave no indication of any interest in the company, especially not her son. Rex watched his mother in a kind of awed fascination, eager to help her in any way he could, passing her the salt and hastening to pick up her napkin for her when she dropped it. She smiled and thanked him vaguely, as she might a stranger, and he slid back into his seat and resumed watching her. Harriet was surprised to feel a pang of pity for him, but she tried to suppress it. Thousands of children had lost their entire families during the war; at least Rex still had his, and, if they didn't exactly shower him with love, at least he was reasonably well looked after.

Sébastien was in a chatty mood.

'An old friend of Papa's came to Piotrowski's yesterday,' he said. 'Name of Fernand Quinault. I seem to remember the name, although I'd never met him. He was very interested when he heard who I was.'

'I should imagine he was,' replied Rose, who had paused for a second at the mention of the name. 'Your father was far too kind to him in my opinion. He was a hanger-on of the worst sort. He was a Jew, and tried to use your father's influence to save himself from being thrown out of his job, as these people will do if given the opportunity. It didn't work, of course, and he had to leave France. I didn't think we'd hear from him again.'

'He lives in America, but he's thinking of returning to France,' said Sébastien, as Harriet raised her eyebrows, taken aback at the unjustness of her employer's remark. 'He writes film music nowadays, apparently.'

'Oh, *film* music,' replied Rose dismissively. She had become stiffer and colder than usual. 'I hope you weren't foolish enough to invite him here, Sébastien.'

'Certainly not. I take it he's not our type.'

'No, and you'd do well to avoid him as much as you can. Let me know if he's bothering you. I expect he wants something, as usual.'

'Oh, he won't bother me. I'll make sure of that,' Sébastien said with a smirk, and the conversation turned.

As soon as dinner was finished, Cécilia said she was worn out and wanted to go to bed.

'You do look fagged. It must be hard work, all that sitting about feeling sorry for yourself,' said Sébastien slyly. It was such an uncalled-for remark that Harriet glanced up in surprise. Cécilia hesitated and flushed, but did not reply.

'Don't be a beast, Sébastien,' said Rex heatedly. 'You'd feel sorry for yourself too if you had to sit in a wheelchair all day. And anyway, she doesn't feel sorry for herself, do you Maman?'

'*Non, mon petit*,' said Cécilia with an attempt at a smile. 'I'm just tired, that's all.'

She put her hand on his head, the lightest touch, just for a second, then turned her chair to leave the room.

'Let me open the doors for you,' said the boy eagerly.

She consented in silence, and the two of them went out.

'I don't know why he bothers,' drawled Sébastien. 'She'll never pay him the slightest bit of attention.'

'I regret to say my daughter has no backbone, Miss Conway,' said Mrs Brouillard unexpectedly. 'She is unfortunate enough to have been bereft of the full use of her legs, but there is nothing wrong with the rest of her, and no reason at all why she should have given up a very promising musical career. With a few adjustments, she might easily have kept up with her violin, and nothing but talent and a lively brain are required to compose music. And yet as you see she has chosen to leave it all behind and sit in seclusion all day every day.'

This seemed a harsh judgement upon a sick woman.

'Perhaps she lost her inspiration after her accident,' suggested Harriet. 'It must have been hard to adjust.'

'Her "accident", as you call it, was entirely her own doing,' replied Mrs Brouillard coldly. 'She knew the likely consequences of her actions, and yet chose to continue.'

'Continue what?' Harriet asked, but Estelle came in just then to take away the plates, and Mrs Brouillard began to talk to her about some matter of housekeeping, and the moment was lost.

Harriet lay awake for a long time that night. There seemed no happiness in the Brouillard family. Of course they had lived through tragedy – one son had been lost, the daughter seriously injured, and the man who was the source of their wealth and fame, Jean-Jacques Brouillard himself, had died early in the war. Their case was hardly unique, however, and there ought to be some relief, surely, that the rest of them had made it through relatively unscathed? But perhaps Harriet was doing them an injustice. How could she criticise them when she herself had dealt with her own unhappiness so badly? Who was she to judge how people chose to work through their misery?

She turned over and tried to sleep, but the dinner had been over-salted and her mouth was dry. There was an empty glass by her bed, and she got up and took it along to the bathroom to fill it. The bathroom was near the top of the stairs, and as she came out she stopped short, hearing a noise from below. She crept to the head of the staircase. The sound of muffled, raised voices was coming from downstairs – from the sitting room, she thought. Mrs Brouillard and Sébastien were having a row about something, but she couldn't hear what, although she strained her ears, listening. Then came the sound of a door opening, and Sébastien's voice, angry, frustrated:

'I can't do it! Don't you understand? I'll never be able to do it, no matter how much I practise. Oh, what's the use?'

The last sentence was uttered in desperation. He was coming upstairs. Harriet darted back into her room, shutting the door as quietly as she could, then stood against it, listening. Sébastien passed her door and went into his own room. Harriet got back into bed and lay down, and shortly afterwards heard Mrs Brouillard come upstairs. All was silent now, apart from the ticking of her little bedside alarm clock. Or was it? Harriet sat up and listened. She was almost certain she could hear the sound of someone sobbing. Rex, perhaps? She slipped out of bed and out into the corridor. There was no sound at Rex's door. The noise had stopped now, but as she listened it started again, muffled, anguished. This time there was no doubt whose room it was coming from. Harriet hesitated a moment, then returned to her room and got back into bed. She might have gone in to comfort Rex, but Sébastien was a different matter.

*

Harriet's first week passed uneventfully. Sébastien went away again, this time to stay with friends in London, while Cécilia mostly remained in her quarters, emerging once or twice a week to eat dinner with them, presumably on the instructions of her mother. She never said much – nor did she eat much – but she would reply with a vague kindness to every remark made to her by Rex, then, as soon as decently possible, would bid them goodnight and retire to the other wing, oblivious to her son's crestfallen face. Harriet felt more and more sympathy for the boy, who was evidently desperate to win his mother's love, although she, equally evidently, was far too wrapped up in herself to show anything other than a polite interest in him. Still, at least he had his studies to occupy him:

now that the school holidays were over, Mr Caldicott the tutor had returned, and Rex's mornings were spent in the schoolroom.

'Here is the post,' announced Estelle, coming into the dining room one day as they sat at breakfast. Harriet held out her hand for the little bundle of letters and began to sort through them as she sipped her coffee.

'One from the Performing Rights Society,' she said. 'One from the Berlin Philharmonic. Two marked private.' She handed the two personal letters to Mrs Brouillard. 'One for Sébastien from the Royal College of Music.' She began to open the others. 'Now, who's this from? I can't read his writing very well.' She squinted at the scrawled signature. 'Quinet? Quinault?'

'I'll take that,' said Mrs Brouillard. 'Give it to me.'

Harriet handed her the letter. Her employer gave it the merest glance, then to Harriet's surprise tore it deliberately into two, then four, then eight pieces. She stood up, the scraps of paper still in her hand.

'I want you to make some telephone calls for me this morning, Miss Conway,' she said, as though nothing had happened. 'Finish your coffee quickly then come into the office.'

Harriet raised her eyebrows as her employer left, and did as she was told. Although Rose Brouillard's manner had seemed uniformly chilly at first, Harriet had begun to recognise in her degrees of chilliness. Today she seemed to be in a particularly bad mood, and so Harriet judged it best to do her work with as little fuss as possible. Even so, she received some sharp words before the morning was over. She hadn't slept well the night before, having been plagued by bad dreams in which she wandered down endless corridors in pursuit of a shadowy figure that remained frustratingly out of reach, so she found it more difficult than usual to bite her tongue when told off for some imagined error.

But at last Mrs Brouillard left her alone and she was able to get on with her work in peace. There were several letters to type and get to the post before the end of the day, and she set to work.

One contained several names in unfamiliar languages, and after the third mistake she swore under her breath, tore the paper out of the typewriter and screwed it up. As she went to throw it in the waste-paper basket, she noticed it contained the torn scraps of a letter. It was the one Mrs Brouillard had received that morning. Why had she ripped it up? Harriet was suddenly overcome by curiosity. She reached into the basket and picked up some of the pieces, but she hadn't got further than glancing at them to make sure that it was the same letter when the door opened and her employer came in again. Harriet jumped and let the pieces of paper fall back into the basket.

'I forgot to mention that I shall be out for dinner,' said Mrs Brouillard. 'I shall stay overnight with a friend in London and will be back tomorrow by lunch-time.'

She seemed not to have noticed what Harriet had been doing.

'Shall I order you a taxi?' asked Harriet.

'No, Sébastien will take me to the station in the car.'

'Oh, he's back, is he?' Harriet had been too absorbed in her work to notice his arrival.

'So Estelle says. Go and find him, will you, and tell him I want to catch the four-twenty train.'

Harriet departed obediently to look for Sébastien, and at last found him pacing moodily up and down the sitting room, smoking. He grunted when she delivered the message, and didn't seem inclined to chat, so she returned straight to the office, which was now empty. Harriet glanced up and down the passage then shut the door, went across to the waste-paper basket and looked inside. She was not entirely surprised to find that the torn pieces of letter had gone, but her curiosity was now fully aroused. Why had Mrs Brouillard been so anxious that she should not see it?

Harriet tried to remember what she had seen of the letter. It had been handwritten, not typed, and was signed as far as she could remember by an F. Quinault. She suddenly remembered Sébastien's casual remark a week ago, about how he had met a Fernand Quinault, a Jewish musician who had escaped France and gone to write film music in America. Her employer had talked of him as being a hanger-on of the worst sort, whatever that meant. Why was Quinault writing to Mrs Brouillard when she obviously wanted nothing to do with him? Harriet had no idea, but she had work to do so she forced herself to dismiss it from her mind for the present.

She had just finished her typing when the doorbell rang. She knew Estelle had gone out, so went to answer it herself. The visitor was a man; youngish, and as far as she could judge from appearances, well-bred.

'Yes?' she said.

'I hope you don't mind my troubling you, but I'm looking for a Miss Brouillard,' replied the man carefully. It sounded as though he'd rehearsed his little speech.

'Cécilia? Is she expecting you?' asked Harriet doubtfully.

'Not Cécilia. Maggie. Marguerite.'

'There's no one of that name here, I'm afraid. I think you must have got the wrong house.'

'Oh, but I was sure I must have the right place.' He seemed disconcerted.

'Well, I'm sorry, but I can't help you.'

'This is the Brouillard house, yes?'

'Yes.'

'You're the family of Jean-Jacques Brouillard, the composer?'

'Well, I'm not, myself, but yes.'

'How odd. I don't suppose there are any other famous musicians with that surname, are there?'

'Not that I know of.'

'How odd,' he said again.

She was about to bid him good day and close the door, but then she glanced around and spotted Mrs Brouillard, who had just come out of the sitting room with Sébastien.

'I don't suppose you know a Maggie Brouillard, do you?' asked Harriet. 'This gentleman is looking for her.'

Mrs Brouillard stood stock still for perhaps a second, then came to the door and stared coldly at the man, who was still standing there uncomfortably.

'Who are you?' she asked.

'My name's McLeod. Alec McLeod. I was looking for a Maggie Brouillard.'

'Then you have come to the wrong place. There is no Maggie Brouillard here.'

'So this young lady told me. But I was sure she said her father was the famous musician. Perhaps I misunderstood.'

'It appears you did. I hope you have not come a long way only for your time to be wasted.'

'No, just from Little Hambourn. I'm staying in the area and someone happened to mention that the Brouillards lived nearby, so I thought it wouldn't do any harm to come and see.'

'Well, there is nothing *to* see, Mr McLeod,' said Mrs Brouillard with finality. She turned away, the interview clearly over as far as she was concerned.

Harriet glanced around again, and saw Sébastien, standing frozen in the doorway of the sitting room, wearing the most curious expression. She would almost have said he looked shocked and frightened, but she couldn't think why he should. When he noticed her staring at him he seemed to come to himself and withdrew back into the sitting room. Harriet turned back to the door, disconcerted.

'I'm sorry I can't help,' she said to the visitor.

'No matter.' He smiled politely, and Harriet said goodbye and shut him out. But she stood behind a curtain and watched him through the window as he walked away from the house and down the drive. Once or twice he stopped and turned to look back, a puzzled frown on his face, but eventually he disappeared from sight.

Harriet guessed Maggie Brouillard was a girl he'd had a fling with during the war. She hoped he'd find her.

*

The weather was better than it had been for a fortnight, and it had turned out to be a fine, crisp, November day. Harriet suddenly felt the urge for some fresh air, so after lunch she said she would walk into Royston and go to the post office, if Mrs Brouillard didn't want her. Rose was caught up in some business with Sébastien, as it happened, and had no further use for her secretary that day, so Harriet threw on her shabby old coat and hat and left the house, a sheaf of letters stowed safely in the handbag she carried over her arm. She took the path through the back garden and across the wooden bridge, which Rex had informed her was a short-cut into town. It was chilly but not too muddy; an enjoyable walk in the country air.

Harriet breathed in deeply, reflecting that it was nice to get away from the cloying, closed-in atmosphere of Chaffingham. It would be pleasant to take a walk like this every day, and explore the area. As a girl she'd walked often with her father. He'd been something of a nature-lover, and she remembered how their outings had always proceeded very slowly, because he was forever pausing to point out a blackbird's nest in a hedgerow, or an interesting cloud formation, or the different leaf shapes of various trees. She'd missed all that since his death, and she spent far too much time indoors these days. But there was no reason she couldn't start going out again. Perhaps she would go into Royston a couple of times a week and sit in a tea shop. She might strike up a friendship with another girl – there must be plenty of them in her position, working in offices and schools and houses. It was time she stopped brooding on her own and made some friends. Harriet had had friends in the past, but most of them had been Jim's friends too, and she hadn't been able to bear their exclamations of sympathy, their pitying looks, their well-meaning offers to help, and so eventually she'd cut contact with them. She hadn't meant to abandon them, but at the time it had seemed the easiest way to begin to forget. These days they were probably all far too busy to think of her, and some of them likely hadn't forgiven her for having cut herself off so abruptly.

Just ahead and to the left of the path was a barn, against which was leaning a sort of tumbledown shed. As she approached it, Rex suddenly emerged. He started when he saw her and looked guilty. Harriet was about to call his name, but he placed a mysterious finger over his lips with an air of suppressed glee, then ran off down the path.

'What on earth is that boy up to?' said Harriet to herself in amusement, and continued on her way.

There was a queue at the post office, and Harriet had one or two other errands to run, so she did those first then returned to post her letters. As she waited and glanced idly around at the people in front of her, she saw someone at the front of the queue she thought she recognised. She could only see his back view, but it looked like the man who had come to Chaffingham House that morning looking for Maggie Brouillard. As Harriet was still trying to decide whether it was the same person, he stepped forward and asked the postmistress for a postal order and some stamps. Yes, it was the same voice: quiet and pleasant, with just a slight hint of a Scottish accent. He paid for his purchases, turned away from the counter and walked past her and out of the door, apparently without seeing her. She was wrong in her assumption, though: having completed her own business, Harriet came out into the street and immediately saw him standing nearby. He was occupied in lighting a cigarette, but his eyes snapped straight towards her as she emerged, and she knew he had been waiting for her.

'Hallo again,' she said.

'Look here, I'm sorry if I intruded earlier,' he replied. 'I didn't mean to offend anybody by turning up out of the blue like that.'

'You didn't offend anybody. At least, not me.'

'That other lady didn't seem particularly pleased to see me.'

Harriet threw him a smile.

'Mrs Brouillard has her ways. Don't take it personally.'

'Oh, so that was Mrs Brouillard I saw? And what about the young man with the red hair?'

'Sébastien Brouillard, her son.'

'But you're not one of the family.'

'No. How do you know?'

'You told me before,' he said simply, looking at her. 'And anyway, you don't look anything like them. You're too fair, and your eyes are too blue, and your face is the wrong shape – a different shape, I meant,' he went on hurriedly, with a half-laugh. 'There's nothing *wrong* with it. Quite the contrary, in fact.'

Harriet was disconcerted to find herself feeling suddenly self-conscious about her coat sleeve, which was frayed. She rested her left hand over her right wrist to hide it, but immediately remembered the stitching was coming away on her left glove. She dropped both hands to her sides.

'Who is Maggie Brouillard? A friend of yours?' she asked, to cover her discomfort, although he didn't seem to have noticed it.

'Not exactly. She helped me get out of France a few years ago when my plane was shot down. I never had the chance to thank her, and never really expected to see her again, but I happened to be here in the area and somebody mentioned a Brouillard family who lived nearby. So I thought I'd drop in on the off-chance, since it's not exactly a common name, and she said she was from round here. But it seems I was wrong.'

He frowned and drew on his cigarette. Harriet looked at him. He was tallish, with dusty brown hair and blue-grey eyes that slanted down a little at the corners, giving him something of a melancholy air when his face was at rest, but a slight look of mischief when he smiled. His clothes were good but shabby, and hung a little loose on him.

'I wonder why she said it?' he said at last.

'Said what?'

'Why, that she was the daughter of Jean-Jacques Brouillard. Or rather,' he corrected himself, 'she didn't actually say that, but she said her name was Brouillard and that her father was a famous musician.'

'You said she helped you get out of France. Was she in the Resistance? Perhaps she gave you a false name.'

'Perhaps she did.' He was still frowning. 'Ah, well, never mind. One of those things, I expect.'

'You're just visiting the area, I think you said. What brings you here?'

'There's a flying school in Little Hambourn that's for sale, and I came to take a look at it. There's not much to it, as it turns out – just a tin hut and an overgrown landing-strip – but it might fit the bill. It was an RAF station originally.'

'You're a flying instructor?'

'For what it's worth.' He glanced at her with rueful amusement. 'There was a good job waiting for me in an insurance office when I came home, but I couldn't seem to settle down to that kind of life after five years of flying planes.'

Jim had been just the same – hadn't wanted to return to his old job in the civil service after the excitement of life as a pilot. He'd rather go down in flames at thirty than rot away behind a desk, he said. Well, he'd had his wish, she thought bitterly.

'I prefer a life on the ground myself,' was all she said. 'Shall you buy the school?'

'I don't know. I'm to see the chap about it this afternoon.' He glanced at his watch. 'In five minutes, in fact. At the Dog and Duck. Which should tell you all you need to know about why he wants to sell it.'

Again there was that gleam of amusement. Harriet laughed.

'Well, I won't keep you. I'm sorry you didn't find Maggie, but at least your trip here wasn't for nothing.'

'Not completely,' he agreed. 'My name's Alec McLeod, by the way.'

'I know, you told me before.' It was her turn to say it now. 'I'm Harriet Conway.'

'Pleased to meet you, Miss Conway,' he said, and with that he took his leave. Harriet watched him stroll off unhurriedly in the direction of the Dog and Duck, then she set off back for Chaffingham.

When she arrived home, she remembered that Mrs Brouillard was going up to London that evening, and would in fact be on the train now. She had left no particular instructions about dinner, which meant that Harriet would need to speak to Estelle about it. She was about to go and hunt her out, when it occurred to her that Cécilia might be more inclined to join them if Mrs Brouillard was not there. There was no harm in asking, at least. Harriet went into the smaller wing of the house and along to Cécilia's room. As she pushed open the right-hand double door she paused, hearing voices in French. One of them was raised, excitable, contemptuous, the other low and murmuring.

'Look at the state of you,' Sébastien was saying. 'Nobody wants you here, you know. You hang about like a great useless lump and make people feel uncomfortable because you won't make any effort to help yourself. We'd all be far happier if you left and took the little brute with you.'

'Don't call him that,' said Cécilia. 'He's not a little brute.'

'How do you know? You hardly even speak to him. He's a brat. And he knows you can't stand him. That's why he crawls all over you whenever you poke your head out of this godforsaken pit of yours. He's simply dying for you to pay him some attention. "*Let me open the doors for you, Maman.*" "*Would you like me to pass you the salt, Maman?*" Ugh, it's enough to make one sick! No wonder you hate him.'

'I don't hate him!'

'You do. And you'll never escape him. He'll always be there, as a reminder of your mistakes. So *many* mistakes, Céci.' His voice was taunting now, merciless. 'Not only do you foist the little bastard on us, you don't even bother to pretend to be a good mother to him. He'll hate you too when he grows up, you know. And you'll both deserve each other.'

'Stop it!' said Cécilia, sounding distressed. 'I can't help this, you know I can't.'

'You don't want to help it either. You're all right, aren't you? You got out of it. You can sit here all day and pretend to be sick, but I have to keep on practising day in, day out, and being told I'm not good enough, and sent off to doctors if I say I can't do it, and being put in hospital and having pills forced down me to "cure" me. Well, they might think they can cure me but they can't make *you* walk again, can they? You've got the perfect excuse. Oh, yes, you knew what you were doing, all right.'

'Please, Sébastien, don't!' Cécilia's voice was almost a cry of pain. Through the crack in the door Harriet could just glimpse her, crouching in her wheelchair, her hands over her ears, as her brother spat out the words in disgust.

'You'll never have to play another concert again if you don't want to. Not like me. Of course *you* would have done it perfectly, but now it's all fallen on my shoulders, and everyone's coming to watch me perform that damned piece of Papa's that I can't stand and can't play. Why is it always me who has to suffer? Nobody else has this pressure put on them. I never asked for this and never wanted it, but I'm the only one left so I have to do it. *Your* fault!'

'I never meant it to happen. I thought—'

But Sébastien was in no mood to let her finish.

'By the way,' he said, changing the subject abruptly. 'I don't suppose Maman told you about the man who turned up this morning, looking for Maggie?'

'*What?*' It came out as a gasp.

'Oh, yes. An old friend of hers, I imagine, come to look her up. Maman sent him away, naturally. Doesn't want the whole thing raked up again, I expect, and who can blame her? Still, it's nice to know that I'm not the only one who remembers her fondly. You don't, of course. I suppose you hate the very thought of her nowadays. But then you started it all when you stabbed her in the back. Couldn't help yourself, could you? You women are all the same. And look what it led to. Why, you might as well have killed her yourself!' The words dripped out relentlessly with poisonous relish. 'And now look at you – crippled and pathetic. It must be galling to know that nobody will ever want you again in that state. To be perfectly honest I don't know why you haven't done away with yourself long before now. After all, what sort of life do you have? No friends, no men – only the blood of your sister on your hands. I despise you.'

Cécilia began to moan softly under her breath. Harriet, frozen just outside the door, couldn't hear her words, but there was genuine anguish in the sound. She was half-inclined to creep away and leave them to it, but she couldn't bring herself to leave Cécilia in such a state of misery. Besides, she'd been arrested by Sébastien's words. What did he mean, Cécilia had the blood of her sister on her hands? She hovered outside the door uncertainly, wondering whether she dared enter and put an end to the argument. But Sébastien did it himself. As Harriet gazed through the gap in the door he threw himself to his knees in front of Cécilia's wheelchair, took her hands and put them to his face.

'Oh, damn,' he said in English, and in quite a different voice. 'Oh, God. I'm sorry, Céci, I'm sorry. I didn't mean it, you know I didn't. I can't help it when I get like this. The words come out before I can stop them. You'll forgive me, won't you? Please say you will.'

The words were muffled, and Harriet saw that he had buried his face in his sister's lap, his hands grasping hers tightly. Cécilia was even paler than usual, and she stared straight ahead, her eyes dry and unseeing. At length she pulled her hands free of Sébastien's and touched his head gently. He raised his face again and gazed at her, contrite.

'My little brother,' she said, and the words held only despair.

'Darling Céci.' He raised himself up on his knees and threw his arms around her. She bore it patiently, but continued to stare straight ahead.

'You're right. I need to get out,' she murmured, almost to herself. 'How can I get out? If only I could sleep. There's peace in sleep. I could sleep for a hundred years.'

'I can help you,' said Sébastien suddenly, sitting back. 'Do you want me to help you?'

At last Cécilia looked into her brother's eyes, and a look of understanding passed between them. At that moment they looked very alike.

'Do you want me to leave them for you? I'll never tell Maman, I promise. It would be so easy. I have plenty to spare. I used to pretend to take them, you see, and hide them. The doctors never knew.'

'So easy,' repeated Cécilia in a whisper. 'I could be free again.'

'As free as you like,' said Sébastien softly. 'Nobody will ever know.'

Chapter Six

Cécilia didn't come in to dinner, after all. Harriet, Sébastien and Rex ate their meal in silence. After the almost painful brightness of the afternoon, storm clouds had begun to gather as darkness fell, and now the loudest sounds that could be heard in the dining room were the scrape of knives and forks and the spatter of rain against the windows. Nobody had thought to draw the curtains, and Harriet, idly watching the water run in rivulets down the glass, could see the back of Sébastien's head reflected in the window, oddly distorted by the frames that divided one pane from another.

Sébastien himself was miles away, absorbed in his own thoughts as he ate. Only once did he look up and catch Harriet's eye, and the expression on his face was one she couldn't quite interpret. She might almost have called it defiance, although why he should look at her like that she couldn't think, since she was sure he had no idea that she'd overheard them that afternoon. Rex, too, was quiet; perhaps because Sébastien was there. Had Mrs Brouillard been at dinner with them, Harriet would have felt the need to keep the conversation going, but she wasn't sorry to be excused from that duty.

Her eyes strayed across to Sébastien again, thinking of the strange row between him and his sister. She had no idea what had led to it, but one or two things were clear to her now – not least the real reason why Sébastien wasn't already out in the world, earning his living as a professional musician. What had Mrs Brouillard said about him? That was it – that he was delicate, and required careful handling. But there was obviously much more to it than that. He'd mentioned a hospital, but it was clear he wasn't referring to somewhere one went with a broken leg or an attack of pneumonia. He must have spent time in a mental institution of some kind. They wouldn't call it that, of course. They'd call it a convalescent home, or a clinic for nervous disorders, and it would be a modern, attractive building, with well-tended lawns, a tennis court and a swimming pool, and it would be astoundingly expensive. One would meet one's own kind there – former captains and majors for whom the war (or its aftermath) had been just too much; wealthy widows with nothing to do but waste away to nothing on a diet of sedatives; sons and daughters of aristocratic families who had 'never been able to settle down to anything', and the like. 'Highly strung' was another phrase Mrs Brouillard had used in connection with her son, and he was certainly that – presumably so much so that he had been thought in need of private treatment.

Her thoughts were interrupted by Rex, who had finished his dinner and wanted to leave the table.

'May I go and say goodnight to Maman?' he asked, addressing Harriet, but it was Sébastien who replied.

'Better not,' he said, without looking up. 'She said she was going to turn in early.'

'But it's only half past seven,' objected Rex.

'She's feeling under the weather and said she wasn't to be bothered.'

Rex screwed up his face but didn't argue. He got down from the table.

'Go and get ready for bed now,' said Harriet. 'You may read in bed for a little while if you like.'

Rex slunk off and Harriet rose to clear away the plates. Estelle was nowhere to be seen. Presumably when Mrs Brouillard was away she didn't feel the need to work so hard. Sébastien made no move to help; instead he yawned and stretched, saying he'd promised to look up a chap in Royston that evening, and that he'd take the car since it was such a filthy night. He disappeared, and Harriet soon after heard the sound of the car engine starting up. It faded away into the distance, and she breathed a sigh of relief at the prospect of an evening alone with the wireless or a book, with no need to continually think up intelligent remarks or polite nothings. Mrs Brouillard was not a comfortable evening companion; her manner was far too formal for that, and Harriet rarely had the chance to relax. Now she would have the sitting room to herself, and she meant to make the most of it.

She was on the most comfortable sofa, her shoes off and her stockinged feet tucked under her, listening to some light music that she knew her employer wouldn't approve of, when she heard the door creak, and a face showed itself warily through the crack.

'Why, Rex, what is it? Shouldn't you be in bed by now?' she said, glancing at the clock. It was a quarter past eight.

He came in fully. He was in his pyjamas, and his face was very white.

'Can you come, please?' he said. 'I think Maman is sick. I can't get her to wake up.'

There was an undercurrent of urgency in his voice. Harriet took one look at him, then stood up and slipped her shoes back on. Rex had already turned and was heading out of the door and towards Cécilia's wing of the house. Harriet followed him down the corridor and into his mother's living room. Cécilia was on the sofa, wrapped in a peach-coloured dressing-gown that revealed a glimpse of dark grey nightdress underneath, her head flopping back against the cushions, the whites of her eyes mere slits under the nearly closed lids. One hand rested on her lap, while the other was thrown out, palm upward, on the sofa cushion. Completing the tableau was a rather grubby stuffed bear, which had been dropped on the floor in front of her. Rex darted forward and picked it up.

'I went to say goodnight to her, just in case she was still awake,' he said, hugging the bear to him like a shield. 'Is she dead?'

Harriet put her hand to Cécilia's forehead. It was warm. She felt for a pulse and found one, weak and slow. She glanced around. On a nearby table was a little bottle of clear glass, half full of tablets, and a glass of water. Harriet looked at the label but was none the wiser.

'No, she's not dead, but we'd better fetch a doctor,' she said.

Rex swallowed. His eyes looked huge in his pale face.

'But will she die?'

'Oh, no, I don't think so,' replied Harriet, although she had no idea whether it was true. 'Where is Léonie?'

'She's gone out. I think Maman gave her the night off.'

'I suppose that makes sense,' Harriet muttered to herself. If Cécilia had been planning to do this, she would hardly want a nurse inconveniently in the way. 'Now, listen, Rex, I'm going to phone the doctor, and he will come and wake her up. In the meantime, you must go to bed.'

'But—'

'No arguments,' said Harriet firmly. 'You want to help her, don't you? Well, the best thing you can do is to keep out of the way instead of getting under everybody's feet.'

He glanced at his mother and still seemed inclined to object, but Harriet continued:

'I promise I'll come up and tell you how she's getting on, all right?'

He nodded, and they left the room together and hurried towards the hall.

'Now, off you go,' said Harriet, picking up the telephone. She glanced up. Rex was hesitating on the stairs, his bear dangling loosely from his right hand. She motioned to him impatiently and he turned and continued on his way.

Harriet had no idea who normally looked after Cécilia, but there was an entry marked 'Doctor' in the address book that lay on the table by the phone. After some delay she was put through to a gruff-sounding voice which immediately became sharp and alert when she explained what had happened.

'I'll be there in fifteen minutes,' said the voice. 'Do you know what it is she's taken?'

'The label says barbitone.'

'Hmm. And how much?'

'I'm not sure. The bottle's half empty, but I don't know how much was in it before.'

He grunted, but whether from irritation or satisfaction Harriet couldn't tell. Twenty minutes later Dr Taylor arrived in person, a short, stocky man with a no-nonsense air.

'What on earth was Rose thinking, letting the girl get hold of sedatives, after what happened last time?' he said, as he gazed down at Cécilia's pale, immobile form. 'Help me move this table out of the way so I can get at her, will you please?'

Harriet did as he asked, then hovered anxiously as he made his examination.

'Where is Mrs Brouillard, by the way?' he said, as he held Cécilia's wrist and looked at his watch. 'Or the boy?'

'Rex?'

'Sébastien. One of them ought to be fetched, at least.'

Harriet didn't want Sébastien to be fetched. She was experiencing a wave of guilt at what she had overheard earlier and what she ought to have done, and the last thing she wanted was to have to confront him with her knowledge of where Cécilia had got the pills.

'Mrs Brouillard is in London until tomorrow,' she said. 'I don't know where Sébastien is. He went out about an hour ago.'

'Pity. It would be useful to know whether this is all she's taken. There's no other bottle here so I think we can assume it is, which may be good news for her.'

'Why didn't she take all of them?'

'Perhaps she meant to, but passed out before she got the chance. Or perhaps she changed her mind. Either way, it's the stomach pump, I'm afraid. Where's the nurse? That silly Frenchwoman who's no use?'

'Out. Shall I fetch Estelle?'

'She'll fuss and flap. You don't mind, do you? You seem as though you've a calm head about you, and that's what I want.'

Harriet found herself agreeing to assist.

'Good. Then go and fetch me a basin. I warn you now, this won't be much fun.'

As he had said, the next few minutes were not exactly pleasant as the doctor did what he could to empty Cécilia's stomach of the sleeping tablets she had put into it, but at the end of them he gave a grunt that might have been approval.

'Well, all we can do is wait now. I've done all I can. Help me get her to bed. You'll stay with her, won't you? Take her pulse every half an hour and give me a call if she takes a turn for the worse. If we're lucky she'll wake up some time tomorrow, although she'll most likely have a stinking headache – and serve her right.'

Between them they lifted Cécilia and took her into her bedroom. The doctor looked down at her for a minute as she lay in bed, still unconscious.

'Did you say she's tried this before?' asked Harriet.

'Mmm. Got hold of some stuff of her mother's. Luckily Rose called me out just in time, but it was touch and go. If you ask me, there have been other attempts too, but you'll never catch Rose admitting it. Silly girl,' he went on, not unsympathetically. 'She needs an interest in life. All this sitting about and brooding isn't good for the mind. All right, I'll be off. Remember to call if you need me.'

He departed, shutting the front door firmly behind him, leaving Harriet feeling very alone. She wondered where Estelle had got to, and looked at her watch. It was after ten o'clock, so presumably she had gone to bed. Harriet remembered Rex, waiting upstairs in his room for her to tell him whether his mother was still alive. She was – although whether she would be by morning was another matter. Still, she could give him good news now, at least. Taking one last glance at Cécilia, who was breathing quietly but regularly, she went out. Rex was sitting bolt upright in his bed with the light on, reading, or at least trying to. He looked up eagerly as Harriet went in.

'I didn't want to fall asleep, so I stayed sitting up,' he said. Then, hesitantly, 'Is Maman all right?'

'She's sleeping now,' said Harriet as reassuringly as she could. 'I expect she'll be much better by tomorrow.'

He looked at her as though not sure whether to believe her, then smiled and let out a sigh.

'May I see her?'

'Not now. Tomorrow, perhaps, when she's awake.'

'But who's going to stay with her?'

'I'll stay with her tonight, and keep an eye on her. The doctor left me special instructions. I'll see she doesn't come to any harm. Now, you must be a good boy and go to sleep. I can't look after you and Maman at the same time. Do you want your bear? There, I'll just tuck you in.'

He settled down quite happily, and she was about to turn the light out and go when he said:

'Will you kiss me goodnight?'

His eyes peeped out forlornly at her above the bedspread, and she was reminded just for a second of herself as a girl, and how every night her own mother had tucked her in and kissed her goodnight. Rex had nothing like that. She hesitated, then returned and did as he asked.

'There you go. Now, go to sleep.'

He turned over, making himself comfortable.

'Goodnight, Miss Conway.'

'Goodnight.'

Harriet hurried down the stairs back towards Cécilia's room. 'I'll see she doesn't come to any harm,' she had said to Rex. Fine words, and far too late, she thought bitterly. She could have prevented this had she acted in time. After all, she had heard with her own ears Sébastien offering to get Cécilia the pills that had nearly killed her. She hadn't clearly understood what he meant at the time, but it was evident he was up to something. She ought to have realised what he was talking about, or at least followed him and asked him what he intended to do. Then she could have threatened him with his mother. Why hadn't she done that? Because she'd been eavesdropping, of course, and was too cowardly to confess it when by rights none of this was any of her business. Still, she might have spoken to Cécilia before she took the pills, or even taken them from her by force. A woman in a wheelchair could hardly put up much of a fight. And now, if she died, it would be Harriet's fault. The guilt gnawed at her insides and she prayed Cécilia would live through the night.

The bedroom was dim when Harriet went in, lit by a single lamp that stood by the bed. Its olive-green lampshade cast a sickly pallor over the scene. Cécilia herself looked much the same. As Harriet took her wrist to take her pulse, her eyelashes fluttered and she murmured something. Was that a good sign? Harriet didn't know. At least it was an indication of life. Harriet was mortally afraid of what would happen if Cécilia died under her care that night. It had been on the tip of her tongue to ask the doctor to stay, but her pride had baulked at revealing her weakness in front of this brisk, breezy man, who probably dealt with putrid illness and death every day without blinking an eye.

She sat down gingerly in an armchair and steeled herself to remain awake for the rest of the night, trying to fight off the negative thoughts that threatened to overwhelm her. This was not what she had wanted when she came here. She'd had quite enough drama and misery to last a lifetime. She wanted a nice, quiet job, with nice, quiet people who wouldn't do anything to crack the thin, delicate shell that had begun to form around her this past month or two after she'd been so long raw and exposed. She didn't want to *feel* any more. That was for the old Harriet. And now she was plunged into the midst of this family who seemed almost to revel in their unhappiness – and God knew, she could hardly blame Cécilia for feeling hard done by. Whatever had shattered the lower half of her body must have come as a devastating blow, and was probably far worse than anything Harriet herself could claim to have suffered. That was what she told herself, anyway.

Suddenly it was all too much. For a mad minute Harriet fought against the urge to run upstairs, pack her bag and make her escape from Chaffingham. The last train to London was not until just before midnight. She could leave Cécilia in the care of Estelle, call a taxi and be free to start again by tomorrow morning. It was almost too tempting, and she was at the point of rising from her chair and leaving the room when Cécilia stirred a little, and the madness passed. Of course she couldn't think of leaving. She'd never find another job as good as this one, given her previous history. She'd have to go back to the dingy boarding house and scrape a living working in a London shop or eating place, which didn't appeal in the slightest. In the old days she hadn't been the sort of person to run away at the first sign of trouble, and she would cling to that thought and try to summon up something of her old strength of purpose. She had a job to do and she would do it, however unpleasant it might be. The least she could do was to make sure Cécilia was all right, rather than abandoning her to the servants.

Harriet sat a moment until she was quite sure the impulse to flee had left her, then went to take the patient's pulse again. It was still steady. After that, she went into the living room, with some thought of tidying up a little. There was not much to do. A few magazines were scattered on the floor, and a glass of water stood on the table next to the sofa – presumably the one Cécilia had used to take the pills. Harriet picked it up and saw it had left a watermark, adding to the several already on the table. Once she'd tidied it away she came back to straighten the cushions, which were lying in disarray on the sofa. As she was pushing a seat cushion in, she saw that a piece of paper had slipped into the crack between it and the next cushion. She pulled the paper out and saw it was a letter, handwritten, much folded, coming apart along its folds. It seemed to be several years old. Harriet unfolded the paper carefully, intending merely to return it to its right place in the drawer, but her eye was caught by the signature. Glancing around guiltily, she turned the letter over and began reading. It was dated 21st September, 1941, and bore a Paris address.

Darling Céci,

I'm so glad to hear you got to Nice safely and that things are carrying on mostly as normal down there. How is the place? I hope you're getting out and enjoying the glorious Mediterranean sunshine instead of sitting inside all day, poring over those fusty music books of yours. The weather has been beastly here ever since you left, which hasn't done much for Maman's mood, as you can imagine! With Papa and Marcus gone and you away she has less to occupy her time with now, although she's still dining out on your winning the Prix de Rome.

Herr Lissauer and some other people from the German Institute came the other day, which I wasn't especially pleased about. I told Maman it looks very bad to be inviting Germans to our house, but she said that now Papa isn't here it's up to her to keep the Brouillard name alive, even if only for your and Sébastien's sakes. She said that there won't be so much money coming in now – at least, not until you and Sébastien have made names for yourselves – so she wants to keep on the right side of the people with influence who can help you both do that.

I know Maman's still devastated at Papa's death, poor thing, and says she only wants the best for us, but I think she's going about things the wrong way. I miss Papa every day. He always knew how to cheer us up, and I know he wouldn't have let Maman sacrifice all our principles just for the sake of success. At any rate, I was glad you weren't here, as it would make me so sad to see her forcing you to ingratiate yourself with those people.

Sébastien's going through a difficult stage at the moment. He declared the other day that he was sick to death of music and didn't want to study at the Conservatoire after all, but Maman invited Prof. Lefeuvre to tea and he charmed Sébastien into submission. He asked Séb to play for him, and was quite struck with what he heard. He didn't say anything in front of him, but later I overheard him telling Maman in an undertone that if she didn't make sure Séb came to study with him then he would come and fetch him himself, by force if necessary! That cheered her up a bit, at least. Other than that, we're all as well as can be expected. We still haven't enough to eat, but I suppose we're better off than some. M. Courtet has had nothing in stock but leeks and onions for the past month, it seems, and I don't mind telling you I won't be sorry never to eat onion soup again!

Anyway, I won't bore you with a long account of what I've been doing, for obvious reasons. As a matter of fact, the main reason I'm writing, my sweet girl, is to ask you a favour. You remember the stray cat I adopted, don't you? Of course you do – I've done nothing but talk about him for months. Now, I know Maman disapproves of pets, but as I've told her before, we took to one another from the start, and I'm hoping he'll be mine for keeps one day, so it's really none of her business. At any rate, a few weeks ago there was a – well, a sort of roundup, I suppose you'd call it, of stray

*animals, and my own dearest Zazou just managed to escape
in time and hide. But what to do with him now? He's bored
indoors, and I'm scared he'll escape and get into trouble.
Besides, I don't think the air of Paris agrees with him. So,
darling Céci, I've decided to send him to you to look after
for a little while. Now, isn't that kind of me!*

*I can almost see you rolling your eyes as you read this. I
know you're not especially fond of animals, but you do love
me, don't you? And when you've met Zazou I know you'll
understand. Don't worry – he's not a domestic cat, so he
doesn't take much looking after, and there's every chance he'll
run off after a week or two anyway. But I'd much rather see
him loose on the streets of Nice than here in Paris, where it's
so dangerous. I'll send this letter with him so you'll know
he's quite safe and trustworthy. Forgive me, darling, but I
love him so and can't bear to lose him, and I can't think of
anyone I'd trust more with him. Keep him safe for me and
I'll be in your debt forever. Send me news as soon as you can.*

*With all my love,
Maggie*

Harriet gazed at the letter for some minutes after she had
finished reading it, taking in the firm, decisive handwriting and
the confident flourish of the signature. The paper was creased and
stained, and bore all the signs of having been read many times over
the years. Maggie. Maggie Brouillard. The same girl Alec McLeod
had come looking for earlier that day. A girl who did not exist,
according to Rose Brouillard. But here she was in writing, her
vibrancy and energy and humour leaping from the page. She was
dead now, of course. Harriet suddenly remembered what Sébastien
had said earlier, about Cécilia having her sister's blood on her
hands, whatever he'd meant by that. Was he referring to Maggie?

She looked at the letter again. It must have been written not long after Jean-Jacques Brouillard died, and about a year into the Occupation, but despite the difficulties the family must have been experiencing at that time there was a determined cheeriness about the first part, with its bits and pieces of family news. The second part was more guarded, less easy to understand, clearly a matter of important business. Maggie had sent something to her sister. What it was, Harriet couldn't tell, although it was perfectly obvious it wasn't a cat.

She was still trying to decipher the coded message when a sound from the bedroom next door caught her attention. Quickly, guiltily, she folded the letter back up and replaced it where she had found it, then went in to investigate the source of the noise. It was Cécilia, who was murmuring and starting to stir. Harriet perched on the side of the bed and watched her. Cécilia's eyes fluttered and opened, and she stared unseeing at Harriet.

'What is it?' she said indistinctly.

'You weren't well, so I called the doctor.'

'Oh.' There was no sign that she remembered what had happened.

'But he thinks you'll be quite all right now.'

'Oh,' said Cécilia again. She lay quietly for a few moments. 'I'm tired. I think I'd like to go to sleep.'

'Yes, that's probably best. I'll stay here in case you want me.'

Cécilia gave a wan smile but didn't reply, and after a few minutes she drifted off to sleep again.

Chapter Seven

Nice, 1941

The man was watching her, Cécilia was sure of it. She'd seen him that morning when she had overslept and had had to rush out of the house to be in time for her lesson at nine o'clock. He was standing on the corner, by the crumbling old house at the bottom of the hill. His gaze fell on her violin case as she passed, and she hugged it to her, fearful that he would try and steal it. But he made no move; he just stood, leaning against the wall and smoking a cigarette as though he had all the time in the world. In her hurry she forgot about him almost immediately, but when she returned home that evening, there he was again, in the same place. Surely he hadn't been standing there all day? But even as she glanced at him and registered his presence, he pushed himself away from the wall without looking at her and headed off down the hill, in the direction of the old town.

The next morning there was nobody at the corner of the street, and she went about her business. In former years the Prix de Rome scholars had studied at the Académie de France in Rome, but with war raging all over Europe that was impossible at present, so now they were housed in the Villa Paradiso here in unoccupied Nice, where the conflict intruded less. The villa was a large, stately building standing in its own lawned gardens among rows of elegant palm trees, with expansive views of the city from its elevated position. Many of its rooms had been given over to the visual arts, but there were several rooms for musicians, too. Most people were trying to ignore the war and work as best they could, including Cécilia. She liked the warm air of Nice, its clear, fresh colours: a serene blue in the daytime and a soft pink, fading to purple in the evening. The colours and sounds and sights all blended together and found expression in her music; a music that came easily – unlike in Paris, where the grey and the brown and the wet clashed with each other and created only a barrier to inspiration.

As soon as she had arrived in the South she had made her way down to the Promenade des Anglais, there to stand and look out at the gentle, welcoming ocean, breathing in its salt tang and feeling the residual summer warmth of a Mediterranean autumn on her face, while melodies danced through her mind, creating faint colours that spiralled in the air, wreathing together then drifting apart. Cécilia had never spoken to anyone of this blending together of the senses, and of how for her each different note had its own colour that she could see just as clearly as if she were staring at a painting in a gallery. When played out loud, music caused an explosion of fireworks in front of her eyes, shooting and swirling and eddying around her in a tumult of colours, but even when she was merely composing in her head, the notes caused hazy visions, watercolours in motion, to float before her, aiding her inspiration. It had always come naturally to her, as something to be taken for granted, but she knew, without having to ask, that it was not the same for everybody – she'd never met anybody else who had talked of it – so she guarded her secret, kept it to herself, as she knew people would think her odd.

She spent the day alone but not unhappily in one of the music rooms. She was struggling a little with a passage she was trying to compose as part of a larger work for strings and piano. The professor came in and found her scratching out whole pages in exasperation. He made one or two suggestions, but the notes, the colours, were too trite for what she was trying to achieve – a faint pencil sketch when what she wanted was fire and passion in oils.

She acknowledged his ideas politely then went back to shaking her head.

At six o'clock, no further forward, she left the villa and headed down the steep street towards the house in which she was staying, which was not more than half a mile away, down then uphill. And there he was again, at the corner. These were dangerous times and she should have hurried on past, but instead she stopped and met the man's eyes. He took a step forward.

'Cécilia?' He seemed a little unsure, although he didn't strike her as the hesitant type, now that she could look at him properly. He was young and strongly built, with dark hair and eyes; not tall, and not exactly handsome – the broken nose and rough, pitted skin saw to that – but there were lines at the corners of his eyes and mouth that indicated he liked to laugh.

'Yes?' she said.

'I have a letter for you. From Maggie.'

He was taking something out of his inside pocket as he spoke. As he handed her the envelope she saw the long fingernails on his right hand and glanced automatically at his left. On that side they were short.

'Thank you,' she said. She was diffident and awkward, and not accustomed to talking to men in the street, so she couldn't think of anything else to say, and made as if to move on.

'Aren't you going to read it?' He seemed surprised and half-amused.

'I was going to read it at home.'

'There's a message for you. About me.'

'You?' Cécilia stared in puzzlement. She glanced down at the envelope in her hand, and, since he seemed to expect it, tore it open. She skimmed through the first part about Maman and Sébastien without taking it in, then came to the second part about a stray cat, which made no sense on first reading. She frowned, read it again, and suddenly understood.

'Zazou… This is you? You're… Emil, is it?'

'Emil Ginsburg.' He shook her hand formally. His hand was warm and slightly rough, and she felt the long fingernails against her palm. 'Maggie said you would help me, but I wasn't certain, so I watched you a little first.'

'I know – I saw you.'

'I'm sorry, but I wanted to judge for myself whether you could be trusted.'

'Oh, did you indeed?' she said, pulling her hand away sharply. 'Well I hope the examination didn't disappoint.'

He laughed at the sudden tartness in her voice.

'So you do have some life in you! I was beginning to wonder. No, I think you'll pass.'

She ought to have been annoyed at his easy confidence when it was he who needed her help, but it was so obvious that he was being his natural, assured self, and intended no offence, that she wavered. He was smiling at her, and all of a sudden it was impossible to dislike him.

'What do you need?' she asked.

'A place to stay, first and foremost. Just for a little while. I don't have much money, you see, and I'd rather not attract attention just now by asking around for accommodation.'

'I see,' replied Cécilia. She wasn't sure it was wise to let a man, a stranger, into her little apartment, but this was the famous Emil, of whom Maggie had talked incessantly for months. Despite the recent death of their father and brother, and the misery of their daily life in Paris, Cécilia had never seen her older sister as happy as she had been since she met Emil. As soon as the Germans left and all the stupid laws about Jews had been thrown on a bonfire, they were going to be married, Maggie said. In the meantime, she and Emil were going to resist the Occupation until the very end, and do their bit to make sure the enemy didn't have an easy time of it.

Cécilia looked about her. The working day was over, and people were trudging to and fro up and down the street. If they stayed here much longer they would begin to attract attention. She turned back to Emil, who was still smiling at her, and all at once she heard the music and saw it floating around him, sparking and dancing and lighting up the lilac twilight with little bursts of rich blue and indigo and vermilion.

'Oh!' she exclaimed.

So that was what was needed: a brighter red to go with the pink and the yellow! It had all been too soft, too pastel; it needed stronger colours to give it more depth. The music sang in Cécilia's head, causing the air to fizz with iridescence. She must write it down, and quickly, before it slipped through her fingers and disappeared forever.

'We have to go,' she said abruptly, and before he could reply, set off almost at a run up the hill towards her apartment building. He caught up with her as she reached the front door and fumbled with the key.

'What is it?' he said, but she shook her head, wide-eyed, and clamped her mouth shut. She couldn't talk, or she'd lose it. The lift was permanently broken, so she hurried up the stairs to the third floor. She was already rummaging in her bag for her manuscript notebook and pencil as she burst in through the door, and she threw herself down at the nearest table, writing as best she could in the rapidly fading light of early evening. Emil watched in silence as the dots and dashes and squiggles formed under her hand, but did not interrupt her. The notes were bursting to escape from her head, but she couldn't write quickly enough to get them down. After a minute she made an exasperated sound, darted over to an upright piano that looked as if it had seen better days, and played a phrase or two, uncertainly at first, then with more confidence.

'Yes, that's it,' she murmured. She seemed to have forgotten he was there. She played the passage over again and turned to write it down, then stopped as she saw Emil still standing, watching her. She stared at him for a long moment.

'I needn't have hurried,' she said at last. 'It's still there. You brought it with you.'

'What?'

'The music. It needed a deeper blue and more red. I thought it would disappear, but it hasn't.'

As soon as the words were out of her mouth she flushed a deep pink. Now he would think she was an idiot. But he wasn't laughing.

'Play me the blue and red music again,' he said.

She looked at him doubtfully, but he seemed perfectly serious, so after a moment's hesitation she turned back to the piano and played the passage which had been causing her so much difficulty that day. When she looked up again he was standing next to her at the piano.

'It needs a touch of gold,' he said. He sat down beside her and played the passage again, but this time with an addition of his own.

'That's a bright pink,' Cécilia couldn't help saying.

'For me it's gold. And this is a dark chocolate brown, and *this* is an emerald green. Blue for me is this sort of thing…' He played a sequence of notes. 'And as you can see, that wouldn't go with your music at all.'

'No,' she agreed.

'Now, let me play you something, and you tell me the colours. No, no need to get up – you don't take up much space.'

He began to play a jazz tune in a swing style. Cécilia's musical tastes tended towards the heavy and complicated, but this was light, melodic – almost comedic – and she sat next to him and watched as the music lit up the darkening apartment with bursts of aquamarine and purple and salmon pink. He finished in a flourish of spiralling lime green that unexpectedly made her laugh with its quirkiness, and he laughed in turn at her appreciation.

'Like it?' he asked.

'What is it?'

'Just something I wrote. We were going to play it at Club Madagascar, but that was before…'

He shrugged. There was no need to finish the sentence.

'But you're not a pianist?'

'I was a lawyer. Before.'

'Oh yes, Maggie told me. You lost your job because of the new laws. But that's not what I meant. I meant you're a guitarist rather than a pianist, surely.'

He saw her looking at his right hand, and held it up to show her the long nails.

'I had to leave the guitar in Paris. I should cut them, I suppose, but it's a habit to keep them long.'

'You must get another guitar.'

She said it quite simply, because the idea of not owning a musical instrument was foreign to her.

'As soon as I can. But there are other things to think about first.'

'Such as what?'

'There are people down here – Americans and others – who are helping Jews leave France. I'm going to speak to them.'

'You're going to leave France? You're Polish, aren't you? You can't go back there, can you? What will Maggie say?'

'My parents are Polish, but I've lived in France most of my life, so this is the only home I've ever known. But I want to help others get out. They're starting to round us up and send us to camps.'

'Oh, is that what Maggie meant in her letter? They caught you too, but you escaped.'

'Yes, there was a roundup, and they sent a lot of Jews to Drancy. I realised what was going on just in time and got away, but most people weren't so lucky.' His mouth was set in a grim line.

'What do you mean?'

He looked at her, at this shy, innocent girl who quite obviously lived most of the time in her own head, wrapped up in her music, and couldn't bring himself to tell her about the beatings, the shootings, the deportations, and the dawning horror of what was intended.

'Many people are still there,' he said at last. 'Anyway, don't worry, I haven't come here to get in your way and ruin your studies. Maggie says you're very talented.'

'What is she doing? How is she? I miss her.'

'She's fine. She's very indignant about the Germans, but even more so about Vichy and Pétain. She's started teaching piano to Jewish students in secret.'

'That's like her. She was always a Jew-lover,' said Cécilia without thinking.

'You don't like us?'

She looked down, realising what she had said.

'I don't know any Jews. I can't comment.'

'I'm a Jew, and you know me.'

'So I do. But you don't seem like a Jew.'

'What are Jews like?'

Cécilia flushed. She had never given this any thought, and in fact was simply repeating things she had heard Rose say over the years.

'Why, I don't know,' she said after a moment. 'My mother thinks you take over everything.'

'Well, she needn't worry – the Nazis will see to it that we don't,' he said dryly.

The room was getting really dark now. Cécilia found that they were still sitting close together on the piano stool. She could feel the warmth of his thigh along hers, and was suddenly self-conscious. She stood up, and so did he.

'There's a spare room you can have,' she said. 'The bed's not made up. I'll do that now.'

'Is this your apartment? Don't you share it with some other girls?'

'It belongs to my aunt. She retired to Switzerland as soon as the war started. I haven't got any housemates because I've only been here a few weeks and there hasn't been time to find anybody.'

It was a lie. In reality she had been hoping to keep the apartment to herself, although she knew it was selfish of her in the circumstances. Other girls puzzled her; they shrieked and giggled and caked themselves in lipstick and flirted with men, and the idea of having to share a house and put up with all the confusion made her tremble. But it looked as if she had no choice but to share now; here she was, hiding a man on the run – a Jew at that – and risking all sorts of trouble if she was caught.

It seemed that grief over the death of their brother Marcus in the Battle of France had affected Cécilia and Maggie in very different ways. Cécilia had reacted by doing her best to avoid thinking about the war, and all the associated unpleasantness, burying herself in her music until it was all over. She wasn't brave or active like Maggie, who had been protesting and planning and resisting ever since the Germans had arrived, arranging secret performances of banned music among the students at the *lycée* where she taught, passing on radio messages from London, and helping smuggle people out of the Occupied Zone. Resistance wasn't in Cécilia's nature. She had seized upon the opportunity afforded her by her success in winning the Prix de Rome scholarship to escape Paris and come to Nice, where there were fewer Germans, where the sun shone, and where one could almost pretend things were normal. But now here was her sister's lover, hunted by the enemy and demanding sanctuary as easily as he might have asked her for a light for his cigarette. She ought to send him away, but how could she, when he had brought music – such music! – with him and given it to her as a gift?

She made up the bed for him, and went back into the living room. He was leaning on the sill of the open window, gazing out across the rooftops of the city, and he turned around as she came in. She knew she ought to offer him some food, but she didn't have much – just some stale bread from two days ago, a little cheese, and some apples she'd bought yesterday. No meat or vegetables.

But to her relief he didn't seem to be thinking about that, and said he was going out.

'It's safest after dark,' he said. 'There are some people I want to look up. I might be back late, but if you can give me a key I promise not to disturb you.'

She went and dug out the spare door keys and handed them to him, wondering once again whether she was doing the right thing. It seemed he could read her thoughts.

'Don't worry. Everything will be all right, you'll see,' he said, then flashed her a sudden brilliant smile and went out, shutting the door noiselessly behind him, as though to prove he could be quiet.

Cécilia watched through the window as he disappeared down the street into the darkness, before going back to the piano and playing a few notes, very softly, so as not to upset the neighbours. After a few minutes she got up, closed the shutters, switched on the light and went to work creating harmonies with her pencil until past midnight. Then she went to bed and lay awake for a long time, listening for a man who did not come, while music fizzed through her head in bursts of bright blue and scarlet.

Chapter Eight

Cécilia soon got used to having Emil around, and in fact for the first week hardly saw him. As he'd promised, he caused no disturbance: he spent most of the day asleep while she was out, and had usually left the house by the time she got home in the evening. Only the unmade bed and the clothes discarded on the floor – he must have borrowed them from someone, since he'd arrived with no luggage – showed he had ever been there. He was clearly the untidy type, and after a few days she started making the bed for him and folding up the clothes. It was the only way she could think of to show him she was to be relied upon, as she hadn't forgotten his wariness when they first met. He was to be her brother-in-law, so it was important they become friends. Besides, there was new music whenever she saw him; sparkling, joyful music that burst out of her head and spun and darted around him in soaring arcs of colour, much brighter than anything she'd ever seen before. Whenever he was present he brought inspiration and a freshness to her ideas that astounded and delighted her, and she could hardly write it all down fast enough. Such a man was to be preserved at all costs, and she regretted ever having showed she mistrusted him.

After a week or so his hours became less irregular, and she began to see him more. He had managed to get fresh meat and vegetables somehow, and he brought them back to the apartment and they made a *cassoulet* of sorts – stringy and tasteless, but better than anything Cécilia had eaten for months. While they ate, she asked him tentatively what he had been doing, but he shook his head.

'Better you don't know,' he said. 'It's nothing you need worry about, and the less you know the safer you'll be.'

Part of her was relieved at his answer, but another part wished he would tell her. She had started reading the pamphlets and badly printed newspapers that had begun to be left around the city, and her curiosity was aroused. Most of them seemed to come from underground groups of Communists or Socialists, and they carried reports of all sorts of dire events – bombings of synagogues, mass deportations, summary executions – of which she was sure less than half could be true, as well as warnings of terrible things to come, and calls to all patriotic French citizens to stand up against the occupiers. Exaggerated as they were in tone, they nonetheless sparked a curiosity in her that she had never felt before, and she was half-tempted to ask Emil if she might help in any way. She might do some small task – nothing too daring, but something that would at least show she was on his side. She didn't have the courage to ask, however, since he seemed determined to keep his promise and not involve her.

One day she arrived home slightly earlier than usual and found the apartment empty. She supposed Emil would be out for the evening, and was just planning to make herself an early supper and read a book when he came out of the bathroom suddenly and bumped into her.

'Oh, I'm sorry!' she exclaimed. It was only then she noticed that he was naked from the waist up, carrying his shirt and wiping his face with a towel. He'd obviously just been shaving. She blushed before she could stop herself.

'Here you are!' he said, touching her arm in a friendly manner which made her jump. 'I've been waiting for you. Look, I've got something to show you.'

He went into his bedroom, dropping the towel on the floor as he did so and throwing on his shirt in one easy movement. She picked up the towel and returned it to the bathroom, then came out just as he emerged from his room with his new acquisition. It was a guitar in a battered case.

'Oh!' she exclaimed. 'Where did you get it?'

'I borrowed it from a friend of a friend. He doesn't need it at the moment.'

Cécilia envied the social abilities of a man who had been in Nice less than two weeks and already had friends of friends. She was too shy to strike up friendships easily herself; she felt she had nothing to talk about except music, and she was fearful of being a bore, so she tended to avoid people as much as she could. Emil didn't make her feel boring, though; he was easy to talk to, and seemed genuinely interested in what she had to say. It might only have been politeness on his part, but she was grateful for it all the same.

'Let's see what we've got,' he said, bringing the guitar out of its case and giving it a look over. The examination seemed to satisfy him, and he struck a chord or two briefly, then tuned it. 'This is that song I played you before. It sounds much better on guitar. Listen.'

He began to play, strumming first and then plucking. His playing was jaunty, cheerful, and Cécilia watched as his fingers moved like lightning over the strings. Halfway through he grimaced and stopped.

'I need my violinist,' he said.

'Is he still in Paris?'

He shrugged. 'I don't know. He was arrested at the same time as me and I haven't seen him since.'

His brows drew together as he said it, and he was silent for a few moments. He began to play something else, all the while looking thoughtfully at Cécilia.

'Will you do it?' he asked at last.

'Do what?'

'Accompany me on the violin.'

'But I don't know the song,' she said, startled. It was a ridiculous idea.

'It's simple enough. Like this.' He picked out a melody. 'You see, it goes just like that, then more or less repeats after eight bars, just with a slight variation, then goes into this part that echoes the guitar.'

'But I've never played jazz. I can't—'

'Of course you can,' he said. His smile was an invitation. 'And it doesn't matter if you can't remember it all. Filip used to improvise half the time anyway. I never could get him to play the music I actually wrote. Just don't slow down, and make sure you give it plenty of yellow and orange.'

That made her laugh.

'It was turquoise and purple.'

'Well, then.'

He was looking at her with such friendly sympathy that it was impossible to say no.

'All right,' she said at last. 'I'll try, but don't blame me if I do it all wrong.'

She took out her violin. Her heart was beating fast with nervousness, but he reassured her then began to instruct her. She played it through slowly, then a little faster.

'Wonderful!' he said, clapping his hands. 'You're a natural.'

She shook her head to disclaim the compliment, then immediately made a mistake and was embarrassed. She lowered the violin.

'I'm not sure—'

'Well, I am. Just remember the turquoise and purple and you'll be fine.'

She played the passage again and got it right this time.

'Now, let's try it together. Ready?'

His confidence was infectious, and she nodded, wondering what her stuffy professors at the Académie would think if they saw her. They began, and she kept up as best she could. She was unsure and a little stilted at first; the colours were jagged and spiky, like winter, but gradually they softened and relaxed to a warm spring, and she closed her eyes and let herself sink into the music. Suddenly the tune seemed to carry her away on its wings, and she was instilled with a confidence she'd never known she had. She had already forgotten the melody Emil had taught her, but it didn't matter – her own was just as good, and it sprang from her fingers as easily as if she had been practising it for weeks. She had never played anything of the sort before, but this was a revelation. Her bow moved almost of its own accord in time with the guitar, then the music built to a crescendo of lilac stars and swirls, and she finished with a dramatic sweep of the bow before opening her eyes, flushed and laughing.

'Oh my goodness!' she exclaimed.

He was laughing too, in a kind of surprised delight.

'You see? You didn't think you could do it.'

'I never liked jazz before,' she said. 'Maggie plays it at home on the gramophone, but it always sounded like so much noise to me.'

'It's no good on record,' he replied. 'You have to see it live to experience it properly.'

She beamed at him breathlessly, then all of a sudden he wasn't smiling at her any more, but was staring at her intently. She came to herself and turned to put the violin back in its case, shy again.

'We'd better stop. It's getting late, and Madame Gauthier complains if I play music after eight o'clock,' she said.

He was still staring at her, and now the room was too small and she felt the urge to run away. Involuntarily, her mind flashed back to earlier, when she'd bumped into him coming out of the bathroom half-naked, and she felt herself flushing again, but couldn't somehow tear herself away from his gaze.

'Come out with me tomorrow,' he said abruptly. She must have looked surprised, because he went on quickly, 'It's nothing unsafe, I promise. Just some friends who live in a villa outside Nice. They're mostly musicians, but there are some artists and writers as well.'

'But why?' She couldn't stop herself from asking the question.

'Because you look like you need company,' he said lightly. 'And Maggie told me to look after you.'

So that was it. He felt sorry for her. He thought she must be lonely, and wanted to do her a kindness by introducing her to some of his friends. Or rather, it was Maggie who was behind it; Maggie, who had always taken care of Cécilia in the manner of a much older sister, even though there were barely two years between them, and who had told Emil to keep an eye on his soon-to-be sister-in-law as a brother might. So it was stupid to feel uncomfortable under his gaze. He was family – or would be one day – and there was nothing more than friendliness behind his invitation; nothing she need be afraid of.

'Come on, it'll be fun,' he said. 'I promise I won't throw you in among a bunch of strangers and then abandon you.'

How he'd guessed that that was her deepest fear she didn't know, but his words reassured her.

'All right,' she replied.

'Perfect.' He looked at his watch. 'Damn it, it's getting late. I was supposed to go out half an hour ago. Listen, I'll see you here tomorrow at six. Why don't you practise the song, and we'll play it tomorrow night?'

She found herself nodding an agreement, although the thought of such a thing would never have crossed her mind this time yesterday. He packed the guitar away and prepared to leave the apartment. Cécilia had a sudden thought.

'What's it called?' she asked. 'The song, I mean.'

'I don't have a title yet – couldn't think of one.' Then came that brilliant flash of a smile. 'But you've given me an idea. I'm going to call it *Cécilia*.'

Chapter Nine

The Villa Rocquefort was up in the hills towards Villefranche, and they went very late on foot. Despite the chill of the evening, several windows were open and the sound of music and voices issued from inside. Emil rang the bell.

'Who lives here?' whispered Cécilia, looking up at the building, which was on the palatial side, with a red tiled roof, pink stuccoed walls and balconies surrounded by ornate stone balustrades.

'It belongs to an American woman, Marion Zimmerman. She's very rich and she likes to collect people. Artistic people in particular.'

'Why hasn't she left?'

'She likes it here,' said Emil, just as the door opened to reveal a woman. She was perhaps forty-five or fifty, squarely built with dark hair and a heavy brow, but exquisitely dressed in a way that spoke of money.

'Emil, darling, you came!' she exclaimed in French with a strong American accent. 'And who's this?'

'I have a present for you,' said Emil. 'This is Cécilia Brouillard. Now don't tell me you don't know the name.'

'Of course! The winner of the Prix de Rome!' She clapped her hands together. 'My dear, I was so sorry to hear about your father. It must have been a great loss to you, as it was to all of us. I hear they're going to perform his last work in a few weeks. Fernand was getting ready to conduct it, but they fired him, poor thing, and replaced him with Robiquet – ugh! Not that Robiquet doesn't know his job, but to treat your father's protégé like that smacks of ingratitude if you ask me.'

Cécilia didn't know how to reply to this barrage of speech, but found there was no need to, as Marion Zimmerman had quite enough to say on her own account. She swept Cécilia into the house and through a grand hallway, talking over her shoulder to Emil all the while.

'I do wish you'd have a word with Gerhard. He's refusing to leave. Did you know Nina had her baby last week? She had it badly, poor thing, and he won't go until she's well, if at all. So frustrating for the Rescue Committee, just after they'd managed to get exit visas for the lot of them. Do you know Gerhard Varady, dear?' She turned to Cécilia. 'If you're from Paris you must have seen his exhibition a few years ago. We're trying to get him to the States but he's a little stubborn and doesn't want to go, even though the police are trying to deport him to Germany. We've been bribing them for weeks to stay away while we waited for the baby to arrive, and I told him we didn't have the kind of money to keep on doing it indefinitely, but it looks like it might all have been for nothing anyway. You will speak to him, won't you, Emil?'

'I'll try, but if you can't persuade him I don't see how I can.'

'I'm sure you'll do wonders. Just play him that song you wrote for him and he'll be like putty in your hands. Oh, by the way, we couldn't get a real passport for Eugen, so it looks as though we might have to get him a fake one, which always increases the risk. They were going to try and get him over the mountains to Spain, but his leg is bad again and he doesn't think he can manage the walk, so it'll have to be a boat. Now, come in and meet everyone, dear.'

She opened a door and the volume of chatter and music increased as they entered a room seemingly full of people. Cécilia glanced around and saw a spacious living room with high, beamed ceilings and whitewashed walls that were almost invisible behind dozens of works of modern art, which had been hung from waist-height to ceiling. The tiled floor was covered with rich, Persian rugs in a riot of colours, and there were several comfortable-looking sofas which had been pushed back against the walls. The dark wood shutters were closed, and the room was dimly lit, but Cécilia didn't have much opportunity to take it all in, because Marion still had hold of her arm, and conducted her firmly over to a young man whom Cécilia recognised immediately as an art scholar from the Villa Paradiso.

'Now, I'm sure I don't need to introduce you, as you must already have met,' said Marion. 'How marvellous, to have two Prix de Rome winners here at once!'

Cécilia was immediately embarrassed, as although she'd seen the young man around and knew perfectly well who he was, she had no idea of his name. He came to her rescue.

'Florian Haillet,' he said. 'And you're Cécilia Brouillard. I've seen you about, but you don't stay at the villa, I think?'

'No, I have an aunt who has an apartment not far away—' she began, then stopped, as she didn't want him to think she was above sharing accommodation. But he didn't seem to be thinking of that, and immediately started talking about people they knew in common. Cécilia was glad of his presence – at least the place wasn't totally full of strangers – and she began to relax. A languid young woman handed her a glass of wine, a tall man with a limp changed the gramophone record to a patriotic song, and an elderly man with a German accent, who according to Florian was a writer of satire, made a clever remark, and everyone laughed.

'Ah, Flory, there you are!' said a girl, coming up to them just then. 'I was looking for you. Tell Jérôme about what those Germans in Marseille said to us, because he won't believe me.'

She looked Cécilia up and down briefly and flashed her a smile as she led Florian away. Cécilia stood and sipped her wine for a minute until she was joined by Marion.

'Quite a crowd this evening,' said Marion in English, then repeated it in French.

'No need to translate, I speak English,' said Cécilia in that language. Marion made a surprised noise.

'So you do! And without a hint of an accent.'

'I'm half-English,' said Cécilia. 'I went to school in England when I was younger.'

'Well, what a relief to speak my own language for a few minutes! My dear, you must have noticed how awful my French is. I can simply never get my nouns and my adjectives to agree. So difficult! I've been here twenty years, so you'd think I'd have improved by now, but I guess I'm just one of those people who don't have a talent for languages.' She dismissed the subject and nudged Cécilia. 'Look, it's Fernand Quinault.' She indicated a man who was sitting on one of the sofas with a giggling young woman on his knee, although he didn't look particularly pleased about it. 'But I dare say you knew him in Paris.'

'No, I've never met him.'

'No? And yet he and your father worked so closely together. Fernand!' she called.

Fernand Quinault glanced up, politely removing the young woman from his lap and coming over to be introduced to Cécilia. He brightened immediately when he heard who she was, and shook hands cordially, as Marion melted away to do her duty by her other guests. It was difficult to judge his age from his appearance, as he was tall and tended to stoop, had a shock of brown curly hair speckled with grey which stood out wildly from his head, and wore spectacles. But his voice and face were those of a young man, and his manner was calm and pleasant. He, too, expressed his regrets at Jean-Jacques Brouillard's death.

'He was by way of being a mentor to me,' he said. 'Almost like a father. He was the one who recommended me for the Paris-

Montparnasse Symphony Orchestra. For a few weeks I was the youngest conductor they'd ever had.' He grimaced.

'I'm sorry you lost your job,' said Cécilia.

'It was nice while it lasted. And others have been through worse. At least I managed to escape to the South before they decided I'd be better off in an internment camp. Not like Emil, eh, Emil?'

'What's that?' said Emil, who had just joined them.

'I was just saying I was lucky not to have been arrested in Paris. Marion says the news is bad up there.'

'I think it is,' said Emil soberly. 'They've started deporting foreigners to Germany. I was arrested, but a few of us managed to create a diversion and get away. I hid for a couple of weeks then came down here, where it's a bit safer.'

'It won't be safe forever, though,' replied Fernand. 'The prefecture has been making noises about arresting all the *undesirable foreigners*, as they call them.'

'But you're not a foreigner,' said Cécilia to Fernand.

'I am on my mother's side,' he said. 'She was an Austrian Jew.'

'Then you're only half-Jewish.'

'No, my father's a French Jew,' he said with a rueful smile. 'I'm half-foreign and all Jew. Why do you think they fired me as conductor? I can't get a job, and nobody will perform my music any more.'

'So you've come here to try and get out of France?'

'That was the idea. Marion and her friends are the people to go to if you want travel papers. But I'm worried about my father. He stayed in Paris. I wanted him to come with me but he has a business he doesn't want to leave, and he said he was too old to be running away now.'

A week or two ago Cécilia wouldn't have believed Monsieur Quinault senior was in any danger, but the arrival of Emil and the things she had read in the papers had led to the dawning realisation that she had been shutting her eyes to the truth for the past year.

'Will you leave without him if he doesn't come?' she asked.

'I don't know. I don't want to be arrested, but I don't like to desert my family and my country either.'

'Well you'd better decide one way or the other,' said Emil practically. 'There's no use in just sitting here waiting for events to overtake you.'

'Always the man of action,' said Fernand with a smile. 'I prefer a quiet life.'

'There is no quiet life nowadays. I don't see how anyone can see what's happening and do nothing about it.'

'Perhaps you're right. Well, I'll think it over. If I can get back to Paris just for a few days I might have a shot at persuading him to come with me. He's stubborn and difficult but perhaps I can talk him round.'

'They're all stubborn and difficult,' said Emil in a low voice to Cécilia when Fernand had moved away. 'All these celebrities and artistic types are. You see the trouble we have. They want to go, then they don't want to go, then they want to go but they don't want to walk across the mountains in the rain, and they're supposed to be incognito but they get offended when the border officials don't recognise them. I'm surprised any of them get out at all.'

Cécilia looked around at the crowd of people laughing and drinking.

'Is this what you've been doing, then?' she asked.

'Yes. Being a lawyer, I know all the legal channels – and quite a few of the illegal ones, too. We're trying to get refugees out of the country.'

'All Jews?'

'Jews and Communists, mostly.'

'But some of them are famous.'

'Perhaps, but they're all degenerate and dangerous, according to the Nazis. I don't give much for their chances if they don't leave France soon. And that one in particular.' He nodded towards a man, self-important and gracious, who had just entered the room in company with a laughing woman, to applause from the rest of the guests. Marion greeted him enthusiastically, and from the general exclamations from people around her, Cécilia understood that this was Gerhard Varady, the painter, who had aroused the ire of the Nazis with some of his recent work, which was highly political in tone.

'Is that his wife?' she said to Emil. 'She must be feeling better now. Didn't Marion say she'd just had a baby?'

'Yes, that's Elsa,' said Emil, amused, 'but she's not the one who had the baby. That was Nina, Varady's model.'

Cécilia stared. 'But is he the father?'

'So they're all claiming.'

'And doesn't Elsa mind?'

'Who knows?'

Cécilia looked more closely at the Varadys. A group of people had gathered around them and they were holding court. Elsa had her hand on her husband's arm and they were both laughing at something. This was the man who would not leave France because his mistress had just given birth and was ill. She couldn't imagine how the three of them got along together, but at the same time it suddenly struck her that there was something vivid, something vital about all these people. They had lives and loves and happiness and disappointments, just like anybody else, but their very existence was constrained by laws and difficulties that didn't apply to others, simply because of who they were.

Cécilia stood in silence for a while. She was remembering things she'd seen in Paris and had never paid much attention to. The signs in the shop windows that said '*Interdit aux Juifs*' – 'no Jews', the disparaging articles she had read in newspapers and periodicals, the ugly posters she had seen for a propaganda exhibition entitled *Le Juif et la France*. It had been easy to shut her eyes to things that didn't concern her – things that affected people she'd never met and didn't care about – but here in this very room were people who had been vilified by their own countrymen and even by the state, had lost their jobs and their livelihoods, and had had to uproot themselves from their homes and their businesses in order to escape from France, rather than submit to arrest and deportation and who knew what else.

Emil was watching her.

'What are you thinking?' he asked.

'I was thinking about Maggie. I laughed at her for throwing herself into all this. I thought she was stupid for risking herself for a cause that had nothing to do with her. I thought she'd be better off staying out of it. But now I think perhaps I was the stupid one.'

'You're not stupid. Just innocent.'

'It comes to the same thing in the end. I wish there were something I could do to help, but I don't know anything except music.'

'Music is just as important as anything else now,' he said gravely. 'We need something to take our minds off the real world. Keep on playing and you'll be doing your part. Which reminds me—'

He caught the eye of a man Cécilia had seen him talking to earlier and nodded.

'Who's that?' asked Cécilia.

'He's our pianist for this evening. You don't think Marion will let us get out of performing, do you? She's very generous, but she exacts a price. You're part of her collection now, and she'll want to show you off. Ready, Georges?'

At Emil's insistence they had brought their instruments, and it looked as if this was to be the moment of truth. Of course Cécilia was well used to performing classical pieces in public, but jazz was something new. Still, perhaps it was the wine, or the relaxed atmosphere, but she found she wasn't as reluctant as she'd expected. The man addressed as Georges cocked his head in acknowledgement and strolled over to a piano in the corner. He nudged the piano stool's current occupant out of the way, then sat down and played a few bars experimentally as Emil and Cécilia got their instruments ready. Cécilia glanced at Emil, perched with his guitar on the arm of a sofa, who smiled encouragingly and gave the instruction to begin.

After a false start, covered over with much laughter, the three of them settled easily into the music, and Cécilia was soon lost in the tune. She closed her eyes, never missing a note, her bow flying merrily and assuredly across the strings. This time she was more confident in her improvisation, and became more daring, adding contrasting and even clashing colours to the mixture; here a splash of russet, there a hint of crimson, supplementing the cheeriness of Emil's music with a touch of intensity, even poignancy, that was all her own. Then it was finished, and the room broke out in cheers and rapturous applause, and she took a bow, laughing. Suddenly Emil was up on his feet, his arm around her shoulder, showing her to the room.

'Ladies and gentlemen, our newest swing jazz star!' he announced, then before Cécilia knew what he meant to do, he swept her off her feet and kissed her. The cheering grew louder, and he let her go, laughing at her blushing reaction. Before she could think or speak, there were calls for an encore, and so they performed it again, then it was somebody else's turn to play, and Cécilia was kept busy between putting her violin away and talking to all the people who had come up to congratulate her on her performance. The noise of the party had got louder somehow; the sound of chatter and laughter rang in her ears, and the cigarette smoke was beginning to make her eyes sting. Emil had disappeared and suddenly she felt very tired. After a few minutes she sought out a quiet corner and sat down, hoping to be left alone, but it was no use – everyone wanted to talk to her so she was forced to make conversation. Everyone was kind and friendly enough, but still, it was hard work, and she was unaccustomed to the effort.

It was nearly three when they left the villa at last to start the two-mile walk back to the flat. The moon was nearly full, which gave them enough light to see by, and with their instruments strapped to their backs they made quick progress down the steep, winding road. Emil was in a state of exhilaration and kept up a stream of talk as they walked, while Cécilia listened in silence, only half taking in what he was saying. Her head was spinning, although she didn't think she'd drunk more than half a glass of wine. At length he fell quiet and finally seemed to notice her silence.

'What's wrong?' he asked.

Cécilia was too inexperienced to tell anything but the truth.

'You kissed me,' she said, not looking at him.

He laughed.

'So I did.'

'You shouldn't have done that.'

'Why not? Didn't you like it?'

'That's not the point.'

'Then what is the point?'

'You can't do that to Maggie,' she said. 'It's – it's not right.'

'It was just a kiss, that's all. I couldn't help it. How could I help it? You played the music as I've always heard it in my head. Nobody's ever done that before, but you did, and you were…'

'I was what?'

'I don't know, exactly. Glowing. You were glowing.'

'Glowing?' Cécilia stared.

'Look, I'm sorry. I got carried away. It was just a silly thing. I didn't think you'd mind – most girls wouldn't.'

'I'm not most girls.'

'No, you're not, and I beg your pardon. Will you forgive me?'

Perhaps she'd made too much of it. She was trying to deal confidently and elegantly with an unfamiliar situation, but she felt as though she were flailing blindly in the dark, and he looked so serious that she was fearful she might have upset him. She was about to tell him it was quite all right when he suddenly stiffened.

'Shh!' he whispered.

She listened, and heard the sound of footsteps approaching.

'Police,' he said in a low voice. He was glancing around. To their right was a steep flight of steps cut into the hillside between two silent houses. 'Quick!'

Motioning to her to be quiet, he pulled her off the road and up the first few steps. Here they were hidden from view, and they watched from the dark recess as two men in police uniforms passed at a leisurely pace and continued up the road. As their footsteps receded into the distance, Cécilia whispered:

'They weren't looking for you, were they?'

'No, it's just a patrol. But there's no point in taking any chances. The police around here arrest anyone they don't like the look of.'

'Is it safe to go yet?'

'Wait a minute or two.'

The steps were narrow and he still had hold of her arm. In the darkness it was impossible to see his face, but he was standing so close to her that she could smell the tobacco on his clothes, overlaid with the scent of Marion's best cognac. She could feel the warmth of his hand through her coat sleeve and her heart began to beat rapidly. It was the wine, it must be the wine. A silence hovered between them.

'You didn't answer my question, by the way,' he said at last, very softly.

'Which question?'

'I asked whether you liked it.'

There was no escape. Cécilia knew nothing about men but she understood his intention. He turned her towards him and took her face in his hands gently.

'Did you?' he asked again.

She wanted to break away from him. The answer was no; of course it was no.

'Yes,' she heard herself whispering.

She couldn't see him but she sensed his amusement.

'Let's try it again without an audience,' he said, and brought his face down to hers.

She should have stepped back, turned away, but she couldn't. Everything about him – his ready charm, his laugh, the dizzying scent of him – conspired to draw her in, and she could no more resist him than she could resist the melodies that drifted perpetually around and above him like wisps of smoke. She melted into the kiss, and the colours of his music snaked around them both, vivid, insistent, drawing them into a closer embrace. How long it lasted, Cécilia couldn't say; she couldn't seem to think at all, in fact – only feel. His arms were around her and his lips were warm on hers, and there was nothing to do except let herself be carried away by the overwhelming sensation of it all.

At last she had to pull away to catch her breath, and he stared at her, touching her face. He seemed as startled as she was by the whole thing.

'You're quite extraordinary,' he murmured. 'Why didn't I see it before? I thought you were shy and quiet – perhaps even a little dull. But you're not, are you? There's fire in your soul, I can feel it. It's buried deep, but it's there, and I want it. Will you give it to me?'

There was a raw undercurrent to his voice that pierced the moment, and suddenly it was too much, too quick. The colours all whisked out of sight, the cold chill of the night air hit her, and she realised where she was and what was happening. What was she doing? This man belonged to Maggie; her mind told her that much, but then why was he gazing at her with such intensity? This was something she had no experience of. She couldn't explain it but she knew she was balancing precariously on the edge of a precipice, and that one step forward would cause her to plummet straight into the unknown.

She shook her head and shrank back, and he saw the moment was lost. She turned away and without a word walked quickly down the steps and onto the road, then hurried as fast as she could all the way home. He walked briskly to keep up with her, but she turned her face away and wouldn't speak to him, and when they got back to the apartment she shut herself into her room and locked the door, then leaned against it, her heart hammering. He didn't knock, but she heard him moving about, and listened until she heard his bedroom door close. Then she went to bed herself and lay awake for a long while, until the dawn light began to filter under the blinds.

The next day she told Emil he couldn't stay at her flat any more. He saw she was serious and didn't argue the point, but made arrangements to move in with an acquaintance in the old town. Two days later he was gone.

Chapter Ten

For the next week or two Cécilia threw all her efforts into getting back to normal and trying to forget what had happened that night on the way back from the Villa Rocquefort. She went to the Villa Paradiso every day as usual, and tried her hardest to concentrate on her studies, but she couldn't; something got in the way. She wanted to complete her strings and piano piece, and she buried herself in the music, trying her best to make progress, but the notes wouldn't come — or if they did, they came in a burst of reds and blues that reminded her of that first evening when she had met Emil. In a fit of defiance she had crossed out the passages they'd produced together on her aunt's old upright piano, but without them the music was flat and uninspired; besides, the deleted notes jostled noisily at the edge of her consciousness, demanding to be let back in. At last she gave up and restored them to their rightful place, but instead of behaving correctly and forming themselves into an orderly progression, it turned out they had intended only to deceive her, because the reds immediately began to melt into purple and the blues into the turquoise of the swing jazz song she and Emil had played together, which he had said he was going to name after her.

Try as she might, she couldn't stop her mind from casting back to that night at Marion's party, when the music had seemed to blend seamlessly together with the crowd and the laughter in one perfect performance. It had affected him as much as it had her, and he'd acted on impulse then, but after? That kiss on the steps had not been an impulse; it had been a deliberate, considered move.

She tried not to remember the feel of Emil's rough woollen coat sleeve against her cheek, the warmth of his hands and the taste of his lips, yet it was difficult, almost impossible, to put them out of her mind. But she would struggle through it. She'd come very close to betraying her sister – had betrayed her, in fact – but that was all to stop. She couldn't say who had been most to blame. Certainly, Emil had done wrong, but hadn't she been just as complicit in allowing the kiss? *Enjoying the kiss*, a little voice said in her head. That was the worst of it, of course. Without that voice it would have been easy enough to say it had been a stupid mistake.

Cécilia was confused and upset, and for several days didn't stray far from home. She kept to her well-worn route between her flat and the Villa Paradiso, fearing to bump into Emil, although there was no reason why she should meet him at all in such a big city. He had given her his address, somewhere in the old town not far from the harbour. She could reach him there if she needed anything, he said. Cécilia had no intention of needing anything, telling herself she'd be quite happy never to see him again.

It was late October, and an autumnal rain had set in. Cécilia felt a gloom settle upon her, and began to think that perhaps she had made a mistake in coming to Nice. She was lonely; the music wasn't coming along as she wanted, and she missed her family. More than anything she wanted to see Maggie again. Maggie always made her feel better. She was kind and supportive – the older sister to whom Cécilia had always run to confide her troubles, since her mother wasn't the sympathetic type. Of course, there was one particular trouble that Cécilia could never confide, but that was all to be forgotten. She would pretend it had never happened, and then everything would go on as normal.

As if Maggie had read her thoughts, Cécilia shortly afterwards received a letter from her, hand-delivered by another student who had just arrived from Paris, since there was no use in trying to send personal messages via the official channels. Naturally Maggie couldn't talk in a letter about the work she'd been doing for the Resistance, but she sent cheerful, chatty news of their family and friends, and of life in Paris. The food situation hadn't got any better, she said. They were still surviving on limp leeks and onions, and whatever scraps of meat they could get. As for the coffee – well, it was better not to talk about it. Chicory was no substitute for the real thing. There was no mention of Emil until after the signature, where Maggie had squeezed in another few lines in quite a different tone:

> *I hope you got my message about Zazou. I was just about to send this off when we got some bad news about another stray, Filip. It seems he met with an accident, and didn't survive. Obviously we are all devastated. Please look after my Zazou – I wouldn't want anything similar to happen to him.*

There the letter ended, as if Maggie couldn't bear to continue. Cécilia frowned. She seemed to remember the name Filip. Who was it, now? Then she remembered: Filip was the name of Emil's old violinist. They had been arrested together, he said, and he hadn't seen his friend since. Now it seemed he was dead – killed, presumably. Cécilia knew she would have to find Emil and tell him what had happened. After all, it was only right that he be told he'd lost his friend – in fact, that was the only reason Maggie had put it in her letter, of course: she wanted Cécilia to pass the news on. Cécilia dreaded seeing him, but at the same time had to force down a little spark of something that to her dismay she recognised as excitement. She shook herself. This wouldn't do. She would go and find him and deliver the message, and then she would say a polite goodbye.

The address he'd given her turned out to be a squalid, narrow alley a few streets away from the cathedral. It was a grey, damp afternoon, and Cécilia huddled into her coat as she looked for the number of the building. Eventually, she found it: a dilapidated place with crumbling walls and a narrow doorway. The deserted entrance hall echoed with the sound of her footsteps as she went in. There must be several flats in the building, but she couldn't hear a sound from any of them. Emil was staying on the third floor. Cécilia set off up the dark staircase and arrived at last on a tiny landing that was lit only by an even tinier window. She peeped out, but there was no view to be had; only the yellow, peeling plaster on the wall of the building opposite. She listened at the door of the flat. All was silent; perhaps there was nobody in. She hesitated a moment and then knocked lightly. There was no answer so she knocked again. He must be out. Cécilia felt a sense of relief, and was about to turn and walk back down the stairs when she heard the sound of bolts being drawn and Emil opened the door. She gasped at the sight of him.

'Oh, goodness me!' she exclaimed before she could stop herself.

The injuries weren't fresh; it must have happened a few days ago. Even so, his face was still swollen and battered. A bruise around his eye was an ugly purple, and there was a nasty graze on his forehead which had crusted over thickly. Although he was a sorry sight, his face lit up when he saw her.

'It's you,' he said. 'I hoped you'd come.'

'What happened?' she asked.

He shrugged ruefully. 'Occupational hazard.'

He didn't want to say any more, and instead motioned for her to enter the flat. Cécilia spared it no more than a glance, enough to note that it was small and messy, because all her attention was concentrated on Emil.

'Who did this?' she asked.

He was reluctant, but she pressed him and at length got out of him that he had been set upon in the street by a group of men. Beyond that he maintained a stubborn silence.

'But as you can see, I'm fine,' he said. 'It looks a lot worse than it is. Bruises always do.'

'Are you sure you're all right?'

'Of course! Now, tell me why you're here. I'm rather hoping it's because you missed me as much as I've missed you.'

He was smiling, and she felt a mixture of emotions, but she couldn't keep the news from him, much as she'd have liked to.

'I've heard from Maggie,' she said. His smile switched off, and he became serious.

'Go on.'

'It wasn't really a proper message. Obviously she couldn't say anything straight out. Maybe I misunderstood it.'

'What is it?'

'It's Filip.'

She didn't need to go on. A shadow passed across his face and he drew in his breath.

'He's dead, isn't he?'

She nodded.

'How did it happen?'

'I don't know. She just said something about an accident. I'm sorry. Was he a good friend of yours?'

He swallowed, and the desolate look on his battered face at that moment almost broke her heart.

'He was my brother,' he said at last.

She put her hand to her mouth, distraught. 'I'm so very sorry.'

He shrugged.

'It happens. You lost a brother too, didn't you?'

'Yes, but that doesn't make it any better. I wish there was something I could do.'

He turned away and made some indeterminate gesture.

'He wasn't much of a violinist anyway,' he said with grim humour. 'He would never practise, and he used to make the music up half the time.'

'Emil.' She placed her hand on his back in a gesture of sympathy, and he flinched. For a second she thought it was rejection, but then she realised she'd hurt him. He must have more injuries than she knew about.

'You're bleeding,' she said suddenly. It was true; she had just seen a small patch of blood seeping through the back of his shirt near his shoulder blade.

'Am I?' He reached over his shoulder and tested the area gingerly. 'Ah, yes. I'd have bandaged it but I couldn't reach it properly, and I thought it would heal better without. The cut must have been deeper than I thought.'

'I can bandage it for you. Let me see.'

'No!' he said fiercely.

'Why not? What is it? I can help. I know how to dress wounds. If you don't look after it you'll get an infection.'

He was still reluctant, and looked away. There was something to this she didn't understand. She forced him to meet her eye.

'Look at me,' she said firmly. 'You won't help anybody by getting sick. Let me see what I can do.'

He stared at her, and at last seemed to reach a decision.

'All right, I'll show you. But I warn you, it isn't pretty.'

He began to unbutton his shirt, his eyes on her all the time. Then he turned around, and she gasped once more. Most of the wounds had begun to crust over, but some of them were still open and weeping. His back was a mess, but there was no mistaking what had been done to him. Carved deep into his skin in big, jagged letters was the word *JEW*.

Cécilia felt a sob rising in her throat.

'Who did this?' she managed at last.

'Who knows? I don't know who they were. They might have been anyone.'

'Did you report it to the police?'

'Don't be ridiculous. The police were there at the time – two of them. They watched and didn't do a thing. Now don't be like that. It's much better than it was. You should have seen it the other day!'

The tears were rolling down Cécilia's face, and she tried to pull herself together. There was no good in crying like a baby. She ought to be comforting him, not the other way round.

'I'm sorry,' she said. 'I just got a shock, that's all. Let me get some water and I'll clean it for you. Where's your friend? Couldn't he have done something?'

'He left Nice last week on a boat to Gibraltar. I'm here alone now. But I'd rather have you than him looking after me anyway – you're much nicer to look at.'

A touch of the old humour gleamed in his eye, and she managed to hiccup out a laugh. There was no question of walking away from him in his condition, and she took off her coat and set to work, digging out old cloths that could be used for bandages and boiling some water on a little gas stove. He sat quite still on the edge of his bed as she dabbed his wounds clean and bandaged him up as best she could. He said little, his brow pulled low over his eyes.

'There, that's a bit better,' she said at last. 'I don't think there's any infection, but make sure you keep it all clean until it heals.' She glanced at her watch. 'I'd better get back.'

'Won't you stay?' He wasn't going to show weakness in words, but he didn't need to; there was a plea, a sort of quiet desperation in his eyes that he couldn't disguise. He didn't want to be alone. 'Please, Cécilia. Stay and keep me company. Just for a little while.'

They were sitting side by side on the bed, and she hesitated. She knew she ought to refuse, but they were so close together, and the music was coming back again, the colours swirling around them both, very faint at the moment, but getting brighter. He took her hand and placed the palm against his face, and without knowing what she was doing she sank against him and felt the roughness of his cheek against hers. Then suddenly he was kissing her fiercely with his bruised lips, and she was responding eagerly to the taste of him, and feeling the bandages and the bare skin of his chest under her hands. He whispered softly, telling her how beautiful she was and how much he wanted her, fumbling at the buttons of her dress as she helped him, her hands trembling with the urgency of it, but clear-intentioned and purposeful as though she were someone else, not herself at all.

And it was easy, so easy. How could she ever have feared it? Her skin against his, his lips against hers, demanding as much as she was prepared to give. The colours were bright now, glowing gold and coral and violet against the white of the walls, and he pushed her down onto the bed and she gave herself up to him, gave him all the comfort he needed in his unhappiness, because that was the most important thing right now, right at this moment.

Afterwards, they lay quietly together as the grey daylight gathered into darkness. Cécilia allowed her thoughts to be filled with a hazy, pleasant nothingness. Then she saw he was leaning up on one elbow, watching her, and she pulled the sheet over herself, suddenly self-conscious.

'Don't,' he said. 'I want to look at you.'

She drew in her breath as he pulled the sheet away and gazed at her. He ran his hand lightly over her breast and down to her hip. She shivered a little.

'I knew you were extraordinary,' he murmured. 'Will you stay tonight?'

She hesitated.

'I can't, I have a concert this evening – just a little thing, but I have to play. But I'll come back tomorrow if you like.'

'What time?'

'After lunch. Two o'clock. I'll come at two.'

'Good. And you'll look after me again? I like it,' he said, and she laughed, flushing. She gave the promise without thinking too far ahead, shutting her mind to what it meant and to the fact that she was supposed to be keeping away from him. Then she dressed and left, because she'd missed a class and her teachers would be wondering where she was. When she got to the Villa Paradiso she had an hour free before the concert, so she sat in one of the practice rooms and bent to her composition, which had suddenly become easier again – so much so that she wondered why it had been difficult before.

The next day she went back, knowing full well she was lost but unable to stop herself. He opened the door at her first knock and this time there was no hesitation at all. She went straight into his arms and loved him in a way that seemed to come wholly naturally. It was easier than she'd ever imagined, and she put Maggie out of her mind, pushing the consequences away from her to a future day, because the present had closed around her like a cloud of fog. She could see and hear nothing else except Emil and the vibrant shades of music he brought to her pale existence.

Chapter Eleven

Hertfordshire, 1949

Cécilia slowly recovered, and within a couple of days was almost back to her old self, such as it was. She had taken a relatively small dose of the barbitone – hardly enough to knock her out, in fact, the doctor joked as he took her pulse. Cécilia smiled wanly but did not reply. Harriet, who was in the room at the time, wondered whether Cécilia had in fact intended to kill herself. Perhaps she had started with that intention, but had changed her mind partway through, since the dose that was left in the bottle would have been ample to do the job had she taken it all.

Rose, meanwhile, said little when she returned and found out what had happened. Harriet had half-expected her to lose her temper, but something seemed to stop her – perhaps Harriet's presence – and she merely pressed her lips together tightly when the doctor broke the news to her. As for Sébastien, he went about as normal, and didn't even mention the incident, but merely gazed defiantly at Harriet whenever he saw her. Harriet longed to confront him, but dared not. She chided herself for her cowardice, but told herself it would do no good to interfere. After all, what business was it of hers?

None at all – and yet her thoughts returned repeatedly to the letter she'd found in Cécilia's room, and particularly the mysterious Zazou who was not a cat. Harriet had read of the Zazous in the newspapers during the war – young Frenchmen and women who loved swing jazz and rebelled against the occupying Germans by wearing unconventional clothes. Was this what Maggie was referring to? Whatever the case, she'd obviously asked Cécilia to shelter someone. Harriet wondered very much what had happened to Zazou, but given Cécilia's fragile mental state she couldn't possibly ask, not at present anyhow. But Harriet's curiosity had been awakened, and she couldn't help determining to keep her eyes and ears open for further hints about what had happened all those years ago.

More and more Harriet felt her sympathies aligning with Rex, who was overjoyed that his mother was still alive and well, although she showed no more interest in him than she had before. He hung about her until sent packing by his grandmother, who was as impatient with him as ever, but even then he found excuses to hover outside Cécilia's room, not quite daring to go in, but not wanting to be far from her. Harriet began to feel an ache in her heart whenever she saw his pale face and wide eyes, and his pathetic attempts to attract his mother's attention. Poor boy, she thought. He needed friends his own age and a family who loved him; not this empty life in this tomb of a house. But here again, it wasn't her place to say anything, and so all she could do was resolve to keep an eye on him and be as kind to him as she could without attracting the disapproval of her employer.

Less than a week after Cécilia's suicide attempt, it already seemed as though the whole thing had been a dream, such was everybody's determination to go on as if nothing had happened. Rose said nothing about her daughter, but remained as stern and implacable as ever, while Sébastien went off for a few days to stay with friends. One Tuesday afternoon Mrs Brouillard gave Harriet the afternoon off and advised her, in that distant way of hers, to go into Royston and buy some clothes.

Harriet might have resented the inference, but it was no more than she'd been planning to do herself now that she'd saved up a little money, and in fact she rather looked forward to the outing.

Lately she'd found herself examining her reflection in the mirror with dissatisfaction, although it was a while since she'd thought of her looks. Now she saw what others must see in her. What had happened to the young, vibrant Harriet Conway? Not so very long ago she'd had pink cheeks and soft blue eyes and hair the colour of cornfields, as Jim had once described it in a rare and slightly absurd fit of poetry which had made her laugh. Now she was faded and worn, pale and harassed-looking, and the blue eyes weren't soft any more, but were a cold, hard barrier against the world. And where had that frown come from? Once her brow had been smooth and clear, but now it was permanently pulled down, her eyebrows meeting in a deep V. She stared at herself and opened her eyes wide. There: that was better. A little rouge and a touch of lipstick, and she almost looked like her old self again – although her hair badly needed doing. Perhaps she might see if she could get a curl and set while she was out.

It was a beautiful day – not too cold considering it was late November – and she felt her spirits lift a little. She was in a mood to be helpful, so before she left the house she went into Cécilia's room to ask if there were any letters she wanted posting. Cécilia had nothing to send, but Harriet looked at her, sitting at the piano, her usual colourless, quiet self, and suddenly felt a wave of sympathy.

'Look here, it's a lovely day, far too nice to be sitting inside. Why don't you come out with me?'

Cécilia regarded her blankly, then with surprise.

'I can't,' she said, indicating the chair. 'My arms aren't strong enough to go very far.'

'That's because you don't go out enough. But I'll push if you like, I don't mind. Really, you could do with getting a bit of colour to your cheeks. It's not good for you to stay here cooped up inside all day.'

'Who cares what's good for me?'

'Rex does, and I do. And your mother does too,' Harriet added, although she was less sure on this front.

Cécilia laughed. It was a scornful sound. 'You think she cares?' she said bitterly. 'I'm nothing but a burden. She'd be much happier if she didn't have to think about me. We're all a disappointment to her, but I'm the worst of them all. If I were whole I could be earning enough money to keep this place standing, but instead I'm crumbling away with the house and reminding her daily of all the nice things we used to have.'

Harriet had nothing to say to that; for all she knew it was true. Cécilia had turned away and was wheeling herself slowly across to the piano, indicating that the conversation was at an end. Harriet didn't press the point, but left the room. As she walked down the corridor towards the main wing of the house, she heard the sound of that mournful music again, drifting after her.

She enjoyed her walk into Royston, the feel of the sharp air on her face under the light of the low sun, which was sinking, casting a golden glow over the trees along the muddy path that led behind the house. There was a scent of smoke mixed with fertiliser in the air, and in the distance she could hear the sound of a tractor ploughing the fields. There was something encouraging about all this preparation for the next year – a sense that the old skin was being shed in expectation of the growth of a new one – and she found her spirits lifting as she walked.

Her shopping trip was more successful than she could have hoped. In the first place she went into she encountered a sympathetic young assistant who had had a quiet day up until then, and was only too enthusiastic at the thought of helping a new customer. Harriet emerged from the shop after forty-five minutes, having bought far more than she had intended to – although it was all last season's stuff, so not too costly – and wearing a smart new coat and gloves. They would send along the rest of her new things the next day, they promised.

After that, she managed to find a hairdresser that was not too busy, and allowed herself to be generally fussed over. When she looked at herself in the mirror afterwards, she hardly recognised herself, except in a vague sort of way, like a far-off memory sparked by the discovery of a faded old photograph at the back of a drawer. Was this really her? It seemed that there was, after all, something of the old Harriet still left in her. She paid the hairdresser, inwardly resolving that she would make more of an effort, as she had in the past, then came out into the street and set off for home. The sun was very low now, turning to twilight as she returned along the path past the farm, and she picked up the pace, so as to be back before it got too dark to see very well.

As she passed the old barn someone came out of the shed next to it: a lad of eighteen or so whom she recognised as belonging to the farm. She seemed to remember his name was Maurice. Harriet would have thought nothing of it, but as soon as he saw her he made a sudden gesture to someone who was just coming out behind him, who promptly whisked out of sight, but not before she had seen it was Rex. If this wasn't an invitation to be curious, then she didn't know what was.

She immediately left the path, and, ignoring Maurice's rueful grin, passed him and entered the shed. It was almost dark inside – or would have been, except somebody had laid a torch down in the corner, which cast an eerie glow upon the scene. The space seemed to be used to store assorted tools, rusty pails, tins of paint and other paraphernalia. The floor was gritty under her feet and there was a strong smell of creosote. Rex was crouched in the corner by a basket, and was gazing at her warily, as though he expected to be told off at any moment. In the basket was the explanation for the mysterious injury to his hand, because there lay a mother dog, complacently presiding over a household of several brown and white puppies which were clambering over her, burrowing under her and wrestling with each other. To her surprise, she saw that there was also someone else she knew in the shed. It was Alec McLeod. He was sitting on an upturned packing-case, an unlit pipe sticking out of his mouth. He glanced up, smiling as Harriet came in.

'Looks like you've been rumbled, Rex,' he said.

'So this is what bit you,' said Harriet to Rex.

He looked slightly sheepish.

'You won't tell Grand-mère, will you? She told me to keep away from them. I don't think she likes animals very much.'

Harriet looked at the puppies, one of which had escaped the basket and was sniffing at McLeod's trouser leg. He picked it up and tickled its tummy. It wriggled joyously and its floppy ears quivered.

'Bessie went for me when I came too near them,' explained Rex. 'She didn't mean to be horrid, she just wanted to protect her pups. Aren't they splendid?'

'They're very sweet,' replied Harriet.

'She's a beagle, but we don't know what the puppies are. They think it might be the boxer from Mr Evans's farm. Maurice says I can have one if I like, but Grand-mère won't let me.'

He looked downcast. Harriet glanced across at McLeod.

'I… er… happened to be passing,' he said, by way of explanation.

'It's time to be going now, Rex,' said Harriet. 'Your grandmother will be wondering where you are.'

The boy stood up obediently but couldn't stop himself looking wistfully at the puppies.

'I wish I was allowed to keep one. Three of them will be going soon. But they haven't found a home for the fourth one. I wish I could have it.'

The longing in his eyes was plain to see. Harriet thought a dog would do him good, but she knew if Mrs Brouillard had made up her mind then there was no use in trying to change it.

McLeod was still playing with the puppy. He looked up at Maurice.

'I was thinking of getting a dog,' he said. 'Did you say you were looking for someone to take the last one?'

'Yes sir. Do you want one?'

'Any in particular, or can I take my pick?'

Maurice shrugged.

'They're all fine dogs. One's as good as another.'

'I don't know – I've rather taken a fancy to this one,' said McLeod, poking gently at the puppy's stomach. It squirmed in ecstasy. 'What do you think, Rex? Shall I take it? I could look after him for you, and you can come and see him whenever you like and help me walk him. How does that sound?'

Rex's face lit up and he glanced at Harriet.

'Could I? I'd like that,' he said.

Harriet didn't see how anyone could object to the plan so she said nothing.

'Good. Then that's settled,' said McLeod.

'I reckon you can have him next week,' replied Maurice.

'Very well. Mind you keep this one for me. I don't want any other.' He stood up. 'It's getting dark. I'll walk you both home.'

They took their leave and emerged into the gathering dusk. Rex ran ahead with a light step, overjoyed that he was to be getting a share in a dog at least.

'That was very kind of you,' said Harriet to McLeod.

'Not really. I did want a dog to keep me company, and it's a pity the lad isn't allowed one of his own.'

'To keep you company? Are you staying in the area, then? You said you were looking at a flying school.'

'I looked at it, and I bought it,' he said.

'So quickly?'

'He wanted to sell it in a hurry, and I got a good price, so we both benefit from the deal.'

'Have you opened for business already?'

'Not yet. In a couple of weeks, maybe. The place is pretty run down, and there's only the one plane, and it needs some attention. Then I'll need to get certification from the Air Registration Board, but after that, there'll be nothing to wait for.'

He was animated, enthusiastic, and her heart clenched as she recognised the signs. Jim's face had lit up in the same way whenever he talked about flying. She felt a sudden pain in her throat and pressed her lips together. Why was it that everywhere she went, or whoever she talked to, some memory of him intruded? Now there was this man, so different from Jim in many ways, but so similar in others, reminding her of what she'd lost. Why couldn't she escape it? She felt the tears pricking at her eyes but forced them down.

'What about pupils? Do you have any?' she asked, trying to sound cheerful.

'Not so far. I've placed some advertisements in the local papers, and we'll see what comes of them. It'll be a slow start, but at least that'll give me the chance to get used to running a school. After that, we'll see. I'd like to buy another couple of planes and take on some more instructors, but that depends on demand – and funds, of course. I was hoping to persuade my father to invest some money in the business, but he said no.'

'That's a pity.'

'I didn't really expect him to say yes. He's never really forgiven me for deserting insurance in favour of flying. He thinks I'm young and wild and reckless, and that I'll come to no good.'

'And are you?'

'Not so young any more, but maybe I am being a bit wild and reckless getting into the flying school business. What do you think?'

'I think you should do what makes you happy,' said Harriet. It was easy enough to say: after all, he was no concern of hers and if he wanted to live dangerously that was his own business.

'All right, then I shall. Will you come out to dinner with me?'

Harriet blinked. She looked at him to see whether he was joking, but he seemed perfectly sincere. He laughed at her surprise. 'Sudden, I know, but I was hoping you'd take pity on me since I'm new to the area and it's no fun eating alone. You can tell me the best places to go around here.'

'I'm afraid I don't know them myself – I haven't been here long and don't get out much.'

'All the more reason to come out, then. We can keep each other company.'

It was unexpected, and her first instinct was to say no. But then something – perhaps a faint echo of the old Harriet – reminded her that Jim was dead, and had been for over eighteen months. Sooner or later she would have to say goodbye to him and go on without him.

'All right,' she found herself saying. 'When?'

'Can you do Thursday?'

'I dare say. Mrs Brouillard doesn't usually want me in the evenings.'

'Excellent, Thursday it is, then. I'll come and pick you up at seven.'

It must be the effect of the smart coat and newly set hair, she supposed. But after all, why not? His manners were pleasant and friendly, and he was nice enough to look at. There was nothing serious to it, of course – she wasn't ready to abandon her grief just yet, and the last thing she wanted to do was to get involved with another pilot – but it would be a pleasant interlude. She felt a flutter inside that she recognised to her surprise as pleased anticipation, even though only a minute or two ago she'd been on the point of tears. Odd how the mind worked, she thought.

They had arrived back at the bridge over the stream which led into the gardens at Chaffingham. Rex was picking up pebbles and throwing them into the swirling water.

'Your shoes are all muddy, Rex,' said Harriet. 'You'd better go in and change them before you catch a chill.'

'All right, Miss Conway.' He turned to McLeod. 'You did mean it about the dog, didn't you?'

'Every word,' replied McLeod solemnly.

Rex beamed.

'Oh, how splendid! May I help you train him?'

'I was hoping you would. But mind, beagles – even mongrel ones – are a frisky breed. You'll need to have your wits about you.'

'I will!' Rex grinned and turned and ran towards the house. Harriet was about to bid McLeod goodbye when she remembered something.

'By the way, I think I might have solved the mystery for you,' she said.

'Which mystery?'

'Your friend Maggie. It's not good news, I'm afraid.'

He looked up. 'She's dead.' It wasn't a question.

Harriet nodded.

'Yes, I think she is, although they never mention her to me. I had no idea she'd ever existed until you turned up.'

'So they did know her. How did you find out?'

'There was a letter. I didn't mean to read it, it was just lying around.' She said nothing about the circumstances under which she had found it. 'I don't know how she died – as I said, they don't like to talk about her. But there was a Maggie once.'

'I wonder what happened to her.'

'I don't know. I don't like to ask.'

Her mind darted back to Sébastien's accusation to Cécilia that night, when he'd said she had Maggie's blood on her hands. Not exactly the sort of thing one could enquire about straight out, but Harriet couldn't help being curious.

'So that's it,' said McLeod. 'I'm sorry I blundered in and asked about her, if they'd prefer to forget her.'

'You weren't to know.'

'I suppose not. Sad, though. She seemed a nice girl.'

'So many nice people died,' said Harriet.

'Yes. That's war for you. Rather a waste, really.'

Harriet glanced towards the house.

'I'd better go. Thanks for what you did for Rex today. He's lonely, and I think it'll do him good.'

'It'll do me good, too, I expect. I've spent too long on my own lately.'

So had she, Harriet realised. They stood together and smiled at one another for a moment, and she thought what a nice smile he had. A few stray strands of tobacco had fallen onto his lapel, she noticed.

'I'd better go in,' she said.

'See you Thursday. Don't forget.'

'I won't.'

She turned and went towards the house, then glanced back and saw him shambling away into the darkness.

*

Dinner that evening wasn't the usual glum meal. By common consent Rex and Harriet didn't mention the dog. Rex wolfed down his food with suppressed excitement, glancing at Harriet every so often to communicate the knowledge of their shared secret, then occasionally at his mother, who was toying with her food as usual. There was an empty place where Sébastien usually sat.

'Isn't Sébastien coming back today?' said Harriet to Mrs Brouillard, by way of making conversation. 'I thought he said he would be back in time for dinner.'

Rose pressed her lips together.

'He decided at the last minute to stay another day with his friends,' she replied. 'It's highly inconsiderate, since Estelle prepared enough for five, and we might have saved the extra beef for something else if he'd thought to call earlier. It's not as though we have a lot to go round these days. Besides, he ought to be here, practising for his concert, instead of frittering away his time in idle fun.'

Harriet had heard the phone ring earlier, and now understood why Mrs Brouillard seemed more irritable than usual.

'Can't he practise while he's away?'

'Not without his violin, which, as I discovered this afternoon, is still in the music room.'

'But he has plenty of time, doesn't he?' said Harriet. 'The concert isn't until a few weeks after Christmas, I think you said.'

'Miss Conway, unfortunately for my son there are some things that will not stay in his head. He has been practising this piece quite long enough to know it by now, but for some unfathomable reason proficiency eludes him. I have told him he needs to practise it a little every day, or he will never manage it.'

'Perhaps it's too hard for him.'

'That is nonsense, and I beg you not to suggest it in front of him. There is nothing especially difficult about this piece, and the only obstacle to playing it properly lies within Sébastien's head, since he continues to insist that it is impossible when the evidence of other, lesser musicians clearly indicates the contrary. But one day he will succeed.' Rose's fist clenched tightly round her fork and she went on grimly, almost to herself. 'He must, he must.'

Chapter Twelve

Nice, 1941

After the first couple of days, Cécilia found it easiest not to think about her sister at all. She was in far too deep to back out now, so the safest course of action from her point of view was to pretend that Maggie didn't exist. There were two realities: Paris and Nice. Paris was a far-off place, brown, damp and murky, to which she might never return, and where anything might happen to save her from having to face the consequences of her own wickedness. There was a war raging on, and Maggie did dangerous things for the Resistance of her own free will, to serve a higher cause than that of love. That was an alien world that Cécilia had nothing to do with. Nice, meanwhile, was her own real world. Here the skies were blue and everything was bathed in a soft light. The colours were joyous, the sea air gave life, there was music and laughter, and above all there was Emil – Emil, with his dark hair and his sparkling eyes and his guitarist's hands and his strength in the face of suffering.

He had shrugged off the news of his brother's death and the injuries he himself had sustained with astonishing resilience, and had gone back to the business of helping refugees escape from the country. Cécilia felt blessed that he was able to find time for her in among such important work, and flattered that he had chosen her of all people. This first love had come upon her unexpectedly, and, shy and introspective as she was, she had fallen harder than most. In her wilder moments she could see no fault in him, although at more sober times, try as she might to keep the thoughts out, that sly little voice whispered in her ear and reminded her that it was not only she who had done wrong by Maggie, but he too. One day Maggie would come back into their lives and there would have to be a reckoning, but who knew what might happen before that? Maggie must meet men every day. There was every chance the same might happen to her as had happened to Emil, and that she would find love with someone else. It was a forlorn hope, but Cécilia clung to it.

As their affair progressed Cécilia started to neglect her studies in order to visit Emil in the afternoons before he went out. As soon as she arrived at the apartment he would take her to bed and there they would stay until the evening, breathless under the covers, shutting out the evil world outside, intent only on each other. After a few remarks from her professors, however, it dawned upon her that she needed to stop drawing attention to herself if Emil was to stay safely out of sight of the authorities, so she returned to her lessons in the afternoon, and instead went to him at night. They went back to the Villa Rocquefort, and to other houses in the hills around Nice, there to meet many of the same people they had met that first evening when they had played together. Then they would come back to his apartment late at night and make love until the early morning, and she would get up at first light and return to her studies, snatching an hour or two's sleep at lunch-time and in the early evenings, before beginning all over again. But it didn't seem to matter how little sleep she got, because her composition was coming along beautifully; although her professors raised their eyebrows a little at the unexpected, almost avant-garde direction her talent seemed to have taken, the music had never flowed from her fingers so effortlessly. She couldn't explain that the music came not from her own brain but from Emil. It hung around him, a swirling, dancing, ever-changing riot of colours, and she had only to snatch it greedily from the air and commit it to paper in all its ready-made perfection.

So the autumn passed in a whirl of happiness. Cécilia's studies were going well, and Emil was making some progress in helping his fellow musicians and artists escape France. Cécilia had almost managed to forget her sister and the moment of truth that loomed menacingly ahead. But one day she was sitting in one of the music rooms at the Villa Paradiso, contentedly buried in her work, when her tranquillity was interrupted by the arrival of a letter from Maggie herself, carried clandestinely from Paris by a newcomer to the villa. In normal circumstances Cécilia would have been overjoyed, tearing it open and reading it immediately. But this time her heart sank as the unwelcome reality rushed in on her all at once. She stared at the grubby envelope for several minutes, half-inclined to rip the thing into a hundred pieces. At length she swallowed and opened it, bracing herself for the punishment. It was worse than she thought. Maggie was her usual effervescent self, full of little bits of news about what the family had been doing in Paris, together with the occasional veiled reference to her underground activities. But then the letter concluded:

> *Do write and let me know how my Zazou is getting on. I haven't heard a word from him since you let me know he'd arrived, and I assume your letters have been going astray too (I'm sorry to say I haven't received one yet), but I know you privileged Prix de Rome scholars do plenty of to-ing and fro-ing between Nice and the north, so I'm sure you can find some way of reaching me. If he's still with you, and if you can, please send me word as to how he's doing. Tell him I love him and I miss him, and give him a hundred kisses from me. I don't mean that literally, of course! In fact, I can picture you recoiling in horror at the very idea of it. But if it's too much for you to say out loud, show him this message and let him read it himself. In fact, I think I'd prefer you to do that in any case – it'll give me some comfort to think that he's reading my words as I wrote them.*

Cécilia crumpled the letter up, her heart stabbing her with every beat. The remorse was crushing. Here was Maggie, fondly supposing that Cécilia's letters were going astray, when in fact Cécilia had not written to her at all since she'd embarked upon her guilty liaison with Emil, trying to put her own duplicity out of her mind as much as possible. And Maggie had laughed at the very idea of Cécilia's having the courage to pass on her love to Emil in words. If her sister only knew the truth – that Cécilia was no longer the shy innocent who'd waved goodbye to her that rainy day in Paris, but a bad, shameless person who'd eagerly taken her sister's place in Emil's affections as soon as the opportunity presented itself.

Then a thought struck. Had Cécilia been duped herself? Was she nothing but a temporary substitute? Had Emil accepted her company idly in Maggie's absence, as a pale, unsatisfactory replacement for the woman he really wanted? Did he care for her at all? The idea made Cécilia feel even more wretched, and she had a sudden urge to go and see Emil right away. She left the Villa Paradiso and hurried through the streets to his apartment. He was at home, frowning and abstracted.

'Is everything all right?' she asked, forgetting her own troubles for the moment in her concern for him.

He smiled and kissed her.

'You're here – of course everything is all right. We had a little problem with some documents, that's all.'

'What do you mean?'

'Well, not so much with the documents, as with the fellow who makes them. Our forger has been arrested.'

'Oh dear,' said Cécilia. 'Is he all right?'

'We're trying to find out. In the meantime, we have several people waiting for passport and exit visas rather urgently.'

'Don't you know anyone else?'

He glanced at her sideways, in an almost calculating fashion.

'As a matter of fact, we do.'

'Well then, why not use him?'

'We will, but…' he tailed off and looked at her. 'You know old Bernard, the caretaker at the Villa Paradiso?'

She nodded. 'He's a forger?' she asked, surprised.

'Not him, his brother. There's only one problem – well, two, actually. The first is that Bernard's brother is old and can't walk very well any more, so he doesn't like to leave home and won't deliver to us. The second problem is that he lives in an apartment opposite his daughter, who is married to a man who works for the prefecture. He's willing to help us, but obviously his son-in-law is going to get suspicious if strange people start visiting him at all times of the day, so we have to go through Bernard at the Villa Paradiso. He can visit whenever he likes, and no one will raise so much as an eyebrow.'

Cécilia understood now why he had looked at her so oddly.

'Do you want me to act as a go-between?' she asked.

He seized at the offer immediately.

'Would you?'

'Of course. Is it dangerous?'

'Only if you're caught,' he said dryly. 'But really, I don't think you'd have any problems. You go to the Villa Paradiso every day, and you're the daughter of the famous Jean-Jacques Brouillard, so you're practically above suspicion. All you'd need to do would be to give him money and take delivery of the documents, then pass them on to me.'

'Of course I'll do it,' said Cécilia. 'I want to help. I would have offered before now, but I didn't think there was anything I could do. Now there is.'

He shot her a look of approval, and she glowed.

'It's not your cause, you know,' he said.

'Yes it is. If it's your cause, it's my cause too.'

He laughed and took her in his arms.

'Jew-lover,' he said teasingly.

'Oh yes,' she whispered, raising her face to meet his kiss. The look in his eyes was enough to convince her. Of course she wasn't a substitute – Emil loved her, and she'd help him with his work, and they'd be together. She would push her sister out of her mind, she told herself, and something would happen – she didn't know what – that would put everything right, and they'd all be happy, including Maggie.

So Cécilia was absorbed painlessly into the Resistance. It was easy work – as Emil said, all she had to do was deliver instructions and money to old Bernard, seeking him out in his caretaker's cupboard and handing over the goods in a plain envelope. Sometimes he would give her a package in return, and sometimes not. If he did, then she would place it in the pocket of her violin case and walk with it down to the old city, there to receive her reward in the form of Emil's love and approval. Often he would take charge of the package and she would never see it again, but sometimes she would leave it where it was in the violin case, and they would go and visit Marion at the Villa Rocquefort and hand it over furtively, or seek her out at the offices of her Rescue Committee, where she would greet them in her usual ebullient manner.

Occasionally they would find Marion in company with a French policeman or a German officer, joking and laughing as though they were her greatest friends, and at those times Cécilia would feel a stab of fear mixed with excitement at the risk they were taking. Indeed, once or twice Emil handed over a package in full view of the enemy, which horrified her, but she saw that he enjoyed the feeling of putting one over on those who had killed his brother in cold blood, and who had stood by as faceless attackers had viciously pinned him down and carved words into his back, and she could hardly blame him for it. The external wounds were healing fast, but she wasn't so sure about the internal ones, because there was a sort of grimness, a desperation about him now that had not been there before. In her company he was as kind and affectionate as ever, but there was no hiding the change from her, who watched him so closely.

After a while the smuggling of illegal documents began to seem almost like a game. Of course, one had to be careful not to draw too much attention to oneself, or attract the notice of the police, but for the most part the authorities left them alone. In this, the unoccupied part of France, it was almost possible to conduct a normal life and forget there was a war on, and with a few adjustments it was possible to live reasonably, if not well. Those weeks were a kind of dream for Cécilia. This new experience of love was a constant wonder to her; she began to blossom as Emil brought her out of her shell, and as Marion took her under her wing and encouraged her to make more of herself, and not to mind being looked at. If Cécilia was to be a famous musician – and she certainly was, Marion said – then there was no use in being shy. It would do her no good to hide her talent from the world. Much better to display it for all to see. It was not often that she met with such genius; it was terribly exciting, and she couldn't help but want to show off her protégée to all her friends.

Marion was flattering and persuasive, and so Cécilia found herself submitting, with not too much reluctance, to playing little solo concerts for whoever happened to be visiting the Villa Rocquefort. On the more formal occasions, attended by music critics and members of the Vichy establishment and even the occasional high-ranking German who thought himself a connoisseur, she would play classical pieces, but at the private gatherings, crowded with friends, hangers-on and refugees, Emil would join her, sometimes together with a few other musicians, in impromptu jazz concerts.

He was writing music again, including a number of guitar and violin duets. They were to remember him by, he said. Cécilia didn't want to think about the implication of his words. They would go on together forever, she told herself, and he would love her and she him, and they would be happy as long as they both lived. 'Do you love me?' she would ask him, and he would assure her that he did, and she would put out of her mind all that was difficult or dangerous about their relationship, all that could go wrong. She would sink into the warmth of his love, curling up in it and wrapping it around her, to ward off the cold, hostile world outside and the fear that one day it might all end.

Chapter Thirteen

Christmas passed, and the old year gave way to the new. The weather had settled into a succession of dull, grey days, not too cold, but still, not the bright, sunny weather and blue skies Cécilia had become used to. She looked forward to the arrival of spring, when the salt air would feel warm on her skin and they could escape Emil's dingy apartment and walk along the Promenade des Anglais, stopping under the shade of the palm trees for coffee or ice cream. She had invited him to return to her apartment, but he had refused, saying that it was easier to remain hidden in the maze-like streets of the old town. On the higher ground of Cimiez he felt more exposed, more likely to be spotted as a foreigner and an undesirable. So every day she threaded her way down from the hills and through the narrow alleys to his door.

One evening in early March they trudged up the road to the Villa Rocquefort, as they had two forged passports to deliver. It was Monday; not the sort of night on which one would expect visitors to come calling, but as usual they found the villa buzzing with activity. It wasn't a large party, but ten or twelve people were lounging about on the comfortable sofas in Marion's spacious living room, smoking, drinking and talking merrily. Marion had somehow managed to get hold of a consignment of fresh fruit – heaven knew how – and she'd placed it in bowls around the place, so the guests were happily helping themselves to pears and plums, blackberries and even strawberries, as well as delicious ripe tangerines which surely must have been imported.

'Darlings!' exclaimed Marion as they entered. 'Do come and have a drink. We're celebrating the departure of the Varadys.'

'Ah, so they've gone at last?' said Emil.

'Yes, thank heaven! He was protesting right up until the very last minute, but Nina and Elsa talked at him, one into each ear, until he finally gave in – although he was very grumpy about it. They're off to Marseille, and from there we should be able to get them on a boat to Casablanca.'

'With the baby?' asked Cécilia, who had never ceased to be fascinated by the Varadys' unusual household arrangements.

'But of course! I don't envy them, though. The poor thing's still very colicky and was screaming fit to burst when they set off. I expect they'll be deaf by the time they get there. So now we must raise a toast to them and their journey, even if they're not here to drink it.'

Marion was pouring them glasses of champagne as she spoke, and Cécilia wondered how she managed to have such rich supplies. It was all part of having useful connections, she supposed. They sat down and Emil began helping himself to the ripe, ruby-red strawberries. They had only come to deliver the documents, but it was difficult to resist Marion's hospitality; she was so generous, and anxious to ensure that everyone was as well fed and watered as she herself was, and so Cécilia resigned herself without too much reluctance to another late night. They had not been there for more than an hour, however, when there was a loud banging at the door, and shortly afterwards a maid appeared.

'It's the police,' she announced, glancing at Marion significantly. There was no chance to say anything more because she was followed closely by two men in police uniform, stern and unsmiling. The most senior of them, a man with a greying moustache, spoke.

'*Madame*,' he said, 'there have been reports of illegal activity. I am afraid we will have to search the house.'

'What do you mean, illegal activity?' asked Marion, looking as surprised as she could manage.

He didn't reply, but left the room and began to bark out orders to his men in the hall. From the sound of it there were four or five of them. He had left his subordinate in the living room, who now addressed them sharply.

'All of you – line up against the wall. Now.'

'Which wall?' asked Marion reasonably, gesturing around her living room. It was true; there was no bare patch of wall for them to line up against, since all the space was currently occupied by her furniture.

'Silence!' snapped the policeman, making them all jump. He caught sight of a young man who had been smirking and whispering to the girl next to him, stepped up to him and pointed his gun deliberately against the man's head. There was a sudden collective intake of breath. 'So you think I'm joking, do you?'

'No sir,' said the young man hastily. The girl started crying and hiccupping, evidently drunk.

'Silence!' barked the policeman again. 'Now, out into the hall.'

He pointed at the door with his gun, and they all trooped out silently, lining up against the stair wall, none of them daring to say a word. Cécilia just then remembered the fake passports they had brought with them, which were in the pocket of her violin case as usual. She felt a sudden chill of fear and glanced at Emil, who returned her look impassively, and with an almost imperceptible shrug. There was nothing they could do now.

They waited with bated breath while the police tramped through the house, pulling rooms apart in their search for anything that might constitute illicit activity. Then came the sound of animated voices from a room upstairs, and the captain of police shortly afterwards appeared, holding something in his hand.

'We have found this gun,' he announced. 'To whom does it belong?'

Marion looked in surprise at the pistol he held in his hand.

'Why, it's mine!' she said. 'Is there a problem?'

'It is against the law to have a weapon of this kind.'

'But it's a rusty old thing I've had for years, and I don't even think it's loaded. I'd almost forgotten about it, in fact. You're not going to be difficult about such a little thing, are you?'

He didn't answer, but motioned to his men to search the living room, which was the only room they had not yet been into. Cécilia felt herself go cold. It was all over now, surely. They listened to the sounds of creaking and scraping, as the men pulled open drawers and moved furniture in their search. Then there was the sound of voices muttering, and one of the policemen came out holding Cécilia's open violin case in one hand and her violin in the other.

'In the inside pocket,' he said to his superior with a nod.

Cécilia ought to have felt fear, but her first instinct was to cry out and tell them to be careful with the instrument. Before she could say a word, Emil got in first.

'Be careful with my violin!' he said in a commanding voice. 'It's very valuable.'

The captain of police glanced up quickly, then back down again. He reached into the case and brought out the little package, which he examined carefully. Then he looked up again and examined Emil closely.

'This is your violin?' he asked.

Emil clamped his mouth shut. Cécilia wanted to speak, but before she could open her mouth he fumbled for her hand and gave it a warning squeeze.

'Where did you get these passports?' said the captain.

Emil shrugged his shoulders, the very image of a guilty and uncooperative suspect.

The captain nodded to one of his subordinates, who moved over to Emil and gestured with his gun for him to leave the line.

'You,' said the captain. 'You are under arrest. The rest of you too. You will come with us.'

Several voices were raised in loud protest, but Marion and her guests were herded unceremoniously out of the house, towards two waiting police vans: one for the men and one for the women.

'I see you came prepared,' said Marion dryly. 'Anyone would think that you had been expecting to arrest a lot of people this evening.'

'Be quiet!' said the captain.

Cécilia looked around frantically for Emil, who was being dragged roughly along by two policemen, his wrists in handcuffs. When he caught sight of her he lifted his hands to his mouth and blew her a kiss, irrepressible to the last. Then one of the policemen shoved him into the back of the van and he was gone. Cécilia drew a deep breath and fought down her tears. This was no time to start crying. She and Marion, along with a few of the other women, were bundled into one of the waiting vans.

'What shall we do?' she whispered to Marion in English as the van bumped and swerved its way down the steep roads into the city. The motion was making her feel sick, but she tried to ignore it.

'Don't worry – if they don't let us go right away I'll make a huge fuss,' replied Marion. 'In the meantime, you just be sure and not say anything.'

'But they think—'

'Shh!' said Marion warningly. 'Do you want his efforts to go to waste?'

It was three o'clock and still pitch black when Cécilia found herself being shoved into a bare cell with Marion and three other female guests. The cell was already occupied by several young women who looked like prostitutes, as well as one old woman who was sitting on the floor in the corner, rocking backwards and forwards, muttering to herself.

'Well!' exclaimed Marion. 'Very rude of them, to break up my party like that.'

Cécilia wrapped her arms around herself to ward against the cold, and tried not to shiver. She was sick with fear for Emil, but also for herself. She'd never been in a situation like this before – thrown into jail and kept there by faceless, nameless guards with weapons. Up until now her life had been so sheltered that she felt completely at a loss. What were they going to do to her? How long would they keep her here?

'Where have they taken the men?' she asked.

'Who knows, dear? But don't you worry, we're going to get out of here as soon as possible – I hope by breakfast-time.'

But they weren't out by breakfast-time. The sun rose and rose, and the day passed, and by sunset Marion was losing her patience. The cell was chilly, cramped and uncomfortable. Several women prisoners had arrived and left, but still the people from the Villa Rocquefort remained under lock and key. Marion was pacing up and down impatiently. She had several times demanded to speak to someone in authority, up to and including the prefect himself, but without success.

'Why are they taking so long?' she asked crossly. 'This is getting ridiculous.'

Cécilia said nothing. She was cold and tired, and felt that she was coming down with something, because the nausea of the journey in the prison van had not yet worn off, and now she felt dizzy in the head. She had refused the meagre rations of food which had been brought to them, and was huddled against a wall, concentrating on keeping very still so as not to worsen the feeling of sickness.

They passed another night in their cold cell. Cécilia longed to sleep, but she couldn't. Her mind was in turmoil. The initial feeling of terror on her own behalf had receded a little, but she was tormented by fears for Emil. Since she'd woken up to the realities of war she'd heard horrific stories of torture and suffering, and she was in agony at the thought of what they might be doing to him. She wanted to confess, say that the violin was hers, but Marion wouldn't let her.

'Don't be silly,' she said. 'It's nothing to do with you – all you did was carry the things. Emil asked you to get them, and he knew perfectly well what he was doing and what might happen. Even if you did tell them the truth they wouldn't let him go, so why make things worse and give them two victims instead of one?'

She was right, of course, but Cécilia couldn't help feeling guilty all the same. She remembered the feeling of Emil's hand as it squeezed hers, warning her to keep quiet. That was the last time he had touched her. What if she never saw him again? She was in an agony of remorse and fear, but she knew that what Marion had said was true, and that a confession from her wouldn't make any difference to Emil's fate. She shivered, huddling deeper into her coat.

The second night passed. Marion continued to pace and assure her friends that they would be out soon, but eventually even she decided to curl up on one of the hard beds and try and get some sleep. Cécilia passed an uncomfortable night. She had been quiet and withdrawn since they arrived; she felt too ill to talk much, and wanted to conserve her energy, as she hadn't eaten anything all day. Marion had looked at her in concern, and tried to press food upon her, but Cécilia waved it away, saying she wasn't hungry. The next morning, at Marion's urging, she managed to eat half a slice of the stale bread that had been brought to them. Almost immediately, however, she realised she had made a mistake.

'Oh!' she said suddenly, clapping a hand to her mouth.

'What is it?' asked Marion. 'Oh goodness, you look dreadfully pale! Are you all right?'

Cécilia shook her head.

'She's going to be sick,' said one of the other women.

There was a filthy toilet in the corner, and Cécilia made it there just in time. At that moment one of the prison warders arrived to take away the breakfast things. Marion, glancing from Cécilia to the new arrival, drew herself up and let loose a torrent of heavily accented French. Cécilia was too ill to hear much of what she said, but she gathered it included dire threats of terrible repercussions if they were not released immediately. Did they not realise that

Marion was an American citizen, and that they were holding her illegally? And this poor, sick child here – did they know who she was? None other than the daughter of one of the most important musicians in France. If her family chose to kick up a fuss then who was to say what kind of trouble they might bring down on the heads of the prison authorities?

Cécilia bent over the toilet again, oblivious to the rest, but whatever Marion had said must have done some good, because after an hour or so they received a visit from a man who clearly had a much higher rank than anyone they had seen up to now. He spoke to Marion, apologising for the inconvenience they had gone through. The orders had come from much higher up, Mme Zimmerman must understand. Here he held up his hands expressively, as though to say: what could he do about it? It was not his fault if his superiors took it into their heads to arrest respectable citizens. At any rate, he went on, they would no doubt be glad to know that the order had been given for their release and they might go as soon as the formalities were completed. At that Marion clapped her hands together, quite restored to her usual self, then began to cluck over Cécilia, who was feeling slightly better, sitting against the wall again, getting her breath back.

Soon afterwards they were free at last, and emerged into the cold air of Nice. Marion had somehow arranged for them to get an official escort home, and she insisted that Cécilia come and stay with her.

'You're not well enough to study today, so there's no point in going home to that little apartment of yours,' she said. 'I can look after you here. Besides, I'm going to make some inquiries to find out what's happened to Emil, and I'm sure you'd rather be on the spot when I get news.'

Cécilia didn't have the strength to argue – and in truth, she was glad to spend a little time in Marion's well-appointed house, with all its modern conveniences and its home comforts, especially while she was feeling so ill. She was sick and frustrated, desperate to have Emil back, living in terror that she might never see him again, but unable to do anything about it. Again and again she begged Marion to do what she could to find him and secure his release. Cécilia had no friends, no connections, but Marion certainly did. If anyone could find out what had happened to him and obtain his release, Marion could.

Seeing what a pitiful state Cécilia had been reduced to, Marion promised she'd do her utmost to get him back. It took a few days, and many visits to the prefecture, but at last her efforts bore fruit. Most of her male guests had been released by now, but three of them, including Emil, had been sent to Le Vernet.

'It's a camp near Toulouse,' she said. 'I'm going to speak to everyone I can, and get him out.'

But after ten days Cécilia was beginning to lose hope that Marion would be able to do anything. She'd been reading in the newspapers about further mass roundups of Jews all over France, and the news made her heart sink. Emil was a Jew, and a foreign one at that, and he'd been caught red-handed with forged documents. The authorities were bound to try and deport him to Germany as soon as possible. She wanted to do something – anything – to help obtain his release. Her father had known important people; perhaps one of them could be prevailed upon to help. But they were all in Paris, and she was stuck here in Nice, far away and sick. She could have wept from fear and frustration, but she steeled herself against it. She wanted to be strong, and crying would do nothing to help Emil. But if she didn't hear news of him soon she'd scream.

'I wish there were something I could do,' she burst out at last to Marion, 'but I feel so ill all the time. What's wrong with me?'

'Don't you know?' asked Marion.

Something in her voice made Cécilia look up. There was a mixture of amusement and pity in Marion's face.

'What do you mean?'

'I should have thought it was perfectly obvious.' Then, as Cécilia continued to look blank, she went on, 'You're going to have a baby, my dear.'

Cécilia caught her breath as the truth rushed in on her all at once.

'No,' she said feebly. 'It's just flu or something, that's all, I'm sure.'

But it was obvious now. How stupid of her not to have realised – and how mortifying that Marion had known it before she had. She stared at her friend.

'What am I to do?' she asked. All at once she looked very young and lost.

'It's Emil's, I take it?'

Cécilia nodded. 'Who else's could it be?'

'I didn't really think it could be anyone else's, but you never know.'

'Well I know,' said Cécilia.

She felt as though she had been plunged into a pool of icy water, or received a sudden slap to the cheek. For nearly three months she had been wandering about in a dream, blind to reality and the possibility of what might happen. It was ridiculous; she had somehow convinced herself that since her entanglement with Emil was not quite real, then there could be no consequences. How could she have been so stupid? She wanted to believe that Marion had got it wrong, but she knew that the symptoms she had been feeling could have no other cause. She looked up and saw that Marion was regarding her with sympathy. The older woman sat down by her and put an arm around her shoulder.

'It looks like it's come as a shock to you,' she said gently. 'Now, I know there's a lot to think about, so don't say anything just yet, but if you need me to, I can find you someone to take care of things.'

Cécilia started a little. In the normal way of things she wouldn't have understood what Marion was saying, but there had been a girl, a maid, at their house in Paris a few years ago, who had found herself in the same difficulty. Rose had helped her, paying to send her away for a 'cure', as she called it. The maid had been ill for several weeks, but had come back eventually and resumed her duties. Cécilia would have known nothing of all this had Maggie not whispered into her ear what was really going on.

She shook her head.

'No!' she said sharply. 'No, thank you, really. I couldn't do that.'

'As you like, my dear,' replied Marion. 'Well, you're braver than I would be. I'll help you in any way I can, of course, and when Emil gets out, perhaps he'll have a new little family to come home to.'

'Is he likely to be away that long?' asked Cécilia in alarm.

'I hope not,' said Marion soberly. 'But from what I hear the authorities are starting to take a harder line with our sort of activities. Don't worry, I have people working on his release – his and everyone else's. As long as I'm here you can trust me to do my best.'

'As long as you're here? Are you going away?'

'I think I'll have to. I'm Jewish too, you know,' said Marion simply.

'Oh. I didn't know.'

'You've probably noticed we're not exactly welcome around here lately. I'm an American citizen, so they shouldn't be able to touch me – at least they *couldn't* have touched me until a couple of months ago, but now the United States has joined the war I guess I'm not as safe as I was. I'll stay as long as I can, but I expect I'll have to return to the States soon – at least until the war is over. God knows, I don't want to go, but I don't know how much longer I'll be safe here.'

As it turned out, Marion remained in Nice only another month, and in that time she was unable to secure Emil's release from Le Vernet. Seeing the way the wind was blowing she departed France at last, in mid-April, and until the last minute was urging Cécilia to leave with her. But Cécilia would not. She couldn't possibly until she had found out what had happened to Emil. She'd sent him letter after letter, but had no idea if they'd been delivered – he certainly hadn't replied, at any rate. But how could she live with not knowing his fate? Besides, France was her home, and she was in no danger here – not now, at least, when the Rescue Committee had broken up and there was no Emil to send her to Bernard for his packages of forged documents.

So Cécilia found herself alone again in Nice, as she had been before it all started, but now she harboured a secret that couldn't remain a secret for long. Alone in her apartment, she had nothing to do in between bouts of sickness but tremble for Emil and wring her hands fruitlessly over his safety and over her studies, which were going badly again. There was no light, no colour, no inspiration any more. How could she compose when the spark that ignited her talent had gone, perhaps forever? How could she play, when his guitar was standing there, against the wall in her apartment, untuned and unused?

All that was good had gone, and now all that was left was this secret burden growing inside her, and the knowledge of how terribly hurt Maggie would be when she found out what her sister had done. She couldn't keep it hidden for much longer – the sickness had mostly passed now, but her pregnancy was becoming more obvious as the spring days lengthened and her belly swelled. She tried to conceal it as best she could, but she knew her fellow students had begun to whisper about her, and her professors were starting to give her looks. A feeling of shame began to wash over her. This was not the sort of thing a girl from a good family was supposed to do. What if they threw her out of the Académie?

A wave of loneliness swept over Cécilia, and she suddenly longed for her family. She dreaded confessing to her mother what had happened, but she knew she'd have to face Maggie sooner or later and beg her forgiveness. She couldn't bear the thought of being cut off from her sister, her dear beloved sister, forever. She would throw herself upon Maggie's mercy, and she prayed that Maggie would be kind and say that she hadn't cared all that much for Emil anyway, and since she could see how much Cécilia loved him it was only right that she step aside and wish them joy. It was a vain wish, Cécilia knew it, but still she had the strongest urge to go home, at least for a while. Perhaps they would be happy for her in her new-found love. They wouldn't be too pleased about the baby, of course, but once Emil got out – *if* Emil got out, the little voice reminded her – then they would be married, the baby would have a father, and the joy would return to her life.

And so, at the end of June, she packed her things and returned to Paris.

Chapter Fourteen

Hertfordshire, 1950

Dinner with Alec had to be postponed in the end. Harriet came down with a severe cold, and by the time she'd fully recovered it was coming up to Christmas and Mrs Brouillard couldn't spare her, as there were parties and dinners and theatre tickets to organise. Not long after that, Alec was called back to Scotland to see his grandmother, who was sick, and didn't return until the new year. Harriet pictured him sitting by the old woman's bedside, tucking her blankets more warmly about her, and telling her about the flying school and his new dog. Would he mention Harriet? What would he say? Silly question; of course he wouldn't mention her – why, they hardly knew each other. And in any case, why should she care what he said about her? Harriet shook her head at her own nonsense and returned to her work.

The weather stayed mild over Christmas – unusually mild – and Mrs Brouillard said Harriet might take a few days off if she liked, but Harriet had nowhere to go and nobody to visit, so she declined politely. The atmosphere in the Brouillard house didn't exactly improve over the festive season; Harriet soon saw that no effort would be made to make the time a special treat for Rex, and in the end she went into Royston and bought him a few playthings, for which Mrs Brouillard thanked her distantly and Cécilia said nothing at all.

Harriet was almost certain he would have received no presents from his mother had it not been for her intervention, and the thought distressed her, since she'd begun to feel Cécilia's neglect of her son more and more. She wanted to do something about it – she didn't know what, exactly, but she thought she might be able to talk to Cécilia and make her see how unhappy the boy was. His mother couldn't be accused of cruelty as such, but it was obvious that she was so wrapped up in her own world of misery that she couldn't find it in her to spare a thought for him. Harriet was waiting for a suitable opportunity to speak to her about it. It would be tricky to find the right moment, but there was some hope in the fact that since Cécilia's suicide attempt a sort of rapprochement had formed between the two young women. It didn't go as far as friendship, but Cécilia, despite her withdrawal from the world in general, seemed to recognise and acknowledge Harriet's kind treatment of her in that period. Her manner warmed just slightly, and occasionally she would even address a remark or a question voluntarily to Harriet. Harriet hoped she might be able to take advantage of this tiny chink in Cécilia's armour to try and bring about a closer relationship between mother and son.

Telling herself she was doing good from a purely altruistic point of view, Harriet did her best to squash all the thoughts that darted into her head and said she was compensating for her own tragedies. She and Jim had often talked about the children they would have, since Jim had had lots of brothers and sisters and was keen to have a numerous family just like his own. Harriet, an only child, hadn't been so sure, but she knew she'd have gone along with whatever Jim wanted in the end – she always did. His enthusiasm had always been enough to carry her along, even when she had doubts. All that had gone out of the window with his death, of course, and who knew whether she'd ever have a child at all? The idea of a future stretching ahead without Jim, perhaps never having a baby of her own to care for, gave her an ache in the pit of her stomach. But in the meantime here was Rex, who was a good boy, and he deserved a mother who loved him.

One day Cécilia herself gave her an opening. Christmas was over and done with, the first days of January had set in, and Cécilia had at length been persuaded to leave the house. At first, Harriet didn't take her any further than the garden. Cécilia sat in her wheelchair, well wrapped up, and looked about her vaguely. Harriet thought it would do her good to get outside more, so she chatted brightly, drawing attention to some of the more attractive plants in the garden, and describing the beauty of the scenery around Royston. Then she mentioned something Rex had said that had made her laugh that morning.

'You don't seem to mind about Rex,' said Cécilia suddenly.

Harriet glanced at her in surprise.

'Mind? Why should I mind about him? He's a nice boy.'

'But he hasn't got a father,' replied Cécilia. 'Some people don't like that. There was one woman who came, a few months before you. She was quite old, and very proper. As soon as she found out Rex was... that I'd never been married... she said she couldn't stay any more.'

'Did she?' said Harriet with a laugh. 'A delicate constitution, is that it? No, of course I don't mind. It's not his fault where he came from.'

'No, I suppose not.'

It was too good an opportunity to miss. Harriet pressed on a little.

'You don't talk about his father at all,' she said.

Cécilia shrank into herself a little, but after a moment's hesitation replied:

'It's all in the past now. He's not here any more. He was Jewish. A lot of Jews died in the war.'

'I'm sorry. Was he sent to one of the camps?'

'No. He died in France, fighting with the Resistance.'

'Then at least you can remember him with pride.'

Cécilia looked a little surprised, as if this was a new idea to her.

'Yes, I suppose I can,' she said at last.

'Does Rex know much about him?'

'No. Maman said better not to say anything, given that his father and I weren't married, and in any case it's not something I like to talk about.'

She spoke with finality, and Harriet didn't pursue the subject. Who was she to pry? But at least Cécilia had shown awareness of having a son, which Harriet had half-doubted on occasion. Perhaps she could be encouraged to talk about him more as time went on.

The weather was fine, and it would have been pleasant to take a walk to the bottom of the garden, but the grass was too soft for a wheelchair. Harriet mentioned this, then asked:

'I don't suppose you'd like to try? Can you walk at all?'

'A little. Not much, and not without crutches.'

'But you have some feeling in your legs?'

'Sometimes. A tingling, and sometimes pain.'

'Can anything more be done?'

'There were doctors and specialists at first,' said Cécilia, staring towards the trees at the bottom of the garden. 'They gave me exercises, and told me to do them every day. But I stopped eventually. Maman tells me off for it.'

'I'm not surprised. You ought to keep up with them, you know, if you want to improve.'

'What's the use? I'll never be fully mobile again and it's easier to sit.' The apathy was almost palpable. 'I wouldn't even have the movement I have if it weren't for my father's money. That's what paid for the treatment, and the nurses, and the new wing on the house. I'm lucky, really. Most people wouldn't even have had that.'

'I suppose your father's work still brings in royalties?' said Harriet.

'Yes.'

'They were playing one of his pieces on the Third Programme the other evening,' said Harriet. 'One of his early ones. Your mother was pleased.'

'Yes, the BBC are very good that way. *Les Orchidées* brings in most of the money, of course – by far.'

'Yes, I imagine it does.' Harriet glanced back at the house and saw Sébastien watching them through the window, eyes narrowed. He saw her looking, and gave that slow, sly smile of his, then raised his hand ironically and turned away. 'Does the money pay for Sébastien's tuition, too?'

She wanted to add: and his treatment in mental institutions.

'I suppose so,' said Cécilia. Her interest in the conversation was starting to wane.

'Do you think he'll be a success?' Harriet was determined to keep Cécilia talking one way or another.

'I don't know. Perhaps he will – he has the talent. I had a talent too, once.'

'He doesn't compose, though? You were a composer, I believe?'

'I was. Not now.'

'But why? You can still write music, surely? You don't need your legs for that.'

'I lost it,' replied Cécilia flatly. 'There was no colour any more.' Her voice was as colourless as her words.

'You mean you lost your inspiration?'

'In a way.' She grasped the wheels of her chair and turned it. 'I'm getting cold. I'd like to go back in now.'

She'd obviously had enough for today, but that was understandable, since she wasn't used to either going outside or talking much these days. Still, Harriet felt encouraged, as she'd got more out of Cécilia than she'd ever expected. She couldn't always have been this way. There must have been a time, before she lost the use of her legs, when she'd lived something close to a normal life – or as normal a life as a gifted musician could live. Harriet wondered what she'd been like before her accident. Had she been happy and outgoing? It was hard to imagine. Even at her most animated, there was still a self-contained quality about her that spoke of lifelong introspection. She'd obviously been pretty once – even now she was still very striking. What she needed was a friend – or was it Harriet herself who needed a friend? She didn't like to admit it, but the thought of having another woman to talk to was appealing. They'd both suffered loss, and perhaps their shared experience gave them something in common; if so, she didn't admit it to herself consciously, but still, she felt herself drawn towards Cécilia. She was so young; too young to want to die when she had a son to live for.

Ten days later Harriet had an afternoon off, and had arranged to spend it with Rex and Alec. It wasn't the sunniest of days, but an insipid mid-January glow was filtering through the clouds, and there didn't look to be any danger of rain. Cécilia was sitting on her sofa, just falling into a gentle doze, when Harriet came in.

'I'm going to take you out,' she announced.

Cécilia turned her eyes towards her.

'I don't want to go out.'

'No arguments. You spend too much time stuck in this house. You need some fresh air.' She went into Cécilia's bedroom and brought out a coat, hat and muffler. 'We'll take a blanket and put it around your legs. And I'm going to bring your crutches too.'

'What?' said Cécilia in alarm. 'No, I can't—'

'Just in case,' replied Harriet persuasively. 'If you don't feel up to it then we won't, but we might as well take them in case you feel like trying.'

'I don't know why you're bothering. I won't.' But she let Harriet fuss around her, helping her on with her coat and hat and wheeling her out through the door into the hall. There Rex was waiting.

'Ready?' asked Harriet.

His eyes widened when he saw who she had brought.

'Are *you* coming, Maman?'

'So it appears,' said Cécilia dryly. 'Although I don't know where we're going.'

Rex beckoned to Harriet to bend down, and whispered in her ear, audibly enough for Cécilia to hear:

'Is she allowed to know the secret?'

'I think she'll have to.'

'Oh!' He gazed at his mother with an air of suppressed mischief, and Cécilia drew in her breath sharply.

'What is it?' Harriet asked, noticing it.

'I was just reminded of…' She paused, shaking her head, and murmured, almost to herself, 'Just a passing resemblance. It was nothing.'

Her brows knitted together in a frown and Harriet saw her glance several times at Rex. Just then came the sound of a car horn.

'There he is!' exclaimed Rex. He threw open the front door and raced out, leaving Harriet and Cécilia to follow. Outside, Alec McLeod was leaning against the side of a battered old Morris Twelve. He stood up and came towards them as they emerged from the house.

'Alec McLeod, this is Cécilia Brouillard,' said Harriet. 'She's Rex's mother.'

'Pleased to meet you,' replied Alec. He looked doubtfully at the wheelchair. 'We've plenty of room for passengers, but does that contraption fold? I'm not sure it'll fit in the car otherwise.'

'This one doesn't, but I have one that does,' Cécilia said. 'Harriet, would you fetch it?'

'I'll get it!' said Rex, running off. He returned a moment later struggling behind a wheelchair that was better designed for travel than the one Cécilia spent most of her days in.

Alec glanced at the three of them in turn.

'Miss Brouillard, you can go in the front. You two, I'm afraid you'll have to squash up in the back with this thing.'

Somehow Rex and Harriet were stowed uncomfortably in the back with the wheelchair and the crutches.

'You don't mind sharing the front seat, do you, Miss Brouillard?' He opened the front passenger door and Cécilia let out an exclamation as something bounded out and leapt up onto her lap.

'Come here, you.' Alec scooped up the puppy. 'I'm sorry, he's a bit boisterous.'

Cécilia was helped gently into the car and given custody of the excited dog.

'His name's Patch,' said Rex from the back seat. 'Mr McLeod let me name him.'

'Where are we going?' said Cécilia. She looked a little taken aback, but had not so far protested.

'You'll see,' said Alec. 'You don't mind a bit of bumping, do you?'

'I don't think so.'

'Just remember Rex and I have a hundredweight of ironmongery on top of us,' said Harriet. 'Don't bump too hard or you'll hurt somebody.'

'Don't worry,' replied McLeod cheerfully, throwing the car into gear and pulling away.

Cécilia was occupied with trying to stop Patch from jumping up on her lap and licking her face enthusiastically.

'Isn't he splendid?' said Rex. 'This is the secret. I'm sharing him with Mr McLeod. I can take him for walks whenever I like.'

'Wouldn't you rather have a dog of your own?' said Cécilia. 'I'm sure Mr McLeod doesn't want you bothering him.'

'I don't mind,' replied Alec, at the same time as Rex said sadly, 'Grand-mère said no.'

Cécilia glanced back.

'She said no? Well,' she went on after a pause, 'it's her house so we have to follow her rules.'

Patch had wormed his way up onto her shoulder and she was trying vainly to pull him off. Rex leaned forward and took him.

'You mustn't crawl over Maman like that, she's delicate,' he said.

'I'm not that delicate.' Cécilia laughed. 'I think I can manage a puppy.'

'Not this one,' said Alec. 'Nobody can manage this one. He's a little terror.'

'We're going to train him,' replied Rex. 'That's where Mr McLeod is taking us now.'

The Morris had turned off the main road, bumping down a lane which was deeply rutted.

'Here we are,' announced Alec as they passed through a gate. They were in a large open field of tufted grass, in the middle of which was a strip of tarmac several hundred yards long. At the edge of the field was a big, brown-painted barn and a dilapidated white building with a flat roof. In the distance something orange at the end of a tall pole flapped half-heartedly in the gentle breeze.

'It's an airfield!' said Cécilia.

'It's a flying school,' corrected Harriet.

'Not quite yet, but it will be,' said Alec. He pulled the car up next to the white building. 'Better get you two out before that thing squashes you completely.'

The folding wheelchair was, with some difficulty, extricated from the car, and Rex and Harriet emerged. Patch immediately jumped out of Rex's arms, running to sniff at the walls of the building. Rex followed him, while Harriet and Alec helped Cécilia out of the car and installed her safely in the wheelchair.

'Shall I get the crutches out?' said Harriet.

Cécilia opened her eyes wide, looking almost fearful, and shook her head quickly.

'Where are the planes?' asked Rex.

'There's only one plane, and it's in that hangar over there,' said Alec, nodding to the big barn.

'May I see it?'

'If you like.'

The hangar was secured with a large padlock which Alec unlocked, throwing open the doors. Inside was a small biplane, red and, from the smell, freshly painted.

'I say,' said Rex, impressed. 'It's very big.'

'Not big for a plane, but she'll do. This is a Tiger Moth. They used it in the war, but it's been decommissioned now. It came with the business,' he explained. 'I've also inherited an old fellow who keeps the place from falling to bits, and he knows of another fellow who might be able to put me on to another of these cheap.'

'I didn't know there was a flying school round here,' said Cécilia.

'It lost a lot of business after the war and the former owner let it slide, but I think it could be a success if it was only run properly.'

Rex was still gazing at the Tiger Moth.

'Is it a fighter plane?' he asked breathlessly.

Alec laughed.

'No, this one was used to train pilots. It's quite an old model as you can see, but it's still in pretty good working order.'

'May we go up in it?'

'I don't think...' Alec glanced at Cécilia, then decided upon the safest course. 'Easily distracted, aren't you? Weren't we supposed to be training Patch?'

'Oh, yes, Patch! Where is he?' exclaimed Rex, looking about him.

The puppy was eventually located halfway across the field, doing his best to chase a flock of crows that were bigger than he was. He was having far too much fun to bother with the humans, and at first darted away from Alec's grasp, but after a short chase he was eventually caught.

'Let's get that collar on you,' said Alec. Patch protested at the indignity, and spent several minutes trying to get it off, but Rex managed to distract him with a ball, upon which he pounced with glee, allowing Alec to attach a lead.

'Right then, young fellow,' he said to the protesting puppy. 'You are going to have a lesson in behaving yourself.'

'I'll just watch, if you don't mind,' said Harriet. She had joined in the chase after Patch, but Cécilia was still sitting in her wheelchair by the office building, so she went across to keep her company. Cécilia's cheeks had taken on a touch of colour in the brisk air, and she was looking less lethargic than usual.

'You need to get out more,' said Harriet, giving her a searching look.

'Perhaps. It's difficult, though. Maman hasn't got the patience to push me about, Sébastien is away all the time, and Léonie does nothing but talk about herself until I want to scream, so most of the time it's easier to stay indoors.'

'There's Rex.'

'He's too small. I need someone who is strong enough to push me or help me up and down.'

'He is strong. He fetched that heavy chair for you, and I can't believe it would be much heavier with you in it. You must be as light as a feather. He'd be awfully happy to spend more time with you, you know.'

'What does he need me for? I'm useless. I can't play with him, or go for walks with him. I can't teach him maths or Latin or geography. I can't look after him if he's ill.'

'You don't have to teach him maths or geography – he has a tutor for all that. But you could help him with his French if you liked. And you could talk to him, or even just listen when he talks to you. He's very lonely, you know. He needs someone to love him.'

'I don't know if I *can* love him,' said Cécilia dully. 'I don't know if I can love anyone any more.' She made a sudden movement, half frustration, half resignation. 'I don't suppose you can understand that.'

'I do understand, believe me, I do. Love brings misery, so you decide in the end that it's best not to love at all. That way you can't be miserable.'

'Yes, that's it,' said Cécilia. 'That's it exactly.'

'But are you any happier for not loving?'

A fine question, coming from her, Harriet thought ironically. Here she was, lecturing someone else about happiness when she wasn't exactly the best model for it herself.

'I suppose not,' said Cécilia.

'I wish there were something I could do to help you,' said Harriet impulsively.

Cécilia looked surprised.

'Help me? Why do you think I need help?'

'Because you're wasting away from unhappiness all alone in that room of yours, and I can't bear to see it.'

'I'm perfectly all right,' said Cécilia, turning her eyes away uncomfortably. 'I'm no unhappier than anyone else.'

'But you took all those pills, and the doctor said it wasn't the first time.'

Cécilia was silent.

'Why did you do it if you weren't unhappy?' asked Harriet.

'I don't know. Perhaps I thought everyone would be better off without me.'

'Rex wouldn't be better off without you. And I wouldn't either. I'd have been dreadfully upset if you'd died that night. You gave me a terrible fright, you know.'

'Oh.' This seemed to be a new idea to Cécilia. She plucked at the blanket that lay on her lap, turning the matter over in her head.

'So I'd rather like to be sure you're not going to try that sort of thing again – for my sake as well as yours,' Harriet went on. 'I'm sorry if you think this is an awful cheek, but I had to say it. You won't do it again, will you? It would be such a waste.'

'I didn't plan it,' said Cécilia. 'Most of the time I go along without thinking very much about anything, but once in a while it all gets too much and then I can't help myself. I can't explain it, but sometimes it just seems as though the world would turn much more smoothly if I wasn't in it.'

'That's nonsense.'

Cécilia looked at her thoughtfully. 'You're very blunt.'

She said it without rancour. Harriet laughed.

'I'm not usually this blunt. But I wanted to let you know it didn't pass unnoticed, in case you thought nobody cared.'

'I take it Maman hasn't said anything about it? No, that's like her, to pretend it never happened.'

You'd have done the same if I hadn't brought the subject up, thought Harriet. It struck her that Cécilia was more like her mother than she realised.

They were silent for a while, watching Alec and Rex and the dog. The first lesson didn't seem to be going well, and the sound of Rex's laughter drifted over to them as he set off once more after Patch, who had decided he would much rather run around than learn how to walk to heel. Alec looked over at the two women with a rueful shrug and a smile. His gaze lingered a moment on Harriet.

'He likes you,' said Cécilia.

It wasn't like Cécilia to notice anything outside herself. Harriet credited the fresh air.

'Does he?' she replied.

'I should say so. Where did you meet him?'

Harriet glanced at her before answering. Cécilia had already opened up to her slightly that day, so she decided to push a little further.

'He came to the house a few weeks ago, looking for Maggie,' she said deliberately. 'He knew her in France during the war.'

She watched to see Cécilia's reaction. Cécilia said nothing.

'Your mother sent him away, saying there was no such person and that he'd got the wrong house. But that wasn't true, was it? Maggie does exist – or she did.'

Harriet held her breath, hoping Cécilia wouldn't realise that she must have read the letter.

There was a long pause, then Cécilia said, 'She was my sister.'

'Was?'

'Yes. She died in the war.'

'I'm sorry. What happened?'

A shrug. 'She was in the Resistance.'

'Like Rex's father?'

'Yes. Like me, too.'

'You?' Harriet looked at Cécilia in surprise. 'I hadn't realised you were in the Resistance.'

'Of course I was. How else do you think this happened?' She indicated herself and the wheelchair.

'I thought perhaps a bomb, or a car accident.'

'No. It was a bullet.'

'Good heavens! I'm awfully sorry. I never knew.'

'I was one of the lucky ones, they told me,' said Cécilia bitterly. 'Although I can't say it feels like it.'

Harriet remembered again what she had overheard Sébastien saying, about how Cécilia had Maggie's blood on her hands. She longed to know what it meant. Did it have anything to do with Zazou? Had the incident that had put Cécilia in a wheelchair been the same as the one that killed Maggie? She didn't know how to ask without sounding impertinently curious, so instead she said:

'You must all have been very brave.'

'Perhaps.'

Harriet was about to press further, but Cécilia went on:

'If it's all the same to you I'd prefer not to talk about it. It was a long time ago and there's no use in dwelling on it.'

'But—' began Harriet.

'Don't you remember what you just said, about love bringing only misery? Well, it's just as true with family as it is with… anyone else. And if you knew the whole story you'd understand why sometimes a little bottle of pills looks like the easy way out.'

She wouldn't say any more after that, but retreated back into herself, leaving Harriet to watch the antics of Patch and Rex in silence, her mind working busily.

'That's enough for today, I think,' said Alec, as he came across to the two women.

'Any luck?' asked Harriet.

'We've made a start. He's a good-natured little thing and I think he'll do very well.'

'Are you talking about Patch or Rex?'

He laughed, a warm sound, and held her gaze with his own, smiling.

'It might suit either of them. What do you think?'

The signals he was giving were strong enough, and Harriet had more than enough experience to know when a man was interested, but she wasn't sure she was ready to respond in that way. She turned her eyes away from his.

'We'd better go,' she said. 'I think Cécilia is getting cold.'

'I'm all right,' replied Cécilia, but she didn't object when the others made a move to return to the car. Rex, Harriet and the wheelchair were safely stowed in the back, and they set off back to Chaffingham, talking and laughing. Only Cécilia remained silent, staring out of the car window, her expression unreadable, as she absently caressed the head of the little dog on her lap.

Chapter Fifteen

Darkness was falling when they returned to Chaffingham. Alec drew the Morris up a little way from the front door, getting out and unloading the wheelchair carefully.

'Who's that?' asked Rex, as he emerged and stretched his legs. Two people were standing at the door, occupied in animated conversation. Mrs Brouillard had evidently had a visitor and was just seeing him out. It seemed she was displeased; even from where Harriet stood ten yards away she could see her employer bristling with anger. The visitor was a tall, stooped man with a domed forehead, the balding top of his skull forming a stark contrast to the wild shock of hair which stood out from the rest of his head. They were speaking rapid French.

'There is nothing more to be said,' came Rose's voice, sharp, biting.

The man began to say something in a low voice, but she wouldn't let him finish.

'I have told you already, you are wasting your time with me. I have no idea where you dreamt up this wild story, but I certainly have no intention of letting you put about such untruths about my husband and sullying his reputation in this way.'

'There's no question of sullying his reputation,' said the man. 'I owe him a great deal, but we had an agreement, and since he is no longer here to keep his promise I am appealing to you, Madame Brouillard—'

'Enough!' said Rose, who had just caught sight of them approaching, Harriet pushing Cécilia in her wheelchair. The man turned and saw them too. He stared at Cécilia.

'Cécilia!' he exclaimed.

She looked up blankly.

'*Oui?*'

'You're Cécilia Brouillard, yes? I don't suppose you remember, but we've met before, at Marion's house. Fernand. Fernand Quinault.'

He was staring at her in surprise. A spark of something like recognition, followed by shock, came into Cécilia's face, and she went pale.

'Yes – yes, of course, I remember.'

'Cécilia! Go in at once!' snapped Rose in English. 'You too, Rex. Miss Conway, where have you been? I was expecting you back half an hour ago.'

Rex ran inside without saying goodbye to Alec, who had wisely got back into the car to try and keep Patch out of sight. Harriet went across to him.

'I'd make yourself scarce if I were you,' she muttered. 'She's on the warpath.'

'Will you be all right?'

'Quite all right. I know how to handle her. Thank you for today.'

'My pleasure. We still haven't been out to dinner, you know.'

'I know.'

'So how can I get you to come out with me? I've been here long enough that I can't use the excuse of being new to the area any more.'

'Was it an excuse?'

'Of course it was.'

'And to think I took pity on you.'

'Pity? You mean to say that's the only reason you said yes?'

She laughed. 'No. Not really.'

'Good – I'd hate to think you saw me as a charity case.' There was that smile again, which transformed his look from melancholy to mischievous. 'Then shall we try again?' He straightened his face and adopted a formal manner. 'Miss Conway, would you like to come out to dinner with me?'

'Yes, Mr McLeod, I'd like that very much.'

'Then shall we say Friday?'

'Yes, that will do very nicely, thank you.'

They both laughed.

'I'll see you on Friday, then,' he said. 'Mind you look after yourself and don't catch another cold.'

'I won't,' she promised.

He started the car and drove off. Harriet watched him go, then crossed to the front door where the three others stood. Cécilia seemed inclined to talk to the visitor, but her mother was scolding her sharply. She ought not to have gone out in the cold like that. What if she caught pneumonia? Hadn't they already spent enough on doctors? She was to go inside at once.

'But—' began Cécilia, glancing at Fernand Quinault.

'Miss Conway, take her inside please, and see that she gets a hot drink immediately. Monsieur Quinault, I have nothing further to say to you. Goodbye.'

In an instant she had chivvied the two women inside and shut the door in the face of her hapless visitor.

'Go and get that hot drink, Cécilia,' she said. 'Then I expect to see you at dinner.'

She stalked off in the direction of the sitting room without a backward glance. Cécilia was still pale, breathing rapidly.

'Are you all right?' asked Harriet in a low voice.

Cécilia nodded.

'I will be. Listen, Harriet, you must go out and find out what he wants. Quickly, before he goes away.'

'But—'

'Go out through the French windows here, so Maman doesn't see you. Tell him I'm sorry I couldn't talk to him. Find out where he's staying. Get an address, a phone number, anything. Quick!'

Astonished at the sudden change in Cécilia's manner, and wondering what it was all about, Harriet did as she was told. She slipped out through the French windows and skirted the edge of the house. Fernand Quinault was nowhere to be seen, but he couldn't have gone far, so she hurried and caught him up just as he was leaving the drive.

'Monsieur Quinault?'

He turned.

'Yes?'

'Cécilia sent me. She's sorry she couldn't speak to you just now, but she'd like to see you. Where are you staying?'

She'd spoken to him automatically in English, just as it occurred to her that perhaps he didn't understand. It seemed he did, as he replied in the same language.

'What happened to her?' he asked. He spoke with a strange accent, half-French, half-American. Now that she came to look at him more closely, she saw that his style of dress altogether suggested that he had spent time in the United States.

'She was shot, although I'm not sure exactly how – she doesn't like to talk about it. They don't like to talk about anything,' she said, with a bitter laugh. 'It happened during the war though.'

'She's paralysed?'

'Not completely, I don't think, but her legs are pretty useless.'

'What sort of advice has she had? Has she seen specialists? There are doctors in the States who can do wonders with this sort of injury these days.'

Harriet shook her head.

'She's seen the best doctors here in England. It's expensive, of course, but I understand the royalties from her father's estate just about cover the costs.'

'Ah!' There was an odd look on his face as he said it.

'Are you a musician? I seem to recognise your name.'

She remembered perfectly well who he was; he was the man whose letter Mrs Brouillard had torn up, but she wanted to know more.

'Yes. I write movie scores,' he replied.

'In Hollywood?'

Surely Hollywood was too exotic for this shabby, shambling man who wore bent spectacles that made his face look slightly lopsided. He nodded.

'Then you've come all the way from America. Shall you be here long? Cécilia said I was to get your address.'

'I'm staying in Cambridge for a few months, but I couldn't ask her to visit me there. She doesn't look well enough. And as you saw, I'm not exactly welcome at the house.' He smiled wryly.

'I'm sorry Mrs Brouillard was rude to you,' said Harriet. 'I don't think she means it – it's just her way.'

She was too polite to ask directly what it was all about, but her voice held a slight question, an invitation to satisfy her curiosity. He didn't take the hint.

'I'm sorry I offended her. It wasn't my intention. But do tell Cécilia I'd like to see her. How can we manage it?'

'Mrs Brouillard goes away quite a lot. You could come when she's not here – I'd make sure of that. I could telephone first. I think it will do Cécilia good to spend some time with an old friend. She needs to get out of herself more.'

'You're a friend of hers?'

'In a manner of speaking. I'm Mrs Brouillard's secretary – I deal with all her business matters.'

'Ah!' he said again. 'All right, I'll give you my phone number. I'm staying with a friend. We're working on a project together.'

'A film score?'

'More in the classical line. That's how I started out before the war.'

He scribbled down a number on an old bus ticket and handed it to her. She glanced at the figures, written in the peculiar, contorted French style, then folded the paper in half.

'I'll call,' she said.

He nodded, then turned and walked away. Harriet watched until he was out of sight, a tall, bent figure, loping away into the distance. How old was he? It was difficult to judge, but Harriet thought he might be in his late thirties or early forties. What had he wanted of Mrs Brouillard? Whatever it was, her employer had taken great offence at it, accusing him of insulting the memory of her husband. But calm and quiet-spoken as he was, Fernand Quinault didn't seem the type to go around causing trouble.

Still puzzling, Harriet went back in through the French windows, but Cécilia wasn't in her rooms. Perhaps Léonie had been slow to answer the bell again, and Cécilia had gone in search of her own hot drink. Harriet was just hanging up her coat and hat in the hall cupboard when she heard a noise, and looked up to see Sébastien coming slowly down the stairs towards her.

'Well well,' he drawled. 'So you've fallen for it too, have you? Just like Rex.'

'What do you mean?'

'Oh, she knows how to do it all right, and she doesn't even have to lift a finger.'

'Who?'

'My feeble-minded sister. She gets people running around, doing her bidding. All she has to do is sit there, looking pale and wan, until everyone feels sorry for her and does exactly what she wants. I saw you chasing down the drive after that shambling idiot. On her behalf, I assume. She never could leave the men alone, although you'd think she'd have given up on all that now given the state of her.'

'He's an old friend of hers.'

He gave a humourless bark of laughter.

'Friend, indeed! Her sort doesn't have friends. She thinks of men only in terms of sex.'

Harriet gazed at him in sudden dislike, and found herself exclaiming hotly:

'I don't know why you're so hard on your own sister, but I think you're awfully unfair. What is it? Jealousy, perhaps? At your age she'd already won the Prix de Rome and was making a name for herself. Is that it? Is that why you can't say anything nice about her? You can't bear the fact that she has more talent than you do?'

She stopped suddenly, knowing she'd gone too far. She hadn't meant to say so much, but he was so provoking she'd allowed herself to be needled into it.

He flushed angrily and took a step towards her, his fists clenching, but Harriet stood her ground. There was no going back now. She was sick of Sébastien, his insinuations and his casually cruel remarks which seemed to amuse him so much. Her words had hit home, she was pleased to see.

'Let her alone, won't you?' she said. 'She's had enough unhappiness without you making things worse.'

'Oh, I make things worse, do I?'

'Yes, you do,' said Harriet, then before she could stop herself, went on significantly: 'Don't think I don't know where she got those pills. I overheard you offering them to her. I thought at first you were trying to be kind in a queer sort of way, but now I don't think you were being kind at all. I think you were trying to take advantage and goad her on just for the fun of it.'

He looked surprised, then all at once enlightened.

'Oh,' he said with interest. His tone was sly again. 'So you're one of those who listens at doors, are you? We'll have to keep an eye on you. What else did you hear?' He took another step forward, and she was suddenly conscious of the fact that he was much larger than her. Still, she wasn't scared, merely defiant.

'I didn't hear much, just something about Maggie. I don't know what it all meant, or why nobody talks about her. Or why your mother says she doesn't exist.'

He snorted.

'Of course she existed. Brave, wonderful Maggie, the girl everyone was so proud of for her Resistance work. Do you really want to know why Maman never mentions her? She's ashamed, that's why! Ashamed of her own daughter.'

'But why?'

He was very close to her now. Harriet backed away gradually, feeling the panelling of the wall at her back.

'I'll tell you, if you really must know. Or you could ask Cécilia.'

'What do you mean?'

He smirked.

'Why, Maggie was the one who was responsible for putting her in that wheelchair. Do you wonder that we'd all rather forget about it?'

Harriet drew in her breath. A thousand questions rushed in on her all at once, but she was unable to give voice to any of them because Sébastien had suddenly taken hold of her upper arms, pushing her against the wall. The ridged panelling dug painfully into her shoulder blades.

'Now listen,' he hissed. 'Just you keep your mouth shut, you little bitch. You'd better not say a word about those pills to Maman. I suppose you need this job? If so, you'd better keep quiet, because I could have you thrown out on your ear in a minute.'

Harriet up until now had felt more indignation than anything, but something in his voice caused her to experience a sudden chill. His anger had disappeared, and once again he was the sly, superior Sébastien. She stared at him. He was smiling, enjoying himself.

'I could tell her anything and she'd believe me,' he said. 'I could tell her you've been stealing things from the house, or inviting men here, or that you're always rude to me – which is true, incidentally, you really ought to mind those manners of yours. I could make her sack you as soon as winking, *and* make sure she gives you a bad reference so that nobody else will employ you.'

'Don't be ridiculous,' she said.

'Ridiculous, am I? Do you know how many secretaries Maman has been through in the past year? At least four, and possibly five. And who do you think got rid of them? Not Maman. I did. Secretaries like you are two a penny. Maman runs through them like water, and she always believes whatever I tell her. I'm her golden boy, or hadn't you noticed?'

'I had noticed, yes.'

'Well just you remember it. I could have you out on the street by tomorrow and nobody would miss you for a second. Think on that, *Miss Conway*!'

Then he laughed and walked off, leaving Harriet to try and subdue the hammering of her heart.

Chapter Sixteen

Paris, 1942

It was ten o'clock in Paris on a patchy late May morning of sunshine and cloud, and the shadows of the thin green trees on the Avenue Victor Hugo alternately brightened and dimmed as clouds scudded before the sun. A few years earlier the street would have been buzzing with people and cars, but these days the noise had dimmed to little more than a mutter, the shops and cafés that had once brimmed with life were quiet and listless, and the tall, elegant apartment buildings that lined the street seemed to want nothing more than to fade into the background. Few vehicles went by now; only the occasional car, long, sleek and black, its Nazi flags fluttering blood red, passed crosswise on its way to or from Gestapo headquarters. German soldiers of the lower ranks went about on foot, while the Parisians either walked or travelled by bicycle.

Maggie Brouillard had been out early that morning on business of her own, and was now wheeling her bicycle the last few yards up the street to her home on the Avenue Victor Hugo. It had been her father's family home; grand enough, and in an excellent area in which many good families had chosen to live. Not grand enough for her mother, however; Rose had wanted to move when she and Jean-Jacques Brouillard had first married, as she felt that the apartment was too modest for such a famous man and his family, believing they ought to live somewhere more palatial. But he had always refused, and so the Brouillard children had spent their early childhoods travelling between England and this apartment, which occupied the fourth and fifth floors of a handsome building in yellow-grey Paris limestone.

As Maggie approached the tall double doors which led into the entrance hall of their apartment building, she saw her mother's housekeeper, Estelle, standing in the doorway, in conversation with a pair of German soldiers. Maggie hung back and observed from a distance as the men set off down the street, smiling and waving cheery goodbyes. She glared at them until they were out of sight, and then approached. Estelle saw her and held the door open as she wheeled her bicycle through and leaned it against the wall.

'What were they doing here?' Maggie asked. Her eye fell on a wooden crate standing just inside the door, of which Estelle had evidently just taken delivery. 'Did they bring this? What is it?'

'It is from Madame Abetz,' said Estelle. 'She's sent some wine for the party this afternoon.'

'Which party?'

'Oh, there will just be a few people. Someone from the Berlin Philharmonic, I think, and someone else from the Conservatoire. And the German ambassador, of course. Your brother is going to play for them.'

'More Germans,' said Maggie grimly.

'But not only Germans. Mostly French people.'

'Friends of Germans, then.'

Estelle shrugged her shoulders expressively. 'They are here, and there's nothing we can do about it.'

'We don't have to throw parties for them,' Maggie pointed out. 'Here, let me take that.'

The crate was heavy, clinking as they entered the lift.

'I'll give this to Maman,' said Maggie, when they reached the apartment. 'You go and get on with your work.'

Estelle looked a little disappointed. Maggie suspected she had been hoping to see if there was anything in the crate she might take before Mrs Brouillard saw it. When she was alone, Maggie opened the lid of the crate herself. It was packed with straw, and inside were six bottles of good red wine together with some chocolates, a whole wheel of camembert cheese, some fresh bread, two jars of raspberry jam and some cured meat. Quickly, Maggie shook out a few of the chocolates and took one jar of jam, repackaging the crate so that there were no empty spaces. Then she put the stolen items in the bottom of her bag and went to find her mother. Rose was in the drawing room, listening to Sébastien practising the piano.

'Where have you been?' she asked.

'Out,' replied Maggie.

'Out where?'

'It's a beautiful morning, so I went along the river.' This was true, but she didn't expand further. She and her mother didn't see eye to eye about her Resistance activities, and Maggie knew that Rose would be horrified if she knew the true extent of her involvement.

'I hear you're having a party,' she said instead. 'You might have let me know, then I could have arranged to be out.'

'But I need you here to help,' replied Rose. 'I have some important people coming, and it could be a good opportunity for Sébastien if he plays well.'

'But why Germans? Aren't there enough opportunities for him on the French side?'

'Who do you think makes the final decisions about these things?' said Rose tartly. 'It's certainly not the French.'

'Still, I don't like it.'

'You don't have to like it, but we have to live with it.'

'But people will call us collaborators. It's a filthy thing to do.'

'Don't be ridiculous, child. We have no choice in the matter. Do you really think I enjoy courting all these ignorant Germans? Half of them can't tell the difference between Wagner and Vivaldi, even though they consider themselves connoisseurs, and yet I put myself out to invite them here and smile at them and agree with everything they say for the good of the family. What do you think would happen if I didn't keep in with the right sort of people? Don't forget we're English, and could be interned as enemies at any moment now that your father is dead. It's in our interests to keep on the right side of the Germans, and that's what I intend to do.'

'But—'

'But nothing! Where do you think we get all this good food and wine we've been enjoying lately? We'd be starving like everybody else if it weren't for my efforts. If we make the right friends then we can get into the German shops, and get fuel and other good things. Better to live well while we can.'

'The Germans aren't going to win, you know.'

'They've already won, you dolt, so there's no use in your fighting against it. Better just do what they say and we can continue to live nicely. If we keep them on our side, we can get your father's work performed. By the way, Herr Lissauer of the German Institute is coming this afternoon. They're organising a nationwide tour for the Berlin Philharmonic, and he wants to include *Les Orchidées* on the programme, so you had better be on your best behaviour.' She saw Maggie looking mutinous. 'If you won't think of your father, then at least think of your brother. This war has denied him the opportunities that you others had, but at least *I* am trying to make the best of it.'

Here she was sure of hitting home. Maggie was very fond of Sébastien, who was too young to have much independence from his mother yet.

'All right, I'll do my best to be polite,' she said reluctantly. 'By the way, there's a parcel of food and wine from the ambassador's wife in the kitchen.'

'Ah, how kind of Susanne,' said Rose. She went out, and Sébastien, who had been listening to the conversation, resumed his practice.

Maggie went across to him and stroked his head.

'What are you going to play for the guests this afternoon?' she asked.

'"Für Elise",' said Sébastien. 'Maman says it's very important, so I'd better not make any mistakes.'

'What does Professor Lefeuvre say?'

'He says I shouldn't worry, and that nobody expects me to be perfect. But Maman does.'

Maggie laughed. 'I expect she does, but Professor Lefeuvre is right to tell you not to worry. It's only a little party, and everyone will be kind.'

'I want to be as good as Cécilia one day,' said Sébastien after a moment. 'Do you think I can?'

'I don't see why not.'

'But she's brilliant – everybody says so. And she won the Prix de Rome.'

'She was nineteen when she won it. You're only eleven. There's plenty of time for you yet.'

'But what if I don't have the talent?'

'Professor Lefeuvre seems to think you do. And if you don't – well, it's not so bad. Look at me. I don't have anywhere near the ability of you or Cécilia or Marcus, but I do all right.'

'Yes – Maman doesn't shout at you the way she does at me.'

'That's because she knows there's no point. She could shout until the end of time and I'd still never make it as a successful musician.'

'Sometimes I wish we came from a normal family,' said Sébastien resentfully. 'Sometimes it would be nice to get up and not have to practise for hours on end.'

'But you play so beautifully for it.'

'Do I? I'm always worried I'll dry up, or that I'll forget the notes, or that the piano will be out of tune. It frightens me.' Almost unconsciously he began playing a little four-note phrase with his right hand. He wasn't looking at Maggie, but straight ahead. 'I dreamt last night that I was supposed to be playing a piano concerto in public. Mozart, I think it was. I was in a hall, a big hall with thousands of people watching, and I started to play but it came out all wrong. It sounded like that accordion music the old man used to play on the corner of the street. Do you remember him? He always got it wrong. Then everyone started laughing, and Maman came on stage and made an announcement that there had been a mistake, that they'd meant to book Cécilia but she wasn't available, so they had to get me instead. Then I looked across and there was another piano, and Marcus was sitting at it in his uniform, and Papa was next to him, and they were beckoning to me, but I knew they couldn't really be there because they were dead, and I tried to run from the stage but Maman wouldn't let me, and said I had to keep playing. Then I woke up.'

'Poor you,' said Maggie sympathetically. 'That sounds like a horrid dream. But it was just a dream. Now, you'd better start your violin practice before Maman comes back in. If you practise really hard perhaps you'll win the Prix de Rome when you're eighteen instead of nineteen, and beat Cécilia that way.'

He brightened at the thought of that, and went to fetch his violin.

Maggie sat down at the piano stool he had just vacated, and played a few notes of 'Für Elise'. She sometimes felt as if she were two different people, living two separate lives. There was Marguerite Brouillard, music teacher and daughter of a famous composer, whose mother moved in the highest circles, among French intellectuals and the German high command, and mixed with some of the most famous musicians of the age. Marguerite attended concerts and parties, and was occasionally invited with her mother to share a table at Maxim's with the German ambassador. She smiled and handed glasses of wine to the men who had invaded her country, laughed at their jokes and pretended everything was completely normal.

Then there was Maggie Brouillard who led a secret life – a life of early mornings and late nights defying the curfew, of coded messages and secret radio broadcasts, and clandestine meetings with people the Germans would consider the enemy, all with the aim of making things difficult for their unwelcome visitors. It had been exciting at first, but she had found her enthusiasm for resistance waning lately, as a sense of its futility threatened to overwhelm her. When she'd begun, Emil had spurred her on; they'd been together, full of patriotic fervour and an unshakeable determination that they wouldn't be beaten by a few Germans. But as the war went on, it became clear that this wasn't a game, but a very dangerous reality – one which had very nearly cost Emil his life. He was lucky to have escaped when he did. Several of their co-conspirators had disappeared. She had no idea where they'd gone, and didn't know whether they'd been arrested or merely gone into hiding. Others had been taken away, tortured or shot. Filip, Emil's brother, had been rounded up together with Emil and three hundred others one day and had not been seen again until his badly beaten body had been dumped outside the firm of accountants where he had worked.

Maggie wondered whether Emil had received the message about it. He and Filip had been close, and she knew it would be a devastating blow to him. Without Emil, everything seemed like a never-ending struggle with no reward, but she'd had to let him go for his own safety. She missed him daily, and the conviction that she'd sent him out of the way of danger was the one thing that kept her spirits up. He'd managed to get a quick word to her via Cécilia and her friends, to say that he'd arrived and was well, but since then she'd heard nothing, which surprised her. Not even Cécilia had written, although she might easily have passed on a letter via one of the students or professors at the Villa Paradiso, who were not infrequently able to obtain permits to cross the demarcation line between Vichy and Occupied France.

Perhaps it was unfair of her, but Maggie felt as though she'd been left to shoulder the burden alone. She wanted to talk to someone, but of course she couldn't tell her mother what she'd been up to – or about her loneliness without Emil, because Rose disapproved of him. Why couldn't she have picked somebody respectable, instead of a foreign Jew, her mother had said in that frosty way of hers. She was sure Maggie had done it purely to embarrass the family, and it was lucky there were laws against miscegenation, because Rose had no intention of giving them her blessing if they were foolish enough to get engaged.

The party that afternoon was an elegant affair. Rose had used all her connections to make sure there was plenty of food and wine on offer, and the guests had been chosen carefully to meet her mother's high standards of culture and education. There were one or two journalists and critics from magazines which were sympathetic to both the Reich and Jean-Jacques Brouillard's music, as well as representatives of the Paris Opera and the Berlin Philharmonic, and several Germans from the propaganda office and the German Institute who could be relied upon to demonstrate good manners and a certain amount of taste, at least.

Maggie did her best to keep her feelings to herself, but when she saw M Thibaud accepting a third glass of the Bordeaux and Herr Vogel greedily stuffing another chocolate truffle in his mouth, even though most of Paris was going hungry, she was forced to bite her lip to stop herself from making a remark. Then Sébastien began to play, and she was glad she'd restrained herself. He was so talented for such a young boy; he reminded her of Cécilia at the same age, despite his doubts about his own abilities. Whether he would ever achieve as much as his sister had wasn't certain, however. Cécilia, dedicated and self-contained, with the ability to shut out the world as though nothing else existed, had been able to focus all her attention on her music. Sébastien was altogether more mercurial and easily discouraged. Still, if given the right attention and careful management, he might yet come into his own. He finished 'Für Elise' without a mistake, and the room broke into applause.

'*Très bien*,' said Professor Lefeuvre, who had been watching his protégé complacently. 'You shall do very well, young man.'

Sébastien went pink with pleasure, and a note of self-satisfaction crept into his expression.

'Such a talent!' exclaimed one of the Germans from the propaganda office. 'I believe this young man will go far.'

'You see, *madame*,' said Lefeuvre to Mrs Brouillard, and a significant nod passed between them.

Maggie didn't much like the professor. He was large, fat and balding, with a humorous manner and a friendly word for everyone, but Maggie mistrusted anyone who thought he could be all things to all men. She didn't like the way he had favourites among his pupils – all of them boys. Perhaps it was a coincidence, but the tallest, best-looking boys at the Conservatoire always seemed to receive his attention, while the plain, unprepossessing ones and the girls were neglected and passed over. And out of all his favourites, Sébastien, fresh-faced and graceful, was the chosen one: the one the professor talked to most, the one he picked for the solo parts, the one he mentioned in conversation to people of influence. Sébastien, in his turn, hero-worshipped Lefeuvre, always putting in extra effort when he was present. Despite her dislike of the professor, Maggie recognised that he was to be courted, and so was always polite and friendly to him for Sébastien's sake.

The afternoon passed, and Maggie found herself gritting her teeth more and more as it went on. She fell into conversation with a French magazine critic, a pudgy man with a clammy handshake and a monocle; an affectation that didn't suit him. He looked down his nose at her and said distantly that the boy was very good. Clever of him to choose a German piece to play in the traditional style, rather than anything more modern. He didn't quite agree with this German obsession with the old style – thought it had gone a bit too far – but he couldn't argue with them in their desire to expunge the more nefarious influences from music. The Jews had been taking it entirely in the wrong direction, in his opinion; the French had been blind to this for many years, but trust the Germans to see clearly and cut away the dead wood.

Maggie looked at him with inward dislike, but could do nothing but nod and smile. She couldn't help comparing him, drooping and insipid as he was, to Emil and Filip, who had been vibrant and alive, full of laughter and fun and music – real music; not mannered, classical stuff, but lively, joyous, improvised tunes that came straight from the heart instead of following the strict, stultifying rules of composition. She got away from the critic as soon as she could without being rude, and went to help herself to some wine. She was filling her glass when she saw a young man approaching her. She thought she recognised him as one of Professor Lefeuvre's students, and was about to paste on a smile when he came close to her and said in a low voice:

'I've got a letter for you.'

Maggie's heart leapt, hoping it was from Emil. She glanced around. Nobody was watching them.

'Not here,' she said. He followed her into the kitchen and handed her a crumpled envelope. One glance told her it was from Cécilia. 'Where did you get it?'

'A friend of a friend,' he replied.

She thanked him and he returned to the party. It was a disappointment not to hear from Emil, but a message from Cécilia was the next best thing. Maggie felt the need of a break. She locked herself in the bathroom and tore open the envelope, anxious to see what news it contained. The letter was dated six weeks earlier, which was not surprising, since no news of a personal nature could be sent through the official channels, and private communications of this sort often took a while to arrive at their destination. She scanned the letter eagerly, hand over her mouth, her heart beating fast, then forced herself to go back and read it again more slowly.

It was the worst possible news: Emil had been taken, arrested, sent to Le Vernet, a camp for 'dangerous' foreigners. Cécilia had been trying to find out what had become of him, and where he was to be sent after that, but there was no one to help her, she said.

There was a woman called Marion who might have aided her, but she'd gone back to America now, and Cécilia didn't have any more friends in high places she could go to for help.

Maggie shook her head and forced herself to breathe calmly. Of all the people she would have entrusted with the task of getting Emil released, Cécilia was last on the list. Fond as she was of her sister, Maggie knew that Cécilia was not in the least practical, and would have no idea of how to approach the right people or ask for favours. And the tone of the letter confirmed it: Cécilia sounded altogether upset and frantic, her sentences confused and jumbled, as if she didn't quite know what she was writing. She must be feeling to blame for what had happened, although she surely wasn't. Emil was his own man, and had known the dangers he was running, and there had always been a high possibility that he would be caught again and arrested. Poor Cécilia; she had no idea how to look after herself – it was a wonder she'd been allowed to go to Nice at all – and she certainly couldn't cope with a crisis of this sort. Maggie longed to see her and get a full explanation of what had happened, as she might be able to think of a way to help Emil.

A feeling of dread washed over her, and she put her hand to her forehead, which felt cold and clammy to her touch. What would they do to Emil? He'd already escaped once, so his name must surely be on a list. They'd know immediately they had a wanted man in their hands. Perhaps they'd shot him straightaway – please no! she prayed – or perhaps they merely planned to deport him. That wouldn't be so bad, although she'd heard dark rumours about what was happening to the Jews in France. The authorities were rounding up more and more of them now, and a few weeks ago they'd had word that over a thousand of them had been sent off by train to who knew where. A camp in Poland, they said. Emil had never wanted to return to Poland. His family had come to France when he was quite young to escape persecution, and he had no love for the country. Maggie remembered how he'd laughed when they kissed goodbye and she'd told him of her fears for him. She'd been cross at him for laughing, and he'd grown serious again.

'Don't you understand?' he'd said. 'They can take our country and our food, but they can't take our souls. If we let them frighten us then we deserve to be frightened. We have to laugh, because what else is there? Cheer up! We still have each other, and there's always laughter if you care to look for it.'

Maggie had shaken her head at him, but couldn't help smiling at his eternal optimism. But what use had the laughter been to him after all? Perched on the edge of the bath, she realised that tears were rolling down her cheeks. Sometimes it was all too much to bear, but bear it she must. She wiped her eyes, took a deep breath and went back to the party. There she was accosted by the magazine critic, who was in light-hearted dispute with Herr Lissauer from the German Institute about a matter of music and wanted her to act as referee. They were discussing the relative merits of the French and German Romantic composers.

'Berlioz has his supporters,' said the critic, 'but my esteemed colleague here refuses to accept the self-evident truth that the Germans' interpretation of the meaning of Romantic was so much more profound than that of the French. For depth and significance, Berlioz can't hold a candle to Wagner and Schubert, for example – or even to Mahler.'

He was full of himself and yet at the same time quite clearly trying to ingratiate himself with Lissauer.

'Wagner and Schubert, I'll give you those,' said the German. 'But Mahler – no, no, a thousand times no! He was a Jew of the worst sort, from a family of thieves and gipsies. A prime example of how the Romantic movement became tainted over the years.'

'Ah, yes,' the French critic recollected himself. 'I'd forgotten that. How they get everywhere!'

'It's insidious,' agreed Herr Lissauer. 'And the worst of it is, there's something about this degenerate music that appeals to the public. It's a great danger to society.'

'Oh, the public!' said the critic dismissively. 'If only we didn't have to play to such an ignorant lot. One might almost say they deserve Jewish music, except of course we don't want them being any more corrupted than they are already. Some of this jazz music, for example, has a most indecent rhythm to it that can only lead to the worst sort of debauchery.'

'Nonsense!' exclaimed Maggie, who could stand it no longer. 'What rubbish you do talk! You're idiots if you think there's any difference between Jewish music and any other kind of music – it's all just music. And there's nothing at all wrong with jazz. It's not indecent or debauched – it's just music that young people like to listen to. We listen, and we dance, and we have fun. Isn't that the point of the whole thing?'

Herr Lissauer laughed delightedly.

'Aha, I see our pretty Mademoiselle Brouillard has a mind of her own!' he said. He wasn't in the least bit offended by what she'd said, but the French critic had screwed his monocle more firmly into his eye and was looking at her with a touch of distaste. Mrs Brouillard had overheard the exchange, and scented danger. She moved quickly across to where they were standing.

'Maggie! Remember where you are please, and apologise to the gentlemen immediately,' she snapped.

Maggie muttered an apology, and her mother went on coldly, 'Clear those glasses away and stop bothering people. Now, Christophe – Herr Lissauer – I have a little surprise for you that I have been saving till last. You won't say no to a glass of champagne, will you?'

After that, Maggie knew her tongue had been loosened and she wouldn't be able to hold her silence for the rest of the afternoon.

She cleared away the wine glasses, then, instead of going back to the drawing room, she went slowly up the red-carpeted staircase with its wrought iron balcony curving up to the next floor. The sound of gramophone music and laughter drifted up the stairs, but she didn't think she could stand it any more when her own little world had just fallen apart, so she went into her room, shutting the door firmly to block out the noise. She sat on her bed and stared at the wall.

The party was over by six. She could hear her mother saying goodbye to the last of the guests, and she knew she'd be wanted to help clear up, but instead she remained on her bed. At last she heard footsteps ascending the stairs.

'Well, that was quite an exhibition you made of yourself,' her mother said from the doorway.

'Hardly. Herr Lissauer didn't care, and Christophe is an idiot. I might have said so much more, but I didn't.'

'And you expect me to be thankful for that?'

'No.' She was still staring at the wall, refusing to look at Rose.

'Can't you even hold your tongue for a few hours? You know the danger you could put us in,' began Mrs Brouillard, but Maggie had heard it all before. She waved a hand in frustration.

'I can't do this any more,' she said. 'It makes me sick, do you understand that? Sick up to here! How can you do it? How can you invite these people to our house? You stand there, and you give them the best food and the best wine, and you flatter them and speak to them in German. How can you live with yourself for it?'

'Because I know which side my bread is buttered on,' replied her mother crisply.

'But these are the people who killed Marcus! Have you forgotten that? They killed your son, and you're acting like they're your best friends.'

'There was no need for Marcus to do what he did,' said Rose. 'I told him not to enlist, but he would have his own way. He made his own decision and he paid the price for it.'

'That's it, isn't it? That's the real truth of the matter. You can't bear any of us going against your orders. You have to keep us under your thumb at all times, and if we disobey your instructions you take a vindictive pleasure if we come to harm.'

'Nonsense!'

'No, it's true, isn't it? You'd rather have Marcus dead than disobedient.'

'Hold your tongue, girl! You don't know what you're talking about. I am the only thing holding this family together at present. If we are to survive then we need to adapt. There's no use in wishing things were otherwise. This is the situation we have, and we must make the best of it. And yes, if that means being nice to the Germans, then so be it.'

'Do you like them?'

'The Germans? What a question! You might as well ask whether I like the English, or the French, or the Americans. They're people, like anyone else. Some of them are pleasanter than others.'

'I don't believe you mind the Occupation at all,' said Maggie. 'You've done well out of it, so you don't care about anybody else. That's the truth, isn't it?'

'Of course I mind the Occupation! One can't get food, or petrol, and half the hairdressers have closed down. I don't like the Occupation at all. But there's no denying that the Germans have some very sensible ideas about things. Once the war is over, I expect things will settle down and life will resume as it was before – or perhaps even for the better.'

Maggie shook her head, disbelieving. She had often suspected her mother thought differently about things than she did, but this was further than she had ever expected her to go. She felt close to tears, but she knew Rose would see it as a weakness, so she held them back.

'I can't stay here,' she said at last. 'I can't go on pretending things I don't feel. I won't be called a collaborator. Marcus is dead, and my— some of my friends have been arrested, perhaps even killed. You might think all those people at the party this afternoon are friends of yours. They might seem likeable to you, but they're not – they're bad and cruel and evil. They don't even bother to hate us. They think nothing of us. They have no more concern for people than if they were insects – an inconvenience, to be crushed and wiped up and thrown away. We ought to have gone to England when the war first broke out, as Papa wanted to. But you said no.'

'Don't be ridiculous! If we'd gone, then Cécilia would have lost out on the Prix de Rome, and Marcus wouldn't have got his position with the Versailles Orchestra.'

'But he'd still be alive – probably, at any rate. And Cécilia wouldn't be stuck in Nice, all alone. There are lots of musical opportunities in England – just as many as there are in Paris – but none of them are grand enough for you. It was all your ambition, wasn't it? You gave up your own music for Papa, and now you have to live through everyone else. Well, a lot of good your ambition did Marcus, didn't it?'

'Silence!' said Rose, but Maggie could hold it in no longer. All the resentment was pouring out now, at Rose's long neglect of her in favour of her more talented children, at her disapproval of her daughter's lifestyle, and, most of all, at her rejection of Emil, whom Maggie had not dared introduce to the family.

'Why, I'll bet you're secretly glad that Papa died, aren't you?' she went on. 'If he was still alive he'd have made sure we all went to England and were kept safe. But now he's dead there's nothing to stand in your way – you can bully us all as much as you like and Papa can't hold you to account for it.'

At that, Rose finally lost her temper. There was a ringing slap, and Maggie sat back, holding her reddening cheek, as her mother stood over her.

'That's enough!' she hissed. 'I won't have you talking like that.'

There was a silence, then Maggie said in a muffled voice, 'I can't stay here. I have to go. I have to move out.'

'Just as you choose. See how you get on when you've had a few weeks with nothing to eat.'

Rose turned and stalked out of the room. Maggie managed to hold herself together for another five minutes, but then the tears came and wouldn't stop. She drew her knees up and buried her face in her arms. After a while she felt a touch on her hand. It was Sébastien, who had crept in without her hearing.

'Are you leaving?' he asked.

'I think I must,' said Maggie.

'I don't want you to go. I'm frightened of Maman.'

'Oh, darling, there's no need. She loves you, and she's proud of you – or she will be as long as you keep practising,' she was forced to add in all honesty.

'What shall I do without you? Shall I still see you after you're gone?'

'Of course you will. I'll write often, and we'll meet whenever we can. And you'll tell me if anybody is making you sad, won't you? I can't do much, but I'll try and help.'

He promised he would, and she hugged him and gave him one of the chocolates she'd stolen from the crate earlier. Four days later she moved out.

Chapter Seventeen

Cécilia was sick for the whole journey back to Paris. The train was crowded, and she'd arrived late, so there was nowhere to sit, and she had to stand in among a hot, sticky crowd, her eyes closed, willing herself not to vomit. At the demarcation line many people got off, freeing up a few seats. Cécilia hoped she might get one, but then a group of German soldiers got on and she resigned herself to standing the rest of the way.

She was in luck, however, as one of the soldiers saw her and gave her his seat. He was fair-haired and pink-faced and spoke no French, but he clearly meant it kindly. Cécilia wondered what the soldier would say if he knew the baby was half-Jewish. Would it make a difference? But she was too tired and had too much of a headache to wonder for very long, or to think very hard about anything, and at length she fell into an uncomfortable doze which lasted until just before the train pulled into the Gare de Lyon.

Then there was the struggle to get herself and her suitcase and her violin into a crowded metro carriage and across the city to the Avenue Victor Hugo, where she would once more sleep in her comfortable room, with its cool, white-painted walls and its polished parquet flooring, and her bookshelves full of music scores, and her music stand and stool in the corner. All she wanted to do was to crawl into bed and sleep for at least a week, until the sickness went away. Then perhaps she'd wake up and find out it had been all a dream, and there was no baby after all, and she was eighteen again and had never entered the Prix de Rome, and she could be the music teacher she'd always intended to become and live a quiet life forever.

Useless to wish, however – the fluttering and kicking in her stomach were too real to ignore, becoming more insistent by the day. She forced herself not to think about what her mother would say when she found out the state her daughter was in. She'd be horribly angry, Cécilia knew. But Maggie would protect her – Maggie had always looked after her. She wouldn't think about her sister's reaction to the revelation of what she'd done. It would all come out all right; she knew it would.

She arrived home at last, exhausted and almost dropping on her feet, and let herself in at the front door. Leaving her suitcase in the downstairs hall, she took the lift up to the fourth floor. It was June, and the weather was warm, but she was wearing a winter coat in a vain attempt to hide her belly. If she could only conceal her pregnancy from her mother until a suitable moment had come to confess to it, perhaps things would not be so bad – although even Cécilia, with her ability to avoid uncomfortable truths, had trouble convincing herself of this. She took a deep breath and put her key in the lock.

'Hallo?' she called as she came in. There was no reply. Everyone must have gone out. It was close to five o'clock, so presumably someone would be back soon. It was warm, almost stifling with the windows shut. Cécilia moved across to the grand arched window that overlooked the Avenue Victor Hugo and opened it to let in the breeze. She still felt hot and sticky, so she removed her coat and dropped it onto a chair. She was staring out of the window, lost in her own thoughts, when her mother arrived silently. Cécilia heard a long drawn-out hiss of a gasp and whirled round. So much for not springing a surprise upon her: Rose's eyes had gone straight to her belly – not yet huge, but unmistakably full and rounded under the thin dress. From there they lifted to meet Cécilia's eyes, and there was a short silence.

'I wasn't expecting you home,' said Rose.

'Where's Maggie?' was all Cécilia could think of to say.

'She's not here.' There was another silence, then her mother came further into the room with a deliberate, measured step. Cécilia braced herself. 'And what, exactly, is this?' she said, her voice grating into the empty air.

She had not so much as gestured, but she didn't need to. Cécilia glanced down at her stomach and put her hand over it – an involuntary movement which confirmed the truth more than anything else could have – and was silent.

'How did you get permission to travel?'

'Professor Morillot arranged it. He said it was for the best.'

'Do you mean they threw you out?'

'Not exactly – at least, I don't think so.'

'You don't think so? Don't you know?'

'They never said… I don't know. All they said was that I'd better come home, as there was no one to look after me in Nice.'

'What happened?' As Cécilia lowered her eyes, Mrs Brouillard went on, 'Stupid question on my part. It's perfectly obvious what happened. What I meant was: how could you let it happen? I take it you haven't gone and got married behind my back?'

'N-no.'

'And what of the man who did it? Is he standing by you?'

Cécilia shook her head mutely. She couldn't tell her mother about Emil when she hadn't even confessed to Maggie yet.

Rose began to mutter.

'I knew it was a mistake to let you go by yourself. I ought to have sent you in the care of someone. Why didn't they have someone to look after you at the Académie, and keep you out of mischief?'

'I don't need anyone to look after me!' said Cécilia.

'Clearly you do, imbecile girl, since you didn't have the sense not to throw away the only bargaining asset a woman has! How far gone are you? You're not showing too much yet.'

'I don't know exactly. About six months, I think.'

'Oh, good heavens! It's worse than I thought. Far too late to get it seen to, even if we could still get hold of Madame Amiot. I heard she was arrested, so where she is now is anybody's guess, and there's no one else that I know of.'

'I don't want it seen to,' replied Cécilia. 'It's mine.'

'And I suppose it means nothing to you that you are ruining your career, your future, any chance you had of making a name for yourself?'

'I don't see why. I can still compose with a baby. I can still play.'

'Without a husband? Don't be ridiculous! Who's going to be bare-faced enough to put a spoiled woman in front of an audience of German officers? How will that look on the programme, or in the newspaper reviews? If you were married, it might be different, although Lord knows even that's difficult enough, as I have reason to know. Why do you think I abandoned my own music? I'll tell you why: because I couldn't possibly find the time for it while I was looking after four children. And I was married respectably, with a husband and servants. Think on that, my girl. If I couldn't do it, then what hope do you have, all alone and with a bastard child?'

Mrs Brouillard's face was pale, and she seemed to be holding in her temper with difficulty.

Cécilia didn't know what to say. The music wasn't important to her any more – not with Emil gone, and his baby growing inside her.

'It doesn't matter,' she said at last. 'I've been too sick to study lately anyway. I can always go back to it later.'

'Are you quite mad? Do you really think they'll hold the place open for you? Why, I shouldn't be surprised if they strip you of the scholarship. I don't know why they haven't done it already, in fact. What did Professor Morillot say when he found out the state you're in?'

'He was very kind,' said Cécilia. 'He said it was better that I come home, because I had more important things to think about from now on.'

'I knew it! They won't let you back, mark my words! And all your hard work will have been for nothing – all *my* hard work will have been for nothing. All the sacrifices I made when you were young, all the times I made you practise when you didn't want to, all those times I pushed you to do better when you didn't think you were capable. *I* knew you were capable. And now it's all gone to waste – years of work thrown away, just like that!'

She was walking up and down, her agitation was starting to get the better of her. Cécilia sat down, as a wave of exhaustion swept over her.

'And how dare you sit down when I'm talking to you?' said Rose.

'I'm very tired, and I feel sick,' replied Cécilia.

'I imagine you do, yes! That's what you get for being free and easy. I suppose you do know who the father is? Don't tell me you've been handing out your favours to all-comers? I hope you know his name, at least.'

Cécilia flushed and nodded, and her mother came close to her, eyes narrowed.

'Then you'd better tell me. Yes, perhaps that's the best thing. I'll speak to him and get him to do his duty and marry you. It's not ideal, but we must make the best of the situation. Who is he? Some student at the Académie, I suppose?'

But Cécilia was shaking her head. 'It's no use,' she said. 'It's impossible.'

'Why? Don't tell me he's already married. Or don't for goodness sake say it's one of the professors.'

'Of course not.'

'Then who was it?'

'He – he was someone I met in Nice. He wasn't a student.'

'I suppose he told you he loved you, did he? And you fell for it. You always were ridiculously naive. What's his name? We'll see if we can't get in touch with him through the Académie.'

'The Académie don't know him,' said Cécilia. 'And we can't get in touch with him. He went away, and I don't know where. I haven't seen him in months.'

She didn't tell her mother that he was a Jew and had been arrested. But Rose was already angry enough at what she had heard.

'Of all the stupid, idiotic things you could have done, this is the stupidest! Do you mean to say you don't even know where he is? Do you mean to say this child of yours will have no father at all?' She was working herself up into a temper. 'Then we have no option – we must find someone who can deal with it. There are people I can ask. There's bound to be someone. We won't tell them you're six months gone – we'll say it's four months and you've put on weight.'

'No!' said Cécilia. 'I won't!'

It was rare that she stood up to her mother, but not for an instant would she submit to being poked about by an elderly woman in a grubby room until she bled all her hopes away onto a stained mattress. She stammered as she said it, but she had no intention of giving in. The baby was hers. Nothing Rose could say would change her mind.

At that, Mrs Brouillard flew into a rage and began beating her daughter about the head, shouting all the while. Cécilia cowered back in her chair and covered her head with her hands.

'I'm sorry,' she said. 'I'm sorry, I'm sorry. I didn't mean this to happen, but I can't do what you say. I won't. It would be wrong.'

Rose stood back, breathing heavily. She said nothing for a minute or two, but watched Cécilia crying silently in the chair.

'I see you've made your decision,' she said at last. 'In that case, there is nothing more to be said. Are you hungry, or are you too sick to eat?' Then, as Cécilia stared at her in surprise, she went on, 'Dry your tears, child. You could hardly expect me to be pleased, surely. But if you've made up your mind, then there's nothing I can do. Let's just hope you don't live to regret it. At any rate, I assume I can trust you not to embarrass me? If you care for me at all you won't parade about in the street like that and draw attention to yourself.'

Cécilia couldn't argue with that, and she was only relieved that her mother's fury seemed to have burned itself out.

'Where is Maggie?' she asked.

'Your sister moved out of this house some weeks ago. It appears she disagreed with the way I choose to conduct my life, so she left.'

Cécilia was dismayed.

'Where did she go?'

'As to that, I couldn't tell you. She didn't give me her address, and I certainly haven't asked for it.'

This was a blow, but she couldn't say anything because just then Estelle came in followed by Sébastien, who had just returned from his lessons at the Conservatoire. He gave her a noisy greeting and, in the boyish self-absorption of eleven, didn't notice anything different about her at first. He wanted to know whether she'd seen any Italian soldiers in Nice, and whether she'd been to the beach, and whether she'd brought him a present.

'Leave your sister alone for now – she's tired and doesn't want you fawning all over her,' said Rose. 'You'd better go and have a rest,' she said to Cécilia. 'I take it that was your suitcase downstairs in the hall? Estelle can bring it up. Go and lie down, and I'll expect you at dinner at seven.'

Cécilia gratefully made her escape and went upstairs. Her room was just as she had left it ten months or so before. Such a short time ago, but how much had happened in those months! She was a different person now; she'd been still practically a child when she left, but today she was a grown woman, and she'd already taken her first steps as an adult by standing up to her mother. Tired and sick as she was, she couldn't help feeling a twinge of self-satisfaction at her own bravery.

The sun was beginning to sink in the sky, casting a beam of light onto her bed, with its crisp, white cover. Cécilia kicked off her shoes and lay down, enjoying the coolness of the pillowcase under her head. She hadn't intended to fall asleep, but it had been a long day, and after a very few minutes her eyes closed and she was dead to the world. When she awoke, it was dark. She raised her head as she heard her bedroom door open. It was her mother, who came in, pulled down the blinds and switched on Cécilia's bedside lamp.

'I missed dinner,' said Cécilia.

'You were tired,' replied Rose. 'Are you hungry now?'

'No.'

'But you must have something to drink. There's some hot chocolate. I'll go and make you some.'

She was gone a few minutes, and came back with a cup of steaming hot chocolate.

'No milk, I'm afraid, but it has sugar in it. You'd better drink it before it gets cold.'

Cécilia wasn't thirsty either, but she felt as if she'd crossed her mother enough that day, so she sat up and took a sip of the drink. It tasted insipid and full of chemicals, like everything did, but she didn't think anything of it. Nothing tasted nice nowadays.

'Finished?' said Rose, who had been watching her carefully. 'Your luggage is here, so you can get ready for bed.'

Cécilia saw her suitcase standing against the wall. Estelle must have brought it in while she was asleep, although she hadn't heard a thing.

'I'll get your nightdress,' said Mrs Brouillard. 'I don't suppose bending down is easy for you.'

She was being oddly kind. She found Cécilia's nightdress and dressing-gown and handed them over.

'There. Now, you'd better go and wash your face. If there's nothing else you need, then I'll say goodnight.'

'What time is it?'

'Half past ten. Everybody else is in bed.'

She gave one last glance at her daughter before she left the room, carrying the cup and saucer which had held the chocolate. Cécilia slowly undressed and got into her night things, before going into the bathroom. She was beginning to feel very strange. She couldn't describe it, exactly, but her head was spinning a little and her vision had begun to blur. It didn't feel like any of the normal pregnancy symptoms she'd experienced up to now, but what else could it be? Her head was heavy and drowsy and she wanted nothing more than to lie down. A good night's sleep would set her right, she was sure. As she brushed her teeth she gazed into the mirror, staring at her reflection with a kind of groggy detachment, then headed back to her bedroom, which was at the head of the curved staircase with its red carpet and its wrought iron banister. She paused for a minute, her hand resting lightly on the rail as she fought down the rising feeling of dizziness. Her limbs felt so weak that she was finding it difficult to stand up.

It was then that everything turned upside down. Cécilia had no time for thought: she only knew that one minute she'd been standing unsteadily at the top of the stairs, and the next she was pitching headlong down them. She flailed uselessly, trying to catch hold of the banister, but everything was blurred and she couldn't see properly. A series of violent bumps, three seconds of deadly panic, then with a sharp cry she landed on the cold, hard parquet floor at the bottom. At first there was only shock, then after that agonising pain and a feeling of overwhelming terror. The fall had been brutal enough to break bones, and although she'd managed to avoid a direct blow to the stomach, there must have been damage, surely. She lay, winded and in pain, on the unyielding floor, but all her faculties were gone and she couldn't begin to figure out how to get up. Someone was moaning quietly, and it was a minute or two before she understood that the sound was coming from her. She gathered what was left of her thoughts.

'Help me.'

It came out as a whisper, but she couldn't manage anything louder. Then she heard voices. First, her mother's, impatient, snapping:

'Get back to bed, Sébastien.'

Then Sébastien's:

'But Cécilia's fallen downstairs. Is she all right?'

'She tripped, that's all. She's fine. Get back to bed, I'll see to her.'

'But—'

'Get back to bed!'

Then footsteps, descending softly on the red carpet, and someone was crouching beside her.

'Those stairs are dangerous,' said Rose briskly. 'You ought to have been more careful. Can you move? No bones broken?'

The dizziness persisted. Cécilia felt half-asleep, and through the haze in her mind wondered why the fall hadn't woken her up fully.

'Anything broken?' repeated Rose.

Cécilia didn't know. She felt her mother take hold of her under the arms and lift her to a sitting position.

'What about your wrists? No sprains?'

How like Maman, Cécilia thought fuzzily, to be more worried about whether I can still play than about anything else.

'The baby,' she said weakly, as she felt a stabbing pain. 'No, don't move me!' There was an agonising contraction of muscles, and Cécilia let out a cry.

'What is it?' demanded Rose eagerly. 'Is something hurting?'

Cécilia could do nothing but nod, as the pain was so sharp it left her breathless.

'We'd better get you to bed. Can you walk now?'

She helped Cécilia slowly to her feet. Nothing seemed to be broken. Her mother guided her slowly up the stairs and into her bedroom, but before Cécilia could reach her bed another wave of pain hit her and she felt a wetness between her legs.

'I'm bleeding,' she said. 'I need a doctor.'

'No you don't,' said Rose. 'This is the best way, don't you see? You'll thank me for it one day.'

Cécilia looked at her mother, only half-understanding, and was shocked to see the glittering determination in her face.

'No!' she said – or at least, that was what she wanted to say, but nothing came out. Her head was whirling, her limbs were weak, she was aching everywhere, and the pains in her stomach were coming every minute. The blood felt unpleasantly damp and sticky on her thighs, and she wanted to insist on a doctor. The baby was in danger, didn't her mother understand? The baby would die. But of course, that was what Rose wanted. The thoughts came through in snatches as she fought against the wooziness in her head, which was broken only by contractions that made her double over in agony.

'Get into bed,' said Rose.

She helped Cécilia in between the covers, then looked her over assessingly. Her lips were pressed together firmly. Cécilia felt waves of pain washing over her.

'Am I going to die?' she asked.

'No!' said Rose. 'I won't allow it. Now, try not to move. I'll fetch Estelle.'

She went out. Cécilia breathed deeply in an effort to dull the pain, and tried to convince herself that she was asleep and this was all a nightmare. But she knew it wasn't, not really. She couldn't have dreamt the hard shove in her back which had sent her crashing down the stairs to the floor below, or the satisfied glance her mother had thrown back at her as she left the room. Rather than be thwarted, Rose had decided to take matters into her own hands.

'Why did you push me?' whispered Cécilia to the empty room, and began to cry.

Chapter Eighteen

The next morning Sébastien rose very early, dressed and crept out of the house in the Avenue Victor Hugo. From there he made his way, half-running, half-walking, to where Maggie was living, a couple of miles away on a seedy street off the Boulevard des Batignolles. The door to the street was open, and he went in, climbed to the third floor and rang the doorbell of one of the apartments. After a few minutes, in which the person on the other side presumably examined him through the spy glass, he was admitted by an unshaven man who was still half-asleep.

'Maggie? Yes, she's here,' he said. 'But you needn't have come so early.'

He led Sébastien into a small, dingy living room. A woman appeared at a bedroom door, yawning.

'It's too early to get up. Come back to bed,' she said to the man.

'Just a minute. Maggie!' he called, then disappeared into the bedroom with the woman and shut the door.

Maggie came out of another room, fully dressed.

'Sébastien! I thought I told you not to come here!' she said. 'I can meet you at school if you want to see me. Does Maman know where you are?'

He shook his head.

'Why, what is it? You look terrified.'

'Something dreadful's happened. It's Cécilia.'

She turned pale.

'Cécilia? Have you had a letter?'

'No, she came home yesterday.'

'Did she? Why on earth did she do that?'

'I think she's going to have a baby,' Sébastien said.

'*What?*'

'I didn't notice it at first, but then she said she didn't feel very well and I saw her stomach had got all big, and I overheard Maman and Estelle talking about it and discussing what to do about it.'

'But how…? *Cécilia?* Who…? Is she at home now? I'll come and see her. How's Maman taken it?'

He blinked, as though trying to hold back tears.

'She was very cross. She fell downstairs. I'm worried she's going to die.'

'Maman fell downstairs?'

'No – Cécilia. Oh, Maggie, Maman pushed her!' He said it in a whisper.

'She *pushed* her? How do you know?'

'I saw her. I wanted to say goodnight to Céci and I was just coming out of my bedroom and I saw them. Cécilia was standing at the top of the stairs and Maman came up behind her and gave her a hard shove in the back, and she went flying.'

Maggie was silent for a shocked moment as she took it all in.

'Oh, heavens!' she said at last. 'How's Cécilia? Is she all right?'

'I don't know. Maman saw me and told me to go back to bed, but I heard Cécilia making a sort of groaning noise and asking for a doctor, and Maman said they didn't need a doctor and it was all for the best. Then this morning everything was quiet so I sneaked out before anybody saw me.'

Maggie made her mind up. She grabbed her jacket from where it lay over the back of a couch, then went and knocked on the door of the other bedroom. There was a bad-tempered grunt from inside.

'Marcel, I need your help. It's urgent! He's a doctor,' she said to Sébastien.

Marcel emerged and she explained the situation in a few words, but without giving the worst of the details.

'You will help, won't you? Please, Marcel.'

'All right,' he grumbled. 'But I don't like it. What if your mother reports me? I'm supposed to be in hiding and from what you say her house is always crawling with Germans.'

'There won't be any there at this time of the morning, and she has no idea who you are or where you live. We don't need to tell her anything about you. Please, Marcel, it's urgent.'

She got him out of the house, still muttering, and the three of them hurried the couple of miles to the Avenue Victor Hugo. Marcel looked wary and hovered uncertainly at the street entrance, but Maggie urged him through the door and into the lift.

'I hear Cécilia's had an accident,' said Maggie to Rose, who met them as they came in. 'I've brought a doctor to see her.'

Mrs Brouillard glanced from Maggie to Sébastien, and her mouth tightened in a thin line.

'I see I can't trust you not to go behind my back,' she said.

'You'd better leave Sébastien alone – he was only doing what he thought was best. It's upstairs,' Maggie said to Marcel.

They went up. Rose did not follow them, but stalked off into the drawing room. Her manner said quite clearly that she had washed her hands of the whole affair.

They found Cécilia lying in bed, pale but awake. Her sheets were bloodstained, yet she seemed quite calm. Her eyes brightened when she saw her sister.

'Maggie!' she said.

'Hallo darling,' replied Maggie, hurrying forward to kneel at her bedside. 'Well, what a mess you've got yourself into! No, don't try and talk, Marcel is going to look at you. You'll be quite well, I promise.'

'Once I got into bed I didn't dare move again,' said Cécilia by way of explanation. 'I was scared something would happen.'

Marcel was feeling her stomach.

'Any movement?' he asked.

'A little. There wasn't any for a while, but it started again this morning. Do you think it might be all right?'

'Perhaps, but I'll have to examine you properly to get a better idea.'

'Go and have your breakfast, Sébastien,' said Maggie.

He left the room reluctantly. Marcel made his examination, then at last gave a noncommittal grunt.

'You've bled quite a bit, but as far as I can tell the baby hasn't been harmed. But you'll need to stay in bed from now on or I can't answer for the consequences.'

'We have to get you away,' said Maggie, lowering her voice. 'Sébastien told me what happened.'

'Did he see?'

Maggie nodded, as Cécilia's eyes opened wide, and turned to Marcel.

'She can stay with us, can't she? She won't be any bother. She can have my bed and I'll sleep on the floor.'

'There's not a lot of room.'

'She doesn't need much. I can look after her, but we have to get her away from here. She won't get the care she needs if she stays here.'

'You can get perfectly good care if you've got the money,' said Marcel, glancing around at the opulent surroundings.

'You don't know my mother,' replied Maggie. 'And the situation is a little complicated. Now, how are we going to get you there? You can't possibly walk.'

In the end they were forced to hire a horse and cart at an exorbitant fee from the grocery shop around the corner. Cécilia was helped out of bed, dressed, and assisted gently down in the lift to the street. Sébastien wanted to come, but Maggie said, 'No, you'd better stay with Maman.'

'I'm going to be in the most awful trouble,' he said.

'No you won't. You're her favourite. You might get a telling-off, but that's all.'

'May I come and visit?'

'Of course. Do it after school, so Maman doesn't find out. There's no need to irritate her any more than necessary.'

They set off, leaving Sébastien gazing down the street after them. Cécilia, who was lying across Maggie's knee, saw him turn slowly and go inside. It was a bumpy ride, but Marcel drove the old horse as gently as he could, while Maggie did her best to keep Cécilia from being jolted too much.

Eventually they arrived, and Cécilia was installed safely in Maggie's bed.

'You look as if you need something to eat,' said Maggie, gazing at her sister's wan face.

Cécilia shook her head. 'I'm not hungry.'

'But you have a baby to feed now.' She began to laugh in a resigned sort of way. 'Oh, Céci, how on earth did you get yourself into this mess? Of all people, I should never have expected it of *you*!'

Cécilia put her head down, embarrassed.

'And what about the father? Who is he? You never mentioned anyone in your letters. What were you thinking?'

Now was the time to confess. Cécilia had been dreading this moment for months. She'd played out the conversation in her head countless times, always attempting to bring it to a satisfactory conclusion, but had never yet managed to find any words that sounded right. In the end it had always come down to the hope that Maggie would have fallen in love with someone else. Cécilia didn't want to have secrets from her sister, but she didn't know how to begin.

'You must tell me all about him,' said Maggie. 'Are you in love with him? Will he marry you?'

Cécilia shook her head mutely.

'Oh, but why not? And who is he? How did you meet him? Was it someone at the Académie? Or – no – I hope it wasn't one of Emil's friends. Some of them are pretty disreputable.'

Her tone was light, but there was a sort of desperation behind it, as if she were putting on a brave face about something. Cécilia remembered that Maggie must be just as frantic with worry about Emil as she possibly could be herself, and at that thought the full enormity of what she had to confess suddenly swept over her.

'About Emil…' she said hesitantly. 'I'm sorry.'

It was the only preliminary she could think of, but the words were hardly strong enough, and in any case Maggie misunderstood them.

'It wasn't your fault. He knew what he was doing, and the risks he was running. I don't suppose you've managed to discover anything more about where he is? I can't find out anything from here. If I could I'd go south myself and try and get him out – that's if they haven't shot him already. He's not just someone they might round up in the street along with all the other Jews; he's wanted by name for some of the things he did in Paris.'

Here there was a sort of gulp, as if she were trying to hold back tears. She reached for Cécilia's hand.

'How was he, when you last saw him? Was he happy? Did he mention me at all?'

How could she answer that? Maggie's name had barely been uttered between them from the time they began their guilty association. Cécilia couldn't bring herself to do it, wanting only to pretend that Maggie didn't exist, while Emil had presumably had the sense not to talk about her for fear of bringing on a row. But now she had to say something.

'He did talk of you sometimes,' she said at last. 'He was very proud of you and what you were doing for the Resistance.'

That was true enough, at any rate. He had always spoken fondly of Maggie's bravery and activity.

'I never thought I would miss him so much,' said Maggie. She looked at her sister's stomach. 'I almost wish now…' she hesitated.

'What?'

'It's stupid, really, but seeing you like this… I don't know… one oughtn't to talk of these things, but I can't help wishing now that we *had* gone to bed together, since we were going to be married sooner or later anyway. I wanted to wait, but now it looks as though it's all too late. But if we had… if we had… and if he doesn't come back then at least I might have a baby to remember him by.'

It wasn't exactly coherent, but it was clear enough. Cécilia felt suddenly cold and sick as the reality of the situation hit her. So fate hadn't intervened at all, as she'd been hoping against hope that it would. Her sister was just as much in love with Emil as she'd ever been. How could Cécilia live with the guilt? What she'd done was shameful, indefensible. Just to make things worse, Maggie saw her look of distress and was contrite.

'I'm sorry,' Maggie went on. 'There I am, being selfish and talking about myself when there are far more important things to think about. Did Maman really push you? What was she thinking? Why, she might have killed you!'

'She doesn't want me to have the baby,' said Cécilia.

'Well, I won't deny it's not the best thing that could have happened, but to do that to you! You do want it, don't you?'

'Yes.'

'Will you tell me about it? I won't tell Maman, I promise.'

She couldn't do it. Not now, after the things Maggie had just said. And so Cécilia did the unforgivable. She turned her head away, not wanting to look her sister in the eye.

'It wasn't a love affair,' she muttered. 'There was a man – I don't know who he was. I was on my way back to the apartment. It was dark. I don't like to think about it.'

Lies, all lies. But she didn't need to say any more, because Maggie understood immediately. She clapped a hand to her mouth.

'Oh, good heavens! You don't mean to say it wasn't a love affair at all? Do you mean someone – someone attacked you?'

Cécilia was appalled at what she'd just done. She couldn't bring herself to either nod or shake her head, but she didn't need to. Maggie threw her arms around her and held her close.

'Did you tell anybody?'

Cécilia shook her head.

'Not even Maman?'

'I couldn't. She was so angry that I didn't dare.'

'But who did it? Was it a civilian? A soldier?'

'Perhaps a soldier, I'm not sure,' said Cécilia desperately. 'I went home and tried to forget about it, as it didn't seem there was any use in telling anybody. Who would believe me?'

'Oh, you poor darling. I believe you, of course I do.'

Cécilia felt even worse now. What had she done? How could she have lied to her sister like that? What a coward she was! She'd betrayed her in the worst possible way and was too weak to admit to it, and now she had made things worse by her dishonesty. At that moment she felt she'd deserved the push downstairs. The baby hadn't been harmed as far as they could tell, but perhaps it would have been simpler all round if she'd lost it in the fall, she thought in despair. Then there would be no evidence of her shame, and of the wrong she'd done her sister. She longed for someone to comfort her and, despite everything, wished Emil were there. But she shouldn't even be wishing for him, when he'd never been truly hers.

Chapter Nineteen

That summer was a long, hot and dreary one. Cécilia, who was mostly confined to bed, chafed at her enforced inactivity. The days were stifling and lonely; everyone was out during the day – Maggie teaching and Marcel and his wife on business of their own – and she didn't even have her music to keep her company, as there was no piano in the apartment and her arms got tired whenever she tried to play the violin. News from outside brought no relief either: in July many thousands of Jews were rounded up by police and imprisoned for several days in inhuman conditions at the Vélodrome d'Hiver, then subsequently deported to the concentration camp at Auschwitz.

When Cécilia heard what had happened she tormented herself with the conviction that Emil had escaped from Le Vernet and come back to Paris, only to have been caught in this latest mass arrest. Maggie brought her books to read, but they did nothing to ease her restlessness and longing to escape from the tiny apartment and get out into the street, in among the people. It was odd; a few months ago she'd have jumped at the chance to spend time on her own, but now it was forced upon her she could hardly bear it. The baby seemed healthy, as far as they could tell, and she begged to be allowed to go for a little walk, at least. One day, after she'd pleaded particularly hard, Marcel at last agreed that she might leave the flat for a few minutes. She went out with Maggie, walking slowly arm in arm, but the street outside was a steep one, and the baby was heavy inside her, grating painfully against her hip bones. Then the heat was so intense she began to feel faint. She didn't want to admit it, but Maggie saw how uncomfortable her sister was and made her return to the apartment. There was no break in the weather, and so Cécilia reluctantly submitted to staying inside, at least until it turned cooler.

The only relief was in the form of visits from Sébastien, who came as often as he could without arousing his mother's suspicions, for twenty minutes or half an hour after school. He was doing very well at the Conservatoire – at least, that was what Professor Lefeuvre said – so much so that he was receiving private tuition during the summer holidays. They'd held a little concert one afternoon for some dignitaries of the German music world, and one of them had said he'd never heard such playing from someone so young. Then he'd given Sébastien a music book as a gift. It was in German, but Maman was teaching him how to read it.

'Lefeuvre thinks I have more talent than you do, Cécilia,' he said one day. He glanced at his sister slyly, to see how she took it.

'Does he? I shouldn't be a bit surprised if he were right,' replied Cécilia.

'Well, you're not practising any more, are you? You can't expect to stay on top form if you don't practise. That's what the professor said, anyway.'

'Sébastien…' said Maggie warningly.

But Cécilia wasn't offended. She couldn't even begin to think about music in her current situation, and she was happy for her brother.

'He asked how you were getting on,' went on Sébastien. 'He thinks you're still in Nice. I didn't know what to tell him, so I said I didn't know.'

'That's probably best,' said Maggie. 'We don't exactly want it put about that Cécilia is expecting.'

Just then Marcel came in and grimaced when he saw Sébastien, whom he considered to be something of a brat. Sébastien knew this, and enjoyed provoking him deliberately.

'*Bonjour*, Marcel,' he said brightly.

Marcel grunted. 'Isn't Albertine home yet?' he asked.

'No,' replied Maggie.

Marcel was evidently not in the best of moods. He tramped about the apartment, lifting cushions and opening drawers, as if looking for something.

'I can't stand this heat,' he grumbled. 'Has anybody seen my watch?'

Nobody had, so he continued in his search. On his way to his bedroom, he tripped over something and swore.

'Blasted violin!' he said.

Sébastien darted forward. 'It's mine! Be careful, won't you?'

'Well, if you wouldn't leave it lying around, I wouldn't need to,' said Marcel.

'I put it well out of the way. Somebody must have knocked it over onto the floor. But you ought to be careful with it, it's very valuable.'

'Sébastien is going to play it at the Palais Garnier one day, aren't you?' said Maggie, who could see a row brewing and wanted to defuse it. 'His professor is very proud of him, as are we.'

'What use is playing the violin?' said Marcel carelessly. 'Completely pointless activity. You'd better off employing your hands to train as a surgeon, or even a mechanic. Although I doubt you'd be physically suited to either of those,' he said, with a glance at the delicate-looking Sébastien. It was a careless remark, but Sébastien flushed.

'Why must he always be so rude?' he asked in a low voice, after Marcel had disappeared into his bedroom and Cécilia had gone into the kitchen to get drinks.

'Don't let him get to you,' said Maggie. 'He can't help it. He's a doctor, and he's got nothing to do because he's Jewish and he can't practise medicine any more, so he's grumpy.'

'That doesn't mean he can take it out on everybody else.'

'No, but you'd be the same if they stopped you from playing the violin, wouldn't you?'

'I suppose so. I say, I'm hungry. You haven't got anything to eat, have you?'

'Not these days,' said Maggie. 'Maman's the one who has all the food. If you want something to eat you'd better go home.'

One of the disadvantages of leaving the Avenue Victor Hugo apartment was that she no longer had access to the treats the Germans brought, which had proved very useful, enabling her to help people she knew who were suffering under the food shortages. Sébastien was looking at her curiously.

'Maggie,' he began hesitantly. 'I meant to ask you: why did you take the food?'

'Which food?'

'You know, at home. You gave me some chocolate one day, but it was Maman's. Somebody sent it to her.'

'Maman doesn't eat chocolate.'

'No, but still. There was cheese as well, and coffee, and bread sometimes.'

'What of it?' asked Maggie.

'Did you eat it all yourself?'

'Of course not!' She laughed. 'I gave it to other people. You must have noticed there's not a lot of food to go around these days.'

'But we might have kept it for ourselves.'

'There's a war on,' said Maggie. 'We're lucky to have as much as we do, and sometimes we have to go without to help people who have nothing at all.'

'Are you in the Resistance? Paul's brother is in the Resistance. He went south and they haven't seen him for months.'

'Paul? Your friend at school?'

Sébastien nodded. 'Is that what you do, too?'

'I don't do very much,' said Maggie. 'Nothing too dangerous. It's best you don't ask, though, because then nobody can make you tell.'

'You're passing on information, aren't you?' he said suddenly.

'Of course not. What information could I pass on? I don't know anything.'

She'd had plenty of practice in telling a lie with a straight face, but Sébastien wasn't stupid.

'Yes you do. We have Germans here all the time, and they talk about things, and I see you listening to them. That's what you're doing, isn't it? You're telling the Resistance what the Germans are getting up to.'

'No I'm not, and you'd better stop asking. It's none of your business.'

'You shouldn't be doing it,' he insisted. 'Professor Lefeuvre says the Germans are shooting ten prisoners for every German killed by the Resistance.'

'I'm sure that's an exaggeration. You mustn't fret about it. I promise you I have no intention of killing any Germans, so nobody will die on my account.'

She said it to reassure him, although he was still frowning, unconvinced, and when he left, his face wore a brooding expression.

*

The summer wore on, and August melted into September, and at long last they heard news of Emil. One day Marcel brought home a man to stay with them, just for a couple of nights, he said. Anatoli Ivanovitch was an anarcho-communist agitator, as he readily described himself. He'd fought with the Durruti Column in Spain until 1939 and, after fleeing across the Pyrenees from the advance of General Franco's forces, had been caught and interned at Le Vernet. Eventually he'd escaped and was now on his way to Switzerland, where he had other Communist and anarchist friends whom he hoped to persuade to come back to France and cause trouble for the Germans.

He was a small, wiry man, with ears that stuck out comically from the sides of his head, and a shock of black hair. Despite his diminutive size, he ate like a horse. He also drank all their wine, smoked all their cigarettes and established himself in the most comfortable chair. He seemed to be enjoying the war hugely, and spoke cheerfully of the privations of the concentration camp, and the brutality of the guards. He was also dirty and smelly, with a headful of lice and an aversion to washing, but Maggie would have forgiven him anything, because she soon found out he had seen Emil, since they'd both been at Camp Vernet at the same time, six months ago. Ivanovitch gave a wheezing cackle of laughter as he told the story.

'We were a bunch of troublemakers in that place,' he said. 'It's where they put all the political types, and the intellectuals and the writers and the Spanish fighters. They couldn't take their eyes off us for a second or we'd be hatching a plot of some sort. Anyway, they decided that some of us were just too much trouble, so they put us on a train to Castres, and a group of us managed to escape when it stopped just outside the town, including your fellow.'

'Cécilia, did you hear?' said Maggie, her eyes shining. Cécilia had gone pale, and was breathing rapidly. 'Go on, what happened next? Where is he now?'

Ivanovitch shrugged.

'No idea. We could hardly stay together for too long without being captured again, so we all split up after a bit. I headed for Toulouse, and he said he was going to Marseille, I think. Whether he got there I don't know.'

'But was he all right?'

'As all right as any of us were. We gave the guards a hard time and they didn't like that, as you can imagine.'

'But at least we know he survived the camp and escaped, so there's a good chance he's still alive,' said Maggie joyfully. 'I knew it! I knew they couldn't keep him down for long. But where did he go? If he was heading for Marseille then perhaps he managed to get out of the country.'

Cécilia shook her head. 'He said he wasn't going to leave France. He wanted to stay,' she said.

Maggie looked surprised.

'Is that what he told you?'

Cécilia flushed, although she didn't know why she should have. There was nothing guilty about it, but she was acutely conscious of everything she said about Emil, and was careful not to talk of him too often, or make it seem as though she had got to know him too well.

'I— I think so,' she said.

'Well, I think he'd be better off getting out of France,' said Maggie. 'There are things he can do from abroad. He might have gone to North Africa, or made it to England and carried on the resistance from there.'

'I—' began Cécilia, then drew in a sharp breath. She'd been feeling twinges for some days now, and the baby was due at any moment. Ivanovitch saw her grimace and put her hand to her belly.

'Not long now, eh?' he observed. 'Going to have another little fighter?'

'Of course she is,' replied Maggie.

'Well, let me know when he's on his way, won't you?' he said. 'I can't stand screaming babies and I'd like to be elsewhere when it happens.'

As it happened Ivanovitch had already been gone two days before the baby put in an appearance. Cécilia's waters broke at five o'clock in the morning, and she woke Maggie, who ran to fetch Marcel. It was painful but quick, and by mid-morning Cécilia was sitting up in bed, slightly dazed, cradling the new arrival. Marcel examined the baby and said that as far as he could tell, he hadn't come to any harm from his fall downstairs. Maggie sat by the bed as Cécilia held the baby and stared at him, not quite believing she had made this beautiful little thing.

'He's perfect,' she said in wonder.

Maggie laughed. The baby was a comical-looking creature, with a fringe of black hair around the top of his head which stuck up like a crown.

'He's a little king,' she said. 'You should call him Rex.'

It wasn't a serious suggestion, but Cécilia liked the name and it stuck. After a day or two Maggie sent a message to the Avenue Victor Hugo, and soon enough Sébastien turned up. Their mother hadn't written, which was only to be expected, but to their surprise Sébastien had brought food and some blankets for the baby.

'Maman says you're too thin and need to keep your strength up now you have a child to look after,' he explained.

'You may tell her thank you,' said Maggie. 'And if she wants to send anything else we certainly shan't turn it down.'

Sébastien peered at Rex. 'He's very small,' he said. 'Are you going to teach him music?'

'Only if he wants to learn,' replied Cécilia.

Sébastien went off to report to Mrs Brouillard, and Maggie said to Cécilia, 'You ought to get some sleep now. You've hardly slept in days.'

But Cécilia couldn't think of sleeping now she had her darling Rex. He was her only connection to Emil, and he was all her own and so beautiful. She would love him and care for him and keep him safe from harm as long as she had breath in her body, even if she had to fight a hundred invading Germans to do it. Emil might or might not be alive, but while she had Rex she would never forget him, and if he did ever come back then this would be her gift to him – a token to show that she had kept his memory alive while she waited for him.

Chapter Twenty

Hertfordshire, 1950

For a couple of days Harriet avoided Sébastien. She was fairly sure he'd been talking at random and making idle threats about nothing, but he'd dented her confidence severely just when she'd been starting to feel more like her old self. Much to her exasperation, she found herself making mistakes at work and forgetting things, so much so that Mrs Brouillard noticed and remarked upon it in that crisp way she had. At any other time Harriet might have shaken off her cutting comments, but she seemed to have lost her nerve, and it brought back memories of her last few positions, from which she'd been let go for one reason or another – mostly her own incompetence. After the tragedy she'd completely lost the ability to concentrate on a task, and she'd ended up either doing things badly or leaving them undone altogether. She was upset at this relapse, as she'd really thought she was getting better, but if she wasn't careful she'd end up losing this job too. For a day she hovered on the brink of a complete collapse in confidence, until she suddenly realised that after their encounter Sébastien's manner had almost immediately resumed its old veneer of superior civility, and it was obvious that he'd entirely forgotten the exchange.

She ought to have felt relieved, but instead she was angry. How dare the little beast talk to her like he had and throw her into a panic? What on earth had she been thinking to let someone who was practically still a child have such an influence over her? If she'd had any sense at all she'd have given him short shrift there and then, instead of cowering away and slinking about the house all week as she had been. As it happened, the anger was the best thing that could have happened to her, because it stiffened her resolve and caused her to pull herself together. Sébastien had caught her at a bad moment, but she wouldn't let him get away with anything like that again. She was feeling so much better than she had been – if not quite her old self then certainly something resembling it, and if he thought he could threaten her, well, let him try it.

*

On Friday Alec McLeod called to take her out to dinner. She was still feeling full of fire and resolution, so she made an extra effort with her appearance, more to prove to herself she could still do it than anything else. He arrived, quite unembarrassed, in his old Morris Twelve, and she couldn't help comparing him to Jim, who would have scorned to drive anything less than the latest model. Mrs Brouillard had regarded her with something approaching surprise when she'd come down in one of her new frocks; Harriet might almost have said she looked impressed at the transformation, although she said nothing and merely reminded Harriet not to stay out too late.

'I don't suppose you want to go into Cambridge?' said Alec, once he'd seen her into the passenger seat and got in himself. He was looking at her sideways, as though unsure of her reply.

'Not especially,' she replied. 'As a matter of fact, I'm not used to cities these days and I like the quiet.'

'I was hoping you'd say that. There's a place the other side of Baldock I saw a few weeks ago, out in the country. It looked rather nice.'

'Then let's go there.'

He needed no further encouragement. They soon found the place, and Harriet silently approved his taste. It was an old-fashioned country inn of the sort one didn't see much nowadays: unpretentious and unassuming, with a roaring fire and comfortable chairs. The food was simple but fresh, and the wine surprisingly decent for such an out-of-the-way place. The conversation came easily, and Harriet, who hadn't realised she was tense, felt herself relaxing slightly.

'Tell me about Cécilia Brouillard,' said Alec. 'I don't quite know what to make of her. I can't see any physical resemblance to Maggie – as far as I can picture her, at any rate. I know it was years ago, and I only knew her for a few days, but she was one of those people who stick in your mind, if you know what I mean.'

'What was she like?'

'Small and fiery. The forthright and practical sort, you know. Completely different from her sister. Cécilia has a kind of other-worldly quality, as though she doesn't really belong on this earth with the rest of us.'

'She does, doesn't she? But I think she's just very unhappy. She lost people she loved in the war, as well as the use of her legs, and the only thing that might have kept her going – her music – has deserted her, or so she says.'

'What about Rex? You'd think he'd give her something to live for, but she seems to neglect him entirely.'

'She doesn't mean to, I'm sure. I think she does love him underneath it all, but I suppose he reminds her of the past.' She wasn't sure why she was defending Cécilia, but the conversations they'd had recently had revealed a deep sadness which Harriet was sure – or at least hoped – was the only thing coming between Cécilia and her son. 'I feel sorry for Rex too, and I've made it a sort of project to bring her out of herself if I can and remind her he exists. She needs a friend.'

'And that friend is you?'

'Perhaps. It won't happen quickly, because I think she's spent far too much time by herself, but she talks to me a little now. I don't know how long I'll be at Chaffingham, but I mean to do what I can as long as I'm here.'

'You have a kind heart,' he said. 'Most people are far too wrapped up in their own concerns to worry about other people's happiness.'

'Do you think so?' Harriet realised that until she came to Chaffingham she *had* been wrapped up in her own concerns. Was that what she needed to exorcise her own demons? To occupy herself with someone else who was even unhappier than she was? It was a startling thought, and she wasn't sure she liked it.

The evening stretched on, and Harriet found she was enjoying it far more than she'd expected. Alec told her about his time in the RAF, and about his plans for the flying school, then she told him about her years as a translator for the War Office. She'd done the initial stages of training for SOE, the Special Operations Executive, but they'd rejected her in the first round, as despite her fluency in French they thought she was temperamentally unsuited to espionage and undercover work.

'I'm useless at telling lies,' she confessed, 'and I don't know that I'd have had the courage to do it. I felt like an awful coward compared to some of the women, but I'm afraid I'd have been a liability.'

'There's more than one type of courage,' he said. 'It's not everybody that's suited to running around with a gun, sabotaging telephone lines, and I'm sure you did your bit.'

'I hope so. One feels lucky just to have got through the war, somehow, when so many others didn't.'

'Did you lose many people?'

'My parents. My father was a professor of languages, and they'd gone to New York so he could give a talk. Their ship was torpedoed on the way back. My mother didn't want him to go, but he insisted and said it would be quite all right, and she hated to be apart from him so she went with him. He could be terribly pig-headed at times.'

'I'm sorry.'

Harriet thought of her father, tall and absent-minded, wrapped up in his latest book on linguistic theory, and her mother, capable and humorous, who had smoothed his path through life before him. What would they have thought of Alec? They'd have liked him, she thought. She felt a pang, wishing her mother were still here. She missed having someone to confide in. 'What about you?' she asked.

'I lost two brothers, one at El Alamein and one at Monte Cassino. And there was a girl I was rather fond of, too. She died in London when a bomb dropped on her house. She was a teacher.'

'I'm sorry,' said Harriet in turn.

'Beastly thing, war, isn't it?'

'Beastly,' she agreed, and they smiled ruefully at each other and sat in silence for a minute, each thinking of the past. Harriet gazed into her glass of wine. He cleared his throat.

'So, I hope you don't mind my asking, but why are you working for the Brouillards?' he asked.

'Why, because I need to earn a living, of course. Why else?'

'I meant, I'd have expected a girl like you to be married, or at least engaged, instead of living at the beck and call of a grumpy old lady.'

'You mean I should be at the beck and call of a grumpy old man instead?'

He laughed. 'I'm sorry, rude of me to ask. You don't have to answer if you don't want to.'

She thought about it a second, and decided she did want to. 'As a matter of fact, I was engaged, but he died.'

'In the war?'

'No. It was a plane accident, as it happens, a couple of years ago.'

He looked sympathetically curious, but didn't pry. To her surprise, she found she could talk about it.

'You probably read about it in the papers. Group Captain Jim Blacklock. He was trying to break the air speed record in a Gloster Meteor. There were a group of them competing against one another, and we all went down to Eastbourne to watch. One of his engines caught fire and he went into the sea. He never did break the record.'

The irony of Jim's having escaped the war unscathed only to die while messing about in his plane for fun one sunny afternoon had never been lost on her.

'Ah, yes, I remember it well. It's all rather recent, isn't it? And here's me blathering like an idiot about flying all evening. I do beg your pardon.'

'It's all right, although I admit I've rather avoided aeroplanes lately – not that there's any reason for me to fly anywhere.'

'That's a pity, as I was going to ask if you'd like to come up with me one day.'

'In your Tiger Moth, you mean?'

'Yes.'

She blinked, flustered. A few months ago, she knew, she'd have said no immediately. She couldn't say she was keen even now, but she could hear the old Harriet scolding her, telling her to buck up and not be such a snivelling coward.

'Why, I… I don't… I hadn't…' she faltered.

'Forget I asked. It wasn't fair of me. I'm sorry.'

'No need to be sorry. I'd love to,' she said, and her voice was stronger than she felt.

His face spread into a smile, and all of a sudden she was pleased she'd agreed.

'Splendid! We'll wait for a really nice, clear day. The countryside around here is beautiful seen from the air. You'll love it, I promise.'

She sipped her wine, wondering what on earth had got into her. Presumably the drink, she thought ironically.

It was getting late when he took her back home. They sat in silence as he drove, then he looked at her and laughed.

'What is it?' she asked.

'I'm sorry. When I picked you up from Chaffingham earlier you looked as though you were bracing yourself for some sort of ordeal.'

'Did I? Goodness, I didn't mean to.' Had it been so noticeable? She was embarrassed. In any event, there'd been no need for it, as it hadn't been anywhere near as hard as she'd expected – in fact, she'd enjoyed herself very much. She wanted to apologise but he didn't seem at all offended.

'It's all right. You seem to have relaxed a bit now,' he said imperturbably, and flashed her a quick grin.

They got back and he saw her to the door.

'Well, goodnight,' he said. 'I'll call you soon, and we can talk about that flight I promised you.'

'I'll look forward to it.'

He nodded, hesitating for a second, then turned away and got back into the Morris. He hadn't even tried to kiss her, and she was disconcerted to feel slightly disappointed at the fact. But then she reminded herself that she didn't want anything like that; it had been a friendly outing, nothing more, and she hadn't nearly finished grieving Jim.

At that she was almost sure she heard the old Harriet snort in her ear and ask sarcastically how much more grief she expected to wring out of it.

'Be quiet,' she told herself severely, and went in.

*

It was two weeks before they saw Fernand Quinault again, and during those two weeks Cécilia was unusually agitated and impatient.

'Isn't Maman going away soon?' she would ask Harriet every day, and every day Harriet would shake her head and say, 'Not until the end of the month.'

At last, Mrs Brouillard prepared to depart for a visit of a few days to some friends in London, and Cécilia brightened.

'You must call him,' she said to Harriet. 'Invite him here. But don't tell Maman.'

'Why don't you do it?' asked Harriet. 'He's *your* friend, after all.'

Cécilia shrank back.

'I couldn't,' she replied. 'What would I say?'

'Why, that you'd like to see him,' said Harriet, laughing.

'But what if he says no?'

'I don't think he will. Is he a very old friend of yours?'

'Not exactly. He was a friend of my father's, and I met him once or twice when I was living in Nice. But we had some friends in common during the war, and perhaps he can give me news of them.'

She wouldn't make the telephone call, so in the end Harriet did it. She had no objection really, since it seemed that Cécilia was starting to emerge from her shell and show an interest in something at last. She'd even begun to ask Rex occasionally about his music, and about what he'd been studying each day. It wasn't much, but at least it was a start. Harriet saw Rex's increasingly frequent smiles and approved it all. And it wasn't only the Brouillards who seemed to be improving. Harriet had thought often of her evening out with Alec, and how enjoyable it had been. He was good company, easy to get along with, and she found him more attractive than she liked to admit, but her thoughts on the subject were conflicted. Ought she to be thinking of one man when she was still mourning another? Was it disloyal of her to move on so soon? It wasn't something she could think about rationally just yet, so she put the question out of her head for another day.

At last Rose departed for London, and Fernand Quinault came to Chaffingham. Harriet answered the door. There he stood, a tall, stooped figure with a shock of wild, salt-and-pepper hair. Harriet noticed he had dressed more smartly this time, and had made some attempt to tame the hair.

'Come in,' she said. 'Cécilia will see you soon. Her doctor's just come.'

'She's not ill?' he asked in concern.

'Oh no, it's just a routine visit. I think he mainly comes to tell her off for not doing her exercises.'

'Can she walk at all?'

'Not well. She can move herself about on crutches when she tries, but she prefers to stay in the chair.'

She led him into the small sitting room, which was more comfortable and less formal than the grand drawing room.

'I gather you're an old friend of Jean-Jacques Brouillard's,' she said, once they had sat down and she had told Estelle to bring tea.

'Yes,' he replied, in that curious French-American accent of his. 'He was a kind of mentor of mine years ago. He helped me get the job as conductor of the Paris-Montparnasse Symphony Orchestra.'

'You're a conductor too?'

'I was, but not for long. The war started and I lost my job. Then the Nazis began deporting Jews, and I didn't like the idea of that, as you can imagine, so I escaped to Nice and stayed there for a while. That's where I met Cécilia. There were a bunch of us, mostly exiles from Paris – artists, musicians, writers, that kind of thing. A lot of us were Jewish and we couldn't get work, so we hung around in the South of France waiting for a ticket out of there.'

'So you went to America?'

'Eventually, and only by the skin of my teeth. I went back to Paris to try and get my father to leave,' he said, in answer to Harriet's questioning look. 'He wouldn't come with me, so in the end I had to leave without him – just in time, because that's when the Germans really started to round people up.'

'Was your father one of them?' asked Harriet, although she could see the answer in his face.

'Yes. He was sent to Auschwitz, and didn't come back.'

'I'm sorry.'

He shrugged ruefully. 'He was a stubborn old man, but I was very fond of him.'

It was almost an exact echo of what Harriet herself had said to Alec about her own father. So many pointless deaths, so much unhappiness, and for what?

There were voices in the hall.

'Ah, I think the doctor has finished,' said Harriet. She stood up and went out.

The doctor had come from Cambridge. He was an expert in his field, and he knew it. He bristled with his own importance, although his manner wasn't unkind.

'Miss Conway, you must make sure my patient does her exercises,' he said. 'She's been neglecting them for too long. There's a very good chance of progress if she does what she's told, but I'm afraid she's a stubborn one.'

Harriet glanced at Cécilia, who was looking resigned, as though she had just endured a telling-off.

'Don't worry, I'll keep reminding her,' she said. She went to let the doctor out. He bade her a brisk farewell, then added quietly, 'She seems a little better. Has she been getting out in the fresh air?'

'Yes,' said Harriet. 'I made her do it.'

'Good girl,' he said approvingly. 'Keep at it. It can only help. I've recommended physiotherapy, too. See if you can persuade her into it.'

He went off, and Harriet returned to find that Cécilia had already joined Quinault in the sitting room, and they were exchanging polite nothings in the slightly awkward way of people who haven't seen one another for a long time.

'Do we have any of Estelle's shortbread left?' asked Cécilia, glancing up as Harriet entered. 'Didn't she make some yesterday?'

'I'll ask her,' said Harriet.

She went out in search of the old housekeeper, who informed her that Sébastien had been helping himself and there was none left.

'Who's that man?' came a voice as Harriet came out of the kitchen. She turned and saw Rex standing at the bottom of the stairs.

'His name is Fernand Quinault. He's an old friend of your mother's.'

'Is it the same man who came before? The day we went out with Mr McLeod?'

'Yes, he came a few weeks ago.'

His brows drew into a worried frown. 'Grand-mère didn't want him here.'

'Well Grand-mère isn't here, and doesn't have to speak to him if she doesn't want to,' said Harriet.

Rex cogitated over her words, and at last seemed to find them acceptable.

'I left my geography book in the sitting room. May I go in and fetch it?'

'Yes, but be quick,' said Harriet.

She went in with him, in case explanations were needed. Rex pounced on his exercise book, glanced curiously at the visitor, and was about to leave the room when Quinault said:

'Well, well, who is this?'

Rex glanced at his mother, who nodded at him encouragingly. 'I'm Rex.'

'This is my son,' said Cécilia. 'Rex, this is Monsieur Quinault. You must speak to him in French.'

'*Bonjour*, Monsieur Quinault,' said Rex obediently.

Fernand Quinault looked at Rex with interest.

'Well!' he replied. 'It's clear you're related. You look just like your mother.'

Rex looked as if he didn't know whether to say thank you or not.

'Am I needed?' asked Harriet.

'Stay and have some tea if you like,' said Cécilia. 'Estelle always makes too much, and it'll get cold before we can drink it all.' Her words were accompanied by a glance which indicated that she wanted moral support. Harriet stayed.

'And do you play violin like Maman?' asked Quinault to Rex. Rex shook his head shyly.

'I play the piano a little, and Grand-mère wants me to play the clarinet.'

'But you don't want to?'

'I shouldn't mind,' said Rex hesitantly. 'But I think there are other instruments I'd rather play.'

'Not the violin?'

'Perhaps. But I think I'd rather play guitar.'

'The guitar is a grand instrument,' agreed Quinault solemnly. 'Why don't you learn that, then? Is there a guitar in the house? You could try it.'

'You have one, don't you?' said Harriet to Cécilia. 'I'm sure I've seen it on top of your bookshelves.'

Cécilia shook her head. 'No!' she said quickly. 'It can't be played. It's old, and broken. The strings have all snapped, and it's not worth fixing.' She sounded almost agitated, and must have realised it, because she went on more calmly: 'If you'd like a guitar we shall certainly look into it, Rex.'

'Will you play the piano for me?' said Quinault to Rex. 'I'd like to hear you.'

His manner was gentle and friendly. Rex, who was not used to being asked to play for any reason other than to be criticised, looked at his mother again.

'Shall I?' he asked.

'Yes, why not?' she replied. 'Just for fun. Let's show Monsieur Quinault how you do at the grand piano.'

They went into the drawing room and Fernand Quinault sat next to Rex on the piano stool.

'Show me what you can do,' he said.

Rex dutifully pulled out a very serious piece of music he had been practising and began, but almost immediately Quinault shook his head and tutted.

'Oh, but this is dull – music for old men, not young children. Don't you have anything fun to play?'

'N-no,' stammered Rex.

'Then I'll teach you something. We'll play something together. Look, you shall play this part with your right hand.' He demonstrated an easy pattern of notes. 'Now you try.'

Rex did as he was told.

'Excellent! Now you keep playing that, and I will play the left hand. Now we try together. That's right!'

Within a very few minutes they were playing the tune together more or less competently.

'Bravo!' said Quinault. 'Now, you hear how easy the left-hand part is. Do you think you could manage that as well? Here. It takes a little stretch of the hand. Can you manage an octave?'

'Not yet,' said Rex.

'Then we'll just play the lower note until your fingers grow long enough. Now try it.'

Rex did as he was told and very soon could play the short tune by himself. It was a cheerful, modern song, rather than the serious piano exercises he was accustomed to playing.

'*Formidable!*' exclaimed Quinault, after Rex had run through it once without a mistake. 'You are as talented as your mother.'

Rex flushed and was shy, and Cécilia laughed at him. It looked as though the ice had successfully been broken between Cécilia and Quinault, so Harriet said, 'You'd better go and start on your geography exercise, Rex, or Mr Caldicott will tell you off tomorrow.'

'Yes, you'd better go,' agreed Cécilia. Harriet followed Rex out of the room, judging that it was safe to leave Cécilia to it. As she went out she heard the two of them conversing in rapid French.

Fernand Quinault stayed for two hours, and Harriet hoped he was doing Cécilia good. He seemed to have taken over the piano, because she heard snatches of music of various types – classical, jazz and something she was sure must be one of his film scores – drifting from the drawing room. At least, Harriet assumed it was Quinault who was playing; the style was bold and cheerful, quite unlike Cécilia's soft, dreamlike manner of playing. Towards dinner-time she heard the sound of voices in the hall as Quinault prepared to leave, and came out.

'I tried to persuade him to stay for dinner, but he won't,' Cécilia said. She looked almost animated for once.

'A prior engagement, I'm afraid,' he replied easily. Harriet thought it was more likely that he didn't want to sneak around behind Mrs. Brouillard's back, knowing Rose's feelings for him, and she couldn't blame him. 'Anyway, it was very nice to see you,' he said, turning to Cécilia.

'Likewise. Will you come again?'

'Of course! I want to hear what you've been writing lately.'

'I haven't written anything in years,' said Cécilia, looking startled.

'Haven't you? But this is a terrible pity. You mustn't let this,' he gestured at the wheelchair, 'stand in your way. Next time I come we'll play together.'

Cécilia flushed.

'Oh, I don't know – I don't really play much these days either.'

'Yes you do,' said Harriet. 'I've heard you. There's that sad tune you play all the time.'

'That's nothing,' replied Cécilia. 'It's not finished.'

'Then you must finish it,' said Quinault. 'Or if you're having trouble with it, we can finish it together if you like. Sometimes another point of view can help the ideas flow.'

Cécilia looked taken aback, but didn't respond, and Harriet went to show Quinault out.

'I'll call you the next time Mrs Brouillard goes away,' Harriet said.

'Good. I'd like to come again.'

'I think you did Cécilia good. It's a shame you have to wait until her mother is out of the way. Why is she so angry with you, by the way?'

'It's nothing,' he replied. 'We had a little disagreement, that's all, but I've come to the conclusion it's probably best to let things lie.'

Chapter Twenty-One

Some of Fernand Quinault's enthusiasm seemed to have rubbed off on Cécilia. She didn't exactly wake up a new woman, but after one or two more visits, which they were careful not to mention to Rose, Harriet noticed that Cécilia had begun to take far more interest in what was going on around her, especially if it related to music. She'd dug out some of her old compositions and had begun crossing bits out and adding others, shaking her head as she did so.

'Listen to this,' she said to Harriet one day, and played a little snatch of music on the piano.

'What is it?' said Harriet.

'It's the piece I wrote for the Prix de Rome when I was eighteen.'

'You wrote that when you were eighteen? Goodness! It's quite wonderful.'

Cécilia grimaced humorously. 'Wonderful, do you call it? I was just thinking how dreadful it was. I'd never write anything like that these days.'

'Have you been writing, then? How marvellous!'

Cécilia flushed. 'Well, I haven't written anything as such, but I've had one or two little themes running around in my head the last week, and I was thinking of putting them down.'

'Don't think – do it!' said Harriet firmly.

'It's just that it's been such a long time. There are people now who have far more talent than I ever did, and certainly more drive to succeed. What can I offer?'

'What does it matter? You oughtn't to compare yourself to other people. Your music is yours; write it for yourself, and don't worry about anything else.'

'That's what Fernand said.'

'And he's right, too.'

Cécilia toyed with a pencil that was lying on top of the piano. 'He suggested I write some film music,' she said hesitantly.

'Did he? What did you say?'

'That I wasn't sure. Then he said if I was worried about it, then perhaps we could try writing something together.'

'He seems very kind.'

'He is.'

Harriet glanced at her sideways. 'And he doesn't pity you, I notice,' she ventured tentatively.

'No, he doesn't, does he?' said Cécilia, as if struck by this new idea. 'Most people see the wheelchair and start talking in hushed tones, but he hardly seems to notice it.'

'If you ask me, he's good for you. You've been brooding and feeling sorry for yourself for far too long now.'

'You said you weren't usually blunt, and yet here you are telling me off again.'

Harriet laughed. 'I'm sorry. It's just that I'm happy to see you've started taking an interest in things.'

She didn't mention Rex, but she'd been pleased to see that he and Cécilia were spending more time together lately, and that he was looking much happier for it. The attention he was getting from his mother, combined with his outings with Alec and the dog, had made him blossom. He'd started running noisily around the house, which didn't endear him to Rose. She scolded him constantly, but whereas before he would have slunk off to his room afterwards to cry, now he shook it off quickly and was soon cheerful again. Harriet saw he was turning into something much more like a normal boy, and was happy for him. Perhaps time and some new interests in life were all the family needed to emerge from their self-absorbed misery and attain some kind of peace. As the thought ran through her head, she found her mind unaccountably wandering towards Alec McLeod, and it brought her up short. It had never occurred to her, but perhaps she had more in common with the Brouillards than she realised.

*

The weather was dismal throughout February; winter came late with a series of violent storms, one after the other, followed by several days of snow which kept everyone indoors. At last, towards the end of the month, the snow finally thawed and the sun came out, warming the ground and the air. There were signs of an imminent spring all around: despite the snow, the daffodils had begun to flower and some early blossom was beginning to show on the trees. Harriet had felt cooped up in the house for too long, so she was more than ready to take a trip out when Alec called to suggest it. One afternoon he picked her up from Chaffingham in the Morris Twelve. Patch leapt out of the car as soon as Alec opened the door for her, and danced around her enthusiastically.

'Goodness, I do believe he's grown in the last couple of weeks,' she said.

'He never stops eating,' replied Alec. 'Get down, Patch, there's a good fellow.'

Patch dropped away and sat.

'You've trained him!' said Harriet in surprise.

'Not quite, but he knows down, and sit, and heel – sometimes. As for the rest, we've some way to go yet.'

Indeed, Patch had already tired of being good, and was racing up and down the drive. Alec managed to bring him to heel, and Harriet sat in the front while Patch sat in the back, gazing out of the window, his tongue out.

'Where are we going?' asked Harriet.

'I'm going to keep my promise. I said I'd take you up in the plane, remember?'

'Today?' Harriet's heart gave a thump, but she ignored it.

'Why not? The conditions are splendid. Best get out while the weather's good enough. Ah, here we are.'

He parked the car and they got out. The grass was damp underfoot as they walked across to the hangar where the Tiger Moth was kept.

'I'm glad the weather's cleared up,' said Alec. 'I hate sitting about on the ground when I could be flying.' He stopped and regarded her woollen coat analytically. 'That get-up of yours is no good. You'll need a flying jacket.'

'I haven't got a flying jacket. What's wrong with this?'

He gave a laugh. 'You'll freeze to death in half a minute.'

He led her into his office, and she looked about her. The place was a mess: boxes stood everywhere, while bits of machinery and cans of oil cluttered every available surface. A pile of letters on a desk had toppled over, and several had spilled onto the floor.

'You ought to tidy up,' she observed.

'I haven't had time yet.'

Harriet went across to the stack of letters and began sorting them into piles. Some of them were unopened bills, she noticed.

'You need someone to manage the office for you,' she said.

'I know. The old chap I inherited isn't much good. Are those bills? Pass them over, will you?' He flicked through them and opened one or two. 'These need paying,' he said, tucking them into his inside pocket. The rest he put down absently and appeared to forget about them. Harriet shook her head. A heap of what looked like old clothes had been thrown onto the floor in one corner, and he was now burrowing in among it.

'Here.' He brought out a leather sheepskin jacket that was clearly made for a man.

'I can't wear that,' she said, eyeing it askance. 'It won't fit.'

'Well, it's all we've got. You'll need one of these too.'

He unhooked a leather flying helmet from where it hung on the back of a chair and handed it to her. She put on the jacket, which was far too big, and hung the helmet over her arm, and they went out and across the grass to the hangar.

'I refuelled her this morning,' he said, as he unfastened the padlock. Inside the barn stood the Tiger Moth, smelling faintly of paint and oil. 'Help me bring it out, will you? It's quite light,' he added as he saw her doubtful face.

He was right: the Tiger Moth lifted easily by the tail, and they brought it out and wheeled it across to the landing strip.

'Now, you'd better get that helmet on,' he said, putting his own on as he spoke.

Gingerly she placed the helmet on her head. It felt cold and strange.

'I look ridiculous,' she said.

'No you don't, you look beautiful.'

He said it quite unselfconsciously, and she blinked. He'd already turned away and was fiddling with a rudder cable. Patch began dancing around the wheels of the plane.

'I forgot about you,' Alec told him. 'You can't come.'

He took the dog back to the office and tied him up.

'Will he be all right?' asked Harriet, as he returned.

'I left him some water and a bone to play with, and we won't be gone long in any case. He'll be fine.'

He examined the rudder cable again, then gave the body of the plane an affectionate slap, indicating to Harriet that she should get in first.

'You go in the front,' he said.

'I can't fly this thing!' she exclaimed in alarm.

He laughed.

'Don't worry, I'll be controlling it from the rear cockpit. All you need to do is enjoy the view.' She must have looked hesitant, because he looked at her searchingly and said, 'You don't have to if you don't want to.'

She set her jaw and took a deep breath. It would be fun, she told herself. 'I want to.'

'Good. I'm glad.'

He handed her up onto the wing and she climbed into the cockpit and sat down. In front of her were several mysterious-looking dials, and above that at head level was some leather padding, presumably to help in case of a crash landing. She hoped it wouldn't come to that, and took deep breaths to calm herself. It was just a short flight, and everything would be fine.

'All set?' he asked. She nodded, and he flipped the ignition switch then swung himself down and set the propeller spinning. The engine started up, first a chug, then a buzz, then a roar. Alec hopped back nimbly onto the wing and jumped into the rear cockpit. They waited for a minute or two, until the engine warmed up, then the plane taxied slowly towards the overgrown runway. It picked up speed, and Harriet gritted her teeth as she felt every bump and jolt. She closed her eyes, and for one awful moment nearly lost her nerve and thought she would have to wave her hand to make him stop. Then the bumping ceased and she felt an odd sinking feeling. She opened her eyes and found they'd left the ground and were rising lightly into the air. The earth fell away and the plane banked to the left and she gasped, half in fear and half in exhilaration, as she saw the Hertfordshire countryside laid out below her at an angle, golden and green and brown in the low winter sunshine.

He turned the plane and righted it, then headed towards the north-east, away from the sun. It was cold up here, the wind raw against her cheeks, and Harriet was glad of the flying jacket and the helmet. Her gloves were too thin to provide much warmth and her hands tingled with the cold, but she hardly noticed it. The elation had begun to drive out the fear, and she took a deep breath, relishing the almost painful sharpness of the air in her mouth and nostrils.

Now at last she understood what Jim had loved about flying: the freedom, the sheer joy of defying gravity, the escape from the tedium of everyday life. He'd never once taken her up in his plane, and at that moment she felt almost angry with him: he'd kept all this to himself, not wanting to share it even with her. But there'd been no need for him to guard it so jealously. She would never have spoiled it for him had she known what it felt like. Still, it came as a jolt to realise that had he lived she would always have come second to his real passion.

Soon the fields and trees gave way to houses and buildings and a city which Harriet quickly recognised as Cambridge. Alec didn't fly over it, but turned in a large arc back towards the south, then gradually veered westwards towards the sinking sun. They were approaching another town; as far as Harriet could tell it must be Royston. Then she saw Chaffingham below her, and the farm, and peered out to see if she could see Rex or anybody else she knew. But the plane passed overhead before she could spot anyone. It was losing height now, and she felt her fear return momentarily, but swallowed it down determinedly. The plane described one final arc and touched down on the landing strip with one, two, three bounces, then pulled up to a stop. Alec switched off the engines, and they tailed off with a drone and a whine into silence. Harriet sat, collecting her thoughts, as Alec hopped out and ran to fetch the chocks to put under the wheels.

'Everything okay?' he asked, unfastening his helmet and pulling it off as he came back. 'Here.'

He leapt up onto the wing to help her out. She stood up unsteadily and fumbled at the buckle of her own helmet. It was a little too tight, and he quickly took off his gloves to help her with it.

'There!' he said, as the stubborn buckle at last came free.

Harriet shook the cold breeze into her hair, laughing. He stepped down and she took his hand to jump down lightly to the ground. She landed closer to him than she'd intended, bumping against him and losing her balance. He took her arms to steady her.

'I didn't do any aerobatics,' he said, without moving away.

'I almost wish you had, it was tremendous!'

She was flushed and breathless. His hands were still resting lightly on her arms, and she felt a tingling warmth spread through her sleeves and up to her shoulders and neck. She froze. They stared at one another for a long moment, then he said, 'Damn,' and kissed her, right there next to the plane, with the heat of its cooling engine radiating out and the smell of oil all around them. It was so long since she'd been kissed, and she'd thought it would be awkward, but instead it all came back to her quite easily, feeling perfectly natural and wonderful. All practical considerations were driven out of her head momentarily, and she closed her eyes and enjoyed the feeling of his lips against hers, filling her full of warmth after so many months of emptiness.

'Damn,' he said again after a minute. 'I'm sorry, I didn't mean to—'

'That's quite all right.' She felt dazed, and didn't know what to say; how funny that they should fall back on polite British nothings at such a moment. And now that she'd had a second to get her breath back the reality of the situation was beginning to wash over her. They weren't in the air any more, they were back in the prison of the here and now, and she'd just kissed another man without sparing even a thought for Jim. How could she have done it? It was too much, too soon.

'I think perhaps we'd better go home,' she said, turning away. He saw her sudden change in mood.

'I'm sorry,' he said again. 'It's just you were standing there, and—'

'Yes, I—'

'And then—'

They were uncomfortable now, looking away from each other. Perhaps polite British nothings were useful, after all. They put the plane away, exchanging remarks as though nothing had happened, and he locked it up while Harriet went to see to Patch and change back into her woollen coat. They drove back in silence, and Harriet thought determinedly of Jim, and how much she'd loved him, and how she'd kept his memory alive for nearly two years now. But she couldn't stop uncomfortable questions from intruding. How would Jim have acted if the situation were reversed? Would he still be mourning her after so long? However much she wanted to believe he would, her knowledge of him told her that he would have got over it a lot sooner than she had. He'd lived for danger and the moment, and while she was sure he would have been saddened at her death, she had to admit to herself that he would almost certainly have found someone else by now. Why, then, had she kept the flame burning all this time? The little voice of logic inside her kept hinting insistently that it had very little to do with Jim himself, and that the problem lay with her. And it didn't take a genius to work out what that problem was: by clinging to the memory of one already lost, she'd run no risk of losing another. It was a depressing conclusion; she wanted to move on but she didn't know how to get over the fear. A little more time was all she needed, she told herself.

Once back at Chaffingham Alec brought the car to a stop and went round to open the door for her. She got out and they stood together. She couldn't avoid the subject now.

'Thank you,' she said. 'The flight was wonderful.'

'But not the rest?'

'Yes… no. I…'

She couldn't think how to express herself and shook her head at him in mute appeal. He came to her rescue.

'I understand. I won't push you.'

'Thank you. It's not that I don't like you, I do, but—'

'I know. It's early days.'

'Yes.'

'Well, just so you know, I like you too. Quite a lot, in fact. I can wait until you're sure.'

'But what if I'm never sure?'

He smiled.

'We'll cross that bridge when we come to it.'

Chapter Twenty-Two

Paris, 1943

In 1943 the tide of war began to turn. In February news filtered through that the Germans had surrendered at Stalingrad, and this was the first indication that all might not be well with the Axis. In September, the Allies invaded Italy and an armistice was signed. Maggie heard all this, listening to the BBC in secret, and began to think that perhaps there was a chance of victory after all, after so many hard months of desperation and despair.

It was only a spark of hope, however; here in Paris things hadn't got any better, and every day they heard of arrests, and disappearances, deportations, and killings. The Germans had swept through the rest of France the previous November, and the whole country was now occupied. Young Frenchmen were being co-opted as compulsory workers for the Reich, and the Vichy government had created the Milice française, a brutal and merciless paramilitary organisation which tortured and executed people suspected of being Resistance members. In early April the police came and took Marcel away, and three weeks later, to Maggie's devastation, they received word that he had died at the Pithiviers internment camp. Albertine, his wife, was Catholic, and so escaped the roundup, but on news of Marcel's death she was immediately plunged into a deep depression. She shut herself up in her room, and Maggie, also grief-stricken, had great trouble in persuading her to come out for meals.

Paris was becoming a more dangerous place by the day, and anyone with even the slightest connection to the Resistance was forced to take elaborate steps to make sure they weren't caught. Spies were everywhere – not just Germans, but ordinary Parisians, who were sick and tired of their daily lives being even more disrupted than they already had been by the activities of their fellow Frenchmen. Every time the Resistance blew up a railway line, or sabotaged an industrial plant, or killed a German or French official, the Nazis would retaliate ten- or even fifty-fold, executing prisoners and other hostages by the dozen. Innocent people were being killed, and many Parisians believed it was far better to keep their heads down and live with the Occupation rather than risk more people being hurt or killed in the name of freedom. Some were even prepared to betray their countrymen to the enemy in exchange for rewards, or even just the hope of a quiet life.

Maggie, too, had had a near escape. One day in May several teachers at her school, including her, were arrested in a roundup, as the authorities had received reports of illicit activities at the school. They were all taken to Gestapo headquarters and interrogated. Fortunately, Maggie had no incriminating evidence on her at the time, and the interrogators couldn't find any proof that she'd been involved in anything untoward, since she hadn't organised any performances of banned music for a while now, and she carried out most of her Resistance activities a long way from the school.

Still, they were reluctant to let her go until she mentioned her mother's name. Mrs Brouillard was summoned, and within an hour or two had secured her daughter's release. Maggie hated the fact that she had to rely on her mother and on her father's name, but she knew she had no choice.

One good thing came of the whole episode, however, as it led to a thawing of relations within the family. Rose would never admit she had been wrong, and nor would Maggie, but by an unspoken agreement they chose to ignore their differences, and after a little negotiation, Maggie and Cécilia began to visit the apartment in Avenue Victor Hugo, although they both refused Rose's invitation to move back in with her and Sébastien. Cécilia, in particular, couldn't forget how her mother had tried to put an end to her pregnancy, and although Rose showed no signs of wishing Rex harm now that he was a reality – and indeed expressed a certain distant interest in him – the trust had been irrevocably damaged between them.

And there was another good reason not to move back to Avenue Victor Hugo: Mrs Brouillard was still holding her *salons*, and the apartment was frequented far too often by people who couldn't be trusted. Rose knew the dangers of being pegged as an outright collaborator, and was careful to tread a fine line, inviting not just Germans but also French people who were known to oppose the Occupation to the house. Once in a while she even passed on little titbits of information to Maggie, perhaps as a way of ingratiating herself with her daughter, but still, it was too dangerous for Maggie and Cécilia to return, given their activities.

Cécilia had remembered her promise to Emil, and had committed herself to continuing to resist here in Paris. She'd found that Rex's battered old pram was useful for carrying goods and messages that she wanted to keep out of sight, and she found herself in great demand as a courier. She wasn't doing anything much – she was nothing like as courageous as some of the people she knew – but she got some satisfaction out of feeling she was helping the cause, and hoped that Emil would have approved it if he'd known about it – if indeed he were still alive. Whenever anybody asked, she told them she was a widow, because she felt it was true enough, and did her best not to brood over what might have been, or nurse her heartbreak; after all, people lost their loved ones every day and carried on bravely. She owed it to Emil to continue his work as best she could. Maggie had never guessed the truth, and there was no reason she should ever know of her sister's guilt, although the fact of what she'd done and the terrible lies she'd told gnawed away at Cécilia day by day. She'd turned into something she despised: a cheat and a liar, who had betrayed the very person to whom she owed the most. How could she ever forgive herself? Right now she couldn't; all she could do was hope that Maggie would never discover how she'd been deceived, and then perhaps in time the guilt would gradually fade away and be forgotten.

*

But all Cécilia's carefully constructed walls of secrecy and deception were bound to crumble sooner or later, and crumble they did, although she was out of the apartment when it happened. It was a Saturday afternoon in November, and the weather was murky and cloudy and cold. Maggie had been meeting some people in a distant part of the city, and what she found out made her heart leap. She couldn't wait to get home, and she endured the packed metro carriage in a state of barely concealed impatience, then almost ran all the way back to the apartment. She hurried up to the third floor and burst in. Cécilia was not there – only Albertine, who was sitting on the sofa in her dressing-gown, smoking glumly. The dishes had been left unwashed, and the floor was scattered with cushions and books and cigarette ends.

'Where's Cécilia?' asked Maggie, then, without waiting for a reply: 'Oh, Albertine! Emil's back! He's here! François told me.'

She threw herself onto the sofa and clasped Albertine's hand.

'Who?' said Albertine.

'Emil. You remember? I told you all about him. He was arrested in Nice and I thought he was dead, but he's not. He escaped and went to London, and they've sent him back with SOE. He's here in Paris right now! General de Gaulle sent him personally. There's to be a meeting this afternoon about something awfully important. I'm not strictly invited but I'm going anyway. They can't keep me away. Oh, Albertine! I can hardly believe it!'

'Oh *ma petite*, this is wonderful news!' said Albertine, doing her best to seem pleased, although she'd been very low ever since Marcel had died.

'It is!' Maggie was surprised to feel tears in her eyes, and put a hand breathlessly to her forehead. 'Goodness, I didn't think I'd feel so overcome. What an idiot I am! But it's been so long, and I was so sure he was dead. Oh, Albertine!' She looked around. 'But where's Cécilia? Is she out?'

'I think she's gone to your mother's.'

Maggie jumped up and began hunting about for some paper.

'Well, I can't wait for her. I'll write a note. I'll bring him back later if I can. She'll be so relieved to see him. Will you be here? I'd like you to meet him.'

Albertine shook her head.

'No, I'm going to see my sister-in-law. But make sure you tell me all about it.'

'Don't worry, I shall!'

Maggie scribbled a note on the back of an old newspaper, and hurried out.

*

The meeting was in a back room at Club Madagascar. The Germans didn't frequent this bar, and it was quiet and dimly lit, with only a few patrons. A man was pushing a broom around in a desultory fashion. He recognised Maggie when she walked in, and nodded to a door at the back of the room. She went through it into a corridor which led to the kitchen and the backstage quarters.

'Maggie! What are you doing here?' asked a young man who was standing guard in the corridor. 'You'd better not have been followed.'

'Of course I wasn't. How stupid do you think I am?'

'This is important. They won't let you in.'

'I'm not interested in what they're saying,' said Maggie. 'Has it started yet?'

'No. He's not here yet.'

Maggie waited in agitated impatience for what seemed like an hour, but couldn't have been more than ten minutes. She was just wishing that she'd thought to look in the mirror and attend to her hair before she came out, when at last she heard the sound of footsteps and voices coming through the kitchen. They must have sneaked in through the back door. Then she saw him. He was with two other men and a woman, and they were talking in low voices. He was thinner than when she'd last seen him, and his face was pale and drawn. She even thought she could see a touch of grey in his hair. But it didn't matter – he was her Emil, unchanged in all the essentials, and back at last from the dead. Her heart thumped hard, and she swallowed, trying to subdue the agitation within her.

Just then he looked up and saw her, and his eyes brightened in surprise and recognition. A smile spread across his face.

'Maggie!' he said, and it was his old voice, warm and welcoming.

She'd meant to be dignified, but somehow she couldn't. She ran to him and threw herself into his arms, and he laughed.

'What a welcome!' he said.

Her eyes were shining. 'I thought you were dead!' was all she could say.

'Well, as you can see, I'm not. And how are you? Are you well?'

'Quite well. When can we talk?'

'After the meeting.' He glanced around. 'This isn't really the place.'

'I'm so pleased you're back,' she said. He'd let her go but her hands were still clutching at the damp wool of his coat sleeves.

'Stay here,' he replied. 'Or can she come in?' He looked around. One of the men he'd arrived with shook his head quickly.

'Better not,' he said briefly.

'I'll tell you all about it afterwards,' Emil promised. He took her by the shoulders and kissed her on the forehead, then disappeared into another room.

They couldn't take long – it was dangerous to linger in groups these days – and after an hour the meeting broke up. Maggie had been sitting on the floor of the corridor, and she jumped up as they all came out. Emil was talking to two of the leaders of her own network, and she waited impatiently until they'd finished.

'Where are you staying?' she asked, when at last he turned his attention to her. 'You'll come back and have dinner, won't you?'

'To your mother's?' he said, amused.

'Of course not! I have an apartment. There's some wine I was saving for a special occasion, but if this isn't a special occasion then I don't know what is. Come back and tell me all about what you've been doing. We heard you'd got out of Le Vernet, but we've been frantic with worry, wondering what had become of you. Come to dinner. It's only a couple of streets away, and it should be safe enough as long as nobody knows you're here.'

He agreed, and they went out into the street. Darkness hadn't quite fallen, and she turned to take a good look at him. There was a distance to him that disconcerted her, although on reflection she supposed it was only to be expected after two years apart. But he hadn't even kissed her, apart from that one peck on the forehead. She'd missed being in his arms so much, but here they were walking along the darkening street as though they were merely old acquaintances, not the lovers they'd once been. They'd been practically engaged – or at least had talked of marriage as if it were only a matter of time. He knew her feelings – she was hardly the sort to hide them – and she was sure he'd reciprocated. Maggie fought down the hurt that was trying to rise in her, and reminded herself that there were other things to think about now. He'd been through a lot, and she couldn't expect things to return to normal immediately.

'Tell me everything about what you've been doing,' she said. 'We heard from Anatoli Ivanovitch that you'd been sent to Castres but escaped. Where did you go after that? He said you were heading for Marseille.'

'I started that way, but there were patrols on the roads and it was too dangerous, so in the end I doubled back and went inland. I'd somehow picked up a dose of pneumonia, so I had to take shelter with some people at a farmhouse near Rodez. It turned out I'd trusted the wrong people, though, and they turned me in. After that I was sent to Lyon for interrogation.'

She looked up at him quickly. She'd heard about what went on at the Gestapo headquarters in Lyon.

'Did they hurt you?'

'A bit.' His lip curled in dry amusement. 'Luckily I managed to escape before they decided to do away with me altogether.'

She laughed.

'Escape! Again! You have more lives than a cat. How on earth did you manage that?'

'As luck would have it, there was a German fellow I knew in Paris before the war working in the building. I'd given him some legal advice at no charge a few years ago, and he remembered me and turned a blind eye for old times' sake. Good old Bruno – there's some humanity left in the world, at least. I wasn't in the best shape, but somehow I managed to get across country to Grenoble and hooked up with the Maquis there. They looked after me until I was well, then rather than spend the next few months or years skulking about secretly in my own country I decided to try and get to London. I thought they might have a use for me there.

'As it happened they did. Special Operations Executive got hold of me and sent me back in to support the Resistance. One of the biggest escape networks has gone down and they need me to set up another one. I'm to establish contact with some of the other underground groups and we'll see if we can't get something going through the South and into Spain. That's what we were discussing in there. There's a lot of stuff happening at the moment. There are rumblings of an Allied invasion soon, and they're making a big push to unite all the Resistance movements. I don't know exactly what they're planning, but without a trained army of sorts on the ground here in France, they'll have trouble making headway. They sent me here because I know a lot of people in the Paris networks. I'd rather be fighting, but this will do for the present.'

'If anyone can set up a new escape network you can,' replied Maggie.

She was hanging onto his arm, relieved that he was starting to seem something like his old self. They reached her apartment building, and she said:

'Here we are. I wonder if Cécilia's back. She'll be so surprised to see you. She's had to listen to me maundering about you for months now.'

He stopped dead.

'Cécilia? Isn't she in Nice?'

'No, she gave up her studies last year and came back to Paris.'

'But why?'

'Never mind why, you'll see.'

He seemed hesitant, but at last followed her into the building and up to the third floor. Maggie opened the door and the first thing they saw was Cécilia, who had evidently just got back, because she was still wearing her coat. She was reading Maggie's note, pale in the face. She looked up as they entered.

'Look who's here!' said Maggie gaily.

Cécilia stared at Emil and he stared back. For a few moments, nobody spoke. Rex was crawling about on the floor, picking up cigarette ends and trying to put them in his mouth.

'Oh, no you don't!' said Maggie, sweeping him up into her arms. '*Tante* Maggie says no! As you can see, Emil, we have a new member of the family, and he's a darling, but very mischievous.'

She handed the baby to Cécilia and began clearing up the mess from the floor. Cécilia hugged Rex to her and removed a stray cigarette end from his hand. She still hadn't said anything. Emil watched them both.

'How old is he?' he asked after a long minute.

'Just over a year. Fourteen months,' said Cécilia.

She waited as he calculated in his head. He seemed lost for words. At last, he said, 'I thought you were still in Nice.'

'No. I came home. You know…' She indicated Rex.

His face twisted in a rueful grimace. 'No wonder you never replied to my letters.'

He went across to her and took the baby, who looked so much like him there couldn't be any doubt. Cécilia had often been terrified that Maggie would notice the resemblance, which seemed obvious to her, but she never had. Emil looked into his son's face for the first time.

'What's his name?' he asked.

'Rex.'

'Is he healthy? And you? Are you well?'

'Yes. He's quite well, and so am I.'

He absorbed the new discovery in silence. Something in the atmosphere must have alerted Maggie, because she looked up suddenly from the floor, her hand suspended in mid-air, clutching a piece of crumpled paper. She saw her sister and Emil, standing close together, occupied with Rex, the three of them forming a self-contained unit and looking for all the world as though they belonged together, and at that moment she might as well not have been in the room for all the attention they were paying her. She took in a breath. Had Emil's actions not been enough to give the game away, the expression on Cécilia's face as she watched Emil and the baby would have said it all. It was as though a curtain had been drawn back unexpectedly to reveal the inner workings of a piece of complicated machinery, and Maggie saw in one enormous, terrible revelation what Cécilia had been hiding from her all this time. She rose from her kneeling position, her fist clenching around the screwed-up piece of paper.

'Emil? Céci?' She looked from one to the other uncertainly. 'Tell me.'

Cécilia wouldn't look at her. She took Rex back and wiped some mess from around his mouth.

'You told me you were...' Maggie laughed uncertainly. Her heart was pounding and she was having difficulty in catching her breath. 'This isn't true, is it? I'm being an idiot as usual. You didn't...'

'I'm sorry,' said Cécilia, still not looking at her. She was focusing very hard on her son. 'I'm so sorry. I was a coward. I didn't know how to tell you, and he wasn't here, so in the end I told you a lie. It was awful of me, I know, but I couldn't bear to hurt you. I'm so sorry, Maggie.'

Maggie turned to look at Emil, who glanced away at the sight of the devastation in her eyes, but said nothing. The air rang with heavy, unspoken betrayal, and their silence confirmed everything. Maggie opened her mouth as though she wanted to say something, but how could she? What was there to say when the door had been slammed in her face with such violence? She swallowed, then without a word turned and ran from the apartment.

'Maggie!' exclaimed Cécilia. She started after her sister, but she could hear the sound of her footsteps running down the stairs, followed by the bang of the outer door. 'Oh, heavens, what have we done?'

The appeal was to Emil, who was glancing this way and that and rubbing the back of his neck uncomfortably. He couldn't have expected this.

'She didn't know?' he said at last.

Cécilia shook her head.

He swore under his breath and began to pace up and down.

'I'm sorry,' he said. 'I thought you were still in Nice, and I had no idea...' He paused and gestured towards Rex.

'But what shall we do?' asked Cécilia.

'I don't know,' he replied simply.

They stared at one another. Then his expression softened, and he went across to her and took the baby again. Rex appeared to find Emil's nose hilarious. He grabbed it and giggled. Emil tweaked Rex's nose gently in return, and Rex laughed even more. Then Emil looked up and saw Cécilia watching them, waiting.

'We'll have lots more just like him once this damned war's over,' he said.

Chapter Twenty-Three

For Cécilia, this was a period in which the colours became darker, more sombre. If she'd expected Emil to bring with him the music that had coloured their early days together in vibrant blues and pinks and reds, then she was disappointed. Things had changed now; the war had changed them both. Emil had no time for his music any more, and Cécilia herself had for a long while considered the Prix de Rome as something from a past life – something which had seemed important in the days when she'd been ignorant and shut out from the world, but which now seemed frivolous and useless. The music, when it did come, was spiky, discordant, jarring, and gave her no pleasure. She seemed to have lost whatever talent she'd had in among the confusion of war, but she couldn't say she regretted it. This was the new reality, and there were far more important things to think about now. Emil had stayed in the apartment with her for the first few days, but it was an unsatisfactory arrangement that made them both uneasy, since they had in effect thrown Maggie out of her home in addition to all the other wrongs they'd done her, and in the end they moved to another apartment in the same building that had fewer guilty associations.

Emil had changed in the past year and a half: he'd become grimmer and more focused, and the ready humour and easy laughter that had once brought Cécilia out of her shell had almost disappeared. Whatever he'd been through – and although he didn't say much about it, Cécilia suspected he'd suffered – had made him a different man. Still, for her part, she was ready to accept him as he was. She loved him, and Rex had a father at last, and after the war they would be together – Emil had said as much. The initial awkwardness at the circumstances of his return had swiftly been replaced by a kind of astounded delight on both sides, although there was a guilty, half-shameful element simmering under the surface of their relationship now, since both were fully aware that their love had come at a cost to an innocent person. Cécilia had been almost sure Emil was dead, and he'd told her that he'd thought she must have come to her senses once he'd gone and decided she wanted no more of him. Whether that was true or not Cécilia couldn't say, but if it was then he couldn't have been more wrong. Despite her guilt, she did everything in her power to show him that she wanted their relationship to return to what it had been.

But things couldn't possibly be exactly as they were, of course. For a start there was Maggie, who had moved back to the Avenue Victor Hugo. Cécilia and Emil had both betrayed her, and there was no getting over it. Cécilia was heartbroken at the loss of her beloved sister, but didn't know how to put it right. She also tried not to think too hard about what Emil might have been doing in the time he was away. She never asked him about other women, but she suspected there must have been some in the past year and a half, as he attracted them easily and wasn't the sort to turn down willing female company, as she knew only too well. She couldn't even be sure there wasn't someone else now – he was out half the time and had plenty of opportunity – but she shut her eyes to any hint of it and thought only of her son. Rex was her certificate that gave her greater rights to the prize than anyone else, and she was confident that however far Emil strayed, he would always return to her.

So the winter went on. Emil was working hard to establish a new escape network to replace the ones that had been interrupted. Cécilia, wanting to help in any way she could, performed her part as before, carrying messages to and fro in Rex's pram. She wanted to do more, but Emil wouldn't let her.

'Your job is to keep our son safe,' he said. 'He needs his mother, and I need you safe and well.'

Cécilia saw that it was true, and that her role, as Emil saw it, was to be there for him, and comfort him, and help him forget the stresses of his duties – although she didn't think she was doing a very good job of it, because she could see that he was itching to do something more. Since he'd been away he'd come to embrace ever more left-wing ideas, and even went so far as to talk of a Communist France once the war was over. He'd also developed a deep-rooted hatred of the Germans, wanting nothing more than to shed some German blood. It would be a fitting revenge for his brother's death and the deaths of so many friends of his over the past few years. Once he'd set up this escape network and seen it running properly, he would rejoin the fighters, he said. Cécilia said nothing, but prayed the war would end before that happened. She'd already lost him once and couldn't stand to lose him again.

*

In the Avenue Victor Hugo, meanwhile, Maggie's shock had given way to tears, and then to a deep depression, and she was struggling with self-doubt in a way she never had before. Of the two sisters, she'd always been the confident one, the one with countless friends and boyfriends; the one who had the open, charming manner which attracted people to her and made her popular. Cécilia had been the shy, delicate, introspective sister who needed sheltering from the harsh realities of life. Maggie had taken on the job of looking after her, but now she wondered whether it had all been a mistake, whether she'd done her job too well. If she'd encouraged her sister to get out more and meet people, perhaps Cécilia would have been less likely to be bowled over by the first man who got close to her.

It was clear from their initial encounter after Emil's return that there had been no malice in Cécilia's betrayal of her. It was obvious her sister had fallen hard for Emil – and equally obvious, a painful, pricking little voice told her, that Emil had fallen for Cécilia too – so Maggie couldn't in all honesty accuse her of having deliberately set out to act in bad faith. Even so, there was that terrible lie Cécilia had told, which could have had no reason behind it except a cowardly desire to avoid a confrontation. How could she have done it? Maggie was hurt; more hurt than she had ever supposed she could be by such a thing. She was still in love with Emil – had clung to his memory ever since she sent him away to safety – and to find that the very person she had chosen to give him refuge had won over his heart and lied about it was a double blow.

For several days Maggie stayed at home, leaving the house only to go to school. When not working she stayed mostly in her room, lying on her bed, staring at the ceiling, her thoughts wandering and coming to no good conclusion. All she knew was that her world had been pulled from under her like a rug on a slippery floor, and all the ideas she had held dear didn't seem to mean much any more. She'd been putting herself in danger for nearly three years now, working for the Resistance, and where had it got her? Where had it got them? Nowhere. They were no further forward in freeing France from the Germans than they had been back in June of 1940. Her brother had been killed fighting, and her father had died suddenly of a heart attack – brought on, she was sure, by the shock of Marcus's death and the effects of the invasion. But none of this had discouraged Maggie: she was determined they shouldn't have died in vain, and she still had loved ones who had lives to live and bright futures ahead of them. She'd look out for Cécilia and Sébastien and protect them as far as she could. Then there was Emil, whom she was going to marry. They were all worth fighting for – or so she'd thought, until in the space of one heart-freezing moment the very people she'd been trying to help had made it clear they didn't need her, wrapped up in each other as they now were.

In those far-off days of their early idealism, Emil and Maggie had planned to fight together, side by side, until the Germans were forced out. But the years had rolled by, and the Germans were still here, and now it wasn't Emil and Maggie any more but Emil and Cécilia, and Maggie was left with no one. Even Sébastien was doing better under the Occupation than anyone might have expected: he was a favourite of Professor Lefeuvre, who brought important Germans to see him and express their delight at his young talent. If the Germans went away what would his future be? There would no doubt be a period of upheaval, and all his musical opportunities might be swept away – just as all Maggie's certainties had been. There seemed no way out of the gloom, and Maggie gave herself up to it completely.

Rose could see, of course, that something had happened, but she wasn't the sort of mother a daughter was likely to confide in. She made a few impatient efforts to find out what the problem was, but in the end washed her hands of the matter. She supposed Maggie and Cécilia had fallen out over some trivial thing, and left them to it. Maggie would never have confided in her mother, but her heart was heavy and she did want to talk to someone. Sébastien also knew something had happened, although nobody would tell him exactly what, and he was watching his eldest sister with concern.

One Saturday afternoon, after Mrs Brouillard had gone out, Maggie, bored and fidgety, emerged from her room and began prowling around the drawing room, pausing occasionally before the bookshelf to scan the titles, then abandoning them impatiently to pace restlessly up and down again. Sébastien watched her from the doorway.

'Do you want to hear "Winter Wind"?' he said, coming into the room. 'I've been practising really hard, and Professor Lefeuvre says it's coming on well although I'm not fast enough yet. Even Cécilia couldn't play it at thirteen, he says.'

'I don't know why you always feel like you have to compete with Cécilia,' said Maggie half-absently. 'There's no use in comparing yourself to someone else.'

'But I want to beat her,' replied Sébastien simply.

'It's not a race.'

'Well, then, I want to be better than her. She's just a girl. I won't be beaten by a girl.'

'Don't be silly. I don't think you need worry in any case. She seems to have forgotten all about her music since Rex was born. You ought to have a clear run.'

She stopped pacing and threw herself onto a sofa with a great sigh. Sébastien glanced at her, then went across to the piano and began to play. He made several mistakes and stopped halfway through with an exclamation of frustration.

'That's very good,' said Maggie. 'You have been practising, haven't you?'

She'd hardly been paying attention. Sébastien struggled with a sulk for a minute or two, then his face cleared.

'Why did you come back?' he said at last. 'Has something happened to Cécilia? You've hardly mentioned her since you came. Have you fallen out?'

There seemed a touch of hope in the question; he'd always been jealous of the close relationship between the two sisters, and of the attention Maggie paid Cécilia.

'No, we haven't fallen out, exactly,' said Maggie dully.

'Not exactly?' Sébastien pressed.

There was a band of pressure around Maggie's head, and she rested her forehead in her hand.

'She upset me, rather.'

'What did she do?'

Sébastien stood up from the piano and came over to sit next to her on the sofa. He put his hand on her shoulder and rested his chin on it. The small gesture of concern went straight to Maggie's heart. Sébastien cared about her, even if nobody else did. He was only thirteen, but he was growing so tall now that he looked almost grown up. He was sensitive for a young boy, too, and she badly needed a confidant. But even so she couldn't bring herself to set Sébastien wholly against Cécilia.

'It's not much,' she said. 'Only, I was engaged to someone – or at least, I thought I was. But Cécilia likes him too, and it seems he prefers her to me. They met in Nice after he left Paris.'

'Is that the man you used to talk about? The one with the foreign name?'

'Emil. Yes.'

'But she's got Rex,' said Sébastien. In his thirteen-year-old world view, women with babies could not be the object of romantic interest.

'Emil is Rex's father,' replied Maggie before she could stop herself, then wished she hadn't. It hurt to say it, and she shouldn't have told Sébastien. It was meant to be a secret.

'But he's a Jew, Maman said. That's not allowed, is it?'

'Not strictly. But the law wouldn't have let me marry him either, to be fair, so it's not as though it was an easy situation in the first place.'

'He left you for her?'

'So it seems.'

Sébastien thought about this.

'I'm glad,' he said finally.

'Sébastien!'

'I'm sorry you're sad, but you shouldn't be marrying someone like that anyway. Professor Lefeuvre says they're sending all the Jews out of France. There'll be none left soon, and good riddance!'

'You mustn't talk like that,' said Maggie.

'Why not? It's the truth. You were going to marry a Jew, and he went with another woman behind your back. That's the sort of thing they do – everybody says so.'

'Nonsense! Jews are no different from you or me, and they do good things and bad things just like the rest of us.'

'Well he did a bad thing. And you're being far too kind to Cécilia. I'd be furious with her if I were you, after what she's done to you.'

'I can't be furious,' said Maggie. 'I haven't the energy.'

And it was true; the shock seemed to have taken all the fight out of her, and all she wanted to do was go to bed and sleep until the war was over.

They sat silent for some time. Maggie was wrapped up in her own thoughts, while Sébastien, frowning, played with a tassel on the arm of the chair.

'Does that mean you're leaving the Resistance?' he asked tentatively at last.

'Probably. Yes... no. I don't know. It all seems so useless.'

'I'm frightened of the Resistance,' said Sébastien quietly. 'The Germans shot forty-eight people last week – ordinary people, not criminals or prisoners – just because the Resistance killed a German soldier. Frédéric's uncle was one of them.'

'Oh, darling, I'm sorry,' said Maggie. 'How's Frédéric taken it?'

'He's very angry. He says he's going to join the Milice as soon as he's old enough, and fight against the Resistance.'

'I suppose one can't blame him for feeling like that, if the Resistance were indirectly responsible for his uncle's death. I can understand why people don't like us.'

'Don't say "us" – you're not one of them.'

'But I am one of them, Sébastien. Or at least, I was. I love France, and I want us to be free.'

'If you really loved France then you wouldn't do things that make the Germans want to kill French people,' he said.

She looked at him. The weak winter sun trickled in through the window and glanced off his red hair, causing it to glow like fire. He was gazing at her now, a wounded expression in his light brown eyes. The answers were so easy for him.

'Please, Maggie,' he went on. 'Don't do it any more. And if you know anything, report it. I'm frightened, and I don't want to die.'

'Nor do I,' she replied simply.

*

A few days later Cécilia turned up at Maggie's school, waiting for her as she came out. Maggie was with some colleagues, and hesitated when she saw her sister, but at last said goodbye and came slowly over to her.

'Where's Rex?' she asked.

'With Albertine,' said Cécilia.

'Why have you come?'

'To say I'm sorry.'

'Is that all?' Maggie turned away and started walking very fast. Cécilia followed her.

'You know I never meant it to happen, don't you?' she said. 'I would never have done it...'

Maggie waited. There was no possible way to finish the sentence which could put things right. Cécilia must have realised it, because she didn't continue.

'But you did do it,' said Maggie, at last, pointing out the obvious.

'I know. It was... it was a sort of overwhelming thing. I didn't know what I was doing. I didn't realise what was happening to me until it was too late, and then I couldn't stop. Then Emil went away and I came home and I didn't know how to tell you, so I told that horrible lie. It was a dreadful thing to do, and I just want you to know how sorry I am.'

Maggie slowed down and allowed Cécilia to catch up with her.

'I loved him, Céci,' she said sadly. 'You knew I did.'

'Yes, and I'm terribly sorry, please believe me. I wish I could explain it to you, but I can't. It's all so long ago I can't even remember how it happened. But it's been agony these last few weeks without you, thinking how badly I've treated you, especially after everything you've done for me, taking me in when Maman didn't want me. I miss you so badly, and I'd do anything to make it up to you.'

She stopped. 'Except one thing. I can't give him up. I don't think I could bear to.'

'You don't think I want him back, do you?' asked Maggie sharply.

Cécilia looked down. 'No. Of course you don't. You're proud. I wish I were proud, but I have no pride when it comes to Emil. I can't let him go. I always was weak, you know I was. And now I've proved it.'

'Why did you come?' asked Maggie again. She felt tired.

'We need you, Maggie,' said Cécilia. 'Emil needs you. We're getting more people by the day, and you're so good at organising everything. Besides, Henri and Gérard have been asking where you are.'

'Oh, for heaven's sake, you didn't tell them our private business, did you?' said Maggie irritably.

'Of course not! I'd never do that. We said Maman was ill and you'd gone to look after her.'

'That's almost worse,' muttered Maggie.

'Please come and join us again. Hate me and Emil if you must, but don't give up the fight on our account. We're not worth sacrificing your principles for.'

'I'm not certain I have any principles any more. Everything I've done up to now has been for nothing, it seems.'

'It hasn't been for nothing, it hasn't. Things are happening – I don't know what, exactly, but there's been lots of activity lately. I really think there's going to be an invasion. They haven't said when, but we've had lots of messages to start mobilising on the ground. There'll be a lot more to do from now on, and Emil particularly wants you to help.'

'What can I do that no one else can? You don't need me.'

'We do. Even if you won't help with the organisation side of things, you can keep your ears peeled at Maman's. There are always lots of Germans and suchlike hanging around the house. You can pass on anything you learn. Every little thing is useful.'

They were standing face to face now, two sisters, one small, dark and vital, the other tall, pale and slender. There was not much resemblance between them in the normal way of things, but just at that moment, as they gazed at each other soberly, they looked very alike. A light rain had begun to fall and Maggie felt the chill.

'I don't know,' she said at last. 'I don't know whether I have the stomach for it.'

'I understand. I've hurt you, and nothing can change that, but I'd like you to forgive me some day – if not for my sake, then Rex's. He misses his *tante* Maggie. Come back. Please.'

At the mention of her nephew Maggie felt a stab. Had things been otherwise, Rex might have been hers – or if not Rex, then some other happy, chubby baby who would be all hers to love and care for. Suddenly the pain was too raw, and she felt the tears starting in her eyes.

'I don't think I can, Céci,' she said, with a catch in her voice. 'I don't think I can do it any more.'

*

Maggie stuck to her resolution not to get involved for another two weeks. Then one day she came home to be greeted with the terrible news that the old couple from the flat opposite theirs had been taken away in a roundup and sent to a concentration camp in Poland. She'd known M and Mme Bonnaire for as long as she could remember; they'd given her sweets when she was little, and made her presents of music scores and notebooks for her birthdays. The danger was coming ever closer. If the Germans could arrest a harmless old couple like the Bonnaires, then who would be next?

Maggie lay awake most of that night, then the next day after school she took a detour to Cécilia's apartment en route to the Avenue Victor Hugo. The only person at home was Emil, who had been asleep. When he opened the door, yawning, his look of startled recognition was swiftly replaced by one of wariness. She walked past him into the apartment.

'Don't say anything,' she said. 'I haven't come to chat. All I need to know is: what do you want me to do?'

She'd meant to look him straight in the eye, but at the last minute she couldn't quite do it. Still, she held herself together better than she'd expected.

He seemed relieved.

'I'll take any help I can get right now,' he replied. 'Let me speak to Gérard, and we'll get you fixed up. In the meantime, we need intelligence. Anything you hear – anything at all – pass it on. The Allies are going to invade soon, and we need to keep the Germans on the back foot as much as we can until then, but to do that we'll need to know what they're doing. You hear things at your mother's house, I know you do. Will you tell us?'

She gave a brisk nod. 'You can count on me for that, certainly. For the rest, let me know once you've spoken to Gérard.'

'Maggie,' he said suddenly.

She looked away. 'Don't. What's the use?'

'Won't you let me apologise?'

She was suddenly irritated. First Cécilia, and now Emil was trying to assuage his conscience by obtaining her forgiveness. But why should she make things any easier for them?

'Look, I know one's supposed to take these things on the chin,' she said. 'But I don't see why it's my job to make you feel better about what you did. I trusted you both and you let me down badly. There's no use in my pretending it doesn't hurt so I shan't even try.'

'I wish you could believe it, but I never meant anything like this to happen. I really am sorry, Maggie.'

'Sorry enough to leave Cécilia? No, don't bother replying – I wouldn't want you back anyway. She's desperately in love with you, you know.'

'I know.'

She couldn't help asking it. 'Did you ever love me, Emil?'

She tried to say it unemotionally, but there was an involuntary catch in her voice that she hoped he hadn't heard.

'I thought I did,' he said simply. 'But then everything changed.'

She gave a humourless laugh.

'That's clear enough. It all changed for me too. One minute I had you, and a sister and a nephew I adored, and now I have... what?'

'You could still have them, you know. Cécilia's terribly upset at what happened, and she'd be only too glad if you could forgive her. Blame me if you like, say I took advantage of her innocence – it's probably true enough.'

'I've made allowances for Cécilia all her life, but I'm not sure I can forgive her this time. She's a grown woman, and she knew what she was doing.' He made to reply, but she went on. 'Listen, don't let's talk about it any more. It's not the reason I'm here. I came because there are more important things to think about than our own personal concerns. There's a war on and I want to get the Germans out, so I'll take on whatever job you give me.'

'Even if it means being in company with me and Cécilia?'

'Of course. I can be civil.'

'Promise? You're right that our concerns aren't important in the circumstances, but I need to be sure you can rise above them.'

She was ready to meet him in the eye now, and did so.

'You can depend on me,' she said firmly.

Chapter Twenty-Four

Hertfordshire, 1950

It was now rapidly approaching the date of Sébastien's performance. It wasn't an important concert – just an amateur thing, with an orchestra of student musicians, and he wouldn't be playing the whole of *Les Orchidées*, but it was a long time since Sébastien had performed in public and he knew the importance of getting it right. The orchestra had rather prided themselves on getting the son of Jean-Jacques Brouillard to play the solo part, while Rose had taken every opportunity to make as much of this performance as possible, inviting everyone she knew who had any influence to come and see it. A little concert like this wasn't much, but it might lead to better things.

And better things were urgently needed: Harriet had been doing the household accounts lately and knew funds were running low. The roof of the house badly needed repairs, and several of the rooms were damp, but there wasn't enough money for any of that just at present – nor was there any likelihood of enough coming any time soon. Harriet thought Mrs Brouillard was being a little unrealistic in supposing that the family's fortunes could be restored merely by one successful concert, but she sensed her employer's desperation, and couldn't help feeling some sympathy for her. However, none of this was helpful to Sébastien, who was becoming increasingly agitated as the day approached. He was practising almost constantly, and his moods swung wildly between absurd overconfidence and frustrated rage, so that everybody took care to avoid him.

Harriet herself was feeling increasingly oppressed by the atmosphere in the house. The relentless air of misery and anxiety did nothing to raise her own spirits, and in the days following her flight in the Tiger Moth her sense of guilt at having betrayed Jim grew stronger and stronger, and the self-recrimination so severe, that she couldn't think what on earth had got into her, or why she had ever agreed to go out with Alec in the first place. Her sensible self had retired, defeated, under the unstoppable wave of remorse, and she was in no mood to do anything except follow the example of the Brouillards and indulge her own unhappiness by looking through old photo albums and reading Jim's letters. They were mostly brief, cheerful messages about planes and engines and jokes the men had played on each other in the mess, but all ended with a word or two of casual affection, and sometimes even a few more sober sentences about how he missed her, and about the plans he had for them once they were married.

Had Harriet been in a more logical frame of mind she might have asked herself why she was deliberately attempting to inflict pain on herself – and might even have wondered why she found herself laughing instead of crying at some of the letters – but her surroundings had affected her, and brooding on the past seemed like the right thing to do now. Alec had called once or twice, but she'd told Estelle to say she was out. She'd have to speak to him sooner or later, but not until she'd got her head straight and decided what she really wanted.

A few days before the concert Fernand Quinault paid a short visit to Chaffingham while Mrs Brouillard was out, wanting Cécilia's opinion on some music he'd been working on. Harriet watched them as they sat together at the piano, their heads bent over a score, discussing the technicalities of the music, and thought how well they worked together. Without knowing it, Cécilia was gradually being drawn into a collaboration with him, and Harriet thought it could only do her good. Perhaps at some point she could begin earning some money of her own, then she and Rex could move out and away from the unhealthy atmosphere of Chaffingham.

At length Quinault glanced at his watch and said he had to go, and they all went out into the hall, still talking.

'What's that?' asked Quinault, stopping mid-sentence to listen.

The sound of a violin floated towards them from the music room, playing the familiar sound of the second movement of *Les Orchidées*.

'It's Sébastien,' said Cécilia.

The music stopped abruptly, and they heard an impatient exclamation.

'He has trouble with that part,' said Harriet, just as the door of the music room opened and Sébastien came out. He stopped when he saw them, and his eyes went straight to Fernand Quinault.

'Don't I know you?' he asked, although he must have been perfectly aware whom he was addressing.

'We met a couple of months ago, at Piotrowski's house. Fernand Quinault.'

'Ah, yes,' said Sébastien distantly. 'I remember now.'

'I couldn't help hearing that you were practising the adagio just now,' observed Quinault. 'That part you're having difficulty with – it's easier if you slur it. Start on a down-bow, then a short up-bow on the E to the high C, then it's easier to get back to the open A without scraping, and it sounds better too.'

'Is that so?' Sébastien stared at Quinault with barely concealed dislike. 'And how do you know so much about it?'

His manner was so hostile that Quinault blinked behind his spectacles.

'Well, I played it a little some years ago,' he said uncertainly.

'You and everybody else. Thanks for the suggestion, but since it was *my* father who wrote it, I'm sure you'll agree that I'm more likely to know how to play it than you are.'

Quinault glanced at Cécilia and then again at Sébastien, reassessing.

'I beg your pardon,' he said. 'I wasn't trying to interfere.'

'Good. And you'd better not, either.' Sébastien darted him another venomous look, then turned on his heel and walked off.

'I'm afraid he's a bit sensitive about that particular piece of music, and he's playing it in public in a few days,' explained Harriet apologetically.

'I'm sorry – I didn't mean to offend him,' said Quinault.

'You weren't to know, and you were only trying to be helpful.'

'I'm not very good at being diplomatic, I'm afraid. I can't stop myself from giving my opinion on other people's performances, but next time I'll keep quiet.'

He left, promising to visit again soon, and Harriet wondered how long it would be before Sébastien informed Rose of Quinault's visits. So far they'd managed to keep them quiet with the help of Estelle, who was fond of Cécilia and more than prepared to keep secrets from her employer if necessary, but now it was surely only a matter of time and Sébastien's mood as to when she would find out.

At last the day of the concert arrived, and Sébastien went off in the morning carrying his violin, for a final rehearsal with the orchestra.

'Would you like to come this evening, Miss Conway? I have a spare ticket,' said Mrs Brouillard to Harriet.

'Thank you, I'd love to,' replied Harriet after a moment. And why not? It was years since she'd been to a classical concert – in fact she hadn't attended one since before her parents died, as far as she could remember. At that thought she was jolted by a sudden memory of an evening at Wigmore Hall a few days before she'd waved them off for the last time. She remembered the violet scent her mother had worn, and how she and Harriet had both laughed at her father's comical exasperation as he struggled with his bow tie. It was a characteristic image of both of them, and she felt tears pricking unexpectedly at her eyes as she remembered the light-hearted ease of family life in those days, before her parents had been torn from her.

It was to be an early evening concert, and at half past four a car drew up at Chaffingham, bringing a visitor. His name was Cyril Foulks-Webb and, as far as Harriet could tell from Mrs Brouillard's introduction, he was someone important in the BBC Northern Orchestra, who was coming to the concert to see what all the fuss was about. He'd brought another man, who was also someone important, and they were all to travel to Cambridge together in Mr Foulks-Webb's car.

Harriet was especially pleased to have the chance to see King's College Chapel again, as she hadn't been there in years. Somewhat to her disappointment it was raining when they arrived, and the sky was darkening, and the chapel wasn't looking its best, so they went in immediately and she sat down and admired the ceiling, with its delicate tracery and its fan vaulting. The light inside was dim, and it was too dark to get the best effect from the huge stained-glass windows, so she made a mental note to come and visit again in dry weather and daylight. Mrs Brouillard was sitting next to her, completely uninterested in the architecture of the building, and radiating an air of edginess. Harriet wasn't surprised; this was Sébastien's biggest moment in years, and it was incredibly important for his mother's ambitions that he do well. For herself she hoped the performance would go smoothly. She wasn't fond of Sébastien, but he'd certainly practised hard enough and there was no reason why he shouldn't get it right.

The orchestra came in and tuned up, then launched into a Mozart piece. It was pleasant enough but not outstanding, and Harriet waited impatiently for the main part of the performance. And here it was. Sébastien came on holding his violin. His face was impassive, and from where Harriet was sitting she couldn't read how he was feeling, although she was sure he must be nervous.

The audience fell silent as the conductor held up his baton, then flourished it to begin. The first plaintive notes of the second movement floated out, and Harriet listened, enjoying the way the music sounded in the chapel, which was entirely different from how it sounded in the music room at Chaffingham. At first it went splendidly well. Sébastien was looking increasingly confident; his bow swept across the violin with energy and economy, and he seemed to have decided to approach the difficult passage by taking a run at it and benefiting from the momentum.

Harriet found herself holding her breath as he came up to the part where the music changed tempo, but she needn't have worried – he got over it with aplomb and played on. She let out her breath. The hardest part was over now, and it ought to be all plain sailing until the end. But in that she was mistaken. Whether his success with the difficult passage had lulled him into a false sense of security, or for some other reason, it was then that it all began to go wrong. First he played one note sharp, then another one flat, then as the music changed tempo again his bow slipped and he faltered. He bit his lip and tried to pick it up again, but was too late and fluffed his entrance. The conductor tapped his baton on his music stand and nodded to the orchestra to stop. For a few seconds there was a deadly, awkward silence, then they began again at the start of the phrase and this time Sébastien got it right.

Harriet glanced at Mrs Brouillard, who was staring at Sébastien, stony-faced, then craned her neck surreptitiously to look at Mr Foulks-Webb, who was on Rose's other side. He was shaking his head almost imperceptibly. After what seemed an interminable length of time and one or two more mistakes – thankfully minor ones this time – Sébastien finally ploughed through to the end of the piece and took a deep breath. There was applause – not exactly rapturous, but enthusiastic enough – and Sébastien gave a rueful bow. He was trying to smile but he was pink in the face. Harriet felt all his awkwardness, and was surprised to find herself experiencing a twinge of sympathy for him.

The concert was over; the last applause had died away, and the audience rose and crowded out noisily. Mr Foulks-Webb and his colleague took Rose and Harriet back to Chaffingham, and prepared to bid them goodbye.

'He'll be good one day if he can conquer his nerves,' said Mr Foulks-Webb, as he shook Rose's hand. 'Perhaps the attention is a little too much for him at present. I'd recommend that he start off in among the orchestra, instead of stretching himself too far on the solo parts at this stage. Give me a call, and we'll see about giving him an audition.'

Rose's smile was fixed until the men left, then her expression snapped back to stoniness. She turned and went into the house, and Harriet followed, not daring to say a word.

Sébastien came home later, as they were sitting listening to the Third Programme and reading. Harriet glanced up as she heard him enter. It seemed he planned to go straight up to his room without saying goodnight, but Rose wasn't having that. She opened the sitting room door and looked out into the hall.

'Come in here, Sébastien,' she said. Harriet wanted to escape, but it was too late now.

Sébastien came in, looking sullen. He smelt of drink. 'What is it? I'm tired, and I want to go to bed.'

Harriet wanted to tell him that she'd enjoyed the concert, but she knew it would be a mistake. Rose and Sébastien were glaring at one another, each waiting for the other to speak first.

'How was the concert?' came a voice just then. It was Cécilia, in her dressing-gown. She wheeled herself into the sitting room, her eyes bright. 'I couldn't go to bed without finding out how it went.'

It was the worst possible moment for her to start taking an interest in things, Harriet thought.

'He did well,' she said brightly.

'Don't talk nonsense, Miss Conway,' said Rose, spurred into speech at last. 'You know full well it was a disaster.'

'It wasn't, was it?' said Cécilia, looking in concern from her mother to Sébastien.

Sébastien's expression darkened from sullenness to fury.

'Yes it was,' said Rose.

'Not the usual part? Oh, poor Sébastien, I thought you'd mastered that bit.'

'He had – that part went perfectly well – but as usual he was afflicted by a moment of overconfidence and began making mistakes. After that, one had difficulty in keeping one's seat while he lurched and scraped his way through to the end.'

Harriet winced at the barbs in her tone.

'Yes, it went wrong,' snapped Sébastien. 'No thanks to you, sitting there glaring at me like a spectre at the feast and putting me off. How was I supposed to concentrate? I'd have done it perfectly well if you hadn't insisted on turning up.'

'Let me remind you that I am your mother,' she returned. 'And in case you'd forgotten it, I spent a great deal of time and effort pulling strings in order to make sure that the concert was attended by people who might be able to help you. Much good it did me! I was forced to sit there, humiliated, as Cyril Foulks-Webb sighed and tutted his way through that excuse of a performance of yours, and then I had to smile and nod as he told me you weren't ready for solo parts and ought to audition for some second-rate orchestra in the north. After all the things I've done for you, you might at least have had the good grace to put on a better show!'

Her tone was biting, brutal. 'I sometimes wonder why I bother. Look at how I've supported you all these years since your father's death. You've had ample opportunity to make your name as a musician and start paying your way, and yet every time you let me down. How do you expect to make a living if you fall to pieces every time something is expected of you? You know full well the house is in need of expensive repairs which can't be put off much longer. I was hoping the necessity wouldn't arise, but if I can't rely on your contribution within the next few months I shall just have to sell your father's piano. It will break my heart to do it, but it seems as though I have no choice.'

'Oh, and here we go again. That's it, isn't it? Throw everything onto Sébastien's shoulders now that the talented older sister won't play ball. Make me do all the hard work, drive me into exhaustion just so Cécilia can sit twiddling her thumbs all day and making an art exhibition of her misery, then put all the guilt on me if I make a mistake.'

Cécilia shrank back at his words. More than anything, Harriet wished she'd gone to bed as soon as they'd got home. Sébastien was working himself up into a fine fury now.

'The sheer unfairness of it all,' he said. 'You put all the pressure on me and I'm never good enough. Cécilia does nothing, but she has people tripping over themselves to do her bidding.'

'No I don't!' said Cécilia.

'Oh, really? I've seen how you do it. You've got the little brute, and Estelle, and Miss Conway here, and Léonie, and that frightful Quinault fellow, all running around after you whenever you so much as snap your fingers. You've always had it easy. "Oh, but Cécilia's so talented, we can't ask her to put herself out or do anything for anyone else. She needs to dedicate all her time to her music." Nobody's ever said that about me, you'll notice.'

This was so patently untrue that Harriet wondered how he could be so self-deluded.

'I beg your pardon,' said Rose. 'What do you mean by "that Quinault fellow"? Are you referring to Fernand Quinault? What has he to do with Cécilia?'

'Oh, don't tell me you didn't know,' said Sébastien. 'He's been coming here behind your back for weeks, and they've been cooking up who knows what between them.'

'Is that true?' Rose swung round to Cécilia, who cringed.

'He's been here once or twice,' she faltered.

Rose drew herself up. She looked furious.

'So this is what goes on when I'm not here! I do not want this family to be associated with that man, and yet, as soon as my back is turned, you invite him here and tell him who knows what. How could you be so disobedient?'

'You didn't tell me not to invite him,' said Cécilia sullenly. 'I know you don't like him, but I used to know him a little and I wanted to see him. Besides, what is there to tell that we don't want him to know? He can see well enough what's happened to me, but I'm hardly going to give him all the details, am I? He wouldn't be interested anyway.'

'He's an encroaching sort of person,' said Rose. 'Insinuating, sly. These people are all like that.'

'Which people?'

'You know what I mean.'

'You mean Jews, don't you?' Cécilia demanded.

'I didn't say that.'

'No, but it's what you meant, and I'm tired of it. What would Rex say if he knew how you felt about him?'

'Rex is much too young to understand his situation – and quite frankly, you've done him far more harm by having him out of wedlock than you did by giving him a Jewish father. My dislike of this man has nothing to do with his religion, and everything to do with the fact that he's a sponger, pure and simple. Quinault has been begging me for money for years now, ever since we came to England. While he was just writing me letters from America it was easy enough to ignore him, but now he's here, on our doorstep so to speak, and you, foolish girl, have let him in! Now there's no saying where it will end. He's trying to take advantage of his friendship with your father to scrape an acquaintance with us, and now he's here we'll never get rid of him.'

'But why should you want to get rid of him? I don't believe he wants money. Why should he? He's a successful composer in Hollywood. One of his scores was nominated for an Oscar two years ago. Why should he be asking us for money, when he must be able to see we don't have much?'

'Who can say what motivates these people?' said Rose crisply. 'Yes, he can see we don't exactly have a lot to spare. I told him most of our money goes on your treatment. With any luck, that will put him off, but I daren't bank on it. At any rate, you mustn't invite him here again, do you understand?'

'But—'

'Never mind that. You heard me.'

Cécilia turned hurt eyes to Sébastien.

'Why did you tell her?' she said. 'That was unkind, Sébastien.'

'Unkind? That's rich! You put me in an impossible position. I knew he'd been here and that Maman wouldn't be happy, but I was the one who was forced to keep the secret. Don't you think you were unkind to *me*? You're always trying to twist things round to make me look bad. You pretend to be so calm and kind, but I know how you work against me.'

He strode across to Cécilia and loomed over her as she shrank in her chair, looking for all the world as though he might strike her.

'Sébastien!' snapped Rose.

Harriet had had enough. She'd listened to the row in silence, feeling a groundswell of pressure build up within her, an almost physical turbulence that was nearly unbearable. She couldn't stay quiet any longer.

'Stop it!' she exclaimed. Her voice sounded high and hysterical in her own ears. 'Can't you hear yourselves? You make me sick, all of you!' There was a sudden silence as all three of them turned towards her in astonishment. 'Look at you, fighting like animals. And over what? Do you think you're the only people in the world who've ever suffered? You're all bitter and twisted, eaten up with spite and misery. If you ever thought about anybody but yourselves you'd realise that you have it easy compared to others. But you don't, do you? You're just self-indulgent and full of your own importance, and never give a thought to anybody else. It's not...' She gestured wildly, looking for the right word. 'It's not normal. It's unhealthy.'

She wasn't quite sure who she was addressing, but it might have applied to anyone in the room.

'And what do you know about it?' spat Sébastien.

'I know you're so jealous of your sister that you encouraged her to kill herself and gave her enough pills to do the job.'

There. She'd said it and now it couldn't be unsaid. Cécilia gasped.

'Miss Conway!' snapped Rose. 'Sébastien, is this true?'

'Of course it isn't true!' said Sébastien. 'Cécilia, tell her.'

Cécilia shook her head quickly, but whether in denial of Harriet's accusation or refusal to join the argument wasn't clear.

'Sébastien!' said Rose again.

Sébastien raised his voice petulantly. 'It's all rot! I didn't do anything.' He glowered at Harriet. 'I don't want her here any more, Maman. She listens at keyholes and she's rude and tells lies. Get rid of her.'

'No need,' Harriet heard herself saying before Rose could reply. 'I'm not staying.'

She'd said it louder than she meant to, and she seemed to hear the echo of her words ringing around the room.

She turned to address her employer. 'Mrs Brouillard, you might as well take this as my notice. I'll pack my things and leave as soon as possible.'

Then she went out before any of them could say a word, feeling nothing more than a huge sense of relief.

*

If Mrs Brouillard had been taken aback by what had happened the evening before, she was doing a good job of hiding it. The next day when Harriet went down to breakfast she merely gave her a cool 'Good morning' and began to discuss the arrangements for Harriet's replacement.

'You'd better call the agency – or better still, put an advertisement in the papers, since they haven't yet managed to send anyone who stayed more than a couple of months,' she remarked. She was sipping her coffee, casting her eye over the morning paper, and she hardly looked at Harriet as she said it.

Harriet flushed, but went to do as she was told, half-wondering whether she'd dreamt the last twenty-four hours. There was no going back on her word now, though, and she spent most of the morning fretting over what she was going to say to the agency – and more importantly, how she was going to tell Alec she was leaving. The first task was the easier of the two, and she was just picking up the telephone with gritted teeth, preparing to confess she'd lost another job, when she heard the door open and turned to see a familiar figure in a wheelchair.

'So you're really leaving,' Cécilia said without preamble.

'I am.'

'But why? Maman won't make you go if you don't want to, you know.'

Harriet wanted to tell her that she was sick and tired of the all-pervading air of misery in the house, of the barely concealed enmities between the family members, of the oppressive atmosphere that blanketed the place like a heavy pall of smoke and made it difficult to breathe. But she didn't, because she'd made it clear enough already.

'This place is a little too out of the way for me,' she said. 'I'd prefer to be in London.'

'I wish you wouldn't go. I know this isn't exactly the most cheerful place, but I really thought we were getting better. Rex is so much happier since you came, and I've been... well, I... I've rather enjoyed the company. I thought perhaps we could be... friends.'

She said it as though the word were unfamiliar to her. Harriet saw the appeal in her eyes and felt a pang of remorse. In other circumstances they might have been friends, she thought, but not in this house, not among these people. Harriet needed a change of scenery, and the sooner the better.

'I'm sorry,' she said sincerely. 'I'll write if you like.'

'It's not the same.' Cécilia paused, looking down at something she was holding in her hand. 'I brought something to show you. I thought you might like to see it.'

She held it out and Harriet took it. It was a gold locket, very old, its engravings almost worn away.

'I used to wear it but haven't for years,' Cécilia went on. 'I'd almost forgotten about it.'

Harriet opened the locket. Inside was a faded portrait of a girl with dark, curly hair. She was looking straight at the camera and laughing, and her vitality shone out like a beacon. Harriet glanced up questioningly.

'It's Maggie,' said Cécilia. 'I thought you'd like to see a picture of her.'

'Oh.' Harriet didn't know what to say. She looked down again, at the photo of the lively, spirited girl whose letter she'd read secretly, and who was long dead.

'She reminds me of you in many ways,' continued Cécilia. 'She was blunt, like you, and brave. She wasn't afraid of anything.'

'I'm not brave,' said Harriet, surprised.

'Yes you are. You stand up to Maman much better than I ever could. And you speak up for what's right. Maggie was just the same.' She gazed at the photo for a moment when Harriet handed it back, then snapped the locket shut and closed her fingers tightly over it, as though it were something precious. 'I miss her every day.'

She said it quietly, almost talking to herself. Then she turned her chair to leave. 'Well, if you've made up your mind there's nothing I can do to stop you. I hope you find whatever it is you're looking for.'

What *was* she looking for? Harriet had no idea. She was more sorry than she'd imagined to leave Cécilia and Rex, but she couldn't stay here at Chaffingham. If she did, she knew she'd go mad.

That evening Alec called. He'd been away visiting an old RAF pal in Yorkshire for a few days, but was back now and was calling to see how she was, he said. Her heart gave a thump as she heard the familiar voice at the other end of the line, and she felt suddenly flustered.

'I'm very well, thank you,' she said.

He caught the tone immediately. 'What's wrong?'

There was no use in beating about the bush.

'I gave notice today. Or was given notice. I'm not quite sure which,' she added honestly.

'You're leaving?'

'Yes.'

'Has something happened?'

She couldn't tell him over the phone, but it would be a mistake to meet him and tell him in person.

'Not exactly. It's a little complicated.'

'Where are you going?'

'I don't know yet. I'll find another job somewhere.'

'What about here? I've an office that could do with reorganising.'

Harriet swallowed and braced herself.

'I don't think so, Alec.'

Her words were final enough, and he'd have been a fool not to pick up on them. It had hurt to say it, but she had to escape from Chaffingham, had to break away from him before he drew her in further and stole what was left of herself from her. There was too much turmoil in her head and her heart to cope with anything just now. He was silent for a moment, and she braced herself for a difficult time of it.

'I see,' he said at last. 'That's it, then. I guess you've made your decision.'

'Yes. I'm sorry. It's just—'

'It's quite all right. I understand.'

'I didn't mean—'

He laughed. 'Don't start with the apologies, or you'll end up talking yourself into something you don't want.'

He was right, of course. He'd made it easy for her, and she was grateful to him for it even as she tried her hardest to hold back the tears that were threatening to form in her eyes. She couldn't let him hear any catch in her voice.

'Thank you,' she said.

'The pleasure was all mine. Let me know if you change your mind.'

'I will.'

'Goodbye, Harriet.'

There was a click at the other end of the line and Harriet put the phone down at her end. She was out of breath, and her heart was beating fast. She'd made the right decision, she was sure of it. She wasn't ready to fall in love again, she told herself, and the hollow feeling in her chest and the tears that were now spilling down her cheeks were for Jim, not Alec. She'd have to keep reminding herself of that or she might forget.

Chapter Twenty-Five

Paris, 1944

On the 6th of June 1944, the long-awaited invasion came. In a determined offensive, thousands of Allied troops landed on five beaches in Normandy, with the aim of driving the Germans out of France. For several weeks there was some doubt as to whether they would succeed, but at last, after nearly two months of fighting, the Allies broke out of Normandy and pushed their way further into France. Finally there was a sense that things were coming to a head, and that the tide of war was on the turn for good. The liberation of France had begun, and hope began to spread across the country that Paris would soon be free. Meanwhile, the Resistance doubled their efforts. They wanted to obstruct the Germans as much as they could, so those few weeks saw an upsurge in activity as trains were derailed, depots blown up and communication lines cut.

Emil was impatient to join the action. He'd established his escape network, and it was working well, but he wanted more. Determined to fight, he joined the Francs-Tireurs et Partisans, or FTP, a Communist resistance organisation, and soon he was involved in sabotage operations aimed at preventing the Germans from operating at full capacity as far as possible. As his work became more dangerous he and Cécilia were forced to move from place to place to avoid capture, since the Germans knew about the Batignolles apartment, and it wasn't safe any more. After moving to three or four different houses they finally went to stay with old Suzette, at her house near Le Bourget. Pierre had died the year before, but Suzette had continued to shelter people throughout the war, and had never yet been caught. There was another advantage to Suzette's house, in that it was not far from a major railway line, along which German troops and supplies passed frequently, allowing their movements to be monitored, and so the little cottage became for a while a centre of Resistance activity.

In early August, the FTP received word that there was to be a huge mobilisation of German troops out of Paris, on Hitler's orders, most likely as reinforcements to the troops fighting the Allies in Normandy. As part of this operation, a train full of soldiers was to come in on a local line from the outskirts of Paris, then change to another train and head west out of the city. Their source gave the date of this movement as Saturday the 5th of August, at 5 a.m., and a daring plan was quickly hatched to blow up the first train on its way into Paris. It was a dangerous mission, and there was not much time to organise, but if they could pull it off it would be a serious blow to the German forces. Two separate Resistance cells were allocated to the job, one of them led by Emil. They were to lay explosives on the line just after the station at Épinay-sur-Seine, and then get away as fast as possible and go into hiding.

Maggie knew about the plan, although she wasn't personally involved in sabotage activities. She'd wanted to join in with more active resistance, but Emil wouldn't let her. Her expertise lay elsewhere, he said: in talking, and listening, and passing on intelligence. She'd argued with him but he'd been implacable, and she'd been forced to give way. She was still at her mother's house, keeping her ears to the ground, and being as charming as she could to anyone she met who might have anything useful to tell her. The wine flowed freely in the circles in which Rose moved, and more than one German officer had found his tongue loosened by the generous hospitality, so Maggie was often able to pass on snippets of information. Most of them were of little use in themselves, but they all added up to a bigger picture that was of some assistance to the resisters and that might one day soon, she hoped, help cast out the Germans from Paris forever.

*

Even as all eyes were on the Allies' advance, Rose continued with her musical efforts. A big concert was to be played at the Paris Opera, which would include a gala performance of *Les Orchidées*. It was to be attended by some of the most important people in Paris's cultural sphere: orchestra directors, music critics, and of course many Germans. It was also another chance to show off Sébastien. He wouldn't be playing, of course, but his mother was anxious to put him in the public eye as much as possible and introduce him to as many influential people as she could. In the days leading up to the concert, Rose spent a great deal of time scolding Sébastien and schooling him in how he was to behave. Maggie did her best to interpose, as she could see Sébastien was becoming agitated and nervous, but Rose snapped at her in her usual impatient way and told her not to interfere.

'The sooner he learns the art of making useful friends, the better. You'd do well to learn that yourself. By the way, I don't suppose you're coming?'

'Yes, I'll come,' said Maggie.

'Oh, you will, will you? Very well. In that case, you'd better find something to wear. You can't get away with trousers for this sort of occasion, you know.'

'I'll wear my old black dress,' replied Maggie. She didn't relish the thought of spending an evening among such stuffy people, talking about the intricacies of classical music. She'd far rather have been in a dingy club with her friends, listening to lively jazz and dancing freely. But those days were over now, and she had a job to do, and there would be plenty of Germans at the gala. At this sort of occasion they were unlikely to give anything useful away, but one never knew.

'Why are you so keen to come?' whispered Sébastien, once Rose had left the room. 'You're not still trying to find things out, are you? Please don't, Maggie. What if we get caught?'

'*You* won't get caught,' she said. 'You're not doing anything wrong.'

'No, but if they catch you then we'll all be in trouble. Please, Maggie, give it up, won't you? I'm tired of all this stuff and it puts us in danger.'

'Do you really think anything I can do will make much difference?' replied Maggie, remembering her argument with Emil. 'They won't let me do anything useful anyway – I'm kept out of all the important operations – but I promised to help.'

She hadn't meant to let the bitterness show, but Sébastien saw it and pounced.

'You're still angry at Cécilia, aren't you?'

She sighed. 'No, not exactly. She couldn't help it.'

'I don't understand how you can be so kind to her.'

'One can't go through life feeling angry – it's a waste of effort.'

'But don't you hate her for what she did? If anyone did that to me I'd never forgive them, not for the rest of my life. You do, don't you? You must hate them both.'

He was watching her eagerly.

'Perhaps I do, sometimes,' admitted Maggie.

'Only sometimes? Don't you ever want to get back at them?'

'No, of course not! And that sort of thinking isn't helpful, Sébastien. Have you done your violin practice today? You'd better go and do it before Maman finds out.'

He huffed, but went to fetch his violin, then returned to the drawing room and began to practise, watching her covertly from under his lashes all the while.

The concert was much as Maggie had expected, but afterwards they were invited by one of Rose's German acquaintances to a late dinner at Maxim's. Professor Lefeuvre had somehow managed to invite himself along, and he was doing his best to ingratiate himself with everybody as usual, especially their German hosts. They ate and drank, and talked of music and art, and it was all very dull in Maggie's view. The evening was drawing into night, and she was growing tired. She'd heard nothing useful, so it seemed as though her efforts had been for nothing, after all. But she was wrong.

'Ah, by the way, Mrs Brouillard,' said a smooth German lieutenant, emerging from his brandy glass. 'I must extend my apologies, as I'm afraid I won't be able to come on Friday evening.'

'Oh? How unfortunate,' said Rose graciously.

'So it is, dear madam. I was very much looking forward to it, but duty calls. Orders, you know. I'd much rather be at your house that evening, than on a train out of Paris with the excuse for soldiers they've given me – they're nothing but a herd of swine, frankly – but there's nothing I can do about it. We were supposed to go on Saturday morning, but we've had orders from on high to bring it forward. Think of me at eleven o'clock on Friday night, won't you? There'll be none of this fine cognac for me, more's the pity – only whatever disgusting rations they think we'll put up with.'

Maggie had glanced up momentarily at his words, but now she was doing her best to appear as though she were paying attention to the Austrian conductor they had put her next to, who was talking of something or other. In reality she was listening carefully, her mind working. Emil's cell had formed their plans on the understanding that the troops were leaving Paris on Saturday morning, but now it sounded as though the Germans' schedule had changed. She needed to get the information to Emil as soon as possible.

That night, Maggie waited until the house had fallen silent, then she rose and dressed quietly and stole out of the apartment, taking the stairs to the ground floor so as not to make a noise with the lift. She fetched her bike from the courtyard and wheeled it through the entrance hall, then nearly jumped out of her skin as a shadow slipped out in front of her.

'Goodness, how you frightened me!' she said, as the shadow revealed itself to be Sébastien.

'Where are you going?' he asked.

'It's none of your business. Go back to bed.'

'I knew you'd be going out. I was watching you tonight. You were listening to what that fellow Ackermann said, weren't you? About going away on the train.'

'What train?'

'You know what I mean. I was watching you, remember? You seemed very interested in what he had to say. You're going to tell your friends, aren't you?'

'What if I am? It's nothing important.'

'I don't believe you. If it was nothing important you wouldn't be going to tell them in the middle of the night. You'd wait till tomorrow. Something's happening, isn't it?'

'Not as far as I know,' lied Maggie. 'And I'm going now because I have to work tomorrow. I can't go in the day anyway – it's too dangerous. Somebody might see me.'

'You've been in the day before. Why are you so interested in when the Germans are leaving? There have been lots of train derailments lately. Is that what your group are planning to do?'

'No!' insisted Maggie. 'Don't worry about it. Forget everything you saw, and go back to bed. You're far too young to worry about all this stuff.'

'No I'm not! I'm thirteen – nearly fourteen!' he said indignantly. 'That's almost grown up.'

'Yes, you're growing up a little more every day, aren't you? But you're a child now, and you're in no danger of getting into trouble for anything I do. Go back to bed, and I'll see you in the morning.'

He seemed to be making up his mind to something.

'If you don't come back upstairs I'll call Maman,' he said suddenly.

'What?'

Maggie's heart sank.

'I mean it,' he went on. 'I'll call her and tell her what you're doing.'

'She won't hear you,' she said feebly.

'Well, then, I'll call for help. There must be a patrol around here somewhere.'

'Sébastien!' she said.

'I mean it. I'm sick of all this. You're spoiling things for everybody. You're spoiling things for me. We'll get caught and I'll get thrown out of school and I'll have to give it all up and Maman will never forgive me. Please, Maggie, don't do it. Don't go back to Cécilia and that horrid man. They'll only let you down again.'

His distress was sincere, and she couldn't stand firm when he gave her that wide-eyed look. She sighed.

'All right, I'll come back up. I don't suppose it was very important anyway.'

He smiled with relief.

'Good!'

'But don't say anything to Maman.'

'I won't,' he promised.

Maggie returned her bike to the courtyard and they went upstairs together.

'It's nearly one o'clock,' she said. 'You'd better go to bed or you'll be useless tomorrow.'

'All right. Goodnight.'

'Goodnight.'

Sébastien went into his room and Maggie did likewise. But she didn't go to bed. Instead, she waited another hour, before emerging onto the landing and creeping silently into Sébastien's room. He was lying on his back, sound asleep, one arm flung out to the side and the other resting across his stomach. Maggie listened to his regular breathing for a few moments, then stole out of the apartment, fetched her bike from the courtyard and set out into the dark, silent street.

Sébastien waited until he was sure she'd gone out, then opened his eyes, turned over and stared unseeing at the wall for a long while.

Chapter Twenty-Six

Maggie's information spurred the cell into action. Over the next twenty-four hours there was a flurry of activity as they tried to find out whether the mobilisation was in fact to take place six hours earlier than they'd expected. They couldn't get complete confirmation of it, but there was enough movement among the Germans to make them bring forward their plans. The whole operation was perilous – perhaps the most perilous they had ever attempted in size and scope – and on Friday the atmosphere in the farmhouse was grim and determined as the members of the group prepared themselves and their weapons. They were to equip themselves with explosives, grenades and guns, and once the raid was over, they were to split up and return to the house by separate routes as soon as they could. Emil wanted Cécilia to leave the farmhouse with Rex until it was all over, but she refused.

'I'm not going,' she said. 'You'll need me here when you get back.'

Suzette came bustling in just then, carrying Rex on one hip and a basket over her other arm. The baby saw his mother and reached out for her.

'There, you see!' said Suzette triumphantly. 'I told you you should come with us. The little one needs you – not like these big stupid men who think of nothing but fighting. You'll just get in their way.'

'You know I can't leave, Suzette,' replied Cécilia. 'Take Rex to your sister's and look after him. It won't be for long.'

'Hmph!' Suzette glared at Emil. 'You see what you've done to her? A mother belongs with her child, but you've got her so she's not thinking straight. Tell her, won't you?'

'Suzette's right, sweetheart,' said Emil. 'It's too dangerous to stay here. I don't want you caught up in it.'

'I told you – your cause is my cause now, and you'll need me there to patch you up if you get hurt. I only wish you'd let me do more, but you might as well give up trying to send me away, because I won't go. I'll wait for you here.'

He took her in his arms and kissed her. 'You're so patient. And all I seem to do is make you wait. I'm sorry.'

'I'd wait for you until the end of time, you know that. I can't live without you so what else is there to do? If I have to wait then I'll wait.'

He looked at her. She seemed so fragile, but over the past two years she'd shown an inner strength that he'd never suspected she had. He took her hand and placed it against his chest, and she felt the pulse underneath his shirt.

'Can you feel it?' he said. 'You have my heart. Keep it safe for all of us. Keep it beating even when I'm gone.'

'But you're coming back, aren't you? Of course you're coming back.'

'He'd better,' put in Suzette, who was gathering things from drawers to put in the basket, still carrying Rex in the crook of one arm. 'It's about time he made an honest woman of you, and he can't do that if he's dead.'

'Yes,' said Emil. 'I'll be back.' Just for a second, he seemed tired and defeated. Then he smiled and kissed Cécilia again. 'Don't wait up.'

'Of course I'll wait up. I couldn't possibly sleep.'

Suzette finally departed with Rex, then a little later the men went out and Cécilia settled herself for a long, agonising night of waiting. Only a few more weeks and the war would be over – she could feel it. And then everything that had been put on hold for so long could resume once again, and everybody would be happy.

*

In the apartment on the Avenue Victor Hugo, Maggie was chafing impatiently. She couldn't stop herself from wondering how the sabotage operation was going, and wished she'd been allowed to join it. Instead, she was talking politely to an up-and-coming French clarinettist in whom her mother had taken an interest. It was a quieter party than usual, and Maggie noticed there were fewer Germans than would normally be expected. This gave her some comfort that the information she had passed on was correct, and she was on tenterhooks, knowing that she would not hear anything for some hours yet.

At last the guests departed in defiance of the curfew – although most of Rose's friends had enough influence not to be bound by the same rules as everybody else – and Maggie helped her mother and Estelle clear up. She was wondering whether she'd possibly be able to sleep in the circumstances, but there was nothing else she could do, so she got ready for bed then took a book and prepared to while away the hours until she could receive news of the operation. As one o'clock approached Maggie began to feel a little tired, so she put down the book and decided to try and sleep. Just then, there was a tap at her door and Sébastien sidled in. He wore an air of suppressed excitement mixed with what looked almost like sheepishness.

'Shouldn't you be asleep?' asked Maggie.

'I knew *you* wouldn't be,' he replied. 'And I wanted to see you.'

He came in and sat on the side of her bed. He didn't say anything, but began plucking at the bedspread, glancing up at her occasionally as he did so.

'What is it?' said Maggie. 'You look awfully pleased with yourself. Did your practice go well today?'

He shrugged. 'Maggie, do you remember when we met Paul Ostermann at the gala evening the other night?'

'The composer? Yes, of course. He was talking to you for quite a while, wasn't he?'

'Yes. I wanted to ask for his autograph but I thought he'd think I was stupid so I didn't dare. Anyway, he's been speaking to Professor Lefeuvre and he wants to take me on as a pupil!'

It burst out in a rush of words, and he looked to see Maggie's reaction.

'Paul Ostermann wants to teach you? Violin, you mean? Goodness, Sébastien, that's wonderful! Why, he's world-famous! What an honour for you!' She threw her arms around him and hugged him, and he flushed with pleasure. 'What did Maman say when you told her?'

'I haven't told her yet. I'd have to go to Vienna, you see.'

'Vienna? Yes, I suppose you will. Won't Maman go with you?'

'I hope not – I mean, I'd rather like to go by myself. That way I'd have more freedom, without her breathing down my neck all the time. She prefers Paris, anyway. This is where her friends are, and Papa is more famous here.'

'That's true,' said Maggie. 'If you really want to go by yourself I'll try and help you persuade her if you like.'

'Would you?'

'Of course.' It would do her brother good to get out from under Rose's influence for a while. 'Oh, Sébastien, how marvellous for you!'

'I know. I can't quite believe it! I think Professor Lefeuvre talked to him and suggested it.' He looked down and was silent for a moment, plucking at the bedspread again. 'He gave me a warning.'

'Paul Ostermann?'

'No, Lefeuvre.'

'What kind of warning?'

'He said that Ostermann has friends who are very high up in the Nazi party, and he won't take me on if he thinks I've been helping the Resistance.'

'But you haven't been helping!'

'I know! And I told him so. But…'

'But what?'

'He said there were rumours about you. He said people have been saying you're a Resistance member.'

'You didn't tell him that's true, did you?'

'Of course not! I lied and said you'd never done anything like that.'

He paused, fiddling once more with the bedspread, wearing a half-complacent, half-embarrassed expression. There was evidently something else, because he kept stealing glances at his sister. She said warily:

'But you did tell him something. What was it, Sébastien?'

He avoided her eyes.

'I wanted to help you. And I had to show him I'm not a traitor.'

'A traitor? To France, you mean?'

'Well, I meant a traitor to the Germans. At least, the ones who are our friends.'

'None of them are our friends.'

'Some of them are. Herr Vogel is, and the Abetzes. They've all been very kind to me. And I only told Lefeuvre. He's not German, so it's not as though it matters.'

'But you know he passes on anything he hears. What did you tell him?'

At last he seemed to make up his mind.

'I told him about what's happening tonight,' he said, gazing at her defiantly.

'What do you mean?'

'You know – what we talked about the other day. The Resistance are planning something, aren't they? I'll bet they're going to sabotage a train or something.'

If he'd had any doubt about the accuracy of his guess, it was dispelled by Maggie's reaction. She'd gone white at his words.

'Sébastien, you didn't!' she whispered, horrified.

'I knew you'd gone to tell your pals what Ackermann said about the troops leaving Paris. You oughtn't to have done that, you know, when you promised you wouldn't. I lay awake all that night worrying that if your friends killed any Germans then they'd come and kill us in revenge, or a lot of other poor innocent people, and I couldn't stand the thought of that happening, so I told Lefeuvre. Don't worry – I didn't give you away. I just said I'd overheard someone talking about it in the street.'

Maggie put her hand to her forehead, which felt clammy. She'd known Sébastien wasn't exactly sympathetic to the cause, but she'd never dreamt he would do something like this.

'How could you? Sébastien, don't you realise how many people you've put in danger? Did Lefeuvre report it? Silly question, of course he did. Oh, goodness me! How could you be such an idiot?'

Sébastien was in a state of feverish agitation. His eyes glittered with excitement as the words tumbled out.

'I had to tell him, don't you understand? If I'm ever to make Maman proud I have to be picked by the best schools, and the Germans are in charge, so we can't have people saying we're partisans or all my practice will have gone to waste. I've been working towards this for years. Why, just think what I could do if Ostermann puts me forward!' Suddenly his expression became sly, and he darted a sideways glance at her. 'Besides, I thought you'd be pleased, after what Cécilia did to you.'

'What Cécilia…' Maggie drew in her breath. 'Don't you *dare* say you did this for me. You know perfectly well I'd never have agreed to it if you'd told me. I believe you did it for yourself. You've always been jealous of Cécilia, but I never thought you'd stoop this far. How could you?'

'I'm not jealous of Cécilia!' he exclaimed hotly. 'I did it because she's trying to hurt us all with this stupid Resistance stuff. It's nothing to do with us, and if you had any sense you'd keep out of it yourself. I tried to tell you not to do it, but you wouldn't listen, would you? It won't do us any good. It won't do *me* any good. Don't you want me to have all the nice things Cécilia had? Don't you want me to be a famous musician like Papa?'

Maggie shook her head, seeing him in a new light.

'Oh, Sébastien, I had no idea you could be quite so selfish,' she said sadly.

He opened his mouth to protest, but she had no time to listen to him. She had to get to Suzette's house, and quickly. The men would have gone out by now, but someone would be there and might know where they'd headed. She didn't know what she could do to help but she had to do *something*. Perhaps it would be possible to get a warning to them.

She threw Sébastien out of her room and dressed quickly, then hurried downstairs to fetch her bike and set out into the street, keeping an eye out for patrols. All was quiet, and by avoiding the main streets she reached the outskirts of the city without incident, then headed north-east. When she arrived at Suzette's house all looked dark, so she leaned her bicycle cautiously against the wall and stole around to the back of the house. Here the darkness was thinner, and she peered through the kitchen window and observed that someone had left a candle burning. At her gentle knock on the glass, a shadow rose and came towards her. It was Cécilia, who had been waiting, fully dressed, for the men to come home. She opened the door to admit Maggie, and immediately saw that something was wrong.

'What is it?' she said.

Maggie clutched at her sister's arm.

'Oh, Cécilia, I'm dreadfully afraid we've been found out!' she said.

'What? How?'

'Never mind that – it's a long story, but we need to warn the men.'

'It's too late,' replied Cécilia, aghast. 'They went off ages ago. They were planning the attack for eleven o'clock. That's over three hours ago, and they'll be on their way back by now, assuming they haven't been caught.'

She turned away and sat down at the table, her face paler than ever in the candle-light. Maggie followed her in.

'Then what shall we do?'

'There's nothing we can do. We'll just have to wait.'

'I hate waiting.'

'I'm used to it,' said Cécilia. 'And we have no choice.'

'Is Rex here?'

'No, Suzette took him to her sister's. He's quite safe, even if we're not.'

Maggie started at that. Of course, if the Germans had captured any of the members of their cell, they were likely to torture them for information, and she was cowardly enough to hope that they wouldn't give anything away.

They sat and waited, facing each other at the kitchen table, the candle flickering between them, casting shadows over their pale faces. They said little, each absorbed in her own thoughts. At one time they would have shared those thoughts with each other, but something had been lost between them; the confidence wasn't there any more. The night stretched on, and at last the indigo darkness turned to a deep grey, and then to a lilac. There was no sound but the chirruping of the dawn chorus outside.

'They ought to have been back by now,' said Cécilia, wrinkling her forehead.

'Perhaps they had to hide somewhere.'

'All of them? They were supposed to split up.'

Maggie had no reply to that. She was terribly afraid of the damage Sébastien might have done, but she said nothing about it. Perhaps everything would be all right, and the men would be safe, and there would be no need to tell everybody what had happened and get her brother into trouble – her brother, who was a child still, and who was not yet able to fully grasp the possible consequences of his actions.

At last, Cécilia stood up. 'I'll make some coffee,' she said. 'Do you want some?'

Maggie shook her head. Cécilia didn't want any either, but she felt she should be doing something, so she busied herself about the kitchen, putting things away, getting cups out for the men when they returned – if they returned.

It was after six when they at last heard a sound outside. They both glanced up just as there was a hammering at the door. Cécilia rushed to open it, and gasped as Emil stumbled into the kitchen, he and Gérard carrying Henri between them, badly wounded. Emil himself was soaked with blood all down his right leg from what looked like a bullet wound. He cut short the exclamations of the women.

'Quick! Get some hot water!'

'Where are the other three?' asked Maggie.

'Just behind us. They're coming, and so are the Germans.'

'What?'

'There's no time for questions. You girls get out quickly, before they get here.'

All was confusion now in the kitchen as the other three men arrived. They were all tired, and several of them had some injury, but none was as badly wounded as Henri.

'You'd better get him upstairs,' said Cécilia. 'Is he going to be all right?'

'I don't know,' replied Emil grimly.

'And your leg! What happened?'

'They knew we were coming,' said Gérard. 'Someone must have told them.'

'I know,' said Maggie. 'That's why I came – to warn you.' There was no time for a full explanation. 'Did you blow up the train?'

'No. We didn't get the chance. They intercepted us before we could lay the explosives, and started shooting. We managed to throw some grenades, but I don't know how much damage they did. Then we had to make a break for it. But they know where we are – they'll be here soon.'

'How do you know?'

'They had a search going for us, and nearly managed to cut us off by those fields over there. There isn't anywhere else we could have gone to, so they'll be here searching these cottages soon.'

Two of the men had lifted Henri and taken him upstairs.

'Let me get some bandages,' said Cécilia.

'Bandages won't help him,' replied Emil. 'Listen, you two have to get out.'

'I won't leave you,' insisted Cécilia.

'He's right, Céci,' said Maggie. 'There's no sense in our all being caught.'

'But your leg needs seeing to,' objected Cécilia. She wasn't listening to her sister.

'Never mind that!' said Emil.

'Then you come too.'

'I can't leave Henri, and I can't run with this leg. I'll have to stay here.'

'No!'

'Don't worry – I'm not going down without a fight. Now, get out before they get here. Maggie, tell her.'

'Come *on*, Céci,' said Maggie, pulling at her sister's arm.

Cécilia would have refused until the last, but Emil took her face between his hands and kissed her tenderly.

'Don't stay here,' he said softly. 'I can look after myself, but Rex needs you. Now quick, through the back door!'

Maggie pulled at Cécilia's hand and hustled her out, still protesting, into the pale dawn. They crossed a scrubby patch of grass, soaked with dew, and squeezed through a gap in the hedge that bounded the property, beyond which was a rushing stream, shaded by trees.

'They'll come by the front way first,' said Maggie. 'If we can cross the stream here we can get back onto the road and walk back. I'll have to leave my bike.'

They heard the sound of dogs barking in the distance, and Cécilia wrenched her arm away from Maggie.

'I can't leave,' she said.

'You have to, or they'll shoot us!'

Cécilia didn't care. She ran back, and would have gone back through the gap in the hedge, except at that moment the soldiers arrived and went straight around to the back of the house. There were at least ten of them, with two dogs. Maggie dragged Cécilia back into the undergrowth and they watched as one of the men hammered on the back door with the butt of his rifle. Two of them kicked at the door and broke it open, and there came the sound of shouts from inside the house.

Maggie pulled Cécilia further away from the hedge and behind a large, gnarled shrub growing next to the stream. Cécilia wouldn't go any further, but at least they were less visible here. They watched breathlessly through the hedge from their hiding place as Gérard and three of his colleagues were dragged out and lined against the wall. Emil was not among them. The sound of a shot came from inside the house, and both women jumped. Cécilia was trembling, and Maggie reached out to grasp her hand tightly. Where was Emil? Then two soldiers came out, dragging the dead body of Henri with them. They threw him down on the ground and one of them fired a volley of shots into his body. Cécilia put her hand over her mouth and began to sob quietly. Hidden in the bushes, the sisters clung together in horror.

'Who's next?' said one of the soldiers to the men lined up against the wall. He raised his gun, and before anybody could say a word shot Guillaume, who dropped like a stone.

'Come on!' Maggie was pulling at Cécilia's arm, tears rolling down her cheeks. 'We have to go!'

Just then there was a shout and the sound of another shot, and they watched as one of the German soldiers fell where he stood.

'Emil!' breathed Cécilia, breaking free of her sister and running forward to the gap in the hedge. He had somehow escaped to the attic and was now leaning out of the window, firing a pistol at the Germans. First one fell, then another. At last he had drawn German blood, just as he'd always wanted. The soldiers dashed for cover, and began firing back at him. For a minute he held them off, picking them off one by one, but he was fatally outnumbered, and he must have known he couldn't hold his position for long.

Finally he ran out of bullets, and dropped his gun. But he was not finished yet. Cécilia watched as he reached behind him and brought something out which, in the confusion of her mind, she thought at first was a ball. Then her thoughts cleared and she saw it was a grenade. At the same time, she saw a German soldier raise his rifle and take aim at her lover, standing framed as he was in the window. She wanted to cry out, but the air seemed thick and impermeable, as in a dream, and the sound wouldn't emerge.

At that moment Emil saw her, standing frozen in the gap in the hedge, her eyes seeking his in mute appeal. He looked straight into her eyes, and his old, brilliant smile spread across his face. He turned his head away and made to pull the pin out of the grenade, but before he could do it the soldier fired. Cécilia saw Emil crumple and tip slowly forward. For a second that seemed like an hour he hung, motionless, across the window-sill, then the soldier fired again, hitting him in the neck. He slid almost gently out of the window and fell through the air. Cécilia never heard the sound of his body landing on the path below, because it was drowned out by her own scream.

At that, Maggie was galvanised into action. She grabbed her sister and pulled her away from the gap in the hedge and towards the stream. There was the sound of more shots, and she knew the rest of the men were being executed. Cécilia was sobbing, and Maggie herself felt very close to hysteria, but she urged Cécilia on. This was no time to stop. They were in the stream now, wading across. If they could make it to a thicket about fifty yards away, then they could get to the road, and from there find any number of escape routes.

They clambered up the other bank, their clothes heavy and clinging to their legs, using the low-hanging fronds of a willow tree to pull themselves out. Someone was still shooting, Maggie could hear it. Surely they ought to have stopped by now? After all, there were only six men, and no more than a bullet or two would be needed to finish each of them off. Why were they still firing?

'Quickly!' she exclaimed. 'Before they see us.' She set off towards the little thicket, then looked back to see that Cécilia had collapsed as though exhausted. 'What are you doing? Come on, we don't have time to stop!'

But her sister hadn't stopped because she was tired. She was half-kneeling, half-lying in a patch of mud, pale in the face, sweating and panting. Maggie realised something was wrong. She ran back.

'What is it?'

'Shot,' said Cécilia. It came out as a croak.

'Oh, heavens! Where?'

'I'm not sure – my back, I think. I can't quite tell.'

Maggie looked. A dark red mark was spreading out across the back of Cécilia's pale blue dress, and she gasped. That was why the shooting had continued. Cécilia's scream as Emil fell must have given them away, and one of the soldiers had taken a shot at her as she climbed out of the stream. But they couldn't stay here. The Germans would be here at any moment. Gritting her teeth, she lifted Cécilia under her arms. She was so heavy despite her light weight, but desperation gave Maggie strength. She dragged her sister with brute force the final twenty yards to the hedgerow by the side of the road, then stopped for a second to get her breath.

'There's something coming,' she managed.

It was a truck, piled high with potatoes, heading in the direction of the city. Maggie's heart raced with hope and she breathed a prayer. This was their only chance. Leaving Cécilia by the side of the road, Maggie ran out in front of the truck, which braked sharply just in time. She ran to the driver's side and wrenched open the door. An elderly Frenchman with an enormous moustache began to upbraid her angrily, but she interrupted him.

'My sister's hurt!' she said breathlessly. 'Please, you must help. I can pay you. I need to get her to hospital.'

Cécilia, lying dazed by the side of the road, didn't understand a word of what was going on. All she knew was the fire in her lower back, and that Emil was gone. Nothing else mattered. The burning sensation began to spread throughout her body and her senses dimmed, clouding into shadow. She knew nothing of what happened next – how Maggie and the driver dragged her into the truck and laid her across the seat as best they could, how they set off in a hurry to Paris, or how Maggie broke into deep, uncontrollable sobs once they were fairly away – as the world receded and she sank into a merciful unconsciousness.

Chapter Twenty-Seven

Two weeks later, Paris was liberated. The Allies had originally intended to bypass the city on their march through France, but the Parisians pre-empted them. In the middle of August the French Forces of the Interior, the armed wing of the Resistance, staged an uprising, allowing French and American forces to march into the city. At their head was General de Gaulle, leader of the Free French, who had spent most of the war in exile in London. Paris was free at last. It ought to have been a moment of celebration, and for many it was, but for others it was the start of a period of recrimination and reprisal, as those who were considered collaborators were punished for their association with the Germans. Black marketeers were rounded up, accused of profiting from people's misery; women who'd had relationships with German soldiers – or were even suspected of it – had their heads shaved and were paraded half-naked through the streets; while anyone who was seen to have betrayed his or her countrymen faced being dragged before an unofficial tribunal and subjected to summary justice.

Cécilia knew nothing of this. Rose had insisted on her being taken to the American hospital, where, thanks to her name and her mother's connections, she'd received the best treatment that could be had in the circumstances. The bullet had gone too close to her spinal cord to allow it to be removed safely, and the doctors had decided not to operate on the grounds that she had still a certain amount of feeling in her legs. The sensation came and went, and it seemed doubtful that she would ever walk properly again, but at least the nerve damage was not so great as to prevent her from ever using her legs at all. Better have a little sensation than risk complete paralysis if they tried to remove the bullet, the doctors said.

Throughout her time in hospital, Maggie stayed at her bedside. Cécilia was hardly aware of it for the first few days, but one day she woke up from an uncomfortable doze to find her sister weeping silently by the bed. Cécilia observed her in silence for a few moments, until Maggie looked up and saw her. Cécilia reached for her hand and Maggie clasped it tightly. There was no need for words; with that gesture everything that had gone before was wiped away, and they were sisters again.

'Rex,' said Cécilia. 'Is he all right?'

Maggie nodded.

'Maman has him at home. He's perfectly happy. If you're feeling up to it, I'll bring him to see you tomorrow.'

'Yes,' replied Cécilia. 'Please. He's all I have now.'

'You have me,' said Maggie.

'Do I?'

'Of course you do. I'm here whenever you need me. You'll see – you won't be able to get rid of me!'

Cécilia tried to smile but couldn't.

'I'm sorry, Maggie,' she said. 'Can you ever forgive me?'

Maggie squeezed her hand. Her eyes were bright with tears.

'Let's imagine none of it ever happened,' she said. 'We can start again and forget the past.'

'I wish I could,' replied Cécilia. 'I wish I could bottle it all up, put it to one side of my mind and never think about it again. But I can't. It's all too awful.'

'Hush, now. Try not to think about anything. The doctor said you weren't to be agitated.'

Cécilia shook her head but said nothing. They were silent for a while, then Maggie said:

'The doctor says you can go home in a few days as long as you have someone to look after you.'

'But who will look after me? You have a job, and Maman won't be too keen.'

'Maman is getting you a nurse,' replied Maggie. 'She's talking about taking us to England for a while, too. There are good doctors there, she says, but I think really she's worried that people won't look too kindly on her now the Germans have gone. I can't blame her. The mood has turned ugly here in Paris over the past few days, and collaborators are getting the worst of it.'

Her words reminded Cécilia of something.

'Maggie,' she said hesitantly. 'How did you know the Germans had found out about… about the operation?'

Maggie's heart thumped at the direct question. She couldn't tell Cécilia what Sébastien had done. He'd be in such trouble, and he couldn't have understood the possible consequences of his actions.

'It was just something someone said at Maman's that made me put two and two together,' she replied evasively.

'But who told them about it?'

'I don't know. Don't worry about that now. The main thing is that you have to get well for Rex, and for the rest of us.'

'I don't know that I want to get well,' said Cécilia bleakly. 'Not now. He's gone, Maggie. He's gone. What shall I do without him?'

There was no answer to her cry, and they both knew it. She would have no choice but to get on with her life, in the same way as the thousands of other people who had lost loved ones in this terrible war. Perhaps one day it would get easier, but now there was nothing but desolation and emptiness at what had been torn from her so swiftly and so cruelly.

*

A few days later Cécilia was allowed home. Rose had prepared a bedroom on the downstairs floor of the apartment, and had arranged things as comfortably as possible for her daughter. The nurse was installed in Cécilia's old room to see to all her needs, and so the long, slow process of recovery began. Maggie, Rose and Estelle looked after Rex between them, and as Cécilia grew gradually stronger, they brought the baby to her more and more often, although she couldn't do much more than watch him listlessly as he pulled the books off her bookshelf and clambered on and off her bedside chair. She'd expected to weep – wanted to weep – but she couldn't, not yet. It was all too recent, still too much of a shock. The tears were there, she knew it, multiplying day by day in her heart, which felt as heavy as hot, liquid lead in her breast, but for now there was nothing to give her relief, only long, dry days stretching ahead of her into an interminable future.

Sébastien hardly seemed to notice the change in their arrangements. He was busy practising several very difficult pieces, which he was to play for Paul Ostermann as a sort of informal audition, and the sound of the piano and violin could be heard at all times as he practised for hours on end, sometimes muttering to himself, sometimes terrified, sometimes tearful. He seemed to have completely forgotten – or even be unaware of what he had done. Maggie wanted to confront him about it, but he was so agitated and bad-tempered that it was impossible, as he snapped at anyone who came near him. He had dark rings under his eyes, and had bitten his nails so furiously that there was nothing left of them. Rose didn't help: she reminded him several times a day how important this opportunity was, and continually criticised him for his mistakes. She seemed as agitated as he was – and perhaps she was; this was the best opportunity her youngest son had received so far to make a career for himself, but in the current climate it was anybody's guess as to whether anything would come of it now that the Germans had gone from Paris.

Cécilia wasn't the only one grieving the loss of Emil. Maggie too had taken his death hard, even though he'd been lost to her for a long time before that. The worst of it was that she had nobody to confide in, since she could hardly tell Cécilia how much she missed him, and no one else would have been sympathetic. But that wasn't the only thing on her mind. She was tormented by the knowledge that Sébastien had passed on information about the operation to blow up the train to Professor Lefeuvre, who must surely in turn have shared it with the Germans. The professor was lying low at the moment – not surprisingly, given his outright collaboration – so she couldn't accuse him directly, but she knew that must be the reason the operation had failed. But should she keep the secret or not? Cécilia was sick and unhappy, and didn't need any more trouble heaped upon her just at the moment, while Sébastien was in no condition mentally to defend himself at present. Maggie knew that the secret would have to come out sooner or later, and that Sébastien ought to be called on to at least make an attempt to atone for what he'd done, but it didn't seem like the right time, and so she said nothing.

'I wish we could go back to England,' she said impulsively. 'It was so peaceful there. We haven't seen Chaffingham in years, have we, Céci? I bet it's looking its best at the moment. It was never so much fun in winter when the weather was bad – I always found it dull then, but to be perfectly honest I think I could stand a bit of dullness now. I feel as though I've had enough excitement to last a lifetime.'

She was feeling increasingly nervous, and she didn't know why. They seemed to be held in a sort of limbo, waiting for something, although she didn't know what. The violence in Paris had got worse, and it was becoming dangerous to go out in some quarters of the city. She'd heard of several people she knew who had been shot, accused of collaboration, and she hoped things would be brought under control soon. It would be too bad if, after all they'd been through, France were to descend into civil war. She was anxious for things to return to normal, but in the meantime she didn't want to stay here. She said as much to her mother.

'Of course we're not leaving!' replied Rose, when she suggested it. 'Not while Sébastien still has this opportunity.'

'Oh, but surely it won't go ahead now that the Germans have been sent packing.'

'Paul Ostermann isn't German; he's Austrian, and Sébastien will be going to Vienna if Ostermann takes him on, not Berlin.'

'What difference does it make?'

'Every difference in terms of possibility,' said Rose crisply.

Maggie saw that there was to be no chance of help from that quarter. She felt that Paris was dangerous for her mother and, despite their frequent disagreements and prickly relationship, she didn't want to see her shot as a collaborator. She felt a looming danger; what it was she couldn't say exactly, but every time the doorbell rang she jumped, half-expecting that standing there would be a couple of solemn strangers in uniform, who would take their mother away.

*

But the end, when it did come, was wholly unexpected, because it wasn't a group of strangers at all, and it wasn't Rose they'd come for. It was a parched, dusty afternoon in late August, and they were all sitting at home. Cécilia had begun to be able to sit up a little, so they'd moved her into the drawing room and lifted her onto the sofa, where she was half-reclining, propped up with cushions. Sébastien was playing the piano, while Rex was upstairs having his afternoon nap, and all was peaceful, when there was a knock at the inside door to their apartment. Estelle went to answer it, muttering under her breath about people leaving the downstairs door open for anyone to get in. She opened the door to be confronted by a group of four or five unsmiling men carrying pistols and rifles. They were not in uniform, but each wore an armband with the letters 'FFI' and the emblem of the Cross of Lorraine. Estelle let out a shriek, drawing Rose and Maggie out to see what all the fuss was about.

'Who are you?' said Rose coldly.

Maggie had jumped at the sight of the guns, but then relaxed as she saw who it was – some of her old colleagues from the Francs-Tireurs et Partisans Resistance cell. She hadn't seen any of them for a few weeks, as she'd been too occupied with Cécilia.

'Oh, Daniel, Valentin, I'm so pleased to see you!' she exclaimed. 'Have you come to visit Cécilia? You needn't have brought the guns.'

The man addressed as Valentin was not smiling.

'Marguerite Brouillard,' he said. 'You are to come with us. You are charged with having passed information to the enemy regarding an operation by the French Forces of the Interior, and causing the deaths of six men.'

'What?' said Maggie, taken aback. 'What are you talking about?'

'On the fifth of August—' began Valentin, in that same formal tone, but then the man addressed as Daniel broke in. He had been standing there in agitation, waiting for an opportunity to speak.

'Don't put on that innocent act!' he said. 'You killed my brother!'

'Guillaume?' Maggie was bewildered. 'No, I didn't. The Germans killed him. I was there, and I'm very sorry it happened.'

'You might as well have killed him. The information came from you. You told us to bring forward the operation and sent them all into a trap.'

'Yes, of course the information came from me. I overheard it from a German officer at Maxim's, and passed on the information because otherwise the operation would have failed. But I didn't know the Germans had found out about it.'

Daniel's lips were twisted in an ugly sneer.

'You didn't overhear it. You agreed it between you. He fed you false information to bring to us, and we walked right into it.'

Maggie glanced about in a panic and saw that her mother had gone white, her breast rising and falling rapidly.

'I didn't! You know I wouldn't! My own sister got shot in the raid. I would never have done anything like that.'

'You're lying!' spat Daniel. 'Everybody knows your sister stole your lover and you hated her for it. I expect you thought it was a good opportunity to get revenge.'

'That's not true!'

'You got her shot. And what about Guillaume? He just got married in March, and he left a pregnant wife and a fatherless child behind him, all thanks to you. Don't think we don't know about you and your family of filthy collaborators.'

Rose drew in a breath and shrank away at the word. The piano had fallen silent, and Sébastien had come to the door of the drawing room. On the sofa Cécilia was struggling to sit up further among the cushions, but couldn't. Through the half-open door past Sébastien she could see Maggie's back and two of the men, whom she recognised.

Valentin began again. 'Marguerite Brouillard, you are to come with us to stand trial—'

'There's no need for a trial – I can shoot her myself right now,' said Daniel.

He grabbed hold of her by the arm. Maggie had just begun to realise the danger she was in and tried to pull away. She had never for a second thought that she would get the blame for the failure of the operation, but now she saw it from their point of view in all its enormity. It was true: she was the one who'd told them to bring the time forward, and they thought she'd done that to draw them into a trap, when it hadn't been the case at all. The information had been good; it was Sébastien who had betrayed the details of the operation to the Germans. One of the other men had now taken hold of her other arm and she began to struggle.

'But I didn't do it!' she exclaimed.

They ignored her, and began to hustle her towards the door. She glanced round to where Sébastien was standing, looking scared.

'Sébastien, tell them!' she said.

Sébastien had been standing there in almost a trance. At last he seemed to wake up. His eyes flickered, and his gaze turned to the men with their ugly-looking weapons – weapons which, with one curl of a finger, could snuff out a young life before anyone had the chance to protest. He licked his lips.

'Sébastien!' pleaded Maggie. Even at that moment her gaze held nothing more than reproach. He turned his eyes away from hers and looked at the ground, and said nothing.

'Sébastien!' she repeated, and this time the appeal was genuine, terrified. Again, he stayed silent. She gave a sob and began to struggle in earnest.

Cécilia was in agony, trying to pull herself up from the sofa.

'Daniel!' she exclaimed. 'Valentin! What are you doing?'

Daniel left Maggie to his companions and went into the drawing room. He looked down at Cécilia, his face a mask. She gazed up at him and shook her head, trying to hold back the tears.

'This isn't true, is it?' she said. 'It can't be. Where's Maggie? I want to speak to her.'

Daniel barked an order and one of the men gave Maggie a shove through the door, but didn't let go of her.

'There she is,' he said. 'Your sister. Look at what you did to her.'

The tears were spilling down Maggie's face.

'I didn't. Cécilia, I didn't, I promise!'

'Enough!' said Daniel. 'Let's go.'

Cécilia wanted to cry out, but she couldn't. Maggie gave her one last despairing glance, then two of the men tied her hands behind her back and marched her out of the apartment. The door slammed behind them.

*

The stairs echoed with their footsteps as they walked down the four floors to the street. Maggie had given up trying to argue, as nobody was listening to her, and Daniel in particular seemed on a knife-edge. He smelt of alcohol and looked as though he hadn't slept in a while, and she could see it wouldn't take much for him to lose control. Only the presence of Valentin was keeping him subdued for now, but Valentin didn't want to speak either. Despite her nervousness, Maggie's thoughts came to her with startling clarity, and it suddenly struck her how many of the people closest to her had betrayed her: first Cécilia and Emil, and now Sébastien. Even her own mother hadn't spoken up to try and prevent the men from taking her away – presumably she was reluctant to draw attention to herself and be accused of collaboration too.

Maggie lifted up her head. One thing she was sure of: she wasn't like that. Yes, she'd been betrayed, but she couldn't lower herself to do it in return. She wouldn't be like the rest of her family. She'd wait until they'd got to wherever they were taking her, and then the men would give her a chance to explain herself. She could exonerate herself without needing to get Sébastien into trouble. She'd deny everything and rely on her innocence to win the day. Surely the truth still counted for something?

They had reached the entrance hall now and were walking out into the street. The pavement was dry and dusty, and the bright light reflecting off the ground and walls of the buildings hurt her eyes. The hot air prickled against her skin and she felt perspiration begin to form a sheen over her body. The street was busy for once, and she heard one or two shrieks as the little party emerged into the open. They must look a forbidding sight, she thought: the men with their guns, wordlessly conducting a bound woman towards who knew where. Someone called her name, but she couldn't see who it was; presumably one of her neighbours. The sound was oddly distant, but why did it seem so despairing? Didn't they know she'd be home in no time, just as soon as they'd let her explain what had happened?

They'd stopped now, in the street, under the shade of a tall tree. Why had they stopped? Weren't they supposed to be going to the

FFI headquarters or somewhere like that? They'd mentioned a trial – not that it would have any legal basis, of course, but they had to make it look as if they'd followed some sort of procedure, at least. Yet they were standing in the hot, grubby street, just outside her apartment. She felt sweat forming on her upper lip, but her hands were tied and she couldn't wipe it off.

Her thoughts began to drift in a detached sort of way, and she found herself observing the scene almost as an outsider might – but no, that wasn't exactly true; she knew perfectly well who she was, and who the men were. They were her friends, or had been at one time. There'd been a little misunderstanding, but as soon as they gave her a chance to explain they'd realise they'd made a mistake.

Someone – she thought it was Valentin – began to speak. He was holding a piece of paper and was reading from it. There was a roaring in her ears and the sun was blinding in her eyes, and she couldn't hear or see what was going on. She turned her head to relieve the brightness, and saw a poster on a wall to her right. It was advertising a performance of *Les Orchidées* from two years ago. A crowd had begun to gather a little way away. They must be talking or perhaps shouting, but she couldn't hear anything. She turned her head to look at Valentin, and gradually it dawned on her that she wasn't to be allowed to speak for herself. The other men were standing to attention, not looking at her – except for Daniel, who kept his eyes on her, his face grim. Valentin stopped speaking, although she hadn't heard a word, and seemed to be waiting for her to say something.

'I'm sorry,' she managed. That was no good; it sounded like a confession. She tried again. 'I didn't do anything. Valentin—'

Daniel had moved out of her line of vision, but she knew he was there, just behind her and to the right. She turned her head and saw him out of the corner of her eye, his pistol raised and pointing at her head. Why hadn't she said anything when she'd had the chance? Now it was too late, all too late.

'Please…' she began, but she could see by his expression that it was no good, and what was the use in begging? Valentin nodded at Daniel. This was the end. She was tired and weary, but she straightened up and looked Valentin directly in the eye.

'*Vive la France*,' she said ironically, and Daniel fired the gun.

*

Upstairs, Sébastien had been staring through the window, uncomprehending, at the scene below, ignoring Cécilia, who was weeping silently on the sofa. He flattened his palms and his forehead against the glass. Why hadn't they taken Maggie away for interrogation? They were all standing in the street, and one of them was saying something, and Maggie was standing there, her hands behind her back, a tiny figure in among all those tall men. She hadn't spoken yet as far as he could see, but any minute now she'd tell them the truth – tell them what he'd done – and they'd bring her back in and take him away. Would they treat him more leniently because he was only fourteen? He had no idea, but he was afraid. Perhaps he ought to run downstairs and try to creep away under the cover of the crowd. He could stay with a friend until the fuss had died down.

Then, as he watched, Maggie dropped to the ground. For a moment he thought she must have fainted because the sound of the gunshot didn't come until a split second afterwards. Then he realised what had happened and gasped.

'No!' he cried. 'I never meant—'

'What is it?' said Cécilia urgently. 'What was that shot? Sébastien, what is it?'

She tried again to push herself up from the sofa to see, but she couldn't. Sébastien was fixed at the window, breathing hard. He paid no attention to Cécilia's demands, but watched as down in the street his mother fought her way through the crowd and bent over the motionless body of Maggie. A dark pool of something stained the ground below her head. Rose was busy, slapping her daughter's face, presumably urging her to wake up.

People were still watching, but the little group of men gesticulated and shouted, waving their guns, and the crowd began to melt away to watch from a safe distance. The FFI men strode away without looking behind them, then two old women stepped forward and seemed to be saying something. One of them took out a handkerchief from her apron pocket and laid it over Maggie's face. Rose protested, but the woman shook her head and put a hand on Rose's arm, then crossed herself. Then Sébastien saw Estelle, gesticulating desperately to some of the bystanders to help. Two or three men came forward, lifting Maggie as gently as they could, and carried her towards the downstairs door of the apartment.

All the while, all the time he'd been staring at the horrific sight in the street below, Cécilia had been talking, pleading, demanding to know what was going on, but he couldn't bring himself to say a word. He ran out of the drawing room and up the stairs, intending to shut himself in his room, but he couldn't prevent himself from hovering on the landing until the little procession arrived, which it soon did. First came the sound of Estelle, sobbing loudly, then his mother's voice, snapping:

'Stop that, you silly woman, and help me get her inside.'

Sébastien retreated into his room and pushed the door not quite closed. He peeped through the crack and over the banister as the helpers brought Maggie in.

'Lie her down here,' said Rose. Sébastien crept out again and went to the top of the stairs. They were taking Maggie into the drawing room. He heard Cécilia's voice, raised in one high cry of distress, followed by hysterical sobs – whether from his sister or Estelle, he couldn't tell. He stole down the stairs, unwilling but unable to stop himself. He didn't know it, but he was whispering to himself over and over again: *'Not my fault, not my fault.'*

The men were leaving now. His mother was speaking to them on the landing outside the apartment. Sébastien ventured past her and went to stand in the drawing room doorway. They'd put Maggie on a chaise longue that nobody ever used. The handkerchief had slid partly off her face, but even as he watched, Estelle replaced it, and all he could see was the blank white square of what had once been his sister. His lips moved silently as he stared: '*Not my fault, not my fault.*'

Then Cécilia looked up at him and he flinched, because he thought he could see accusation in her eyes. But what right had she to accuse him? She'd started all this, surely. This was all her doing. Surely fate would have taken a different path and Maggie would still be alive if Cécilia hadn't come between her and Emil. Suddenly Sébastien felt a wave of combined indignation and fury washing over him at the sheer unfairness of it all. This was never meant to happen; the war was over, and they ought to have been free and happy. Instead the family had been left a broken wreck, cripples and failures all. At that moment he hated everybody, but Cécilia most of all. She knew nothing of this, but saw only her little brother, standing in the doorway, looking aghast at the dead body of his elder sister. She held out her hand.

'Sébastien,' she said.

'It's *your* fault!' he spat, then turned on his heels and stormed out.

*

They buried Maggie in Passy Cemetery, in the same plot as her father and her brother. What with the Occupation, Rose had never yet been able to have a family mausoleum built, and so Maggie's name, Marguerite Brouillard, was added to the simple headstone that had been put there for Jean-Jacques and Marcus Brouillard. Many of Maggie's friends from school and elsewhere came to the funeral to pay their last respects and tell Rose how much they'd

liked her. It was small comfort. Cécilia didn't attend the funeral.
She didn't want to think or to feel any more, and wished above
all else that the German bullet which had taken away her legs had
also taken her life.

Maggie's death brought home to Rose just how much danger
she and her family were in. The atmosphere in Paris that late
summer and early autumn was febrile and vengeful. For four years
the people of France had been oppressed by an occupying force,
and each person had reacted differently – some resisting, some
collaborating, others doing neither one nor the other, but keeping
their heads down and waiting for it to be over. Now the deep
divisions between them had emerged, and it looked as though the
situation might descend into open warfare. General de Gaulle was
doing his best to establish a new, strong government, but violence
was still occurring on the streets.

Wilfully blind and stubborn Rose might have been, but
she wasn't stupid, and it was becoming obvious that there was
nothing left for her family in France. Paul Ostermann had left
the country, and any opportunity in that direction had been put
on hold indefinitely; besides, Sébastien's always precarious mental
state had crumbled almost completely after Maggie's death, and
he had become prone to fits of panic and hysteria. He cowered in
his room, refusing absolutely to play his instruments, and neither
threats nor persuasion could change his mind. Rose saw that he
needed a rest, and since she was also frightened that the rest of the
Brouillards might be next on the list for summary justice, she set
about seeking a passage out of France for them all.

So it was that in November of 1944 the family arrived in Hertfordshire and prepared to wait out the rest of the war. Sébastien
was sent away for a rest cure, while Cécilia was taken to doctors
in Cambridge and London, who prodded her and examined her
back and lifted her legs up and down, and gave her exercises to do
daily. Cécilia half-listened to what they said, and nodded her head

at all the right moments, then immediately forgot their instructions and followed her own inclination, which was to withdraw from the world, retreating further and further into herself, thinking as little as possible. It was the only way she could deal with the horrors she'd witnessed, and the deep sting of her sister's betrayal.

Rex, who for a few weeks had been her comfort in her unhappiness, was now nothing more than a reminder of the wrong she'd done Maggie, and of how her sister had repaid her. Besides, he was looking more like Emil every day, and every time she caught sight of him unexpectedly she would feel her heart clench with a pain that was almost agony. It was more than she could bear, and so she left her son more and more to her mother's frosty care, and to Estelle's perfunctory kindness, and tried her best to shut everything out.

The music had gone, now – or rather, if it hadn't gone, it had lost its glow and had become flat, routine, a habit to pass the time. Although she spent hours at a time idly tracing out snatches of music, improvising melodies, it held no colour for her now, no magic. The composition she'd begun in Nice was abandoned. Her violin, too, sat ignored on a shelf, as did Emil's guitar in its battered case, which Suzette had sent her along with some of his papers in an old briefcase. They went into a cupboard, and Cécilia never looked at them, although she couldn't quite bring herself to destroy them. Nurses came and went, and their names were forgotten immediately, and in among it all Cécilia sat, gazing at nothing and allowing time to pass around her.

Rose saw that Cécilia had become quite useless, and so she gave up trying to persuade her to return to her composition and instead invested all her hopes in Sébastien, her darling, her son, who had come out of his rest cure refreshed and almost back to normal and ready to play again. He'd fulfil all her hopes, be a famous musician, and restore the glory of the Brouillards to what it had once been, because she'd lived with the dream for so long that without it she was nothing.

Chapter Twenty-Eight

Hertfordshire, 1950

The scrap-books would never be finished now – not by her, at any rate – but there was still a lot of tidying up to do before Harriet could leave. She'd somehow amassed quite a lot of possessions in her time at Chaffingham, including so many new clothes that she'd need to buy a new suitcase to carry them. She was slightly shocked at her own profligacy, but she couldn't say she regretted it: when held up to daylight, the old clothes she'd arrived in looked horribly shabby next to her new things, and she felt so much smarter now, and more likely to impress a new employer.

In the end she'd decided she couldn't face going back to the agency, who wouldn't be at all happy with her, and instead had begun scouring the situations vacant pages for suitable positions, of which there seemed to be a decent few. What she really wanted was a job with a school or a college, somewhere noisy and exuberant, where the mood was cheerful and she could take refuge in the minor irritations and difficulties that came with a job of that sort, instead of having to absorb an atmosphere of constant unhappiness and mental torment. There she would have space to think and heal properly, away from the misery of the Brouillards and the fear of plunging into a new relationship with another man. It was too much to hope that Alec would wait until she was ready to start again, but he'd set her on the final stretch of the road to recovery, and at least she could remember him fondly. It could never have been serious between them – or that was what she told herself, despite the ache that surrounded her heart whenever she thought of him. The old Harriet made a few efforts to make herself heard and urge her to take the risk, but her emotional side held sway just at present, and she wasn't in the mood to listen to the voice of reason.

Harriet wanted to leave her work in good shape, to make things easier for the next girl – if there was a next girl. To that end, she spent some time one day reorganising the filing system in Mrs Brouillard's office into something simpler to use, and getting rid of old unwanted documents. After that she decided to clear out all the drawers in the desk. The bottom drawer had always given her a bit of trouble, as it wouldn't shut properly, so in a fit of efficiency she pulled it out all the way to see if it could be fixed. As soon as she did that, she realised what the problem was: a sheaf of letters had been shoved to the back of the drawer and had fallen down into the drawer cavity. It must have been the previous girl who'd done it.

Harriet pulled out the crumpled papers. They were all dated months ago, before her arrival, and whatever invitations or appointments they contained would have long since passed, but she opened them anyway, one by one, in case there was anything important that required her attention. One of the envelopes was addressed in a familiar handwriting, but her mind was on other things and she didn't recognise it until she had the letter open in front of her. It was from Fernand Quinault, whose most recent note Mrs Brouillard had torn up before Harriet could read it. Rose had gone out with Sébastien and wasn't expected back until dinner, but Harriet still glanced around half-guiltily, as though her employer might come in at any moment. She read the letter. It was in French, and she had a little trouble with the handwriting, but as she read on her eyes widened. She got to the end then went back and read it again, then a third time. It was evidently a continuation of earlier correspondence between the two of them, as it referred to Rose's refusal to agree to something they had discussed previously. Exactly what she was refusing to agree to wasn't stated in so many words, but it was obvious enough what it meant.

Harriet sat back breathlessly and stared at the paper in front of her in astonishment. So this was what Quinault wanted! If what he was saying was true, then it would be momentous news if the information ever got out, and would most likely cause an earthquake that would reverberate throughout the music world. It was almost too much to take in, and Harriet sat for several minutes, her mind racing. She wished she hadn't read the letter; it was too big a piece of news to keep to herself, but it seemed neither Mrs Brouillard nor Quinault was prepared to make it public, and it was their secret to reveal – or Quinault's, anyway. She pondered for several minutes without reaching a decision, then at last folded up the paper and put it in her pocket. She'd have to sleep on it before deciding what to do.

As it happened, events overtook her that same day, and the decision almost made itself. She was still in the office, clearing things out, when the doorbell rang, and she remembered that Quinault was supposed to be visiting again, in defiance of Mrs Brouillard's orders. It was encouraging to see that Cécilia had decided to make a small stand and disobey her mother, although she had sense enough not to do it openly.

Harriet was about to go and answer the door when she heard voices in the hall and judged she wasn't needed; Cécilia must have answered it herself. Harriet carried on with her work for a while longer and then went out into the hall. The sound of music drifted out from Cécilia's wing of the house; presumably they'd gone there to be more comfortable, away from the formality of the huge drawing room with its concert piano. Harriet went in to ask them if they wanted anything. Quinault was sitting at the baby grand, and to her surprise she saw that Cécilia had brought out her violin and was busy tuning it up. Rex was sitting on the sofa, playing with his toy cars.

'Hallo, Miss Conway,' said Quinault. 'You're just in time. I've managed to persuade Cécilia to get out her violin again. Cécilia, do you remember that song you and that fellow played in Nice that night at Marion's house? It was the first time I ever heard you play. What was his name now? Ginsberg, something like that. One of those Zazous with the long jackets. What happened to him, by the way?'

'I'm afraid he died,' replied Cécilia evenly, as Harriet looked up sharply at the familiar word.

'Oh, I'm very sorry. So many bright talents lost. But do you remember the song? I only heard it the once, that night at Marion's, but somehow it stuck in my memory. Could you teach me it? We could play it together.'

Cécilia looked irresolute.

'I... I don't know. I haven't played it in years.'

'Try it,' he urged.

'Please, Maman,' said Rex. 'I'd like to hear it. You don't play the violin much, do you?'

'No, I don't. I stopped.' She looked at her son, who was sitting there, smiling at her. 'Perhaps I could try it,' she said uncertainly.

'Excellent,' replied Quinault. 'Then you can teach me.'

'Actually, I have the sheet music. I kept it.' She wheeled herself over to a drawer, unlocked it and brought out a battered old manuscript book. She handed it to Quinault, who examined it with great interest.

'It's the first one. I made him write them down,' said Cécilia.

'"Cécilia". He called it after you! I remember it very well.' A smile spread across Quinault's face. 'What an entertaining evening that was – and it reminds me, I must write to Marion soon. I had a letter from her a month ago and I still haven't replied.'

'Marion! Where is she?' asked Cécilia. 'Is she well? I'm sorry to say I'd almost forgotten about her, but she was very good to me at one time.'

'She spent the war in New York, but moved back out to Nice a couple of years ago with her latest husband. Her villa was quite burnt out in the fighting, and she's been rebuilding it. I'll give you her address and you can write to her if you like. Just be aware that she'll force you to come out and visit whether you like it or not.'

'That sounds like her,' said Cécilia with a laugh.

Quinault propped the music up on the piano.

'Here, we'll have to squash up to see the book together,' he said.

'It's all right, I can play it without the music. Yes, I really think I can play it,' Cécilia added in a murmur, almost in wonder. She drew her bow across the strings of the violin and grimaced. 'Ugh! I haven't practised this nearly enough recently.'

She tried a few little phrases while Quinault examined the music and ran his fingers experimentally up and down the piano keys, then he said:

'Shall we try?'

Cécilia took a deep breath and gave a nervous nod, and they began. It wasn't the best performance: Emil's writing was scrappy and difficult to sight-read, and Cécilia had spent years trying to forget the song had ever existed. Still, she set to bravely, and they made it through to the end. Harriet and Rex clapped enthusiastically, and Cécilia found herself laughing breathlessly, her eyes shining, as she had that day long ago, when she and Emil had first played it together in her apartment in Nice.

'I like that,' said Harriet. 'It's such a fun, happy tune. You should play more music like that, Cécilia.'

Rex was rapt. 'Oh!' he exclaimed.

'Did you like it?' asked Cécilia. He nodded.

'I like the colours,' he said. 'Blue is my favourite, and there's not much blue in the practice music Grand-mère gives me.'

Cécilia stared at him.

'Not much blue?' she said.

'No. It's all yellow and brown. I don't like those colours. What kind of music is this?'

'It's called jazz.'

'I like it. Who is it by?'

'Papa wrote it.'

He looked at her uncertainly.

'Do you mean Grand-père?'

'No, *your* papa. His name was Emil. He played guitar and he loved jazz music.'

'My papa!' He thought about this. 'Was he clever?'

'Very clever. And very brave, too. He was a hero in the war.'

'Did the Germans kill him?'

'Yes.'

'Poor Maman. Were you sad?'

'Yes, I was – very sad.'

'Are you still sad now?'

'A little. Perhaps not so much as I was. It was a long time ago.'

'That's his guitar, isn't it?' asked Harriet. She gestured to the instrument lying on the top shelf of the bookcase.

'It was, yes.'

'Is that why you didn't want me to play it? Because it made you sad?' said Rex.

'I suppose it was,' replied Cécilia.

Quinault had been flicking through Emil's music, but he now looked up and glanced from Cécilia to Rex as though he'd just realised something.

'I'm sorry,' he said at last. 'I'd no idea. And there I go, blundering about again and making you play music when you'd rather not.'

'It's all right, really,' said Cécilia. 'I'm glad you did. It wasn't as hard as I expected, and it was rather nice to hear it again after all these years.'

Quinault indicated the music book in front of him.

'Some of these are quite wonderful,' he said. 'I suppose they were never published?'

Cécilia shook her head.

'That's a pity. Who has the rights to them?'

'I've no idea. His family are all dead too, as far as I know.'

Quinault began picking out another of the tunes on the piano.

'What colour is this, Rex?' said Cécilia.

He gazed at the piano, his head on one side as he listened.

'Blue again! Dark blue and light blue. And purple – no – now it's a sort of pink colour.'

'What are you talking about, Rex?' said Harriet, laughing.

But Cécilia was smiling at her son fondly as he stared at the notes floating through the air. Quinault finished and Rex clapped his hands and said, 'Again, again!' Quinault began another piece, and after a minute Cécilia joined in, but they hadn't got more than halfway through it when Rose came in unexpectedly, followed by Sébastien. She stood stiffly until Quinault noticed her and stopped playing. Cécilia glanced round and lowered her violin.

'Maman!' she said. 'I thought you weren't coming back until dinner-time.'

'That's clear enough,' said Rose. 'Monsieur Quinault, I thought I told you not to come here again.'

It was said in rapid, brittle French. Quinault stood up from the piano stool and gave her a polite bow.

'*Pardon*,' he said. 'I wanted to see Cécilia and she said I might come. I didn't mean to intrude.'

'Nonsense!' replied Cécilia suddenly. 'I invited him, Maman. He's my friend, and I wanted to see him. I thought you'd be pleased to see me have a visitor.'

Sébastien was regarding Quinault with contempt.

'You always did have terrible taste in friends, Céci,' he said.

'Hold your tongue, Sébastien!' snapped Rose, then to Cécilia: 'I had very good reasons for not wanting this person here in the house. But clearly you didn't want to listen to me, even though my only purpose in all this was to protect you.'

'Protect me? From what? Fernand comes to play music and cheer me up, and we talk about France and the old days. What's wrong with that?'

'He's out for everything he can get,' said Rose. 'I've told you this before, but it seems you didn't believe me.'

'I beg your pardon, madam,' replied Quinault with dignity. 'I'm not here to ask for anything. You've made your views quite clear on the subject, and for my old friend's sake I have no intention of causing a scandal. I'm here exactly as you see me, and with no ulterior motive, just to see Cécilia and talk about music and the friends we have in common.'

'What do you mean, cause a scandal?' asked Cécilia, looking from one of them to the other.

Quinault shook his head.

'It's nothing,' he said. 'Just a little matter of business between your father and me. It doesn't really matter now.'

'I'll never understand why my father mixed with the likes of you,' said Sébastien suddenly. 'I suppose it was one of his weaknesses, but he certainly wasn't too choosy in his associates.'

Quinault flushed a little but didn't say anything. Cécilia was angry, however.

'Stop that!' she said. 'Don't you dare talk to him like that. Fernand is a friend of mine.'

'Friend of yours, indeed!' snorted Sébastien. 'I'll bet he's come to sponge something from us. Maman says he took advantage of Papa's good nature to get himself promoted to conductor of the Paris-Montparnasse Symphony Orchestra. I'll bet that's how he's been so successful in Hollywood, too. They're all Jews there – they all know each other and give each other jobs. They're parasites, nothing more.'

Harriet had been listening to the exchange indignantly. Quinault was such a polite, unassuming man, and yet all Mrs Brouillard and

Sébastien did was subject him to abuse, based on nothing more than unfounded prejudice.

'Why must you be so hateful?' she demanded, glaring at Sébastien. 'You're horrid to him, and it's not fair, when he's been so good to Cécilia.'

Sébastien rounded on her.

'Oh yes, *Miss Conway*, and what would you know about it?' he spat.

'More than you think. I know he's been cheated out of something that's rightfully his.'

She said it before she could stop herself.

'What are you talking about?' asked Sébastien, at the same time as Rose exclaimed, 'Miss Conway!'

Harriet looked at Quinault. 'It's true, isn't it?'

He glanced uncomfortably at Cécilia. 'I…' he began.

'What's true?' asked Cécilia.

'Are you going to tell?' said Harriet, still addressing Quinault. It was too late to wish the words unsaid now. She'd gone and done it, and now she had to follow it through, however reckless she was being.

'Miss Conway!' said Rose again sharply. 'I insist you leave the room this minute!'

'Tell what?' asked Cécilia.

'Very well,' said Harriet. 'If you won't say it, then I shall. Cécilia, Fernand Quinault wrote *Les Orchidées*.'

Chapter Twenty-Nine

There was a silence, then Sébastien began to laugh. It was an unpleasant sound.

'Don't be ridiculous!' he said. 'Now I've heard it all.'

But Cécilia was looking at Fernand Quinault.

'Is it true?' she asked.

He hesitated, then nodded.

'But what…?' She turned to Rose, whose lips were pressed together in a thin line. 'Maman?'

Mrs Brouillard looked more angry than Harriet had ever seen her, but she was clearly trying to hold it in.

'I expect you're feeling very pleased with yourself,' she said to Harriet. 'I don't know why you felt the need to cause this sort of disruption before you left. I can only assume you take pleasure out of it.'

'Of course I don't!' replied Harriet. 'As a matter of fact, I didn't mean to say anything, but you were both so horribly rude to him I couldn't stop myself.'

'Look here, it's not really true, is it?' asked Sébastien. He was still smiling disbelievingly, but anxious lines had appeared on his forehead, and his face had paled. Rex, meanwhile, had picked up his toy bear and was pressing himself into the cushions of the sofa, as though to avoid being seen.

'There's no proof!' said Rose. 'He might be saying anything.'

'It's true I have no proof,' replied Quinault. 'There was a signed letter containing the terms of the agreement, but I had to leave everything behind when I left Paris and I don't know where it is now. All I have is one or two older letters referring to it, but they're a little vague and I don't know whether they'd stand up in court.'

'Do you mean you and my father agreed it between you?' asked Cécilia in astonishment.

'Yes. I wrote it in 1940 and was hoping to get it performed, but then the Nazis came and I lost my job as conductor, as well as any chance of making a name for myself with *Les Orchidées*, since nobody was allowed to play music by Jewish composers any more. But I was fortunate to have Jean-Jacques as my friend. He loved the symphony and said it was a shame to let it go to waste, so we came up with a plan. He was to publish it in his name and hold any money it earned for me until a future date when things were less dangerous. But then he died suddenly. It was very unexpected, and shortly after that I had to leave Paris and go into hiding. For a long time after that I had other things on my mind, as you can probably imagine. My father died, and I escaped France only by the skin of my teeth. Then after the war I was establishing myself in Hollywood, and in any case I didn't know how to get in touch with Mrs Brouillard. Eventually I found out her address and wrote to her, but I'm afraid she didn't take it too kindly, even when I sent her copies of the letters I had. I was busy in America for a long time so I didn't pursue the matter too hard, but then when I knew I was coming to England, I decided to come and see your mother in person, as I thought I might be able to persuade her. I was wrong.'

'But if you wrote it then you ought to get the credit for it,' said Cécilia. 'Maman?'

She turned to her mother questioningly.

'What proof do we have?' Rose glared defiantly at Quinault. 'None at all, except your word for it. Perhaps you did have a hand in writing it, but I've no doubt it was mostly my husband's work.'

'I'm sorry to contradict you, but it was entirely my own work, and any expert ought to be able to confirm it.'

'Everybody said how different it was from his previous music,' said Cécilia. 'I always thought it was strange that he wrote his most avant-garde piece when he was old. Maman, if Fernand wrote it then we have no right collecting the royalties from it.'

'What do you think pays for your medical treatment, you foolish girl?' snapped Rose. 'Certainly not his older music. It's paid for all those expensive doctors you ignore, and all Sébastien's treatment, and his music lessons, and the upkeep of this house, as far as it goes. *Les Orchidées* has kept us afloat for the past five years. Without it we'd have gone under long ago. It was written by your father, and until Monsieur Quinault can prove any differently, then I am afraid he's out of luck.'

She seemed almost defensive, Harriet thought. Sébastien must have seen it, too. As he listened to the conversation the complacent, contemptuous look had gradually disappeared from his face, to be replaced by something akin to incredulous horror. Now he rounded on his mother.

'It's true, isn't it?' he said. 'Why, of course it is! I don't know why I didn't see it before. *Les Orchidées* is nothing like Papa's usual stuff. He wrote old-fashioned music. *Les Orchidées* is modern and in a completely different style.'

'Yes,' replied Quinault. 'Jean-Jacques said that he was sure nobody would believe it was his, but he said we might as well try it anyway. And the deception worked, luckily for us both.'

Sébastien gave a bitter, sardonic laugh and began to pace up and down.

'Well, this is something of a jolt, I don't mind saying. After all these years, all the time I've spent tearing myself apart trying to play that damned piece of music in honour of my father, the man who supposedly wrote it, now I find it wasn't his work at all, but really belongs to a second-rate vaudevillian who probably dashed it out in half an hour. What a joke! And to think we all fell for it – the Germans included. Tell me, Maman, did Papa write *any* music? Or have you been lying to us all these years?'

'Of course he wrote music!' said Rose.

'But how do we know? He lied about it once, so how do we know his whole reputation isn't founded on a lie? How can we be sure he hadn't been stealing other people's work for years?'

'He didn't steal my work,' replied Quinault. 'As I told you, he published it on my behalf.'

'Then if he didn't steal it, you did,' said Sébastien to his mother. 'You knew about this all along, didn't you?'

'Of course I didn't! But if you're determined to believe this man's lies—'

The normally easy-going Quinault was beginning to lose his patience.

'I beg your pardon, but that is not true. Jean-Jacques told me on several occasions that he had mentioned it to you, Mrs Brouillard. He was always aware of what might happen if he was no longer here to act as my champion, and so he took care to ensure that there was some way of proving the case after he was gone. He kept a copy of the agreement we signed, although I have no idea whether it still exists.'

'Does it exist?' said Cécilia to Rose.

Rose had been completely caught on the back foot. She opened her mouth and then closed it again, as if uncertain what to say.

'If it does exist, then it'll be in the locked drawer of the filing cabinet where she keeps her private correspondence,' said Harriet.

'If she had any sense she'll have burnt it,' said Sébastien sourly.

'No, I didn't burn it!' replied Rose suddenly. She glared round at them all defiantly. 'I see it's no use. I might have hoped that my own children would have more loyalty to me in this matter, after all I've done for you, and after all your father did, but it seems I'm to be disappointed yet again. Very well, there was an agreement – a rambling, ridiculous piece of nonsense which no lawyer would ever have countenanced, and probably full of loopholes.'

'But why did you keep it secret?' asked Cécilia.

'Why do you think? Haven't I already told you? There was very little money after the war. Nobody was playing Jean-Jacques Brouillard's music – not his older pieces, anyway. All anyone wanted to listen to was *Les Orchidées*, and since there was no one else to promote it and make use of it, I did it myself. And I don't regret what I did. Surely Jean-Jacques' family deserves to be able to live after his death? Surely his children deserve the same chance to achieve success as he had? I was certain I was in the right. And look how you all repaid me for my work. Marcus and Maggie got themselves killed, while the two of you have frittered away your talents in useless self-indulgence.'

'Self-indulgence?' said Sébastien. 'You've pushed me and bullied me and forced me to practise until I could hardly stand up, and had me put away when I didn't think I could manage it any more, just because you had to give up your own music and couldn't bear to miss out on the glory, and you call that self-indulgence?'

His voice was becoming increasingly high-pitched, his breath coming rapidly.

'Yes, it was self-indulgence,' returned Rose. 'Don't tell me you didn't enjoy all the attention you got in Paris. What about all those people who complimented you and patted you on the back and gave you gifts when you played so nicely for them? If you'd only tried a bit harder instead of letting your head be turned by the praise, you might be a world-class musician by now. Instead, what are you?'

'Oh, there's no need to continue,' said Sébastien. 'I know quite well what I am – I'm a failure. Too highly strung to make a success of anything. That's right, isn't it? I know what you think, but it didn't stop you from pushing me beyond all endurance, did it? Here, look at us. This is what you have now.' He indicated himself and Cécilia. 'A cripple and a nervous wreck! Much good your ambition did you.'

Fernand Quinault had been looking increasingly embarrassed. Now he spoke up.

'I'm very sorry,' he said to Cécilia. 'If I'd had any idea this was going to happen I'd never have dreamt of coming. I didn't come to cause trouble or beg money off anyone, least of all you. As soon as Miss Conway told me that the royalties from *Les Orchidées* paid for your treatment, I realised it would be better to keep quiet about the whole thing. Whether you believe it or not, Mrs Brouillard, your husband was my friend. Of course I wanted to claim my rights when I first came here, but I know Jean-Jacques would have been disappointed in me if I'd tried to deprive his daughter of the treatment she needed, so I changed my mind.' He shrugged. 'And it's not as though I needed the money – Hollywood pays very well. Mrs Brouillard, please be assured I was telling the truth when I said I didn't intend to cause trouble. I didn't realise the circumstances your family were in. I'm very sorry, Cécilia. I think I'd better go now and let you all talk it over.'

'Yes, perhaps you'd better go,' said Cécilia. 'I'll call you later and we can talk about it then.'

She held out her hand and he grasped it for a moment then went out, leaving them in silence. Rex was still crouching behind a cushion with his bear. As Quinault departed he scrambled down from the sofa and went across to his mother, who put her arm around him and buried her face in his hair.

'Well, I hope you're happy, Miss Conway,' said Rose.

'Of course I'm not!' exclaimed Harriet. She was horrified at what she'd unleashed, and it was taking all her strength not to cover her face and run out of the room. 'Cécilia, I'm so terribly sorry. I didn't plan to blurt it out, but I found one of his letters this afternoon and it came as rather a shock.'

'*It came as rather a shock*,' said Sébastien suddenly, mimicking Harriet with a savageness that took her breath away. 'Rot. You knew this all along, didn't you? You've just been waiting to produce it at the right moment. Couldn't wait to get your own back, could you?'

'It wasn't like that!'

'Yes it was.' His face was screwed up, and he looked like a small boy in a bad temper. 'You hate me, just like everyone else. Everyone wants to get at me and make me suffer. You especially,' he said to his mother. 'Look at all the damage you've done. Look at the mess you turned me into. I was perfectly happy until you decided I had to be famous at all costs and follow in dear Cécilia's footsteps. All the things I hated doing – exhibiting myself in front of all those fat, beastly Germans in the hope that they'd mention my name to somebody important in Berlin – always feeling like a performing dog in a circus. The son of the great Jean-Jacques Brouillard, trying and never quite managing to live up to his father's reputation. I couldn't stand it, I tell you! But you made me do it. And what was the use? His reputation was all hot air!'

'Sébastien—' began Cécilia.

He turned to her.

'And you too. I was always in your shadow, wasn't I? And that's the way you liked it. You somehow persuaded everybody that you were a great talent, so they showered you with adulation and gave you all the attention you wanted. And then I was forced to drive myself into the ground, trying to keep up with you.'

'What?' Cécilia looked astonished. 'That's not true at all!'

Rex raised his eyes and glowered at Sébastien, who ignored him. Years of resentment had welled up in him and he couldn't hold it in any longer.

'Oh, don't play the innocent with me! I recognise you for what you are if nobody else does. You're a manipulator, that's what you are. You use people for your own advantage and then make them feel sorry for you when you're found out. That's how you got round Maggie, isn't it? Poor Maggie – if it wasn't for Maman and her ambition and you and your betrayal she'd still be alive today.'

'What?'

'You left me with no choice, don't you see?' He turned back to Rose. 'You made me do it; you and Lefeuvre, always telling me to be helpful to the Germans and co-operate with them if I wanted to get anywhere. I was too young to know any different. And you—' he swung round to Cécilia '—you stole a man from your own sister and had his bastard child. Maggie was always my favourite. I loved her, and now I have to do without her because of what you did. I wish she was still here. She'd have stood up for me. I never meant her to get killed, I just wanted to help – just wanted to be good and do what Maman told me and help Maggie get back at the people who hurt her. I thought she'd be pleased about it after the way you cheated her, but she wasn't grateful at all when I told her what I'd done. It was all your fault; I never wanted it to turn out like this! And now it seems it was all for nothing anyway. We've been living on borrowed glory all these years and look what it's done to us!'

He was sounding increasingly hysterical. He strode up and down, throwing up his hands in agitation.

Cécilia was staring at him in dawning astonishment.

'What are you talking about?' she demanded. 'What do you mean, you never meant her to get killed?'

He stopped and looked mutinous.

'It wasn't my fault, I tell you,' he said. 'I suppose you could say she brought it on herself in a way, although God knows I didn't mean it to happen. I told her, you know. I told her if she kept working for the Resistance then the Germans would keep shooting innocent people, but she wouldn't listen. She said she had to do it, and I wanted to put a stop to it, but I never thought anyone would kill her for it. Funny, isn't it? It wasn't the Germans at all but her own side who did for her in the end. That's what your fine Resistance friends did, Céci. They weren't interested in saving France at all – once the Germans had gone all they wanted to do was turn on each other like rats.'

His voice had risen to a high-pitched whine, and he stuck out his lip and darted vicious glances at each one of them in turn from under his eyelashes.

Cécilia was breathing rapidly as though she'd been running, and she'd gone even paler than usual. She was staring at Sébastien as if he were wholly unfamiliar to her.

'It was you who passed on the information!' she said in wonder.

He was silent, but his furious, defensive expression said it all.

She wheeled herself across to him and looked up into his face, forcing him to meet her gaze.

'Sébastien? Is it true?'

Still he said nothing. Harriet held her breath and glanced at Rose, who was watching, stony-faced. The silence hung like a guillotine.

Cécilia let out a sharp breath and put her hands to her face, grief-stricken.

'And you let me think she did it,' she said, so quietly that it was almost a whisper. 'All this time, I thought she'd betrayed us because of what I did to her. You've let me think that all these years. My poor, brave sister, and she had nothing to do with it!'

'I couldn't help it!' he said defiantly. 'I didn't want her to die!'

'But you wanted me to die. And Emil – you wanted him to die. And Guillaume, and Gérard, and Henri, and all the others. They're all dead, and I'm in this wheelchair because of what you did. And you stood by and said nothing while they dragged Maggie away and shot her. And you watched me sit here, rotting away year after year, eaten up with guilt, hating myself and thinking I'd driven her to it because I fell in love with Emil and took him away from her.'

Her brother squirmed under her reproachful gaze.

'I couldn't say anything! They'd have shot me instead!'

'Oh, Sébastien,' said Cécilia. The tears had begun to roll slowly down her face.

'It wasn't my fault!' he repeated. 'I told you! You brought it on yourself. Look, you're doing it again! Trying to make me feel bad. I won't stand for it. None of this was my fault!'

'What about Marcel?' said Cécilia suddenly. 'Did you give him away too?'

'Who? Do you mean that idiot doctor? I can't remember. Perhaps I mentioned him to someone, I don't know. Look here, what does he matter? What does any of it matter now? I won't listen to this any more – I'm tired of you all. I have to get out!'

He put his hands over his ears like a small boy, then turned and left the room in a hurry. Rex didn't understand what was going on, but he could see his mother was upset. He crossed to her and threw his arms around her, and she held tight to him and wept. Rose was still standing rooted to the spot, her lips pressed together. What she was thinking was anybody's guess.

Harriet raised a hand to her forehead. It felt clammy and cold, and she could feel herself trembling slightly. What had she done? She'd never meant any of this to happen, but now it seemed she'd turned over a hornets' nest and set the whole family against each other. She stirred uncertainly and took one or two steps towards the door. As she did so, Mrs Brouillard seemed to come to herself. She straightened up and turned her head to Harriet.

'You had better go and speak to Estelle about dinner,' she said.

Chapter Thirty

It was getting dark, and Harriet had spent the last hour in her room fearing to come out, although she could hear no sound from below. Finally she understood the heartache Cécilia had kept buried within her all these years, the story that had been too painful to tell. Maggie had sent this man, Emil, to her sister, trusting her to shelter him, and Cécilia had fallen in love with him herself – had had a child by him, in fact.

It was the sort of private tragedy that happened every day, and would usually have had no other consequences than the unhappiness of the people involved, but in this case it had had terrible, far-reaching repercussions that had ended in Maggie's tragic and unjust death. Out of jealousy or fear, or who knew what other motive, Sébastien had betrayed both his sisters, and they'd paid a heavy price for it. He and Cécilia had had a prickly relationship at the best of times, but how could it possibly be repaired following this new revelation? And Harriet herself had been the unwitting catalyst for the rupture. She'd read private letters like a sneak, and she'd spoken out when she ought to have kept quiet. Whatever happened to the Brouillards now would be on her shoulders. How could she possibly face them?

But it was approaching dinner-time, and she couldn't stay here forever. She'd have to go downstairs sooner or later. She put on one of her new evening frocks and glanced at her reflection in a perfunctory sort of way, then went out and downstairs. There was no sound in the hall. She pushed open the door to Cécilia's wing, took a deep breath, and went in. Cécilia and Rex were sitting at the piano together, not playing, but looking over some music books together. Cécilia looked up as Harriet came in. Her face was drawn and her eyes were pink-rimmed, but she'd stopped crying.

'I came to fetch Rex,' said Harriet. 'Dinner will be ready in a few minutes.'

'Go and wash your hands, Rex,' said Cécilia.

Rex ran off obediently, and Cécilia played one or two notes on the piano.

'I'm sorry.' Harriet was contrite. 'I had no idea.'

'She was always so good to me,' said Cécilia, not looking up from the piano. 'I didn't know what I was doing in those days. I was such a child, but she looked after me and stood up for me, just like she did for Sébastien. She was so brave, Harriet. She never faltered. She fought against the Occupation from the very beginning, and never stopped trying even when things looked hopeless. She really believed in what she was doing. Not like me. I was just a hanger-on, really. I treated Maggie very badly. It's true, you know – what Sébastien said, I mean. I stole the man she loved, and even then she forgave me.' The tears began to roll down her cheeks again, dripping onto the piano keys as she played. 'That's the worst of it all: I didn't believe her. My own sister. I thought she'd lied about forgiving me. I really believed she'd given us away to the Germans. That's the cruellest thing, somehow.'

'But it was Sébastien all along,' said Harriet. 'How could he do it?'

'I don't know. He was just a child at the time, and Maman worked him awfully hard. She thought he had more potential than I did, being a boy, you see. She always felt she'd had to give up music because she was a woman. Men have it easier. But I had no idea he felt so badly about me.'

She let out a breath and raised glistening eyes to Harriet's. 'I've been racking my brains, trying to remember anything I might have said or done to make him think that I felt I was better than him, but I can't. I never thought I was better than anyone – all I wanted to do was play my music. And yet he still hated me enough to do this. I had no idea. I always knew he was a little jealous, but I thought it was just the way he was, and that he'd get over it in time, once he made his own career. But he must really have hated me.'

She looked stricken.

Harriet didn't know what to say, but just then Rex returned so she was spared the necessity. Estelle came in.

'Dinner is ready,' she announced.

'You'd better go, Rex,' said Cécilia.

'Are you coming?' asked Harriet.

Cécilia shook her head. 'I don't think I can. I can't speak to Sébastien just now. I don't know if I can ever speak to him again. I need some time to think.'

'I'll bring you some food, Maman,' said Rex eagerly.

'Yes, please do. I'd like that,' she replied.

'And can I sit with you after dinner?'

'Yes, of course. We can read a book together, if you like.'

Dinner began uncomfortably, as was only to be expected. Harriet and Rex went in and took their seats. Mrs Brouillard was already there, seated, waiting. She looked as unemotional as ever.

'This is where we find out whether you really are as professional as the agency said you were, Miss Conway,' said Rose. 'I hope you can be discreet about what happened this afternoon.'

Harriet was flustered for a second.

'Yes... yes, of course. This is nothing to do with me, really. I didn't mean to... I never intended...' she faltered.

'Well, perhaps you ought to have thought of that before you decided we all needed to clear the air,' said Rose dryly. 'Where is Sébastien?'

'I think he went upstairs to the archive,' ventured Rex.

'Miss Conway, will you fetch him please?' said Rose.

She was so determined to behave as though nothing had happened that Harriet wanted to scream. She stood up and went out of the dining room in search of Sébastien. As Rex had said, he was in the archive, working busily.

'What are you doing?' asked Harriet in surprise. Sébastien had put a heap of scrap-books on the table in the middle of the room, and was arranging it. A half-smoked cigarette hung from the corner of his mouth. He gestured at the pile, but didn't stop working.

'You see these, Harriet? Do you know what they are?'

'Yes. They're your father's newspaper cuttings.'

'And every single one of them a lie!'

'Hardly,' said Harriet. 'Look, I know you're upset about *Les Orchidées*, but I think you're overreacting.'

But he wasn't listening.

'All a lie, all a lie, all a lie,' he was chanting under his breath. He was acting strangely, and Harriet was at a loss to explain it until she saw the bottle of whisky standing open on the window-sill next to a half-empty glass.

'Have you been drinking?' she asked.

'Have you been drinking?' he mimicked nastily. 'And what if I have? God knows there's little enough else to do in this house that doesn't involve playing a musical instrument. Do you play anything, Harriet? Ah, yes, you play the piano a little, don't you? Do you enjoy it? Did your mother make you practise hour after hour after hour until your fingers bled? Did she beat you if you didn't play quite well enough? I'll bet you were allowed friends. Not that friends were forbidden, exactly, but anyone who didn't see music quite as we did would get frozen out soon enough. It was almost a relief to go to the Conservatoire and study there. The teachers there encouraged, rather than threatened. But then one always had to come home at the end of the day to more interminable practising and studying, because Maman would never be satisfied.

'And then there were the Germans and the professors, always hanging around our house, always panting over me and pawing at me because they liked to look at me, promising me presents, getting me alone so they could paw at me again. I hated it – hated every minute of it, but Maman said the Germans were going to win and we should be very clear about which side our bread was buttered on. Selfish, all selfish!' he burst out viciously. 'Nobody thought of me. Nobody thought of anyone but themselves. Even Maggie stopped caring about me when she met that idiot of a Communist Jew. She spent all her time mooning over him while they were together and feeling sorry for herself when he left. Imagine that! She ought to have been thankful, but instead she just threw herself back into the Resistance. Nobody was on my side. Nobody cared about how I felt. There was Maman on the one hand telling me to collaborate, and Maggie and Cécilia on the other, putting us all in danger. I couldn't win whatever I did.'

He turned unsteadily to the window-sill and picked up the glass, then took a large gulp of whisky.

'I don't suppose you can quite understand how much I hated music sometimes. I detested it – despised it – wanted nothing more to do with it. But I wasn't allowed to stop. The only time I ever had a break was just after the liberation, when we came to England and they shut me up in hospital. The doctors said it was nervous exhaustion. Maman told them I'd seen some bad things. She thought it was because I'd been there when they killed Maggie and it sent me mad. Perhaps it did, a little. Nobody wants to see their sister shot dead, after all – especially not over some silly mistake. That was unfortunate. But really, it was because I couldn't stand the music any more.

'And then I came out of hospital and it was the same old thing again: practise, practise, practise, while Maman talked to people and begged for favours to try and get me solo parts, because God forbid I should ever be a plain old second violin in a second-rate orchestra. No, I was the son of Jean-Jacques Brouillard, and it would be shameful to settle for anything less than first violinist or concert pianist. She didn't seem to care that I couldn't do it – no, I must do it or die in the attempt.'

He finished his cigarette, tossing it onto the pile of scrap-books without first stubbing it out. Harriet moved forward and put out the still-glowing end. He didn't seem to notice, but fished out another cigarette and applied a match to it, then held the burning match to the leather edge of one of the scrap-books. He watched almost idly as the leather smoked a little, but didn't catch.

'Be careful, that's dangerous,' said Harriet.

'Dangerous, is it, Miss Conway? Why should you care? After all, this isn't your house, and these aren't your books. You don't have a right to say what happens to them.'

'Nor do you.'

'Oh, but I do – every right.'

The first match had gone out. He struck another and opened the scrap-book and held the flame to the corner of the pages. This time it caught, and he watched with every appearance of enjoyment as the paper curled and blackened under the jagged flame.

'You see?' he said. 'I can burn them, and it'll be as though he never existed.'

'No it won't.' Harriet eyed the table in alarm. She darted forward and slammed the book closed, and the fire went out.

'Now look what you've done,' he said crossly. 'I want them gone.'

'You'll be gone if you keep on the way you are. Have you seen how much paper there is in here? If you're not careful the whole room will go up and then the house.'

'Oh, well, what does it matter? This is a foul place. I never liked it. I want to go back to Paris.' He threw his half-smoked cigarette down onto a heap of newspapers that was lying on the floor. Harriet stamped on it quickly.

'Look here, you'd better stop!' she said.

He ignored her and lit another match.

Harriet could see there was no use in arguing with him. She left the room and ran downstairs. Rose had decided not to wait, and she and Rex had begun dinner.

'Mrs Brouillard, it's Sébastien,' said Harriet breathlessly. 'I think you'd better come. He's setting fire to things.'

'*What?*'

Her employer didn't stop to ask more questions but stood up and left the room quickly.

'He's been drinking,' said Harriet as they headed into the new wing. 'And I don't think he's quite sane.'

'He's never been quite sane,' muttered Rose grimly.

'I don't think he quite realised what he was doing. He wouldn't listen to me when I told him to stop.'

'He'll listen to me,' said Rose. They hurried up the stairs and Rose burst into the archive. Sébastien had given up piling the scrap-books on the table, apparently considering them not flammable enough. Instead he'd shoved a great pile of newspapers over to the base of one of the wall shelves. As they entered they found him just setting light to it. The flame caught quickly and lapped hungrily at the newspapers.

'Sébastien!' said Rose in horror. 'What are you doing? The records!'

He whirled round and came towards her.

'Oh, it's you, is it? I might have known you'd be more worried about the records than you are about me.'

'Of course I'm not,' said Rose.

'Yes you are.' He threw out an arm to encompass the shelves stacked around the walls. 'Look at all this. Nearly nine years Father's been dead. Nine years! And still you keep this shrine to him. But what about the living? What about me?'

The fire had caught some loose papers that were stacked on one of the shelves. Smoke had begun to curl up and run back along the ceiling towards them.

'Get some water, Miss Conway,' commanded Rose.

'It's too late!' exclaimed Harriet, staring at the fire in horror. 'We need to get out.'

'Then I shall get some,' said Rose, as though Harriet hadn't spoken. Opposite the attic room was a small bathroom that was also used as a cleaning cupboard. In it was a pail. Rose went in and ran some water into it. The water pressure wasn't strong up here, and after half a minute she gave up in disgust. Harriet could only watch helplessly as she ran back into the attic room and threw the water onto the fire. There was a hissing sound, but it wasn't nearly enough. Flames had begun to lick against the curtains and curl around the open window. Sébastien watched it all with mild interest.

'Mrs Brouillard, come out!' said Harriet.

'Sébastien!' Mrs Brouillard's voice rose to a scream. 'I insist you come out now!'

'Why should I come out?' replied Sébastien. 'It's fun, I want to watch.'

'Sébastien!' exclaimed Harriet urgently. 'You have to come! It's going to go up any second.'

But he didn't seem to be listening. The paint on the window-sill was bubbling and blackening, and the window frame had begun to buckle. The shadows flickered on Sébastien's face. Harriet retreated, eyeing the fire, which was now nearly at the ceiling.

'You don't care if I live or die,' said Sébastien to his mother. 'I could stay here forever and all you'd care about would be those stupid scrap-books of yours.'

As he spoke, the shelf unit at the end of the room caught fully. The flames roared upwards. The heat was becoming unbearable, and the smoke was getting thicker.

'Sébastien!' exclaimed Rose again.

But Sébastien wasn't listening. Harriet grabbed hold of her employer's arm and pulled her back towards the door just as there was a roaring sound and the whole room went up in an explosion of blinding orange. Rose shrieked, but it was too late for him now. The last thing they saw of him was as a shadowy figure in among the flames, regarding them in wonder. Harriet wrapped her sleeve around her hand and pulled the door shut.

'Come on, before it spreads!' she said.

But Rose wouldn't come. She was leaning against the wall of the corridor, shaking and breathing rapidly. Then she gave a great wail and sank to the ground.

'Sébastien!' she cried.

'Oh no you don't!' said Harriet firmly. 'We haven't time for this.'

She lifted Rose under the arms and dragged her bodily towards the stairs. Rose at last seemed to come to herself, although she was still shaking. She shook herself free from Harriet's grip.

'I'm quite all right,' she said.

Harriet herself was trying to force down a feeling of panic at what she had just seen. Her heart was thumping wildly and her lips were dry.

'I'm going to tell everyone to get out,' she said. She took hold of Rose's hand and pulled her down the stairs. Mrs Brouillard sank onto the bottom stair. She was safe enough there now. Harriet ran towards Cécilia's room, and met Cécilia just coming out.

'What is it?' she said. 'I can smell smoke.'

'Cécilia, we've got to get out, there's a fire. Where's Léonie?'

'She went out for the evening.'

'Come on! And don't argue. We'll get you out.'

'Wait!' said Cécilia. Before Harriet could speak she wheeled herself back into her room, which was directly under the attic room and was starting to fill with smoke.

'What are you doing?' said Harriet.

'I'll only be a second.' She wheeled herself over to the ash dresser and brought out a battered old briefcase. 'Get the notebook from the piano, will you?'

Harriet ran across to the baby grand and picked up Emil's old manuscript book from where it had been left earlier, then threw a shawl around Cécilia and pushed her out of the room. The smoke was drifting down the stairs, and Mrs Brouillard moved away from it, coughing and clutching at her breast.

'Let's get out,' said Harriet.

She chivvied Rose into the main wing of the house. Cécilia followed. Rex had just come out into the hall.

'Is something happening?' he asked.

'Help Maman out of the house. The archive is on fire. It hasn't spread very far yet, but we need to get out. You push her chair.'

'I can wheel myself,' Cécilia began, then saw Rex's face. 'But I'd prefer it if you pushed me.'

Harriet ran to the kitchen.

'Estelle, you'd better get out,' she said. 'There's a fire. *Au feu! Vous comprenez?*'

Estelle gave a little shriek and came out into the hall.

'Where is it?'

'In the archive. We need to get out before it spreads.'

Estelle made her own judgement of the situation. She hurried to the phone and picked it up.

'There is no sound!' she exclaimed. 'But we must call the fire brigade.'

'The line must have gone down,' said Harriet. 'But don't let's wait here and burn to death – we must get out! Estelle, look after Mrs Brouillard, she's not well.'

At last, by alternately coaxing and urging, Harriet got them all out of the house and onto the drive. Cécilia and Rex gasped as they looked back and saw how far the fire had spread in the new wing. The upstairs was fully ablaze, and the roof had begun to catch, and flames were licking at a trellis that was fixed to the outside wall.

'Where's Sébastien?' asked Cécilia.

Harriet didn't reply. The fire had begun to spread across the roof of the new wing, attracting the attention of neighbours and passers-by. Harriet sent Estelle to the farm to ask if she might use the telephone to call the fire brigade, and in the meantime looked about her anxiously, wanting to do something, but unable to think what.

'How did this happen?' said a voice at her side, and she turned and jumped. It was Alec, who'd come out to take Patch for a walk. 'Is everyone all right?' His eyes searched hers in concern.

'Hello Mr McLeod,' said Rex. 'The house is on fire!'

He was hopping from one foot to another, half-appalled, half-thrilled. The fire was spreading further. The flames had escaped from the windows of the upper storey of the new wing, and were now trickling along a low section of roof that jutted out from Cécilia's room.

'Maman! All the things in your room are going to burn!'

'It can't be helped,' said Cécilia.

'But what about Papa's guitar?' asked Rex.

Cécilia wasn't paying attention, but was looking at her mother, who was white and swaying.

'She needs a doctor,' she said. Alec turned and saw Mrs Brouillard, then went across and took her gently by the arm and led her to a low wall nearby, where he made her sit down. Cécilia wheeled herself over to her mother and looked at her in consternation.

'Maman, are you all right? And where's Sébastien?' Rose said nothing, and Cécilia's eyes widened in sudden realisation. 'He's not… he's not still inside, is he?'

Harriet said, gulping back tears: 'We tried to make him come out, but he wouldn't come.'

Cécilia gasped. '*Mon Dieu!*' she whispered.

The fire was burning fiercely now in the new wing, and had begun to spread to the roof of the main part of the house. Just then Maurice and John and the other men from the farm turned

up with Estelle. They took one assessing look at the state of the
fire, then John came up to Harriet.

'There's no one in there, is there?' he asked.

'I'm afraid someone was in that top room,' said Harriet. She
could feel tears pricking at her dry, stinging eyes, but they brought
no relief.

The men were nothing if not pragmatic. One look was enough
to tell them that there was no hope for the unfortunate person who
had remained behind. They shook their heads and tutted, then
turned their attention to that which could be saved.

'We can probably get a few things out for you if you like, miss,'
said John. 'The fire hasn't spread to the main part of the house yet.
What shall we bring?'

But Harriet's mind was blank. Bring Sébastien, she wanted
to say, but she couldn't send them into that wing of the house; it
was futile.

'Musical instruments,' she said at last.

'Can't bring that grand piano of yours out,' said John.

'There are violins and other things. Just what you can. Thank you.'

They went off and in through a side door furthest away from
the fire, and shortly afterwards Harriet saw them bringing out
various small items of furniture and something that looked like a
violin – probably Sébastien's, which he kept in the music room.

'Where's the fire brigade?' she muttered to herself. They seemed
to be taking an awfully long time to arrive.

'Harriet, have you seen Rex?' said Cécilia. She was wheeling
herself around the front lawn, looking agitated.

'Not for a few minutes. Isn't he with you?'

'No, he went off somewhere.'

'Hey! Come back, you little idiot!' came a shout just then, and
they looked and saw two of the men, who had managed to get
into the hall and bring out the portrait of Jean-Jacques Brouillard

and his Legion of Honour certificate through the front door. They were staring into the house, gesticulating.

'What is it?' said Harriet, then her heart gave a great thump as she realised who they must be shouting at. Cécilia had got there before her.

'Rex!' she exclaimed. She turned and wheeled herself towards the house.

'What do you think you're doing?' demanded Harriet. 'He hasn't gone in, surely? And even if he has, you can't go in after him!'

'I have to! I think he's gone in to get the guitar,' said Cécilia in a thin, high voice.

Harriet hurried after her.

'Don't go in there, it's too dangerous,' said one of the men warningly.

'I have to get him!' exclaimed Cécilia. Her breath was coming in gulps of fear, and she coughed as she inhaled a mouthful of smoke. She spluttered, then pulled her shawl over the lower part of her face and tried to hold it there and wheel herself towards the front door at the same time. There was something rather pitiful about her efforts, but she was determined. Harriet ran up to her and pulled her away from the house.

'Don't be ridiculous! Are you sure he's gone in there?' she said, turning to the man, who nodded dismally.

Cécilia had begun to sob, and Harriet gazed at her irresolutely, and then came to a decision: there was nothing for it – she'd have to go in herself, and quickly, before Rex was overcome by smoke. The heat emanating from that side of the house was tremendous. Quickly she unfastened a thin scarf she was wearing around her neck, and ran to dip it in the old water butt which stood to the side of the front door. She took a deep breath, wrapped it around the lower part of her face, and went in through the door. The entrance hall was dark and smoky; the lights had failed, and she could hardly see a thing. She was groping blindly towards the door of the new wing, willing herself to breathe slowly through the mask, and only through her nose, when she heard running footsteps behind her and someone took hold of her arm roughly.

'What do you think you're doing?' said Alec's voice, muffled under his jacket, which he'd pulled across the lower part of his face.

'I have to find Rex! He came in to rescue his father's guitar.'

'He didn't! The little idiot. You go out and I'll get him.'

But Harriet was already pulling open the door to Cécilia's wing. The smoke here was even thicker; it went into her eyes and stung so much she was half-blinded. She bent double and began to cough.

'Get out!' commanded Alec again. 'I'll fetch him.'

She couldn't have disobeyed him even if she'd wanted to; she couldn't see a thing and she could hardly breathe. He'd already disappeared into the smoke, and she realised the futility of staying there and forcing him to rescue two people instead of one, so she retreated and fought her way through the thickening clouds, out through the door. She stumbled to the water butt, then drenched the scarf and put it to her face again and again, until she felt she could breathe once more. Her throat was rough and raw, and there was a ringing in her ears, and she was only dimly aware of what was going on around her. She knew that Cécilia was still sobbing hysterically nearby, and that people were shouting and screaming, but all she could think about in between her gasping breaths was Rex and Alec, and whether they could possibly come out alive. The ringing in her ears grew louder and time seemed to recede and slow, so that hours instead of seconds passed.

Then there was a shriek, and she looked up and the first thing she saw was Cécilia, her hands reaching out to take a bundle of something from the arms of a soot-blackened figure which had just emerged from the house. Harriet had just enough time to understand that it was Rex, covered in Alec's jacket, when a crowd of people swarmed forward, eager to come to their aid, and blocked them from view. Cécilia was crying and scolding at the same time, and Rex was coughing, and the would-be helpers had much ado to make her let go of Rex so he could be attended to. He was given a good dousing with water, wrapped in a warm blanket, and handed back to his mother.

'I wanted to fetch Papa's guitar,' he managed at last.

Cécilia was hugging him and kissing him and gabbling to him in between sobs.

'It's just a guitar,' she said over and over again. 'Just a stupid old guitar. Don't you ever dare do that again to Maman, promise me you won't. Are you all right? You're coughing. Please, my son needs another drink – some hot tea – soup. *Mon petit*, I thought I'd lost you, oh goodness me!'

Rex submitted, somewhat stunned, to the attention. Gradually his coughing subsided and he allowed himself to be given pride of place on his mother's lap – although there was some danger in that too, since Cécilia seemed inclined to squeeze the life out of him.

The fire brigade had arrived at last, and were unwinding their hoses. Harriet found Alec over by the water butt with his sleeve rolled up, coughing and tending to a nasty burn on his arm.

'Let me help,' she said. She dipped her scarf into the water and applied it gently to the burn.

'That blasted guitar came down on me and did it,' he said.

'Your hair's all singed.'

'Everything's singed. I feel like I've smoked a hundred cigarettes all at once.'

She wanted to laugh, but suddenly it was all too much and instead she found she was crying.

'Hey, it's all right. We got him out. He'll be fine, you'll see.'

'I was so frightened, and then there was you, and… and I didn't know if you'd get out, and… and… oh, Alec, Sébastien!'

She could hardly get the words out between sobs, and all he could do was put his arms around her and try to comfort her as she wept. Then there were warning shouts, and Alec was pulling her away from the building, and they turned to watch as the new wing collapsed in on itself. There was a stunned silence, broken only by a harsh, rasping sound. Harriet thought someone was coughing from the smoke until she turned and saw Rose Brouillard, kneeling on the ground, her body racked by sobs as all her ambitions went up in flames.

Chapter Thirty-One

The weather was beautifully warm for late April, with clear skies and hardly a breath of wind. Harriet came out of the station at Cambridge and set off in the direction of the cricket ground. The students had started to return from their Easter break, and the town was abuzz with activity. Young people on bicycles passed to and fro, while bakers' and butchers' vans trundled through the streets making their deliveries. Harriet breathed in and enjoyed the sights and scents of the city as she walked unhurriedly along the road. A young man glanced at her once then again as he passed; she ignored it but appreciated the tribute. She'd only been away a little over a month, but already the past seemed like unfamiliar territory – a place of unhappiness and difficulty that she'd ploughed through slowly, before emerging all the stronger on the other side. On a day like this it was impossible to dwell unhealthily on misery; the sun was shining and the air was fresh and clean, and it was time to look forwards instead of backwards.

She found the street she was looking for: a quiet road of modest-looking cottages. She went to a particular number and rang the bell. Estelle answered it. Her face broke into a smile of recognition.

'Ah, Miss Conway, here you are at last! Mademoiselle has been waiting for you impatiently.'

'Is that Harriet?' came a voice. Estelle stood back, and Harriet to her surprise saw Cécilia on her feet, struggling along the narrow hallway towards her on a pair of crutches.

'What happened to your chair?' she asked.

'Oh, I've still got it,' said Cécilia. 'But I've been told in no uncertain terms that I have to practise on these horrid things. It's a terrible bore, but they won't let me off.'

She didn't seem bored at all, Harriet noted. In fact, despite the terrible events of only a few weeks ago, she looked brighter and more animated than Harriet had ever seen her. She was smiling at the sight of her visitor, and even moved forward to give her a kiss of greeting – slightly awkwardly, as though she wasn't used to that sort of thing, but still, it was a great improvement on her former listlessness.

'Come in, do!' she said. 'Estelle, bring us some tea, won't you?'

She turned with difficulty and led Harriet into a little sitting room. It was a far cry from the decayed opulence of Chaffingham, but it was cosy and comfortable and presumably much easier to manage. Cécilia rested her crutches against the wall and lowered herself carefully into a chair with a thankful sigh. Harriet saw that her hair had grown a little longer, which softened the lines of her face, and made her look younger.

'You're looking very well,' said Cécilia. 'Tell me about your new job. Isn't it awfully noisy working in a school?'

'It is, rather,' replied Harriet. 'Quite a change from Chaffingham, but I don't mind it. It's all very…' she cast around for a suitable word '…uncomplicated,' she finished.

Cécilia laughed.

'I expect it is compared to us. Shall you stay there, do you think? Reading's a long way away, and I was hoping you'd find something nearer here.'

'It was the only thing I could get in a hurry. I don't know how long I'll stay. We'll see. I can't keep on changing jobs every few months as I have been, though – at some point I really ought to pick one and stick with it. Where's Rex, by the way? I was hoping he'd be here.'

'I don't know where he's got to. He took the dog out and promised to be back by the time you arrived, but I dare say they've got distracted as usual.'

'How's he getting on? Will he go to school?'

'Yes, I think so. He's at home with me just at present, but in the long run it'll be much better for him to have the company of boys his own age rather than his lame duck of a mother.'

'What about his music?' Harriet looked around and saw an upright piano standing in the corner. She recognised it as the one which had stood in the music room at Chaffingham.

'He begged to give up the piano, so I've let him have a little time off,' said Cécilia. 'But he's still keen on the guitar, so he's not deserting music altogether, and I expect he'll be happy to start the piano again after a few months. I've been watching him and I think he has talent. I know one oughtn't to say so of one's own son, but I have hopes of him.'

Harriet suppressed a smile. However different she might be from her mother, Cécilia was a Brouillard through and through.

'Well, I'm glad the fire doesn't seem to have done him any harm.'

'No, none at all in the end. There's been a lot to think about, of course, but Fernand has been very kind and has dealt with a lot of the difficult stuff. He found us this house, and he's paying for it too until the insurance people stump up – *if* they stump up, that is. I'm not sure what the position is, given that Sébastien set the fire. There's not a lot of money, you know, so I shouldn't be surprised if Chaffingham had to be sold. Thankfully a good deal of the furniture was saved, although nothing from my room – the baby grand and my violin were destroyed. But Papa's concert piano survived perfectly intact, and that will go to auction with some of the other things and help pay the convalescent home fees for Maman.'

'How is your mother?'

'Just the same,' said Cécilia soberly. 'I knew she oughtn't to have gone to the inquest, but she insisted, and it was all too much for her so soon after the fire, and she collapsed. She doesn't speak. They say the stroke paralysed her left side, but with a little effort she ought to be able to regain some movement. But she won't make the effort. She just sits in her room and stares at that awful portrait of Papa he hated so much.'

'Did he hate it?'

'Oh, he thought it was ghastly. It made him look far too severe, he said. He was always away when I was growing up, so I never got to know him very well, but I remember him as a very kind man, not severe at all.'

'He must have been, after what he did for Fernand. What are you doing about *Les Orchidées*, by the way? Are you going to give Fernand the credit?'

'I want to, but he's refusing to listen to reason about that. He says there's time enough yet, and Maman still needs the money. Her care's rather expensive, you know. Oh – but I never told you, did I? We found Emil's will!'

'Did you? Where?'

'It was in that old briefcase full of his papers. I'd never thought to look through it, but he was a lawyer, and so of course he must have taken care of all that sort of thing. Anyway, when the house caught fire it suddenly occurred to me that the papers might be important, so I decided to take them with me. It's a good thing I did, because it turns out he left everything to Rex, which is the most tremendous good news.'

'Why? Did he leave a lot of money?'

'Barely a penny. But he left his music, and we have plans for that.'

'We?'

'Fernand and I. He thought it would be a good idea to record an album of Emil's songs and release it. Swing jazz is a little out of style these days, but Fernand thinks the story behind the music might help sell it. I'd like to earn some money for once, and be able to buy nice things for Rex. What do you think?'

'I think it's a splendid plan, and it's only a pity you never thought of it earlier.'

'Well, as I said, it was Fernand's idea. He's so full of them I can't keep up. When he's finished the classical project he's working on he wants me to compose some film scores with him. I'm not sure it's quite my thing, but I said I'd give it a try.'

Harriet couldn't help marvelling at Cécilia's new-found enthusiasm for life and music. It was as though the fire had been the catalyst she needed to help her break free from the unhealthy influence of her family, and she seemed almost a different person. One could hardly call her cheerful – after all, she'd recently lost her brother and her home, and her mother's health was failing badly – but there was a determination and a purpose to her that had never been there before.

'I suppose you haven't been back to Chaffingham?' she asked tentatively.

Cécilia shook her head. Her eyes glistened and she blinked and pressed her lips together.

'I'm not sure I can bear to,' she said. 'After the funeral I just wanted to forget about the whole thing for a while. Everything's changed, and it's all so new. I need a little time to think, but not just now.'

Harriet wasn't surprised. Forgetting had always been Cécilia's way of dealing with things. Poor, beautiful, tormented, jealous Sébastien, who'd caused so much damage to his family, tearing his sisters apart just as they were beginning to mend their friendship, and adding to the misery of Cécilia, who'd struggled with an additional burden of guilt for so many years. Harriet could hardly blame her for wanting a little time to make peace with him and herself.

They were interrupted just then by Rex, who had been out with his new dog. He greeted Harriet noisily.

'This is Daisy,' he said, after Harriet had duly admired the dog. 'She's a pointer. I'm training her all by myself. She's a lot easier than Patch was. Look. Daisy, sit!'

The dog sat, and Rex beamed proudly.

'I wanted to call her Maggie, after my aunt, but Maman said there was only room for one Maggie in the family, so she suggested Daisy instead.' He was bouncing up and down excitedly. 'Did you know I'm going to school? And I've started learning the guitar too. The one in the house got burned, but Maman got me a new one. Shall I show her, Maman?'

'Why not?' replied Cécilia.

'Oh, good!' he exclaimed, and ran out of the room. His enthusiasm was infectious and Harriet smiled at how well he was doing. He looked as though he'd grown in the past few weeks, and he was bright-eyed and full of energy. He returned shortly afterwards carrying a guitar and a music book, and handed the instrument to his mother to tune.

'I've only learned a few chords so far, but I've been practising really hard, and I can play the introduction of the song Papa wrote for Maman,' he announced proudly.

Cécilia returned the tuned guitar to him and he sat down and opened the music book, frowning for a moment as he read. Then he began to play. It was hardly a virtuoso performance, but he was clearly a natural at it, and the jaunty notes of the song that Emil had written and named after Cécilia all those years ago floated around the small room, bringing an air of bygone cheerfulness to the place.

'That's the only part I've learnt so far,' said Rex, as they applauded. 'It's much more fun than the piano.'

'I'm not letting you off that altogether,' Cécilia warned him. 'It's just a little break.'

He huffed, then brightened.

'Maman and I are going to have such fun together,' he said. 'We're going to Paris soon. I used to live there when I was a baby, but I don't remember anything about it. Maman says she'll show me where *tante* Maggie is buried, and Grand-père, and the house where we used to live. I want Maman to show me the place where the Germans shot her, but she said no.'

'It is not a matter for fun,' said Cécilia severely.

'Rex!' exclaimed Harriet, shocked.

'They're impervious to everything at that age,' said Cécilia. 'And perhaps it's good for me. I'd been brooding too much. But we'll go back as soon as we can. There's an old woman called Suzette who used to look after Rex, and I know she'd love to see him again. Then I want to make sure that Maggie's grave is being properly looked after, and if I can find out what happened to Emil, perhaps I can arrange a proper Jewish burial for him.' The tears came to her eyes again momentarily, but she shook them off, then took a deep breath and smiled.

'I'm glad you're doing so well,' said Harriet sincerely.

'It'll take time, but the music has come back, and that's the most important thing. As long as I have the music, then everything else will follow.' She took a deep breath, then went on, 'Thank you, Harriet.'

'What for?'

'For being a friend to me, and helping me.'

'Oh, but I didn't do anything,' said Harriet, embarrassed.

'Perhaps it doesn't seem like much to you, but you encouraged me when everybody else had given up on me. You and Fernand.'

'I think he's done more for you than I ever could have.'

'Oh, no! But it's true that he's been incredibly generous. I don't feel as though I deserve all this kind treatment.'

'You mustn't say things like that. That's the old Cécilia talking. It's time to forget the past and look forward to the future.'

'You're right,' said Cécilia firmly. She suddenly looked anxious. 'But you must keep reminding me.'

'Don't worry, I shall,' said Harriet, laughing.

They talked for a while longer, then Harriet glanced at her watch. It was time to go.

'I'll come back as soon as I can,' she promised. 'I want to hear you play me one of your pieces.'

'Are you going back to Reading now?'

'No, to Royston. I said I'd look up a friend.'

'Say hello to him from me,' said Cécilia, and Harriet blushed and laughed.

*

But she didn't get as far as Royston, because when she arrived at Cambridge station there he was, sitting on a bench, waiting for her, while Patch sniffed around a nearby lamp-post. Her heart leapt, but she walked calmly over to him. He stood up. He looked just the same, the turned-down corners of his eyes temporarily absent as he smiled at her.

'What are you doing here?' she asked. 'I thought I was supposed to come to Little Hambourn.'

'I didn't want to wait. It's a beautiful day and the walks are nicer around here.'

'But didn't you have lessons this afternoon?'

'Yes, but I got old Stan to do them.'

'Can he fly?'

'We'll soon find out.'

She laughed.

'Let's walk,' he said. 'I want to walk. You don't mind, do you?'

She didn't mind at all. They headed back into Cambridge and went for a stroll along the Backs. The punts were out in force, and they stopped to watch the little crafts gliding gently up and down the river, some of them steered more expertly than others. Then they walked together towards King's. The chapel was looking glorious in the daylight, its spires soaring upwards into the blue, and they stood and contemplated it for several moments. Harriet had wanted to come back and see it, but the remembrance of the last time she'd been there was touched with sadness.

'Sébastien played here not long before he died,' she said at last.

Alec looked at her sympathetically but didn't say anything. He wasn't the sort to fill every available space with chatter, and there was a companionableness to the silence. Harriet was glad of it, and glad of his presence. She'd spent much of the past month thinking about the past, and the present, and the future, and if her time with the Brouillards had taught her anything, it was that brooding over the past was unhealthy and achieved nothing. It wasn't a startlingly original conclusion, she was forced to admit, but perhaps she'd needed to see an example of it before her eyes so that she could act on it herself. Jim had lived for the day, and she knew he would have been scornful of her for sitting around moping. She'd never forget him, but she could think of him as he was and say goodbye now.

'Let's pass on,' she said at last. 'It's such a lovely day I don't want to think of sad things.'

Patch was sniffing around ahead, and they walked after him along the river path, under the trees, sunlight dappling the ground before them. Harriet glanced at Alec and thought once again how easy it was to be with him. He returned the look and felt for her hand, and she clasped his arm with her other hand and smiled up at him. She and Jim had clashed sometimes, given their strong personalities, but Alec was so easy-going she couldn't imagine ever fighting with him.

Idle thoughts passed through her mind of what they might do together in future, places they might go. His family lived in Edinburgh, he'd told her, and she'd never been to Scotland. Perhaps they might go there together one day. He could show her round the city, and then they could go walking in the Highlands for a few days. She wasn't sure how far it was from Edinburgh but she'd heard the scenery was beautiful. Then she brought herself up short, laughing to herself at the image she'd drawn in her mind. Why, she hardly knew the man. It was far too early to be thinking of that kind of thing. Still, the picture was an attractive one. A little spark danced inside her.

'What are you smiling at?' he asked.

'Nothing,' she replied. Before he could pursue the question, she went on: 'So, I gather the flying school business is going from strength to strength.'

'It is. Those adverts I put in the paper seem to have done the trick. Plus there was one chap who got his licence in record time – he's a natural really, but he seemed to think I'd had something to do with it, so he's recommended me to quite a lot of people.'

'That's good news. You must be very busy.'

'I am. Too busy. The paperwork's getting a bit out of hand, to be honest. I need to find someone to run the office for me.'

'Oh yes?'

They'd stopped again, by a willow tree that was drooping over into the river. With its long, elegant limbs, it reminded Harriet a little of Cécilia. Patch was half-fascinated, half-scared by the river; he'd gone down to the water's edge and was alternately dipping a paw in and running off as though he thought it would rise up and drench him.

'Yes. I was thinking maybe I should look for a young lady with lots of secretarial experience.'

'Secretarial experience? What else?'

He turned to her and took both her hands, examining her with mock-seriousness.

'Blonde, I think. About your height. Nice to look at. We want to impress the customers.'

'I see.' She was doing her best to keep a straight face.

'I don't suppose you'd be interested in the job?' He'd pulled her closer now – close enough for her to see the fine lines at the corners of his eyes as he gazed into hers.

'I've only been at the school a few weeks. They won't be happy if I give notice so soon.'

'Tell them I need you more than they do. I'm sure they'll understand.'

She was already thinking about how it might be done. Perhaps a little flat in Royston, or even here in Cambridge. No commitment, just a few months, to see if it worked out – the job *and* the man. His record-keeping was terrible, but she was sure she could get the place ship-shape within a week or two. Perhaps a new booking system for the lessons and a large planning chart for the wall.

He was watching her as she rearranged his office and her life in her head.

'What do you think?' he asked. 'I'll even teach you to fly. No charge.'

'I'm not wearing that jacket again.'

'We can get one that fits you better. Any colour you like.'

She burst out laughing.

'Is that the best you can do?'

'I thought it was a pretty good offer. I wouldn't do it for just anyone, you know.'

They were smiling into each other's eyes now, and it was all looking very much like a foregone conclusion. His hand reached up and brushed a stray wisp of hair from her face. Her cheek felt hot where he'd touched it.

'I told you I'd wait,' he said quietly.

'Well, you didn't have to wait very long.'

'It felt long enough. I missed you.'

'I missed you too. And thank you for waiting. My head was a bit muddled, that's all.'

'I could see that. And it's understandable. Time to move on?' he asked, gazing at her searchingly.

Her eyes glinted at him, full of mischief.

'Kiss me again and we'll see,' she said.

This time there was no shame, no guilt, no feeling that a kiss was an act of betrayal. The touch of his lips sparked off an electric current that ran down her spine and started all her nerve endings tingling. She felt the warmth spreading through her body, and put her arms around his neck, drawing him closer. He responded eagerly to the deepening kiss, gripping her more tightly as they clung together, oblivious to their surroundings.

'Did that answer your question?' she said, when they finally broke apart.

His blue-grey eyes darkened as he gazed at her, then his mouth curled up in a smile.

'I guess it did.'

It had answered Harriet's question too – if any doubt had remained. She suddenly remembered that they were standing in a very public place, and made a move to disengage herself, but he tightened his hold.

'Not so fast. I just want to be *quite* sure.'

But the second kiss had to wait, because at that moment Patch created a disturbance by falling in the river, and there were several minutes of confusion while they got him out. He then proceeded to shake himself vigorously all over them.

'That dog of yours is a menace,' said Harriet, shaking her head in mock exasperation. 'Rex's new puppy is much better behaved.'

'Perhaps we ought to introduce them. Maybe she'll teach Patch some manners.'

'I doubt it.'

They were laughing, and he slid his arms around her again.

'What were we talking about?' he asked.

'I don't think we were talking at all,' replied Harriet.

'Talking's overrated anyway. This is nicer.' His chin was resting on her head. It felt comfortable there, and she fitted under it perfectly. They stood clasped together, enjoying the warmth of the day and each other's proximity. Harriet let her mind drift idly, the possibilities stretching ahead of her, unknown but untroubling.

'So about this job…' he began after a minute or two.

'I'll take it,' she replied.

He pulled back and looked down at her questioningly.

'Really? Don't you want more time to think about it?'

'I've had enough of thinking. Life is short. Best make the most of it.'

'I couldn't agree more,' he said, and kissed her again.

A Letter from Clara Benson

Dear Reader

Thank you for choosing to read *In Darkness, Look for Stars*. If you enjoyed it, and want to keep up to date with all my latest releases, sign up at the following link. Your email address will never be shared and you can unsubscribe at any time.

www.bookouture.com/clara-benson

In Darkness, Look for Stars is of course a work of fiction, but it was inspired partly by the men and women of the French Resistance who died fighting the German Occupation. Given our relatively peaceful existence in Europe and the West today, it's almost incredible to think of the struggles and suffering people went through at a time which is still within the living memory of many. Of course, not everyone was a hero – in fact, many people were convinced that resisting the Occupation was a futile endeavour, and that it was better to put up with the situation than risk being shot. But among those who did join the Resistance, there are countless stories of bravery and sacrifice in the name of France; countless Emils and Maggies and Cécilias who died, their lives cut cruelly short by global conflict. This story is for them.

I hope you enjoyed *In Darkness, Look for Stars*. If you did I'd be very grateful if you could write a review – even just a sentence or two will do. Reviews are incredibly helpful to authors, and they're also useful for readers looking for new books. And if you'd like to drop me a line you can find me on Facebook, Twitter, Goodreads and my website.

Thanks for reading!
Clara

 facebook.com/clarabensonbooks

 twitter.com/clarabooks

clarabenson.com

Acknowledgements

A book like this takes a fair bit of research, and I'd like to thank Fabien Masvaleix, Laura Viner and Michael Omer, who provided helpful advice in the matters of the French language, violin technique and Jewish burial customs respectively. Much appreciation also goes to my husband Paul, for his seemingly inexhaustible fund of Second World War knowledge. Any factual errors are, of course, my own.

Many thanks also to all the wonderful people at Bookouture, especially Kathryn Taussig, who first suggested I write historical fiction, and Christina Demosthenous, my amazing and talented editor, who took my rough first draft and helped me turn it into something I'm truly proud of. Thanks too, to Kim Nash and Noelle Holten, for their boundless energy and enormous enthusiasm for all things bookish.

Finally, a big thanks to all my author friends of the AC, who provided moral support, and who were always on hand to distract me with silly jokes when I *really* should have been writing.

Made in the USA
Middletown, DE
15 June 2020